A NOVEL BY

CARL HIAASEN

Published by Random House Large Print
in association with Alfred A. Knopf, Inc.
New York 1997

Library of Congress Cataloging-in-Publication Data

Hiaasen, Carl.
Lucky you : a novel / Carl Hiaasen.
p.   cm.
ISBN 0-679-77451-3 (lg. print)
1. Large type books.   I. Title.
[PS3558.I217L83   1997]
813'.54—dc21   97-18570
CIP

Random House Web Address:
http://www.randomhouse.com/
Printed in the United States of America
FIRST LARGE PRINT EDITION

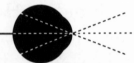

This Large Print Book carries the
Seal of Approval of N.A.V.H.

*For Laureen,
one in a million*

1 On the afternoon of November 25, a woman named JoLayne Lucks drove to the Grab N'Go minimart in Grange, Florida, and purchased spearmint Certs, unwaxed dental floss and one ticket for the state Lotto.

JoLayne Lucks played the same numbers she'd played every Saturday for five years: 17-19-22-24-27-30.

The significance of her Lotto numbers was this: each represented an age at which she had jettisoned a burdensome man. At 17 it was Rick the Pontiac mechanic. At 19 it was Rick's brother, Robert. At 22 it was a stockbroker named Colavito, twice JoLayne's age, who'd delivered on none of his promises. At 24 it was a policeman, another Robert, who got in trouble for fixing traffic tickets in exchange for sex. At 27 it was Neal the chiropractor, a well-meaning but unbearable codependent.

And at 30 JoLayne dumped Lawrence, a lawyer, her one and only husband. Lawrence had been notified of his disbarment exactly one week after he and JoLayne were married, but she stuck with him for almost a year. JoLayne was fond of Lawrence and wanted to believe his earnest denials regarding the multiple fraud convictions that precipitated his trouble with the Florida Bar. While appealing his case, Lawrence took a job as a toll taker on the Beeline Expressway, a plucky career realignment that nearly won JoLayne's heart. Then one night he was caught making off with a thirty-pound sack of loose change, mostly quarters and dimes. Before he could post bail, JoLayne packed up most of his belongings, including his expensive Hermès neckties, and gave them to the Salvation Army. Then she filed for divorce.

Five years later she was still single and unattached when, to her vast amusement, she won the Florida Lotto. She happened to be sitting with a plate of turkey leftovers in front of the television at 11 p.m., when the winning numbers were announced.

JoLayne Lucks didn't faint, shriek or dance wildly around the house. She smiled, though, thinking of the six discarded men from her past life; thinking how, in spite of themselves, they'd finally amounted to something.

Twenty-eight million dollars, to be precise.

One hour earlier and almost three hundred miles away, a candy-red Dodge Ram pulled into a convenience store in Florida City. Two men got out of the truck: Bodean Gazzer, known locally as Bode, and his companion Chub, who claimed to have no last name. Although they parked in a handicapped-only zone, neither man was physically disabled in any way.

Bode Gazzer was five feet six and had never forgiven his parents for it. He wore three-inch snakeskin shitkickers and walked with a swagger that suggested not brawn so much as hemorrhoidal tribulation. Chub was a beer-gutted six two, moist-eyed, ponytailed and unshaven. He carried a loaded gun at all times and was Bode Gazzer's best and only friend.

They had known each other two months. Bode Gazzer had gone to Chub to buy a counterfeit handicapped sticker that would get him the choicest parking spot at Probation & Parole, or any of the other state offices where his attendance was occasionally required.

Like its mangy tenant, Chub's house trailer emitted a damp fungal reek. Chub had just printed a new batch of the fake emblems, which he laconically fanned like a poker deck on the kitchen counter. The workmanship (in sharp contrast to the surroundings) was impeccable—the universal wheelchair symbol set crisply against a navy-blue background. No traffic cop in the world would question it.

Chub had asked Bode Gazzer what type he wanted—a bumper insignia, a tag for the rearview or a dashboard placard. Bode said a simple window tag would be fine.

"Two hunnert bucks," said Chub, scratching his scalp with a salad fork.

"I'm a little short on cash. You like lobster?"

"Who don't."

So they'd worked out a trade—the bogus disabled-parking permit in exchange for ten pounds of fresh Florida lobster, which Bode Gazzer had stolen from a trapline off Key Largo. It was inevitable that the poacher and the counterfeiter would bond, sharing as they did a blanket contempt for government, taxes, homosexuals, immigrants, minorities, gun laws, assertive women and honest work.

Chub never thought of himself as having a political agenda until he met Bode Gazzer, who helped organize Chub's multitude of hatreds into a single venomous philosophy. Chub believed Bode Gazzer was the smartest person he'd ever met, and was flattered when his new pal suggested they form a militia.

"You mean like what blowed up that courthouse in Nebraska?"

"Oklahoma," Bode Gazzer said sharply, "and that was the government did it, to frame those two white boys. No, I'm talking 'bout a *militia.* Armed, disciplined and well-regulated. Like it says in the Second Amendment."

Chub scratched a chigger bite on his neck. "Reg'lated by who, if I might ast?"

"By you, me, Smith and Wesson."

"And that's allowed?"

"Says right in the motherfuckin' Constitution."

"OK then," said Chub.

Bode Gazzer had gone on to explain how the United States of America was about to be taken over by a New World Tribunal, armed by foreign-speaking NATO troops who were massing across the Mexican border and also at secret locations in the Bahamas.

Chub glanced warily toward the horizon. "The Bahamas?" He and Bode were in Bode's cousin's nineteen-foot outboard, robbing traps off Rodriguez Key.

Bode Gazzer said: "There's seven hundred islands in the Bahamas, my friend, and most are uninhabited."

Chub got the message. "Jesus Willy Christ," he said, and began pulling the lobster pots with heightened urgency.

To run a proper militia would be expensive, and neither Chub nor Bode Gazzer had any money; Bode's net worth was tied up in the new Dodge truck, Chub's in his illegal printshop and arsenal. So they began playing the state lottery, which Bode asserted was the only decent generous thing the government of Florida had ever done for its people.

Every Saturday night, wherever they happened to be, the two men would pull into the nearest convenience store, park brazenly in the blue handicapped zone, march inside and purchase five Lotto tickets. They played no special numbers; often they were drinking, so it was easier to use the Quick Pick, letting the computer do the brainwork.

On the night of November 25, Bode Gazzer and Chub bought their five lottery tickets and three six-packs of beer at the Florida City 7-Eleven. They were nowhere near a television an hour later, when the winning numbers were announced.

Instead they were parked along a dirt road on a tree farm, a few miles from the Turkey Point nuclear reactor. Bode Gazzer was sitting on the hood of the Dodge pickup, aiming one of Chub's Ruger assault rifles at a U.S. government mailbox they'd stolen from a street corner in Homestead. An act of revolutionary protest, Bode had said, like the Boston Tea Party.

The mailbox was centered in the headlight beams of the truck. Bode and Chub took turns with the Ruger until they were out of ammo and Budweisers. Then they sorted through the mail, hoping for loose cash or personal checks, but all they found was junk. Afterwards they fell asleep in the flatbed. Shortly after dawn they were rousted by two large Hispanics, undoubtedly the foremen of the tree farm, who swiped the Ruger and chased them off the property.

It was some time later, after returning to Chub's trailer, that they learned of their extraordinary good fortune. Bode Gazzer was on the toilet, Chub was stretched on the convertible sofa in front of the TV. A pretty blond newscaster gave out the previous night's winning Lotto numbers, which Chub scribbled on the back of his latest eviction notice.

Moments later, when Bode heard the shouting, he came lurching from the bathroom with his jeans and boxer shorts bunched at his knees. Chub was waving the ticket, hopping and whooping like he was on fire.

Bodean Gazzer said: "You're shittin' me."

"We won it, man! We won!"

Bode lunged for the ticket, but Chub held it out of reach.

"Give it here!" Bode demanded, swiping at air, his genitals flopping ludicrously.

Chub laughed. "Pull up your pants, for Christ's sake." He handed the ticket to Bode, who recited the numbers out loud.

"You're sure?" he kept asking.

"I wrote 'em down, Bode. Yeah, I'm sure."

"My God. *My God.* Twenty-eight million dollars."

"But here's what else: They's two winning tickets is what the news said."

Bode Gazzer's eyes puckered into a hard squint. "The hell you say!"

"Two tickets won. Which is still, what, fourteen million 'tween us. You believe it?"

Bode's tongue, lumpy and blotched as a toad, probed at the corners of his mouth. He looked to be working up a spit. "Who's got the other one? The other goddamn ticket."

"TV didn't say."

"How can we find out?"

Chub said, "Christ, who gives a shit. Long as we get fourteen million, I don't care if Jesse Fucking Jackson's got the other ticket."

Now Bode Gazzer's stubbled cheeks began to twitch. He fingered the Lotto coupon and said: "There must be a way to find out. Don't you think? Find out who's this shitweasel with the other ticket. There's gotta be a way."

"Why?" Chub asked, but it was awhile before he got an answer.

Sunday morning, Tom Krome refused to go to church. The woman who'd slept with him the night before—Katie was her name; strawberry blond, freckles on her shoulders—said they should go and seek forgiveness for what they had done.

"Which part?" asked Tom Krome.

"You know darn well."

Krome covered his face with a pillow. Katie kept talking, putting on her panty hose.

She said, "I'm sorry, Tommy, it's the way I'm made. It's time you should know."

"You think it's wrong?"

"What?"

He peeped out from beneath the pillow. "You think we did something wrong?"

"No. But God might not agree."

"So it's precautionary, this church visit."

Now Katie was at the mirror, fixing her hair in a bun. "Are you coming or not? How do I look?"

"Chaste," said Tom Krome.

The phone rang.

"Chased? No, sweetheart, that was last night. Get the telephone, please."

Katie put on her high heels, balancing storklike on elegant slender legs. "You honestly won't go? To church, Tom, I can't believe it."

"Yeah, I'm one heathen bastard." Krome picked up the phone.

She waited, arms folded, at the bedroom door.

Krome covered the receiver and said, "Sinclair."

"On a Sunday morning?"

"I'm afraid so." Krome tried to sound disappointed but he was thinking: There *is* a God.

Sinclair's title at *The Register* was Assistant Deputy Managing Editor of Features and Style. He relied on the fact that nobody outside the newspaper business understood the insignificance of his position. At smaller papers it was one of the least nerve-racking and lowest-profile jobs. Sinclair couldn't have been happier. Most of his reporters and editors were young and unabashedly grateful to be employed, and they did whatever Sinclair told them.

His biggest problem was Tom Krome, who also happened to be his best writer. Krome's background was hard news, which had made him impossibly cynical and suspicious of all authority. Sinclair was scared of Krome; he'd heard stories. Also, at thirty-five Krome was older by two years, so he held the advantage of age as well as experience. Sinclair realized there was no possibility, none whatsoever, that Krome would ever respect him.

His fear—in fact, Sinclair's most serious concern as the ADME of Features and Style—was that Krome might someday humiliate him in front of the staff. Figuratively cut off his nuts in front of Marie or Jacquelyn, or one of the clerks. Sinclair felt he could not psychologically endure such an episode, so he had resolved to keep Krome away from the newspaper office as much as possible. To that end, Sinclair committed ninety-five percent of his meager travel budget to assignments that kept Krome safely out of town. It worked out fine: Tom seemed content to be gone, and Sinclair was able to relax at the office.

The most challenging of Sinclair's responsibilities was handing out lame story assignments. Calling Tom Krome at home was particularly trying;

usually Sinclair had to shout to make himself heard above the loud rock music or women's voices in the background. He could only imagine how Krome lived.

Sinclair had never before phoned on a Sunday. He apologized numerous times.

Tom Krome said: "Don't worry about it."

Sinclair was encouraged. He said, "I didn't think this one could wait."

Krome had no trouble containing his excitement. Whatever Sinclair was calling about, it wasn't breaking news. Breaking fluff, maybe, but not news. He blew a kiss to Katie and waved her off to church.

"I got a tip," Sinclair said.

"You got a tip."

"My brother-in-law phoned this morning. He lives over in Grange."

Krome thought: Uh-oh. Crafts show. I will murder this fucker if he makes me cover another crafts show.

But Sinclair said: "You play the lottery, Tom?"

"Only when it's up to forty million bucks or so. Anything less is chump change."

No reaction from Sinclair, who was deep into his pitch: "There were two winners last night. One in Dade County, the other in Grange. My brother-in-law knows the woman. Her name is—are you ready for this?—Lucks."

Inwardly Tom Krome groaned. It was the quintessential Sinclair headline: LADY LUCKS WINS THE LOTTO!

You had your irony. You had your alliteration.

And you had your frothy, utterly forgettable feature story. Sinclair called them Feel Goods. He believed it was the mission of his department to make readers forget all the nastiness they were getting in other sections of the newspaper. He wanted them to feel good about their lives, their religion, their families, their neighbors, their world.

Once he'd posted a memo setting forth his philosophy of feature writing. Somebody—Sinclair suspected Tom Krome—had nailed a dead rat to it.

"How much she win?" Krome asked.

"The pot was twenty-eight million, so she'll get half. What do you think, Tom?"

"Depends."

"She works for a veterinarian. Loves animals, Roddy says."

"That's nice."

"Plus she's black."

"Ah," said Krome. The white editors who ran the newspaper loved positive stories about minorities; Sinclair obviously smelled a year-end bonus.

"Roddy says she's a trip."

Krome said, "Roddy would be your brother-in-law?" The tipster.

"Right. He says she's a character, this JoLayne

Lucks." The headline dancing in Sinclair's brain actually was: LUCKS BE A LADY!

Tom Krome said: "This Roddy person is married to your sister?"

"Joan. Yes, that's right," Sinclair answered, edgily.

"What the hell's your sister doing in Grange?"

Grange was a truck-stop town known mainly for its miracles, stigmata, visitations and weeping Madonnas. It was a must-see on the Christian tourist circuit.

Sinclair said, "Joan's a teacher. Roddy works for the state." Sinclair wanted to make clear they weren't nutcases but were responsible citizens. He noticed his palms had gotten damp from talking to Tom Krome for too long.

"This Lady Lucks," Krome said, in a tone designed to cast scorn on the inevitable headline, "is she a Jesus freak? Because I'm in no mood to be preached at."

"Tom, I really wouldn't know."

"She says Jesus gave her those lucky numbers, end of story. I'm coming home. You understand?"

Sinclair said, "Roddy didn't mention anything like that."

Solemnly Krome played his ace. "Think of the letters we'll get."

"What do you mean?" Sinclair hated letters almost as much as he hated telephone calls. The best stories were those that produced no reaction, one way or another, from readers. "What kind of mail?" he asked.

"Tons," Krome replied, "if we do a piece saying Jesus is a gambling tout. Can you imagine? Hell, you'll probably hear from Ralph Reed himself. Next they'll be boycotting our advertisers."

Firmly Sinclair said: "So let's stay away from that angle. By all means." After a pause: "Maybe this isn't such a hot idea."

On the other end, Tom Krome smiled. "I'll drive up to Grange this afternoon. Check it out and let you know."

"OK," Sinclair said. "Go check it out. You want my sister's phone number?"

"That's not necessary," said Krome.

Sinclair experienced a small shudder of relief.

Demencio was refilling the fiberglass Madonna when his wife, Trish, hurried outside to say that somebody in town won the lottery.

"I don't suppose it's us," said Demencio.

"Rumor is JoLayne Lucks."

"Figures."

Demencio removed the top of the Madonna's head and reached inside the statue to retrieve a plastic bottle that had once held the wiper fluid in a 1989 Civic hatchback. These days the jug held tap water, lightly scented with perfume.

Trish said, "You're almost out of Charlie."

Demencio nodded irritably. That would be a problem. It was important to use a fragrance the righteous faithful wouldn't recognize; otherwise suspicions would be stirred. Once he'd experimented with Lady Stetson and there was nearly an uprising. The third pilgrim in line, a buzzardly bank teller from Huntsville, had sniffed it out instantly: "Hey, Mother Mary's crying Coty tears!"

The woman was discreetly whisked away from the shrine before trouble started. Demencio had vowed to be more careful. Scenting the Madonna's tears was a fine touch, he thought. The devout souls who waited so long in the hot Florida sun deserved more than a drop of salty water on their fingertips—this was supposed to be Jesus' mother, for heaven's sake. Her tears *ought* to smell special.

Trish held the plastic bottle while Demencio poured the last of the Charlie perfume. Again she marveled at how small and childlike his brown hands were. And steady. He would've made a wonderful surgeon, her husband, if only he'd had the chance. If only he'd been born in, say, Boston, Massachusetts, instead of Hialeah, Florida.

Demencio replaced the plastic bottle inside the Madonna. Clear thin tubes ran upward from the bottle's cap to the inside of the statue's eyelids, where the clever Demencio had drilled pinprick-sized holes. A thicker black tube ran internally down the length of the statue and emerged from another hole in her right heel. The black air tube connected to a small rubber bulb, which could be operated by hand or foot. Squeezing the bulb forced the phony tears out of the bottle, up the twin tubes and into the Madonna's eyes.

There was an art to it, and Demencio fancied himself one of the best in the business. He kept the tears small, subtle and paced at intervals. The longer the crowd was made to linger, the more soft drinks, angel food cake, T-shirts, Bibles, holy candles and sunblock they purchased.

From Demencio, of course.

Most everybody in Grange knew what he was up to, but they didn't say much. Some were too busy running their own scams. Besides, tourists were tourists and there wasn't much difference, when you got down to the core morality of it, between Mickey Mouse and a fiberglass Madonna.

Trish liked to say: "All we're really selling is hope."

Demencio liked to say: "I'd rather peddle religion than a phony goddamn rodent."

He made decent money, though he wasn't rich and probably never would be. Not like Miss Jo-Layne Lucks, whose astounding and undeserved windfall he now contemplated.

"How much she win?" he asked his wife.

"Fourteen million, if it's true."

"She's not sure?"

"She not sayin'."

Demencio snorted. Anybody else, they'd be hooting and hollering all over town. *Fourteen million bucks!*

Trish said, "All they announced is there's two winning tickets. One was bought down around Homestead, the other was in Grange."

"The Grab N'Go?"

"Yep. The way they figured out who, the store only sold twenty-two Lotto tickets all last week. Twenty-one is accounted for. JoLayne's is the only one left."

Demencio fitted the fiberglass Madonna back together. "So what's she up to?"

Trish reported that, according to neighbors, JoLayne Lucks had not come out of her house all morning and was not answering the telephone.

"Maybe she ain't home," Demencio said. He carried the Madonna into the house. Trish followed. He set the statue in a corner, next to his golf bag.

"Let's go see her," he said.

"Why?" Trish wondered what Demencio was planning. They barely knew the Lucks woman to say hello.

"Bring her some angel food cake," Demencio proposed. "It's a neighborly thing on a Sunday morning. I mean, why the hell not?"

2 JoLayne Lucks didn't expect to see Trish and Demencio on her front porch, and Demencio didn't expect to see so much of JoLayne's legs. She appeared in a peach-colored jogging bra and sky-blue panties.

"I wasn't ready for company," she said in a sleepy voice.

Trish: "We'll drop by another time."

"Whatcha got there?"

Demencio said, "Cake."

He was transfixed by JoLayne's perfectly muscled calves. How'd they get like that? He never saw her running.

"Come on in," she said, and Demencio—shaking free of his wife's grip—went in.

They stood, each holding one side of the cake plate, while JoLayne Lucks went to put on a pair of jeans. The small tidy house showed no signs of a post-lottery celebration. Trish remarked on the handsome piano in the living room; Demencio eyed an aquarium full of baby turtles—there must have been fifty of them, paddling full tilt and goggled-eyed against the glass.

To Trish he said, "I wonder what *that's* all about."

"You hush. They're pets is all."

JoLayne returned with her hair under a baseball cap, which Demencio found intriguing and sexy—

the attitude as much as the style. JoLayne told Trish the cake looked delicious.

"Angel food," Demencio's wife said. "My grandma's recipe. On my mother's side."

"Sit down, please." JoLayne carried the plate to the kitchen counter. Trish and Demencio sat stiffly on an antique cherrywood love seat.

He said, "Those your turtles?"

JoLayne Lucks gave a bright smile. "Would you like one?"

Demencio shook his head. Trish, by way of explanation: "We've got a jealous old tomcat."

JoLayne peeled the plastic wrapping from the cake and broke off a chunk with her fingers. Serenely she popped it in her mouth. "What brings you folks by?"

Trish glanced at Demencio, who shifted in the love seat. "Well," he said, "here's the thing—we heard about your good fortune. You know. . . ."

JoLayne gave him no help. She was savoring the angel food.

Demencio said, "About the Lotto, I mean."

One of her fine brown eyebrows arched. She kept chewing. Demencio fumbled with a strategy. The woman seemed slightly spacey.

Trish came to the rescue. "We stopped over to say congratulations. Nothing like this ever happens in Grange."

"No?" With a lizard flick of her tongue, Jo-Layne Lucks removed a crumb from one of her sparkling cobalt fingernails. "I thought miracles happen all the time around here. Most every Sunday, right?"

Demencio reddened, perceiving a dig at his Madonna concession. Trish, courageously: "What I meant, JoLayne, was nobody's ever won anything. Nobody I can recall."

"Well, you might be right."

"It's just a shame you've got to split the jackpot with somebody else." Trish spoke with true sympathy. "Not that fourteen million bucks is anything to sneeze at, but it'd be nice if you were the only winner. Nice for Grange, too."

Demencio shot a glare at his wife. "It's still nice for Grange," he said. "It'll put us on the map, for damn sure."

JoLayne Lucks said, "Ya'll want some coffee?"

"So what's next, girl?" Trish asked.

"I thought I'd feed the turtles."

Trish chuckled uneasily. "You know what I mean. Maybe a new car? A place at the beach?"

JoLayne Lucks cocked her head. "You're losing me now."

Demencio had had enough. He stood up, hitching at his trousers. "I won't lie. We came to ask a favor."

JoLayne beamed. "That's more like it." She noticed how Trish's hands had balled with tension.

Demencio forced a cough, to clear his throat. "Pretty soon you'll be all famous, in the newspapers and TV. My idea was maybe when they ask where your Lotto luck came from, you could put in a good word."

"For you?"

"For the Madonna, yes."

"But I've never even been to the shrine."

"I know, I know." Demencio held up his hands. "It's just an idea. I can't promise hardly anything in return. I mean, you're a millionaire now."

Although he sorely hoped JoLayne wouldn't ask for a commission on his take, he was prepared to part with ten percent.

Trish, quietly: "It'd just be a favor, like he said. Pure and simple. A favor for a neighbor."

"Christmas is coming," Demencio added. "Any little thing would help. Anything you could do."

JoLayne Lucks walked them, one on each arm, to the door. She said, "Well, it's surely something to think about. And, Trish, that's glorious cake."

"You're so kind."

"Sure you don't fancy a turtle?"

In tandem, Demencio and his wife edged off the porch. "Thanks just the same," they said, and walked home in silence. Trish pondered the possibility she'd gotten some bad information, as JoLayne Lucks didn't behave like a woman who'd won a free toaster, much less a Lotto jackpot. Demencio, meanwhile, had concluded JoLayne Lucks was either a borderline psycho or a brilliant faker, and that further investigation was necessary.

. . .

Bodean James Gazzer had spent thirty-one years perfecting the art of assigning blame. His personal credo—*Everything bad that happens is someone else's fault*—could, with imagination, be stretched to fit any circumstance. Bode stretched it.

The intestinal unrest that occasionally afflicted him surely was the result of drinking milk taken from secretly radiated cows. The roaches in his apartment were planted by his filthy immigrant next-door neighbors. His dire financial plight was caused by runaway bank computers and conniving Wall Street Zionists; his bad luck in the South Florida job market, prejudice against English-speaking applicants. Even the lousy weather had a culprit: air pollution from Canada, diluting the ozone and derailing the jet stream.

Bode Gazzer's accusatory talents were honed at an early age. The youngest of three sons, he veered astray to develop a precocious fondness for truancy, vandalism and shoplifting. His parents, both teachers, earnestly tried to redirect the boy, only to hear themselves lashingly blamed for his troubles. Bode took the position that he was persecuted because he was short, and that his shortness was attributable to his mother's careless dietary practices (and his father's gluttonous complicity) during pregnancy. That both Jean and Randall Gazzer were genetically slight of stature was immaterial to young Bode—from television he'd gathered that humans as a species were getting taller with evolution, and he therefore expected to surpass his parents, if only by an inch or two. Yet Bode stopped growing in eighth grade, a fact lugubriously chronicled in the family's bimonthly measuring ceremonies, conducted at the kitchen doorjamb. A multicolored sequence of pencil slashes confirmed Bode's worst fears: His two older brothers were still ascending positively, while he himself was finished, capped off at the ripe old age of fourteen.

The bitter realization hardened Bode Gazzer against his MSG-gobbling parents, and society at large. He became "the bad element" in the neighborhood, the cocky ringleader of misdemeanors and minor felonies. He worked diligently at being a hood, taking up unfiltered cigarets, public spitting and gratuitous profanity. Every so often he purposely provoked his brothers into beating him up, so he could tell friends he'd been in a savage gang fight.

Bode's schoolteacher parents didn't believe in whippings and (except for one occasion) never laid a glove on him. Jean and Randall Gazzer preferred "talking out" problems with their children, and spent many hours around the supper table "interacting" earnestly with the insolent Bodean. He was more than a match. Not only had he acquired the rhetorical skills of his mother and father, he was boundlessly creative. No matter what happened, Bode always produced an elaborate excuse from which he would not budge, even in the face of overwhelming evidence.

By the time he turned eighteen, his juvenile arrest record filled three pages, and his weary parents had put themselves in the hands of a Zen counselor. Bode had come to relish his role as the family outlaw, the bad seed, the misunderstood one. He could explain everything and would, at the drop of a hat. By the time he turned twenty-two, he was living on beer, bold talk and a multitude of convenient resentments. "I'm on God's shit list," he'd announce in barrooms, "so keep your damn distance."

A series of unhealthy friendships eventually drew Bode Gazzer into the culture of hate and hard-core bigotry. Previously, when dishing out fault for his plight, Bode had targeted generic authority figures—parents, brothers, cops, judges—without considering factors such as race, religion or ethnicity. He'd swung broadly, and without much impact. But xenophobia and racism infused his griping with new vitriol. Now it wasn't just some storm-trooper cop who busted Bode with stolen VCRs, it was the *Cuban* storm-trooper cop who obviously had a hard-on for Anglos; it wasn't just the double-talking defense lawyer who sold Bode down the river, it was the double-talking *Jew* defense lawyer who clearly held a vendetta against

Christians; and it wasn't just the cokehead bondsman who refused to put up Bode's bail, it was the
cokehead *Negro* bondsman who wanted him to
stay in jail and get cornholed to death.

Bode Gazzer's political awakening coincided
with an overdue revision of his illicit habits. He'd
made up his mind to forsake burglaries, car thefts
and other property offenses in favor of forgeries,
check kiting and other so-called paper crimes, for
which judges seldom dispensed state prison time.

As it happened, the hate movement in which
Bode had taken an interest strongly espoused
fraud as a form of civil disobedience. Militia pamphlets proclaimed that ripping off banks, utilities
and credit-card companies was a just repudiation
of the United States government and all the liberals, Jews, faggots, lesbians, Negroes, environmen-
talists and communists who infested it. Bode
Gazzer admired the logic. However, he proved
only slightly more skillful at passing bad checks
than he was at hot-wiring Oldsmobiles.

Between always-brief jail stints, he'd decorated
the inside of his apartment with antigovernment
posters purchased at various gun shows: David
Koresh, Randy Weaver and Gordon Kahl were
featured heroically.

Whenever Chub visited the place, he raised a
long-necked Budweiser in salute to the martyrs
honored on Bode's wall. Through television he'd

acquired a vague awareness of Koresh and
Weaver, but he knew little about Kahl except that
he'd been a Dakota farmer and tax protester, and
that the feds had shot the shit out of him.

"Goddamn storm troopers," Chub snarled now,
parroting a term he'd picked up at a small but
lively militia meeting on Big Pine Key. He carried
his beer to a futon sofa, where he plopped down
splay-legged and relaxed. Quickly his thoughts
drifted from the fallen patriots to his own sunny
fortunes.

Bode Gazzer hunched at the dinette, a newspaper spread under his nose. He'd been in a spiteful
mood since learning from a state lottery pamphlet
that he and Chub wouldn't be receiving the $14
million all at once—it was to be dispensed in equal
payments over twenty years.

Worse: The payments would be taxed!

Chub, who wasn't bad with numbers, attempted
to cheer Bode Gazzer with the fact that $700,000 a
year, even before taxes, was still a very large piece
of change.

"Not large enough to outfit a patriot force,"
Bode snapped.

Chub said, "Rules is rules. The hell can you
do?" He got up to turn on the TV. Nothing happened. "This busted or what?"

Bode smoothed the wrinkles from the newspaper and said: "Christ, don't you get it? This is
everything we've been talkin' about, everything

worth fightin' for—life, liberty, pursuit and happiness all rolled up in one."

Chub thwacked the broken television with the flat of his hand. He wasn't in the mood for one of Bode's speeches yet it now seemed inescapable.

Bode Gazzer continued: "Finally we hit it big and what happens? The state of motherfucking Florida is gonna pay us in drips and draps. Then, whatever we get is snatched by the Infernal Revenue!"

Listening to his friend, Chub's high feelings about their good luck began to ebb. He'd always viewed the lottery as a potential way to get tons of free money without doing jackshit. But the way Bode explained it, the Lotto was just another sinister example of government intrusion, tax abuse and liberal deceit.

"You think it's a accident we gotta share this money with somebody else?"

With the mouth of the beer bottle, Chub massaged the furry nape of his neck. He wondered what his friend was getting at.

Bode rapped his knuckles on the dinette. "Here's my prediction: The shitweasel holding the other Lotto ticket, he's either a Negro, Jew or Cuban type."

"Go on!"

"That's how they do it, Chub. To fuck over decent Americans such as you and me. You think they're gonna let two white boys take the whole jackpot? Not these days, no way!" Bode's nose angled back toward the newspaper. "Where's Grange? Over near Tampa?"

Chub was stunned at his friend's theory. He didn't understand how the lottery could be rigged. If it was, how had he and Bode managed to win even half?

During the brief span of their friendship, Bodean Gazzer had invoked conspiracies to explain numerous puzzling occurrences—for instance, how come there was usually a big airplane crash at Christmastime.

Bode knew the answer, and naturally it involved the U.S. government. The Federal Aviation Administration was in perpetual danger of having its budget slashed, the crucial vote customarily coming in December before Congress adjourned for the holidays. Consequently (Bode revealed to Chub) the FAA always sabotaged an airliner around Christmas, knowing politicians wouldn't have the nerve to cut the funding for air safety while the world watched mangled bodies being pulled out of a charred fuselage.

"Think about it," Bode Gazzer had said—and Chub did. A government plot seemed more plausible than grim coincidence, all those plane crashes.

Corrupting the state Lotto, however, was something else. Chub didn't think even the liberals could pull it off.

"It don't add up," he said sullenly. Plenty of regular white folks had won, too; he'd seen their faces on TV. Speaking of which, he wished the goddamn thing wasn't busted so he could watch football and not have to think about what Bode Gazzer was saying.

"You'll see," Bode told him. "You'll see I'm right. Now, where the hell's Grange, Florida?"

Chub muttered, "Upstate."

"Big help you are. Everything's upstate from here."

From his studded belt Chub took a Colt Python .357 and shot several holes in David Koresh's cheeks.

Bode Gazzer leaned back from the dinette. "What's *your* damn problem?"

"I don't like the way I feel." Chub tucked the gun in the waist of his trousers, the barrel hot against his thigh. Without flinching he said: "Man wins fourteen million bucks, he oughta feel good. And I don't."

"Exactly!" Bode Gazzer charged across the room and seized Chub in a clammy tremble of an embrace. "Now you see"—Bode's voice dropping to a whisper—"what this country of ours has come to. You see what the battle is all about!"

Chub nodded solemnly, withholding his concern that a battle sounded like damn hard work, and hard work sounded like the last damn thing a brand-new millionaire ought to be doing.

. . .

The downsizing trend that swept newspapers in the early nineties was aimed at sustaining the bloated profit margins in which the industry had wallowed for most of the century. A new soulless breed of corporate managers, unburdened by a passion for serious journalism, found an easy way to reduce the cost of publishing a daily newspaper. The first casualty was depth.

Cutting the amount of space devoted to news instantly justified cutting the staff. At many papers, downsizing was the favored excuse for eliminating such luxuries as police desks, suburban editions, foreign bureaus, medical writers, environmental specialists and, of course, investigative teams (which were always antagonizing civic titans and important advertisers). As newspapers grew thinner and shallower, the men who published them worked harder to assure Wall Street that readers neither noticed nor cared.

It was Tom Krome's misfortune to have found a comfortable niche with a respectable but doomed newspaper, and to have been laid off at a time when the business was glutted with hungry experienced writers. It was his further misfortune to have been peaking in his career as an investigative reporter at a time when most newspapers no longer wished to pay for those particular skills.

The Register, for example, was in the market for

a divorce columnist. Sinclair had made the pitch at Krome's job interview.

"We're looking for something funny," Sinclair had said. "Upbeat."

"Upbeat?"

"There's a growing readership out there," Sinclair had said. "You ever been through a divorce?"

"No," Krome had lied.

"Perfect. No baggage, no bitterness, no bile."

Sinclair's fetish for alliteration—it was Krome's first exposure.

"But your ad in *E&P* said 'feature writer.' "

"This would be a feature, Tom. Five hundred words. Twice a week."

Krome had thought: I know what I'll do—I'll move to Alaska! Gut salmon on the slime line. In winters, work on a novel.

"Sorry I wasted your time." He'd stood up, shaken Sinclair's hand (which had, actually, a limp, slick, dead-salmon quality), and flown home to New York.

A week later, the editor had called and offered Krome a feature-writing position at $38,000 a year. No divorce column, thank God—*The Register*'s managing editor, it turned out, had seen nothing upbeat in the topic. "Four-time loser," Sinclair had explained in a whisper.

Tom Krome took the feature-writing job because he needed the money. He was saving for a

cabin on Kodiak Island or possibly up near Fair-
banks, where he'd live by himself. He intended to
buy a snowmobile and photograph wild wolves,
caribou and eventually a grizzly bear. He intended
to write a novel about a fictional actress named
Mary Andrea Finley, based on a true person
named Mary Andrea Finley, who in real life had
spent the last four years successfully preventing
Tom Krome from divorcing her.

He was packing for the Lotto story when Katie
returned from church.

"Where to?" Her purse hit the kitchen table like
a cinder block.

"A place called Grange," Tom Krome said.

"I've been there," Katie said testily. *A place
called Grange.* Like she didn't even know it was a
town. "That's where they have the sightings," she
said.

"Right." Krome wondered if Katie was one of
the religious pilgrims. Anything was possible; he'd
known her only two weeks.

She said, "They've got a Mother Mary that
cries." She went to the refrigerator. Poured herself
a glass of grapefruit juice; Krome, waiting for
more about Grange. "And on the highway," she
said, between sips, "in the middle of the highway,
the face of Jesus Christ."

Tom Krome said, "I heard about that."

"A stain," Katie elaborated. "Dark violet. Like blood."

Or possibly transmission fluid, Krome thought.

"I've only been there once," Katie said. "We stopped for gas on the way to Clearwater."

Krome was relieved to hear she wasn't a Grange regular. He tossed a stack of clean Jockey shorts into the suitcase. "What was your impression of the place?"

"Weird." Katie finished the fruit juice, washed the glass. She slipped out of her shoes and took a seat at the table, where she had a good view of Tom packing. "I didn't see the crying Madonna, just the road-stain Jesus. But the whole town struck me as weird."

Krome suppressed a smile. He was counting on weird.

Katie asked, "When will you be back?"

"Day or two."

"You gonna call me?"

Krome looked up. "Sure, Katie."

"When you get to Grange, I mean."

"Oh . . . sure."

"You thought I meant for you to call when you get back. Didn't you?"

Krome marveled at how, with no effort, he'd gotten himself into a downward-spiraling conversation before noon on a Sunday morning. He was simply trying to pack, for God's sake, yet he'd apparently managed to hurt Katie's feelings.

His theory: It was the pause between the "oh" and the "sure" that had tripped her alarm.

Surrender was the only option: Yes, yes, sweet Katherine, forgive me. You're right, I'm a total shit, insensitive and self-absorbed. What was I thinking! *Of course* I'll call as soon as I get to Grange.

"Katie," he said, "I'll call as soon as I get to Grange."

"It's OK. I know you'll be busy."

Krome closed the suitcase, snapped the latches. "I want to call, all right?"

"OK, but not too late."

"Yes, I remember."

"Art gets home—"

"At six-thirty. I remember."

Art being Katie's husband. Circuit Judge Arthur Battenkill Jr.

Krome felt bad about betraying Art, even though he didn't know the man, and even though Art was cheating on Katie with both his secretaries. This was widely known, Katie had assured him, unbuckling his pants on their second "date." An eye for an eye, she'd said; that's straight from the Bible.

Still, Tom Krome felt guilty. It was nothing new; possibly it was even necessary. Beginning in his teenage years, guilt had played a defining role in every romance Tom Krome ever had. These days it was a steady if oppressive companion in his divorce.

Katie Battenkill had poleaxed him with her fine alert features and lusty wholesomeness. She'd chased after him, literally, one day while he was jogging downtown. He'd gotten tangled in a charity street march—he couldn't recall whether it was for a disease or a disorder—and clumsily slapped some money in her hand. Next thing he knew: footsteps running behind him. She caught up, too. They had lunch at a pizza joint, where the first thing out of Katie's mouth was: "I'm married and I've never done this before. God, I'm starved." Tom Krome liked her tremendously, but he realized that Art was very much part of the equation. Katie was working things out in her own way, and Krome understood his role. It suited him fine, for now.

Barefoot in her nylons, Katie followed him out to the car. He got in and, perhaps too hastily, fit the key in the ignition. She leaned over and kissed him goodbye; quite a long kiss. Afterwards she lingered at the car door. He noticed she was holding a disposable camera.

"For your trip," she said, handing it to him. "There's five shots left. Maybe six."

Krome thanked her but explained it was unnecessary. Sinclair would be sending a staff photographer if the lottery story panned out.

"That's for the newspaper," Katie said. "This is for me. Could you take a picture of the weeping Madonna?"

For a moment Krome thought she was kidding. She wasn't.

"Please, Tom?"

He put the cardboard camera in his jacket. "What if she's not crying? The Virgin Mary. You still want a picture?"

Katie didn't catch the sarcasm that leaked into his voice. "Oh yes," she said ardently. "Even without the tears."

 The mayor of Grange, Jerry Wicks, complimented JoLayne Lucks on her cooters.

"My babies," she said fondly. Her blue fingernails sparkled as she shredded a head of iceberg lettuce into the aquarium. The turtles commenced a mute scramble for supper.

Jerry Wicks said, "How many you got there?"

"Forty-six, I believe."

"My, my."

"There's red-bellies, Suwanees and two young peninsulars, which I am told will grow up to be something special. And see how they all get along!"

"Yes, ma'am." Jerry Wicks couldn't tell one

from another. He was impressed, however, by the volume of noise made by the feeding reptiles. He was quite certain the crunching would drive him insane if he lingered too long.

"JoLayne, the reason I came by—there's talk you won the Lotto!"

JoLayne Lucks dried her hands on a towel. She offered the mayor a glass of limeade, which he declined.

"It's your own private business," he went on, "and there's no need to tell me yes or no. But if it's true, nobody deserves it more than you. . . ."

"And why's that?"

Jerry Wicks was stumped for a reply. Ordinarily he wasn't nervous around pretty women, but this afternoon JoLayne Lucks possessed an uncommonly powerful aura; a fragrant dazzle, a mischievous twinkling that made him feel both silly and careless. He wanted to run away before she had him down on the floor, howling like a coon hound.

"The reason I'm here, JoLayne, I'm thinking about the town. It'd be great for Grange if it was true. About you winning."

"Publicitywise," she said.

"Exactly," he exclaimed with relief. "It would be such a welcome change from the usual . . ."

"Freak shit?"

The mayor winced. "Well, I wouldn't . . . "

"Like the road stain or the weepy Virgin,"

JoLayne said, "or Mister Amador's phony stigmata."

Dominick Amador was a local builder who'd lost his contracting license after the walls of the Saint Arthur catechism school collapsed for no good reason during a summer squall. Dominick Amador's buddies advised him to relocate to Dade County, where it was safe for incompetent contractors, but Dominick wanted to stay in Grange with his wife and girlfriends. So one night he got hammered on Black Jack and Xanax, and (using a three-eighth-inch wood bit) drilled a perfect hole in each of his palms. Now Amador was one of the stars of Grange's Christian pilgrim tour, touting himself as a carpenter ("just like Jesus!") and assiduously picking at the circular wounds in his hands to keep them authentically unscabbed and bloody. There were rumors he was planning to drill his feet soon.

The mayor said to JoLayne Lucks: "See here, I'm not one to pass judgment on others."

"But you're a religious man," she said. "Do *you* believe?"

Jerry Wicks wondered how the conversation had drifted so far off course. He said, "What I personally believe isn't important. Others do—I've seen it in their eyes."

JoLayne popped a Certs. She was sorry about putting the mayor on the spot. Jerry wasn't a bad fellow, just soft. Thin blond hair going gray at the sides. Pink slack cheeks, a picket line of tiny perfect teeth, and sparse guileless eyebrows. Jerry ran an insurance business he'd inherited from his mother; homeowners and auto, mostly. He was harmless and chubby. JoLayne kept all her coverage with him; most everyone in town did.

Jerry said, "I guess the point to be made, it'd be good for Grange to get a different slant of publicity."

"Let the world know," JoLayne agreed, "there's normal folks who live here, too."

"Right," said the mayor.

"Not just Jesus freaks and scammers."

The blunt words caused in Jerry Wicks a pain similar to an abdominal cramp. "JoLayne, *please.*"

"Oh, I'm sorry to be such a cynical young lady. Don't ask how I got this way."

By now the mayor realized JoLayne Lucks had no intention of telling him whether or not she'd won the Lotto. The rhythmic munch of her hungry cooters had become almost unbearable.

"You want one?" she asked. "For Jerry junior?"

Jerry Wicks said no thanks. He eyed the teeming aquarium and thought: Look who's talking about freaks.

JoLayne reached across the kitchen table and tweaked him in the ribs. "Hey, cheer up."

The mayor turned to gooseflesh at her touch; he

smiled bashfully and looked away. He beheld a
fleeting impure fantasy: JoLayne's blue fingernails
raking slowly across his pallid, acne-scarred
shoulder blades.

Teasingly she said, "You came here to tell me
something, Jerry. So let's hear it already, 'fore we
both die of old age."

"Yes, all right. There's a newspaper reporter
coming into town. From *The Register.* He's got a
reservation at the bed-and-breakfast—Mrs. Hendricks told me."

"For tonight?"

"That's what she said. Anyhow, he's looking for
the lottery winner. To do a feature story, is my
guess."

"Oh," said JoLayne Lucks.

"Nothing to worry about." As mayor, Jerry
Wicks had experience dealing with the press. He
said, "They love to write about ordinary people
who make it big."

"Really." JoLayne pursed her lips.

"Human interest, they call it." The mayor
wanted to reassure her there was nothing to fear
from giving interviews. He hoped she would be co-
operative and friendly, since the image of Grange
was at stake.

JoLayne said, "Do I have to talk to him?"

"No." Jerry Wicks' heart sank.

"Because I'm fond of my privacy."

"The man doesn't have to come to the house. Fact, it'd be better if he didn't." The mayor was worried about JoLayne's turtle hobby, and what cruel fun a snotty city reporter might have with that. "Maybe you could meet him at the restaurant in the Holiday Inn."

"Yum," said JoLayne.

The phone on the kitchen wall rang. She stood up. "I've got some errands. Thanks for stopping over."

Jerry Wicks said, "I just thought you should know what's ahead. Winning the Lotto is very big news."

"Must be," JoLayne Lucks said.

The mayor told her goodbye and let himself out. As he walked from the porch to the driveway, he could hear JoLayne's telephone ringing and ringing and ringing.

Chub said they should drive directly to Tallahassee and claim their half of the $28 million jackpot as soon as humanly possible. Bodean Gazzer said nope, not just yet.

"We got one hundred and eighty days to pick it up. That's six whole months." He loaded a cold twelve-pack into the truck. "Right now we gotta find that other ticket before whoever's got it cashes in."

"Maybe they already done it. Maybe it's too late."

"Don't think so negative."

"*Life* is fucking negative," Chub noted.

Bode spread a striped beach towel on the passenger half of the front seat, to shield the new upholstery from the gun grease and sweat that was Chub's natural marinade. Chub took mild offense at the precaution but said nothing.

A few minutes later, speeding along the turnpike, Bode Gazzer summarized his plan: "Break in, rip off the ticket, then split."

"Happens we can't find it?" Chub asked. "What supposed they hid it too good?"

"There you go again."

"I ain't interested in felony time."

"Relax, goddammit."

"I mean, my God, we's millionaires," Chub went on. "Millionaires, they don't do b-and-e's!"

"No, but they steal just the same. We use crowbars, they use Jews and briefcases."

As usual, Bode had a point. Chub hunkered down with a Budweiser to think on it.

Bode said, "Hey, I don't wanna go to jail, either. Say we go up on charges, who'd take over the White Rebels?"

The White Rebel Brotherhood is what Bodean Gazzer had decided to call his new militia. Chub didn't fuss about the name; it wasn't as if they'd be printing up business cards.

Bode said, "Hey, d'you finish that book I gave you? On how to be a survivalist?"

"No, I did not." Chub had gotten as far as the business on eating bugs, and that was it. "How to Tell Toxic Insects from Edible Insects." Jesus Willy Christ.

"I didn't see no chapter on prime rib," he grumbled.

To ease the tension, Bode asked Chub if he'd like to make a bet on who was holding the other winning Lotto numbers. "I got ten bucks says it's a Negro. You want to take Jews, or Cubans?"

Chub had never met a white supremacist who said "Negro" instead of "nigger." "Is they a difference?" he inquired sarcastically.

"No, sir," said Bode.

"Then why don't you call 'em what they is?"

Bode clenched the steering wheel. "I could call 'em coconuts and what's the damn difference. One word's no better than another."

Chub chuckled. "Coconuts."

"How about you make yourself useful. Find a radio station plays some white music, if that's possible."

"S'matter? You ain't fond a these *Negro* rappers?"

"Eat me," Bode Gazzer said.

He was ashamed to admit the truth, that he couldn't speak the word "nigger." He'd done so only once in his life, at age twelve, and his father had promptly hauled him outside and whipped his hairless bare ass with a razor strop. Then his mother had dragged him into the kitchen and washed his mouth out with Comet cleanser and vinegar. It was the worst (and only) corporal punishment of Bode Gazzer's childhood, and he'd never forgiven his parents. He'd also never forgotten the ghastly caustic taste of Comet, the scorch of which still revisited his tender throat at the mere whisper of "nigger." Uttering it aloud was out of the question.

Which was a major handicap for a self-proclaimed racist and militiaman. Bode Gazzer worked around it.

Changing the subject, he said to Chub: "You need some camos, buddy."

"I don't think so."

"What size pants you wear?"

Chub slumped in the seat and pretended he was trying to sleep. He didn't want to ride all the way to Grange. He didn't want to break into a stranger's house and steal a Lotto ticket.

And he sure as hell didn't want to wear camouflage clothes. Bode Gazzer's entire wardrobe was camo, which he'd ordered from the Cabela's fall catalog on a stolen MasterCard number. Bode believed camo garb would be essential for survival when the NATO troops invaded from the Bahamas and the White Rebel Brotherhood took to the woods. Until Bode opened his closet, Chub had had no idea that camo came in so many shrub-and-twig styles. There was your basic Trebark (Bode's parka); your Realtree (Bode's rainsuit); your Mossy Oak, Timber Ghost and Treestand (Bode's collection of jumpsuits, shirts and trousers), your Konifer (Bode's snake-proof chaps) and your Tru-Leaf (Bode's all-weather mountain boots).

Chub didn't dispute Bode's pronouncement that such a selection of camos, properly matched, would make a man invisible among the oaks and pines. Having grown up in the mountains of north Georgia, Chub didn't want to be invisible in the woods. He wanted to be seen and heard. He especially wanted not to be mistaken for a tree by a rambunctious bear or a randy bobcat.

He said to Bode Gazzer: "You dress up your way, I'll dress up mine."

Bode peevishly scooped a fresh beer off the floorboard and popped the tab. "Remember what the Constitution says? 'Well-*regulated* militia.' Regulated means discipline, OK? And discipline starts with uniforms."

Bode took a slug and wedged the beer can in the crotch of his Mossy Oak trousers, to free both hands for steering. Chub leaned against the door, his ponytail leaving an oily smear on the window. He said, "I ain't wearin' no camo."

"Why not, goddammit!"

" 'Cause it makes you look like a fuckin' compost heap."

Bode Gazzer jerked the truck onto the shoulder of the highway. Angrily he stomped the brake.

"You listen—" he began.

"No, *you* listen!" Chub said, and was upon him in a second.

Bode felt the barrel of the Colt poking the soft part of his throat, right about where his tongue was attached on the inside. He felt Chub's hot beery breath on his forehead.

"Let's not fight," Bode pleaded, hoarsely.

"Won't be a fight. Be a killin'."

"Hey, brother, we're partners."

Chub said, "Then where's *our* ticket, dickface?"

"The lottery ticket?"

"No, the fucking laundry ticket." Chub cocked the pistol. "Where's it at?"

"Don't do this."

"I'm countin' to five."

"In my wallet. Inside a rubber."

Chub grinned crookedly. "Lemme see."

"A Trojan. One a them ribbed jobbers, nonlubricated." Bode removed it from his wallet and showed Chub what he'd done the night before— opening the plastic foil with a razor and folding the Lotto ticket inside the rolled-up condom.

Chub returned the gun to his pants and slid back to the passenger side. "That's pretty slick, I gotta admit. Nobody steals another man's rubbers. Steals every other damn thing, but not that."

"Exactly," Bode said. As soon as his heart stopped skipping, he put the truck in gear and eased back on the turnpike.

Chub watched him in a neutral but not entirely innocuous way. He said: "You understand what coulda happened? That we wouldn't be partners no more if I blowed your brains all over this truck and took the Lotto stub for m'self."

Bode nodded tightly. Until now it hadn't occurred that Chub might rip him off. Obviously it was something to think about. He said, "It's gonna work out fine. You'll see."

"OK," said Chub. He opened a beer: warm and fizzy. He closed his eyes and sucked down half the can. He wanted to trust Bode Gazzer but it wasn't always easy. *Negro,* for God's sake. Why'd he keep on with that word? It troubled Chub, made him wonder if Bode wasn't all he claimed to be.

Then he had another thought. "They a whorehouse in Grange?"

"Who knows," Bode said, "and who cares."

"Just don't forget where you hid our ticket."

"Gimme a break, Chub."

"Be helluva way to lose out on fourteen million bucks, winds up in the sheets of some whorehouse."

Bode Gazzer stared straight ahead at the highway. He said, "Man, you got a wild imagination."

The brains of a goddamn squirrel, but a wild imagination.

Tom Krome didn't wait to unpack; tossed his carry bag on the bed and dashed out. The owner of the bed-and-breakfast was pleased to give directions to the home of Miss JoLayne Lucks, at the corner of Cocoa and Hubbard across from the park. Krome's plan was to drop in with sincere apologies, invite Miss Lucks to a proper dinner, then ease into the interview gradually.

His experience as a visiting journalist in small towns was that some folks would tell you their life story at the drop of a hat, and others wouldn't say boo if your hair was on fire. Waiting on the woman's porch, Krome didn't know what to expect. He had knocked: No reply. He knocked again. Lights shone in the living room, and Krome heard music from a radio.

He walked around to the backyard and rose on his toes, to peer in the kitchen window. There were signs of a finished meal on the table: a setting for one. Coffee cup, salad bowl, a bare plate with a half-nibbled biscuit.

When Krome returned to the porch, the door stood open. The radio was off, the house was still.

"Hello!" he called.

He took a half step inside. The first thing he no-

ticed was the aquarium. The second thing was
water on the hardwood floor; a trail of drips.

From down the hall, a woman's voice: "Shut the
door, please. Are you the reporter?"

"Yes, that's right." Tom Krome wondered how
she knew. "Are you JoLayne?"

"What is it you want? I'm really not up for this."

Krome said, "You all right?"

"Come see for yourself."

She was sitting in the bathtub, with soap bubbles up to her breasts. She had a towel on her hair
and a shotgun in her hands. Krome raised his arms
and said, "I'm not going to hurt you."

"No shit," said JoLayne Lucks. "I've got a
twelve-gauge and all you've got is a tape recorder."

Krome nodded. The Pearlcorder he used for interviews was cupped in his right hand.

"Sure is tiny," JoLayne remarked. "Sit down."
She motioned with the gun toward the commode.
"What's your name?"

"Tom Krome. I'm with *The Register.*" He sat
where she told him to sit.

She said, "I've had more company today than I
can stand. Is this what it's like to be rich?"

Krome smiled inwardly. She was going to be one
helluva story.

"Take out the cassette," JoLayne Lucks told
him, "and drop it in the tub."

Krome played along. "Anything else?"

"Yeah. Quit staring."

"I'm sorry."

"Don't tell me you never saw a woman take a bath. Oh my, is it the bubbles? They sure don't last long."

Krome locked his eyes on the ceiling. "I can come back tomorrow."

JoLayne said, "Would you kindly stand up. Good. Now turn around. Get the robe off that hook and hand it to me—without peeking, please."

He heard the slosh of her climbing out of the tub. Then the lights in the bathroom went out.

"That was me," she said. "Don't try anything."

It was so dark that Krome couldn't see his own nose. He felt something sharp at his back.

"Gun," JoLayne explained.

"Gotcha."

"I want you to take off your clothes."

"For Christ's sake."

"And get in the bathtub."

"No!" he said.

"You want your interview, Mr. Krome?"

Until that moment, everything that had happened in the house of JoLayne Lucks was splendid material for Krome's feature story. But not this part, the disrobing-at-gunpoint of the reporter. Sinclair would never be told.

Once Krome was in the water, JoLayne Lucks turned on the lights. She stood the shotgun against the toilet, and knelt next to the tub. "How you feeling?" she asked.

"Ridiculous."

"Well, you shouldn't. You're a good-enough-looking man." She peeled the towel off her head and shook her hair.

Tom Krome roiled the water to churn up more soap bubbles, in a futile effort to conceal his shriveled cock. JoLayne thought that was absolutely adorable. Krome fidgeted self-consciously. He reflected on the difficult and occasionally dangerous situations in which he'd found himself as a reporter—urban riots, drug busts, hurricanes, police shootouts, even a foreign coup. Yet he'd never felt so stymied and helpless. The woman had thought it out very carefully.

"Why are you doing this?" he asked.

"Because I was scared of you."

"There's nothing to be scared of."

"Oh, I can see that."

He laughed then. Couldn't help it. JoLayne Lucks laughed, too. "You gotta admit it breaks the ice."

Krome said, "You left the front door open."

"I sure did."

"And that's what you do when you're scared? Leave the door open and wait buck naked in the bath?"

"With a Remington," JoLayne reminded him, "full of nickel turkey load. Gift from Daddy." She ran some hot water into the tub. "You gettin' chilly?"

Krome kept his hands folded across his groin. There was no sense trying to act casual, but he did. JoLayne put her chin on the edge of the tub. "What do you want to know, Mr. Krome?"

"Did you win the lottery?"

"Yes, I won the lottery."

"Why aren't you happy about it?"

"Who says I'm not."

"Will you keep your job at Dr. Crawford's?" The lady at the bed-and-breakfast had told him Jo-Layne Lucks worked at the veterinary clinic.

She said, "Hey, your fingers are pruning up."

Krome was determined to overcome the distraction of his own nakedness. "Can I ask a favor? There's a notebook and a ballpoint pen in the pocket of my pants."

"Oh, no you don't."

"But you promised."

"I beg your pardon?" She picked up the gun again; gonged the barrel loudly against the tub's iron faucet, which protruded from the wall between Krome's feet.

OK, he thought. We'll do it her way.

"JoLayne, have you ever won anything before?"

"Bikini contest at Daytona. I was eighteen, for heaven's sake, but I know what you're thinking." She rolled her eyes.

Krome said, "What was the prize?"

"Two hundred bucks." She paused. Puffed her cheeks. Propped the shotgun against the sink. "Look, I can't lie. It was a wet T-shirt contest. I tell people it was bikinis because it doesn't sound so slutty."

"Heck, you were just a kid."

"But you'd put it in the newspaper anyway. It's too juicy *not* to."

She was right: It was an irresistible anecdote—yet one that could be retold tastefully, even poignantly, as JoLayne Lucks would appreciate when she finally saw Tom Krome's feature article. In the meantime he could do little but gaze at the glassy bubbles that clung to the wet hair on his chest. He felt disarmed and preposterous.

"What are you afraid of?" he asked JoLayne.

"I've got just an awful feeling."

"Like a vision?" Krome was fishing to see if she was one of the local paranormals. He hoped not, even though it would've made for a more colorful story.

"Not a vision, just a feeling," she said. "The way you can sometimes feel a storm coming, even when there's not a cloud in the sky."

It was agony, hearing one good quote after another slip away untranscribed. Again he begged for his notebook.

JoLayne shook her head. "This isn't the interview, Mr. Krome. This is the *pre*-interview."

"But Miss Lucks—"

"Fourteen million dollars is a mountain of money. I believe it will attract a bad element." She reached into the water—deftly insinuating her hand under Tom Krome's butt—and yanked the drain plug out of the bathtub.

"Dry off and get dressed," she told him. "How do you like your coffee?"

Demencio was carrying out the garbage when the red pickup rolled to a stop under the streetlight. Two men got out and stretched. The shorter one wore pointed cowboy boots and olive-drab camouflage, like a deer hunter. The taller one had a scraggy ponytail and sunken drugged-out eyes.

Demencio said: "Visitation's over."

"Visitation of what?" asked the hunter.

"The Madonna."

"She die?" The ponytailed one spun toward his friend. "Goddamn, you hear that?"

Demencio dropped the garbage bag on the curb. "I'm talking about Madonna, the Virgin Mary. Jesus' mother."

"Not the singer?"

"Nope, not the singer."

The hunter said, "What's a 'visitation'?"

"People travel from all over to pray at the Madonna's statue. Sometimes she cries real tears."

"No shit?"

"No shit," said Demencio. "Come back tomorrow and see for yourself."

The ponytailed man said, "How much you charge?"

"Whatever you can spare, sir. We take donations only." Demencio was trying to be polite, but the two men made him edgy. Hicks he could handle; hard-core rednecks scared him.

The strangers whispered back and forth, then the camouflaged one spoke up again: "Hey, Julio, we in Grange?"

Demencio, feeling his neck go tight: "Yeah, that's right."

"Is there a 7-Eleven somewheres nearby?"

"All we got is the Grab N'Go." Demencio pointed down the street. "About half a mile."

"Thank you kindly," said the hunter.

"Double for me," said the ponytailed man.

Before the pickup drove away, Demencio noticed a red-white-and-blue sticker on the rear bumper: MARK FUHRMAN FOR PRESIDENT.

Definitely not pilgrims, Demencio thought.

Chub was intrigued by what the Cuban had said. A statue that cries? About what?

"You'd cry, too," said Bodean Gazzer, "if you was stuck in a shithole town like this."

"So you don't believe him."

"No, I do not."

Chub said, "I seen weepin' Virgin Marys on TV before."

"I've seen Bugs Bunny on TV, too. That make him real? Maybe you think there's a real rabbit that sings and dances dressed up in a fucking tuxedo—"

"Ain't the same thing." Chub was insulted by Bode's acid sarcasm. Sometimes his friend seemed to forget who had the gun.

"Here we are!" Bode declared, waving at a flashing sign that spelled out GRAB N'GO. He parked in the handicapped space by the front door and flipped on the dome light inside the truck. From a pocket he took out the folded clipping from *The Miami Herald.* The story said the second winning lottery ticket had been purchased "in the rural community of Grange." The winner, it reported, hadn't yet come forward to claim his or her share of the prize.

Bode read this aloud to Chub, who said: "Can't be many Lotto joints in a town this size."

"Let's ask," said Bode.

They went into the Grab N'Go and picked up two twelve-packs of beer, a cellophane bag of beefalo jerky, a carton of Camels and a walnut coffee cake. While the clerk rang them up, Bode inquired about Lotto tickets.

"How many you want? We're the only game in town," the clerk said.

"Is that a fact." Bode Gazzer gave a smug wink at Chub.

The clerk was eighteen, maybe nineteen. He was heavyset and freshly sunburned. He had a buzz cut and a steep pimpled nose. A plastic tag identified him as SHINER.

He said, "Maybe you guys heard—this store had the winning ticket yesterday."

"Go on!"

"God's truth. I sold it to the woman myself."

Bode Gazzer lit a cigaret. "Right here? No way."

Chub said, "Sounds like a line a shit to me."

"No, I swear." With a finger the clerk crossed his heart. "Girl name of JoLayne Lucks."

"Yeah? How much she win?" Chub asked.

"Well, first it was twenty-eight million, but come to find out she's gotta split it. Someone else had the same numbers, is what the news said. Somebody down around Miami."

"Is that a fact." Bode paid for the beer and groceries. Then he tossed a five-dollar bill on the counter. "Tell you what, Mister Shiner. Give me five Quick Picks, assuming you still got the magic touch."

The clerk smiled. "You come to the right place. Town's famous for miracles." He pulled the tickets from the Lotto machine and handed them to Bodean Gazzer.

Chub said, "She a local gal, this Joleen?"

"Lives acrost from the park. And it's *JoLayne.*"

Chub, scratching his neck: "I wonder if she's lookin' for a husband."

The clerk grinned and lowered his voice. "No offense, sir, but she's a little too tan for you."

They all had a laugh. Bode and Chub said goodbye and walked out to the truck. For a while the two men sat in the cab, drinking beer, gnawing on jerky, not speaking a word.

Finally Chub said, "So it's just like you said."

"Yup. Just like I said."

"Goddamn. A *Negro.*" With both hands Chub tore into the coffee cake.

"Eat quick," Bode told him. "We got work to do."

Tom Krome spent three hours with JoLayne Lucks. To call it an interview was a stretch. He'd never met anyone, politicians and convicts included, who could so adroitly steer conversation in a wrong direction. JoLayne Lucks held the added advantages of soft eyes and charm, to which Krome easily succumbed. By the end of the evening, she knew everything important there was to know about him, while he knew next to nothing about her. Even the turtles remained an enigma.

"Where'd you get them?" he asked.

"Creeks. Hey, I like your wristwatch."

"Thanks. It was a gift."

"From a lady friend, I'll bet!"

"My wife, a long time ago."

"How long you been married?"

"We're divorcing. . . ." And away he'd go.

At half past ten JoLayne's father called from
Atlanta. She apologized for not picking up when
he'd phoned earlier. She said she'd had company.

When Tom Krome rose to leave, JoLayne told
her father to hang on. She led Krome to the door
and said it had been a pleasure to make his ac-
quaintance.

"May I come back tomorrow," he asked, "and
take some notes?"

"Nope."

She gave him a gentle nudge. The screen door
slapped shut between them.

"I've decided," she said, "not to be in your
newspaper."

"Please."

"Sorry."

Tom Krome said, "You don't understand."

"Not everybody wants to be famous."

He felt her slipping away. "Please. One hour
with the tape recorder. It'll be fine, you'll see."

That was the lie, of course. No matter what
Krome wrote about JoLayne Lucks winning
the lottery, it wouldn't be fine. Nothing positive
could come from telling the whole world you're
a millionaire, and JoLayne was smart enough to
know it.

She said, "I'm sorry for your trouble, but I prefer to keep my privacy."

"You really don't have a choice." That was the part she didn't understand.

JoLayne stepped closer to the screen. "What do you mean?"

Krome shrugged apologetically. "There's going to be a story in the papers, one way or another. This is news. This is the way it works."

She turned and disappeared into the house.

Krome stood on the porch, contemplating the hum and bubble of the aquarium pump. He felt like a shitheel, but that was nothing new. He took out one of his business cards and wrote on the back of it: "Please call if you change your mind."

He inserted the card in the doorjamb and returned to the bed-and-breakfast. In his room he saw a note on the dresser: Katie had phoned. So had Dick Turnquist.

Krome sat heavily on the edge of the bed, pondering the slim likelihood that his New York divorce lawyer had tracked him down in Grange, Florida, on a Sunday night to deliver good tidings. He waited twenty minutes before making the call.

JoLayne Lucks worked as an assistant to Dr. Cecil Crawford, the town veterinarian. JoLayne had been trained as a registered nurse, and easily could have earned twice as much money at the county hospital if she hadn't preferred animal patients over human ones. And she excelled at her job. Everyone in Grange who owned a pet knew Jo-Layne Lucks. Where Doc Crawford could be cranky and terse, JoLayne was all tenderness and concern. That she was rumored to be eccentric in her private life was intriguing but immaterial; she had a special way with the animals. Just about everybody was fond of her, including a number of lifelong bigots who confided that she was the only black person they'd ever trusted. JoLayne found it interesting that so many of the local racists owned small, neurotic, ill-tempered breeds of dogs. The women favored toy poodles; the men, grossly overfed Chihuahuas. In Dade County, where Jo-Layne grew up, it was German shepherds and pit bulls.

The job at Dr. Crawford's clinic was only Jo-Layne's second since leaving nursing school. Her first job was at the infamously exotic emergency room of Jackson Memorial Hospital, in down-town Miami. That's where JoLayne had met three of the six serious men in her life:

Dan Colavito, the stockbroker, who on a daily basis would promise to give up cigars, cocaine and over-the-counter biotechs. He'd arrived on a Sat-urday night at Jackson with four broken toes, the consequence of dashing into the middle of Ocean Drive and kicking (for no apparent reason) what turned out to be Julio Iglesias' personal limousine;

Robert Nossario, the policeman, who would spend his road shifts stopping attractive young female drivers, few of whom had committed an actual traffic offense. Officer Nossario had been brought to the emergency room complaining of a severely bruised testicle, the result (or so he said) of falling on his nightstick while trying to subdue a burglary suspect;

Dr. Neal Grossberger, the young chiropractor, who would phone JoLayne at least twice an hour when she was home, and who would weep like a drunk when she'd refuse to wear the portable pager he'd bought her (baby blue, to match her hospital scrubs), and who couldn't get dressed in the morning without calling to ask what socks he should wear. Neal had come breathlessly to the hospital after consuming a suspect gooseneck clam, and had waited seven hours in the emergency room for what he'd predicted would be a virulent onset of salmonella, which never arrived.

JoLayne Lucks finally quit the hospital after meeting and marrying Lawrence Dwyer, the lawyer. Like JoLayne's other lovers, Lawrence had good qualities that were instantly obvious and bad qualities that took a bit longer to surface. It was Lawrence who'd suggested to JoLayne that they move upstate to Grange, where he could concentrate on fighting his disbarment, absent big-city distractions such as vengeful ex-clients. Such was JoLayne's affection for Lawrence (and her deter-

mination to make the marriage work) that she'd
declined to read the four loose-leaf volumes of
trial transcripts from his Miami fraud conviction.
She'd chosen instead to believe her husband's
claim of complete innocence, which relied on a
complicated theory of prosecutorial entrapment,
judicial conspiracy and a careless bookkeeper
whose "zeroes looked exactly like sixes!"

In Grange it had been JoLayne who'd found the
old house on Cocoa and Hubbard, and JoLayne
who'd put up the down payment. She had been
touched and secretly proud when Lawrence took
the job as a toll taker on the Beeline Expressway—
until he got arrested for stealing the jumbo-sized
bag of change. That evening, after boxing all her
husband's clothes, jewelry and toiletries for the
Salvation Army, JoLayne made a backyard bon-
fire of his law books, files, depositions and corre-
spondence with the Florida Bar. After the divorce
she asked Dr. Crawford if she could cut back to
three days a week at the animal clinic; she said she
needed time to herself.

That's when she started exploring Simmons
Wood, a rolling splash of oak, pine and palmetto
scrub on the outskirts of town. Once or twice a
week, JoLayne would park on the main highway,
hop the short wire fence and disappear into the
tree line. Every green thicket was an adventure,
every clearing was a sanctuary. She kept a spiral
notebook of the wildlife she saw: snakes, opos-

sums, raccoons, foxes, a bobcat, a half dozen species of tiny warblers. The baby turtles came from a creek—JoLayne didn't know the name. The creek water was the color of apricot tea, and it ran through a stand of mossy oaks down to a sandy, under-cut bluff. That was where JoLayne usually stopped to rest and eat lunch. One afternoon she counted eleven little cooters perched on flat rocks and logs. She loved the way they craned their painted necks and poked out their scaly legs to catch the sunlight. When a small alligator swam by, JoLayne tossed it part of her ham sandwich, to keep its mind off the turtles.

She never thought of taking the little fellows out of the creek, until that day she'd parked on the edge of Simmons Wood and noticed a freshly painted FOR SALE sign facing the highway: 44 acres, zoned commercial. At first JoLayne thought it was a mistake. Forty-four acres couldn't be right—it sounded too small. The Wood seemed to go on forever when JoLayne was walking there. She'd driven straight back to town and stopped at the Grange courthouse to check the plat book. On paper Simmons Wood was shaped like a kidney, which surprised JoLayne. On her hikes she'd tried not to think of the place as having boundaries, but there they were. The FOR SALE sign had been correct on the acreage, too. JoLayne had hurried home and phoned the real estate company named on the sign. The agent, a friend of JoLayne's, told

her the property was grandfathered for development into a retail shopping mall. The next morning, JoLayne started taking the baby turtles from
the creek. She couldn't bear the thought of them
being buried alive by bulldozers. She would have
tried to save the other animals, too, but almost
everything else was too fast to catch, or too hard
to handle. So she'd concentrated on the cooters,
and from a pet-supply catalog at Dr. Crawford's
she'd ordered the largest aquarium she could
afford.

And when JoLayne Lucks learned she'd won the
Florida lottery, she knew immediately what to do
with the money: She would buy Simmons Wood
and save it.

She was sitting at the kitchen table, working up
the numbers on a pocket calculator, when she
heard a sharp knock from the porch. She figured it
must be Tom, the newspaperman, giving it one
more shot. Who else would be so brash as to drop
by at midnight?

The screen door opened before JoLayne got
there. A stranger stepped into her living room. He
was dressed like a hunter.

Krome asked, "Did you find her?"

"Yes," said Dick Turnquist.

"Where?"

"I hesitate to tell you."

"Then don't," said Krome. He lay on the sheets with his fingers interlocked behind his head. To keep the receiver at his ear he'd propped it in the fleshy pocket above his collarbone. Years of talking to editors from motel rooms had led him to perfect a supine, hands-free technique for using the telephone.

Turnquist said, "She's checked herself into rehab, Tom. Says she's hooked on antidepressants."

"That's ridiculous."

"Says she's eating Prozacs like Pez."

"I want her served."

"Tried," Turnquist said. "The judge says leave her alone. Wants a hearing to find out if she is of 'diminished mental capacity.'"

Krome cackled bitterly. Turnquist was sympathetic.

Mary Andrea Finley Krome had been resisting divorce for almost four years. She could not be assuaged with offers of excessive alimony or a cash buyout. *I don't want money, I want Tom.* No one was more baffled than Tom himself, who was acutely aware of his deficiencies as a domestic companion. The dispute had been brutally elongated because the case was filed in Brooklyn, which was, with the possible exception of Vatican City, the worst place in the world to expedite a divorce. Further complicating the procedure was the fact that the estranged Mrs. Krome was an accomplished stage actress who was capable, as she demonstrated time and again, of convincing the most hard-bitten judge of her fragile mental condition. She also had a habit of disappearing for months at a time with obscure road shows—most recently it was a musical adaptation of *The Silence of the Lambs*—which made it difficult to serve her with court summonses.

Tom Krome said, "Dick, I can't take much more."

"The competency hearing is set two weeks from tomorrow."

"How long can she drag this out?"

"You mean, what's the record?"

Krome sat up in bed. He caught the phone before it hit his lap. He put the receiver flush to his lips and said loudly: *"Does she even have a goddamn lawyer yet?"*

"I doubt it," said Dick Turnquist. "Get some rest, Tom."

"Where is she?"

"Mary Andrea?"

"Where's this rehab center?" Krome asked.

"You don't want to know."

"Oh, let me guess. Switzerland?"

"Maui."

"Fuck."

Dick Turnquist said things could be worse. Tom Krome said he didn't think so. He gave the lawyer permission to round up a couple of expert witnesses on Prozac for the upcoming hearing.

"Shouldn't be hard," Krome added. "Who wouldn't love a free trip to Hawaii?"

Two hours later, he was startled awake by the light graze of fingernails on his cheek.

Katie. Krome realized he'd fallen asleep without locking his door. Moron! He sprung upright.

The room was black. He smelled perfumed soap.

"Katherine?" Christ, she must've run out on her husband!

"No, it's me. Please don't turn on the light."

He felt the mattress shift as JoLayne Lucks sat beside him. In the darkness she found one of his hands and brought it to her face.

"Oh no," said Krome.

"There were two of them." Her voice was thick.

"Let me see."

"Keep it dark. Please, Tom."

He traced along her forehead, down her cheeks. One of her eyes was swollen shut—a raw knot, hot to the touch. Her top lip was split open, bloody and crusting.

"Jesus," Krome sighed. He made her lie down. "I'm calling a doctor."

"No," JoLayne said.

"And the cops."

"Don't!"

Krome felt like his chest would explode. Gently JoLayne pulled him down, so they were lying side by side.

"They got the ticket," she whispered.

It took a moment for him to understand: The lottery ticket, of course.

"They made me give it to them," she said.

"Who?"

"I never saw them before. There were two of them."

Krome heard her swallow, fighting the tears. His head was thundering—he had to do something. Get the woman to a hospital. Notify the police. Interview the neighbors in case somebody saw something, heard something . . .

But Tom Krome couldn't move. JoLayne Lucks hung on to his arm as if she were drowning. He turned on his side and carefully embraced her.

She shivered and said, "They *made* me give it to them."

"It's OK."

"No—"

"You're going to be all right. That's the important thing."

"No," she cried, "you don't understand."

A few minutes later, after her breathing settled, Krome reached over to the bedstand and turned on the lamp. JoLayne closed her eyes while he studied the cuts and bruises.

"What else did they do?" he asked.

"Punched me in the stomach. And other places."

JoLayne saw his eyes flash, his jaw tighten. He told her: "It's time to get up. We've got to do something about this."

"Damn right," she said. "That's why I came to you."

 They took turns examining themselves in the rearview mirror, Chub swearing extravagantly: "Goddamn nigger bitch, goddamn we shoulda kilt her."

"Yeah, yeah," said Bodean Gazzer.

They both hurt like hell and looked worse. Chub had deep scratches down his cheeks, and his left eyelid was sliced in half—one ragged flap blinked, the other didn't. He was soiled with blood, mostly his own.

He said, "I never seen such fuckin' fingernails. You?"

Bode muttered in assent. His face and throat bore numerous purple-welted bite marks. The crazy cunt had also chewed off a substantial segment of one eyebrow, and Bode was having a time plugging the hole.

In a worn voice, he said: "Important thing is we got the ticket."

"Which I'll hang on to," Chub said, "just to be safe." And to make things even, he thought. No way was he about to let Bode Gazzer hold *both* Lotto tickets.

"Fine with me," Bode said, though it wasn't. He was in too much pain to argue. He'd never seen a woman fight so ferociously. Christ, she'd left them looking like gator puke!

Chub said, "They's animals. Total goddamn animals."

Bode agreed. "White girl'd never fuss like that. Not even for fourteen million bucks."

"I'm serious, we shoulda kilt her."

"Right. Wasn't you the one had no interest in jail time?"

"Bode, go fuck yourself."

Chub pressed a sodden bandanna to his tattered eyelid. He remembered how relieved he'd been to learn that the woman who'd hit the lottery numbers was black. What a weight off his shoulders! If she'd been white—especially a white Christian woman, elderly, like his granny—Chub knew he wouldn't have had the guts to go through with the robbery. Much less slug her in the face and the privates, as was necessary with that wild JoLayne bitch.

And a white girl, you shove a pistol in her lips and she'll do whatever she's told. Not this one.

Where's the ticket?

Not a word.

Where's the goddamn ticket?

And Bode Gazzer saying, "Hey, genius, she can't talk with a gun in her mouth."

And Chub removing it, only to have the woman spit all over the barrel. Then she'd spit on him, too.

Leaving Chub and Bode to conclude there wasn't a damn thing they could do to this person, in the way of rape or torture, to make her give up that ticket.

It had been Bode's idea to shoot one of the turtles.

Give him credit, Chub thought, for figuring out the woman's weakness.

Grabbing a baby turtle from the tank, setting it at JoLayne's feet, chuckling in anticipation as it started marching toward her bare toes.

And Chub, firing a round into the center of the turtle's shell, sending it skidding like a tiny green hockey puck across the floor, bouncing off walls and corners.

That's when the woman broke down and told them where she'd hidden the Lotto stub. Inside the piano, of all places! What a racket they'd made, getting it out of there.

But they'd done it. Now here they were, parked in the amber glow of a streetlight; taking turns with the rearview, checking how badly the nigger girl had messed them up.

Chub's multiple lacerations gave a striped effect to his long sunken face. The softest breeze stung like hot acid. He said, "I reckon I need stitches."

Bode Gazzer, shaking his head: "No doctors till we git home." Then he got a good look at Chub's seeping cuts and, recognizing a threat to his new truck's gorgeous upholstery, announced, "Band-Aids. That's what we'll get."

He made a U-turn on the highway and drove back to town at high speed. His destination was the Grab N'Go, where they would purchase first-aid supplies and also settle a piece of militia business.

Shiner's teenage years had been tolerable until his mother had gotten religion. Before then, she'd allowed him to play football without a helmet, shoot his .22 inside the city limits, go bass fishing with cherry bombs, smoke cigarets, bother the girls and skip school at least twice a week.

One night Shiner had returned home late from a Whitesnake concert in Tampa to find his mother waiting in the kitchen. She was wearing plastic thong sandals, a shortie nightgown and her ex-husband's mustard blazer, left over from his days at Century 21—for Shiner, a jarring apparition. Wordlessly his mother had taken his hand and led him out the front door. In the moonlight they'd traipsed half a mile to the intersection where Sebring Street meets the highway. There Shiner's mother had dropped to her knees and begun to pray. Not polite praying, either; moans and wails that fractured the peacefulness of the night.

Shiner had been further dumbfounded and embarrassed to watch his mother crawl into the road and nuzzle her cheek to the grimy pavement.

"Ma," he'd said. "Cut it out."

"Don't you see Him?"

"See who? You're gonna get runned over."

"Shiner, don't you see Him?" She'd bounced to her feet. "Son, it's Jesus. Look there! Our Lord and Savior! Don't you see His face in the road?"

Shiner had walked to the spot and peered intently. "It's just an oil stain, Ma. Or maybe brake fluid."

"No! It's the face of Jesus Christ."

"OK, I'm outta here."

"Shiner!"

He'd figured the Jesus thing would blow over once she'd sobered up, but he was wrong. His mother had spent the whole next day praying at the edge of the road, and the day after as well. Some vacationing Christians gave her an ice-blue parasol and a Styrofoam cooler full of soda pop. The following Saturday, a reporter from a TV station in Orlando came to town with a camera crew. Soon the Road-Stain Jesus was regionally famous, as was Shiner's mother. Nothing much went right for him after that.

One day he came home to find her burning his collection of heavy-metal CDs, which she had taken to calling "devil wafers." She forbade him to drink beer or smoke cigarets, and threatened to withhold his five-dollar weekly allowance if he didn't stay home Friday nights and sing hymns. To get out of the house (and far away from the pilgrims who came regularly to snap his mother's picture) Shiner joined the army. In less than a month he washed out of basic training, and returned to Grange twenty pounds lighter but infinitely more sullen than when he'd left. To a depressed job market Shiner brought neither an adequate education nor practical work skills, so he wound up working the graveyard shift at the Grab N'Go, doubles on Saturday. Not much happened except for the stick-ups, which occurred every second or third weekend. Some nights barely a half dozen customers came through the door, leaving Shiner loads of free time to paw through the latest *Hustler* or *Swank.* He was always careful to sneak the nudie magazines back to the frozen-food aisle, the only place in the store that was blocked from the fish-eye gaze of the security camera. Shiner would dissect the magazines and arrange his favorite snatch shots across the Plexiglas lid of the ice-cream freezer—it was colder than a frog's balls back there, but he couldn't risk getting caught at the front of the store. His mother would be ruined if her only son got fired for whacking off on the job, especially on videotape. Even though Shiner was mad at his Ma, he didn't want to hurt her feelings.

At 2 a.m. on the morning of November 27, he was hunched feverishly over a *Best of Jugs* when he heard the jingle of the cat bell that was fastened to the store's front door. He tucked himself in and hurried up toward the register. It took him a moment to recognize the two customers as the same men who'd stopped by earlier in the evening for jerky and Quick Picks. Clearly they'd been in an awesome bar fight.

"The hell happened to you boys?" Shiner asked.

The short one, dressed in camo, asked for Band-Aids. The one with the ponytail requested malt liquor. Shiner obliged—finally, some excitement! He helped the men clean and bind their multiple wounds. The camouflaged one introduced himself as Bodean Gazzer, Bode for short. He said his friend was called Chub.

"Pleased to meetcha," said Shiner.

"Son, we need your help."

"OK."

Bode said, "You believe in God and family?"

Shiner hesitated. Not this again—more pilgrims! But then Chub said, "You believe in guns?"

"The right to bear arms," Bode Gazzer clarified. "It's in the Constitution."

"Sure," said Shiner.

"You got a gun?"

"Course," Shiner answered.

"Excellent. And the white man—you believe in the white man?"

"Goddamn right!"

"Good," Bode Gazzer said.

He told Shiner to take a hard look at himself. Look at where he'd ended up, behind the counter of a miserable motherfucking convenience store, waiting on Cubans and Negroes and Jews and probably even a few Indians.

Chub said, "How old are you, boy?"

"Nineteen."

"And this is your grand plan for life?" Chub sneered as he waved a hand around the store. "This is your, whatchamacallit, your birthright?"

"Hell, no." Shiner found it difficult to meet Chub's gaze; the split eyelid was distracting and creepy. The closed portion hung pale and unblinking, a torn drape behind which the yolky blood-shot eyeball would intermittently disappear.

"I bet you didn't know," Bode Gazzer said, "your hard-earned tax dollars are payin' for a crack NATO army to invade the U.S.A."

Shiner had no clue what the camouflaged man was talking about, though he didn't let on. He'd never heard of NATO and in his entire life hadn't paid enough in income taxes to finance a box of bullets, much less a whole invasion.

Headlights in the parking lot caught his attention: a Dodge Caravan full of tourists, pulling up to the gas pumps.

Chub frowned. "Tell 'em you're closed."

"What?"

"Now!" Bode barked.

The clerk did as he was told. When he came back in the store, he found the men whispering to each other.

The one called Chub said, "We's just sayin' you'd make a fine recruit."

"For what?" Shiner asked.

Bode lowered his voice. "You got any interest in saving America from certain doom?"

"I guess. Sure." Then, after thinking about it: "Would I have to quit my job?"

Bode Gazzer nodded portentously. "Soon," he said.

Shiner listened as the men explained where America had gone wrong, allowing Washington to fall into the hands of communists, lesbians, queers and race mixers. Shiner was annoyed to learn he probably would have *owned* the Grab N'Go by now if it weren't for something called "affirmative action"—a law evidently dreamed up by the commies to help blacks take over the nation.

Pretty soon Shiner's universe began to make more sense. He was pleased to learn it wasn't all his doing, this sorry-ass excuse for a life. No, it was the result of a complicated and diabolical plot, a vast conspiracy against the ordinary working white man. All this time there'd been a heavy boot on Shiner's neck, and he hadn't even known! Out of ignorance he'd always assumed it was his own damn fault—first quitting high school, then crap-

ping out of the army. He'd been unaware of the
larger, darker forces at work, "oppressing" him and
"subordinating" him. *Enslaving* him, Chub added.

Thinking about it made Shiner angry, but also
oddly elated. Bode Gazzer and Chub were doing
wonders for his self-esteem. They gave him a sense
of worth. They gave him pride. Best of all, they
gave him an excuse for his failures; someone else to
blame! Shiner was invigorated with relief.

"How come you guys know so much?"

"We learned the hard way," Bode said.

Chub cut in: "You say you got a gun?"

"Yep," Shiner said. "Marlin .22."

Chub snorted. "No, boy, I said a *gun*."

In more detail Bode Gazzer explained about the
impending invasion of NATO troops from the Bahamas and their mission of imposing a totalitar-
ian world regime on the United States. Shiner's
eyes grew wide at the mention of the White Rebel
Brotherhood.

"I've heard of 'em!" the young man exclaimed.

"You have?" Chub shot a beady look at Bode,
who shrugged.

Shiner said, "Yeah. It's a band, right?"

"No, dickbrain, it's not a band. It's a militia,"
Chub said.

"A well-regulated militia," Bode added, "like
they talk about in the Second Amendment."

"Oh," said Shiner. He hadn't read the first one
yet.

In a low confiding tone, Bode Gazzer said the White Rebel Brotherhood was preparing for prolonged armed resistance—*heavily* armed resistance—to any forces, foreign or domestic, that posed a threat to something called the "sovereignty" of private American citizens.

Bode laid a hand on the back of Shiner's neck. With a friendly squeeze: "So what do you say?"

"Sounds like a plan."

"You want into the WRB?"

"You're kiddin'!"

Chub said, "Answer the man. Yes or no."

"Sure," Shiner chirped. "What do I gotta do?"

"A favor," Chub said. "It's easy."

"More like a assignment," said Bode Gazzer. "Think of it like a test."

Shiner's expression clouded. He hated tests, especially multiple choice. That's how he'd blown the SATs.

Chub sensed the boy's consternation. "Forget 'test,' " he told him. "It's a favor, that's all. A favor for your new white brothers."

Instantly Shiner brightened.

When Tom Krome saw JoLayne's living room, he told her (for the fourth time) to call the police. The house was a mother lode of evidence: fingerprints, footprints, plenty of blood to be typed. JoLayne Lucks said absolutely not, no way, and started cleaning up. Reluctantly Krome helped. There wasn't much to be done about the gutted piano, or the bullet hole in the wood floor. The blood mopped up with ammonia and water.

Afterwards, while JoLayne took a shower, Krome buried the dead turtle under a lime tree in the backyard. When he came back inside, she was standing there, bundled in her robe.

Dripping water. Shredding lettuce into the aquarium.

"Well, the others seem fine," she said quietly.

Krome led her away from the turtles. "What've you got against calling the cops?"

JoLayne pulled free, snatched up a broom. "They wouldn't believe me."

"How could they not? Look in the mirror."

"I'm not talking about the beating. I'm talking about the Lotto ticket."

"What about it?" Krome said.

"I've got no proof I ever had it. Which makes it damn hard to claim it was stolen."

She had a point. Florida's lottery computer kept track of how many winning tickets were bought and where, but there was no way of identifying the owners. That's because Lotto numbers were sold over the counter with the beer and cigarets; trying to keep track of customers' names—hundreds of thousands—would have been impossible. Consequently the lottery bureau had one intractable criterion for claiming the jackpot: possession of the winning ticket. If you didn't have it, you didn't get the money—no matter what your excuse. Over the years, once-in-a-lifetime fortunes had been lost to hungry puppies and teething infants and washing machines and toilets and house fires.

And now robbers.

Tom Krome was torn between his sympathy for JoLayne Lucks and the realization that he'd stumbled into a pretty good news story. He must have done a poor job of masking his anticipation, because JoLayne said: "I'm begging you not to write about this."

"But it'll flush the bastards out."

"And I'll never, ever get the money. Don't you see? They'd burn the damn ticket before they'd go to jail. Burn it or bury it."

Krome lifted his feet to make way for JoLayne's fierce, metronomic sweeping.

"If these guys get spooked," she went on, "that fourteen-million-dollar stub of paper is garbage. They see a newspaper headline about what they did . . . well, it's all over. Same if I go to the police."

She probably was right, Krome thought. But wouldn't the robbers assume JoLayne would report the theft? That's what most people would do.

He no longer heard the manic whisk of her sweeping. She was in the kitchen, leaning on the broom in front of the open refrigerator, letting the cool air soothe the cuts and bruises on her face.

Tom Krome said, "I'll put some ice in a bag."

JoLayne shook her head. The house was silent except for the drone of the aquarium pump and the turtles' steady munching of lettuce.

After a few moments, she said: "All right, here it is. They said they'd come back and kill me if I told anyone about the lottery ticket. They said they'd come back and shoot my babies, one at a time. Then me."

A chill went down Krome's arms.

JoLayne Lucks went on: "They told me to say my boyfriend beat me up. That's what I'm supposed to tell the doctor! 'What boyfriend?' I say. 'I don't have a boyfriend.' And the short one goes, 'You do now,' and he punches me in the tits."

Suddenly Krome couldn't breathe. He stumbled out the back door. JoLayne found him on his knees in the tomato patch. She stroked his hair and told him to take it easy. Before long, the crashing in his ears faded away. She brought him a glass of cold juice, and they sat together on an iron bench facing a birdbath.

In a raw voice, Krome said: "You can identify these guys?"

"Of course."

"They belong in jail."

"Tom—"

"Here's what you do: Go to the cops and the lottery bureau, and tell them everything that happened. About the robbery and the death threats. Give a statement, file a report. And then let the authorities wait for these bastards—"

"No."

"Listen. These guys will surface soon. They've only got six months to claim that jackpot."

"Tom, that's what I'm trying to tell you. *I* don't have six months. I need the money now."

Krome looked at her. "What in the world for?"

"I just do."

"Forget the money—"

"I can't."

"But these guys are monsters. They're going to hurt someone else the way they hurt you. Maybe worse."

"Not necessarily," JoLayne said. "Not if we stop them first."

The incredible part was, she meant it. Krome would have laughed except he didn't want to hurt her feelings.

JoLayne, pinching his right knee: "We could do it. You and me, we could find them."

"To borrow an old expression: No fucking way."

"They're driving a bright-red pickup."

"I don't care if they're in the starship *Enterprise*."

"Tom, please."

He held her hands. "In my business, fear is a sane and very healthy emotion. That's because death and disaster aren't abstractions. They're as goddamn real as real can be."

"Suppose I told you why I need the money. Would it make a difference?"

"JoLayne, I don't think so." It tore him up to look at her, at what they'd done.

She pulled away and walked to the aquarium. Krome could hear her talking—to herself, to the turtles, or maybe to the men who'd beaten her so badly.

"I'm truly sorry," he said.

When JoLayne turned around, she didn't appear upset. "Just think," she said mischievously, "if I get that lottery ticket back. Think of the fantastic story you'll be missing."

Tom Krome smiled. "You're ruthless, you know that?"

"I'm also right. Please help me find them."

He said, "I've got a better idea. May I borrow the phone?"

Shiner awoke to the sight of his mother hovering over him. She was dressed in the white bridal gown that she always wore on Mondays to the Road-Stain Jesus. The outfit was a smash with the Christian tourists—it wasn't uncommon for Shiner's Ma to come home with two hundred dollars in cash from donations. Monday was her best day of the week, pilgrimwise.

Now she told Shiner to get his fat ass downstairs. There was company waiting in the Florida room.

"And I'm already an hour late," she said, cuffing him so hard that he retreated under the blanket.

He listened to the rustle of the wedding dress as she hurried downstairs. Then came the slam of the front door.

Shiner pulled on some jeans and went to see who was waiting. The woman he recognized, with apprehension, as JoLayne Lucks. The man he didn't know.

JoLayne said, "Sorry to wake you, but it's sort of an emergency."

She introduced her friend as Tom, who shook Shiner's hand and said, "The day guy at the store gave me your address. Said you wouldn't mind."

Shiner nodded absently. He wasn't a young man who had an easy time putting two and two together, but he quickly made the connection between JoLayne's battered face and those of his new white rebel brothers, Chub and Bodean. Out of simple courtesy Shiner probably should've asked JoLayne who popped her in the kisser, but he didn't trust himself with the question; didn't trust himself to keep a straight face.

The man named Tom sat next to Shiner on the divan. He wasn't dressed like a cop, but Shiner resolved to be careful anyway.

JoLayne said, "I've got a big problem. You re-

member the Lotto ticket I bought Saturday afternoon at the store? Well, I've lost it. Don't ask me
how, Lord, it's a long story. The point is, you're the
only one besides me who knows I bought it. You're
my only witness."

Shiner was a mumbler when he got nervous.
"Saturday?"

He didn't look at JoLayne Lucks but instead
kept his eyes on the folds of his belly, which still
bore wrinkle marks from the bedsheets.

Finally he said: "I don't remember seein' you
Saturday."

JoLayne couldn't hear the words, Shiner was
speaking so low. "What?" she said.

"I don't remember seein' you in the store Saturday. Sure it wasn't last week?" Shiner began
fiddling with the curly black hairs around his
navel.

JoLayne came over and lifted his chin. "Look at
me."

He flinched at the prospect of her blue fingernails in his throat.

She said, "Every Saturday I play the same numbers. Every Saturday I come to the Grab N'Go
and buy my ticket. You know what happened this
time, don't you? You know I won."

Shiner pushed her hand away. "Maybe you
come in Saturday, maybe you didn't. Anyhow, I
don't look at the numbers."

JoLayne Lucks stepped back. She seemed quite

angry. The man named Tom spoke up: "Son, surely you know that one of the two winning Lotto tickets came from your store."

"Yeah, I do. Tallahassee phoned up about it."

"Well, if Miss Lucks didn't have the numbers, who did?"

Shiner licked his lips and thought: Damn. This high-stakes lying was harder than he figured it would be. But a blood oath was a blood oath.

He said, "There was a fella came in late off the highway. Got a Quick Pick and a six-pack of Bud Lights."

"Wait, wait—you're telling me," JoLayne protested, her voice rising, "you're telling me some . . . *stranger* bought the winning ticket."

"Ma'am, I don't honestly know who's got what. I just run the machine, I don't pay no 'tention to the damn numbers."

"Shiner, you know it was my ticket. Why are you lying? Why?"

"I ain't." It came out as mush.

The man named Tom asked: "This mystery man who came in late and bought the Quick Pick— who was he?"

Shiner slid his hands under his butt, to conceal the tremor. He said, "I never seen him before. Just some tall skinny guy with a ponytail."

"Oh no." JoLayne turned to her friend. "What do you say now, Mister No Fucking Way." Then she ran out of the house.

The man named Tom didn't leave right away, which made Shiner jittery. Later he watched from the window as the man put an arm around Jo-Layne Lucks when they walked off, down Sebring Street.

Shiner sucked on a cigaret and recalled what Bode and Chub had told him: *Your word against hers, son.*

So it was done. And no fuckups!

Presto, Shiner thought. I'm in the brotherhood.

But for the rest of the morning he couldn't stop thinking about what JoLayne's friend had told him before walking out.

We'll be talking again, you and I.

Like hell, Shiner thought. He'll have to find me first.

6 Mary Andrea Finley Krome wasn't addicted to Prozac or anything else. Nor was she chronically depressed, psychologically unstable, schizoid or suicidal.

She was, however, stubborn. And it was her very strong desire to not be a divorced woman.

Her marriage to Tom Krome wasn't ideal; in fact, it had become more or less an empty sketch. Yet that was a tradition among Finley women, hooking up with handsome, self-absorbed men who quickly lost interest in them.

They'd met in Manhattan, in a coffee shop near Radio City. Mary Andrea had initiated contact after noticing that the intent, good-looking man at the end of the counter was reading a biography of Ibsen. What Mary Andrea hadn't known was that the book had been forced upon Tom Krome by a young woman he was dating (a drama major at NYU), and that he would've much rather been delving into the complete life story of Moose Skowron. Nonetheless, Krome was pleased when the auburn-haired stranger moved three stools closer and said she'd once read for a small part in *A Doll's House.*

The attraction was instant, though more physical than either of them cared to admit. At the time, Tom Krome was working on a newspaper investigation of Medicaid mills. He was on the trail of a crooked radiologist who spent his Tuesday mornings playing squash at the Downtown Athletic Club instead of reading myelograms, as he'd claimed while billing the government thousands of dollars. Mary Andrea Finley was auditioning for the role of the restless farm wife in a Sam Shepard play.

She and Tom dated for five weeks and then got married at a Catholic church in Park Slope. After that they didn't see each other much, which meant it took longer to discover they had nothing in common. Tom's reporting job kept him busy all day, while Mary Andrea's stage work took care of the nights and weekends. When they managed to arrange time together, they had sex as often as possible. It was one activity in which they were synchronized in all aspects. Overdoing it spared them from having to listen to each other chatter on about their respective careers, in which neither partner honestly held much interest.

Mary Andrea had barely noticed things coming apart. The way she remembered it, one day Tom just walked in with a sad face and asked for a divorce.

Her reply: "Don't be ridiculous. In five hundred years there's never been a divorce in the Finley family."

"That," Tom had said, "explains all the psychos."

Mary Andrea related this conversation to her counselor at the Mona Pacifica Mineral Spa and Residential Treatment Center in Maui, a facility highly recommended by several of her bicoastal actor friends. When the counselor asked Mary Andrea if she and her husband had ever been wildly happy, she said yes, for about six months.

"Maybe seven," she added. "Then we reached a plateau. That's normal, isn't it, for young couples? The problem is, Tom's not a 'plateau' type of personality. He's got to be either going up, or going down. Climbing, or falling."

The counselor said, "I get the picture."

"Now he has lawyers and process servers chasing me. It's very inconsiderate." Mary Andrea was a proud person.

"Do you have reason to believe he'd change his mind about the marriage?"

"Who's trying to change his mind? I just want him to forget this absurd idea of a divorce."

The counselor looked bemused. Mary Andrea went on to offer the view that divorce as an institution was becoming obsolete. "Superfluous. Unnecessary," she added.

"It's getting late," said the counselor. "Would you like something to help you sleep?"

"Look at Shirley MacLaine. She didn't live with her husband for, what, thirty years? Most people didn't even know she was married. That's the way to handle it."

Mary Andrea's theory was that divorce left a person exposed and vulnerable, while remaining married—even if you didn't stay with your spouse—provided a cone of protection.

"Nobody else can get their meat hooks in you," she elaborated. "Legally speaking."

The counselor said, "I'd never thought of it that way."

"OK, it's just a silly piece of paper. But don't think of it as a trap, think of it as a bulletproof shield," said Mary Andrea Finley Krome. "Shirley's got the right idea. Could you ask them to bring me a cup of Earl Grey?"

"You're feeling better?"

"Much. I'll be out of your hair in a day or two."

"No hurry. You're here to rest."

"With a wedge of lemon," Mary Andrea said. "Please."

Sinclair scalded his tongue on the coffee, a gulp being his reflex to the sight of Tom Krome crossing the newsroom. Pressing a creased handkerchief to his mouth, Sinclair rose to greet his star reporter with a spurious heartiness that was transparent to all who witnessed it.

"Long time no see!" Sinclair gushed. "You're lookin' good, big guy."

Krome motioned toward the editor's private office. "We should talk," he said.

"Yes, yes, I heard."

When they were alone behind the glass, Sinclair said, "Joan and Roddy called this morning. I guess the news is all over Grange."

Krome figured as much. He said, "I'll need a week or so."

Sinclair frowned. "For what, Tom?"

"For the reporting." Krome eyed him coldly. He'd anticipated this reaction, knowing too well Sinclair's unspoken credo: *Big stories, big problems.*

The editor rocked back in a contrived pose of rumination. "I don't think we're looking at a feature takeout anymore, do you?"

Krome was amused at the collective "we." The

newspaper sent its midlevel editors to a management school that taught them, among other
insipid tricks, to employ the "we" during disagree-
ments with staff. The theory was that a plural pro-
noun subliminally brought corporate muscle to an
argument.

Sinclair went on: "I think we're looking at a ten-
inch daily, max, for the city side. ROBBERS STEAL
LOTTO TICKET, UNLUCKY LADY LAMENTS."

Krome leaned forward. "If that headline ever
appears in *The Register,* I will personally come to
your home and cut out your lungs with a trench-
ing knife."

Sinclair wondered if it would be smart to leave
the door open, in case he had to make a run for it.

"No daily story," Krome said. "The woman isn't
making any public statements. She hasn't even
filed a police report."

"But you've talked to her?"

"Yes, but not on the record."

Sinclair, fortifying himself with another swig of
coffee: "Then I really don't see a story. Without
quotes from her or the cops, I don't see it."

"You will. Give me some time."

"Know what Roddy and Joan said? The rumor
is, the Lucks girl somehow lost her Lotto ticket
and then made up this bit about the robbers. You
know, for sympathy."

Krome said, "With all due respect to Roddy and
Joan, they're positively full of shit."

Sinclair felt a foolish impulse to defend his sister and her husband, but it passed quickly. "Tom, you know how short-staffed we are. A week sounds more like an investigation than a simple feature, wouldn't you say?"

"It's a story, period. A good story, if *we* are patient."

Sinclair's policy on sarcasm was to ignore it. He said, "Until this lady wants to talk to the cops, there's not much we can do. Maybe the lottery ticket got stolen, maybe it didn't. Maybe she never had it to begin with—these big jackpots tend to bring out the kooks."

"Tell me about it."

"We've got other stories for you, Tom."

Krome rubbed his eyes. He thought about Alaska, about bears batting rainbows in the river.

And he heard Sinclair saying, "They're teaching a course on bachelorhood out at the community college. 'Bachelorhood in the Nineties.' I think it could be a winner."

Krome, numb with disdain: "I'm not a bachelor yet. And I won't be for some time, according to my lawyer."

"A minor detail. Write around it, Tom. You're living a single life, that's the point."

"Yes. A single life."

"Why don't you sit in on the classes? This week they're doing sewing—it could be very cute, Tom. First person, of course."

"Sewing for bachelors."

"Sure," said Sinclair.

Krome sighed to himself. "Cute" again. Sinclair knew how Krome felt about cute. He'd rather write obits. He'd rather cover the fucking weather. He'd rather have railroad spikes hammered into his nostrils.

With unwarranted hopefulness, Sinclair awaited Krome's answer. Which was:

"I'll call you from the road."

Sinclair sagged. "No, Tom, I'm sorry."

"You're saying I'm off the story?"

"I'm saying there *is* no story right now. Until we get a police report or a statement from this Lucks woman, there's nothing to put in the paper but gossip."

Spoken like a true newshound, Krome thought. A regular Ben Bradlee.

He said, "Give me a week."

"I can't." Sinclair was fidgeting, tidying the stack of pink phone messages on his desk. "I wish I could do it but I can't."

Tom Krome yawned. "Then I suppose I'll have to quit."

Sinclair stiffened. "That isn't funny."

"Finally, we agree." Krome saluted informally, then strolled out the door.

. . .

When he got home, he saw that somebody had shot all the windows out of his house with a large-caliber weapon. Tacked to the door was a note from Katie:

"I'm sorry, Tom, it's all my fault."

By the time she got there, an hour later, he had most of the glass swept up. She came up the steps and handed him a check for $500. She said, "Honestly, I'm so ashamed."

"All this because I didn't call?"

"Sort of."

Krome expected to be angrier about the broken windows, but upon reflection he considered it a personal milestone of sorts: the first time that a sexual relationship had resulted in a major insurance claim. Krome wondered if he'd finally entered the netherworld of white-trash romance.

He said to Katie: "Come on in."

"No, Tommy, we can't stay here. It's not safe."

"But the breeze is nice, no?"

"Follow me." She turned and trotted toward her car—darn good speed, for a person in sandals. On the interstate she twice nearly lost him in traffic. They ended up at a Mexican restaurant near the dog track. Katie settled covertly in a corner booth. Krome ordered beers and *fajitas* for both of them.

She said, "I owe you an explanation."

"Wild guess: You told Art."

"Yes, Tom."

"May I ask why?"

"I was sad because you didn't call like you promised. And then the sadness turned to guilt—lying in bed next to this man, my husband, and me keeping this awful secret."

"But Art's been banging his secretaries for years."

Katie said, "It's not the same thing."

"Apparently not."

"Plus two wrongs don't make a right."

Krome backed off; he was a pro when it came to guilt. He asked Katie: "What kind of gun did Art use?"

"Oh, he didn't do it himself. He got his law clerk to do it."

"To shoot out my windows?"

"I'm so sorry," Katie said again.

The beers arrived. Krome drank while Katie explained that her husband, the judge, had turned out to be quite the jealous maniac.

"Much to my surprise," she added.

"I can't believe he paid his clerk to do a drive-by on my house."

"Oh, he didn't pay him. That would be a crime—Art is very, very careful when it comes to the law. The young man did it as a favor, more or less. To make points with the boss, that's my impression."

"Want to know mine?"

"Tom, I couldn't sleep Sunday night. I had to come clean with Art."

"And I'm sure he promptly came clean with you."

"He will," Katie said. "In the meantime, you might want to lay low. I believe he intends to have you killed."

The *fajitas* arrived and Tom Krome dug in. Katie remarked upon how well he was taking the news. Krome agreed; he was exceptionally calm. The act of quitting the newspaper had infused him with a strange and reckless serenity. Krome said: "What exactly did you tell Art? I'm just curious."

"Everything," Katie replied. "Every detail. That's the nature of a true confession."

"I see."

"What I did, I got up about three in the morning and made a complete list, starting with the first time. In your car."

Krome reached for a tortilla chip. "You mean . . ."

"The blow job, yes. And every time afterwards. Even when I didn't come."

"And you put that on your list? All the details?" He picked up another chip and scooped a trench in the salsa.

Katie said, "I gave it to him first thing yesterday morning, before he went to work. And, Tom, I felt better right away."

"I'm so glad." Krome, trying to recall how many times he and Katie had made love in the two weeks they'd known each other; imagining how the tally would look on paper. He envisioned it as a line score in tiny agate type, the same as on the sports page.

She said, "I almost forgot, did you take that picture for me? Of the weeping Mother Mary?"

"Not yet, but I will."

"No rush," Katie said.

"It's OK. I'm going back tonight."

"Must be some story."

"It's all relative, Katie. Not to change the subject, but you mentioned something about Art intending to kill me."

"No, to *have* you killed."

"Right. Of course. You're sure he wasn't just talking?"

"Possibly. But he's pretty mad."

"Did he hurt you?" Krome asked. "Would he?"

"Never." Katie seemed amused by the question. "If you want to know the truth, I think it turned him on."

"The confession."

"Yes. Like suddenly he realized what he was missing."

Krome said, "How about that."

He paid the check. Outside in the parking lot, Katie touched his arm and asked him to let her know, please, if the $500 wasn't enough to replace the busted windows. Krome told her not to worry about it.

Then she said, "Tommy, we can't see each other anymore."

"I agree. It's wrong."

The concept seemed to cheer her. "I'm glad to hear you say that."

Judging from the note of triumph in her voice, Katie believed that by sleeping with Tom Krome and then confessing to her low-life cheating husband, she'd helped all three of them become better human beings. Their consciences had been stirred and elevated. They'd all learned a lesson. They'd all grown spiritually.

Krome graciously chose not to deflate this preposterous notion. He kissed Katie on the cheek and told her goodbye.

Demencio took the stool next to Dominick Amador at the counter at Hardee's. Dominick was going through his morning ritual of spooning Crisco into a pair of gray gym socks. The socks went over Dominick's hands, to cover his phony stigmata. The Crisco served to keep the wounds moist and to prevent scabbing—Dominick's livelihood depended on the holes in his palms appearing raw and fresh, as if recently nailed to a cross. Should the wounds ever heal, he'd be ruined.

He said to Demencio: "I got a big favor to ask."

"So what else is new."

Dominick said, "Geez, whatsa matter with you today?"

"That dippy woman lost the Lotto ticket. I guess you didn't hear."

Demencio held the gym socks open while Dominick inserted his hands. One of the socks had a fray in the toe, through which oozed a white dollop of shortening.

Dominick flexed his fingers and said, "That's much better. Thanks."

"Fourteen million dollars down the shitter," Demencio grumbled.

"I heard it was a robbery."

"Gimme a break."

"Hey, everybody in town knew she had the ticket."

"But who's got the balls," Demencio said, "to do something like that? Seriously, Dom."

"You got a point." The only robberies to occur in Grange were the holdups committed by itinerant crooks on their way to or from Miami.

Demencio said: "My guess? She lost the ticket some stupid way, then cooked up the robbery story so people wouldn't make fun of her."

"They say she's a strange one."

" 'Scattered' is the word."

"Scattered," said Dominick. He was eating a jelly doughnut, the sugar dust sticking to the socks on his hands.

Demencio told him about JoLayne's turtles. "Must be a hundred of the damn things inside her house. Tell me that's normal."

Dominick's eyebrows crinkled in concentration. He said, "Is there turtles in the Old Testament?"

"How the hell should I know." Just because Demencio owned a weeping Virgin didn't mean he'd memorized the whole Bible, or even finished it. Some of those Corinthians were rough sledding.

Dominick said, "What I'm thinking, maybe she's putting some type of exhibit together. You know, for the tourists. Except I can't remember no turtles in the Good Book. There's lambs and fishes—and a big serpent, of course."

Demencio's pancakes arrived. Drenching the plate in syrup, he said, "Just forget it."

"But didn't Noah have turtles? He had two of everything."

"Right. JoLayne, she's building a fuckin' ark. That explains it." Demencio irritably attacked his breakfast. The only reason he'd mentioned the damn turtles was to show how flaky JoLayne Lucks could be; the sort of space cadet who could misplace a $14 million lottery ticket.

Of all the people to win! Demencio fumed. It might be a thousand years before anyone in Grange hit the jackpot again.

Dominick Amador said, "Why you so pissed—it wasn't your money." Dominick didn't know Jo-Layne very well, but she'd always been nice to his cat, Rex. The cat suffered from an unsavory gum disorder that required biweekly visits to the veterinarian. JoLayne was the only person besides Dominick's daughter who could manage Rex without the custom-tailored kitty straitjacket.

"Don't you see," Demencio said. "All of us woulda cashed in big—you, me, the whole town. The story we'd put out, think about this: JoLayne won the Lotto because she lived in a holy place. Maybe she prayed at my weeping Mary, or maybe she got touched by your crucified hands. Word got around, everybody who played the numbers would come to Grange for a blessing."

Dominick hadn't thought of that: a boom for the blessing trade.

"The best part," Demencio went on, "it wouldn't be only Christians coming, it'd be anybody who does the Lotto. Jewish people, Buddhists, Hawaiians . . . it wouldn't matter. A gambler's a gambler—all they care about is luck."

"A gold mine," Dominick agreed. With a sleeve he wiped a smear of jelly from his chin.

"And now it's all turned to shit," said Demencio. In disgust he tossed his fork on the plate. How could anybody lose a $14 million lottery ticket? Lucy Fucking Ricardo couldn't lose a $14 million lottery ticket.

Dominick said, "There's more to what happened than we been told, I guarantee."

"Yeah, yeah. Maybe it was Martians. Maybe a UFO flew down in the middle of the night—"

"No, but I heard she was all beat up."

"I'm not surprised," Demencio said. "My theory? She's so mad at herself for losing the ticket, she takes a baseball bat and clobbers herself in the goddamn head. That's what *I'd* do if I fucked up that bad."

Dominick Amador said, "I don't know," and went back to eviscerating doughnuts. After a few minutes, when it seemed Demencio had cooled off, Dominick asked another favor.

"It's regarding my feet," he said.

"The answer is no."

"I need somebody to drill 'em."

"Then talk to your wife."

"Please," said Dominick. "I got the shop all set up."

Demencio laid six dollars on the counter and slid off the stool. "Drill your own feet," he told Dominick. "I ain't in the mood."

JoLayne Lucks knew what Dr. Crawford thought:

Finally the girl gets a boyfriend, and the boyfriend beats her to a pulp.

"Please don't stare. I know I'm a sight," Jo-Layne said.

"You want to tell me about it?"

"Truly? No." That would clinch it with Doc Crawford, the fact that she wouldn't talk. So she added: "It's not what you think."

Dr. Crawford said: "Hold still, you little shit."

He was addressing Mickey, the Welsh corgi on the examining table. JoLayne was doing her best to control the dog but it was squirming like a worm on a griddle. The little ones always were the hardest to handle—cockers, poodles, Pomeranians—and the nastiest, too. Biters, every damn one. Give me a 125-pound Dobie any day, JoLayne thought.

To Mickey the corgi, she muttered: "Be good, baby." Whereupon Mickey sank his yellow fangs into her thumb and did not let go. As painful as it was, the attachment enabled JoLayne Lucks to control the dog's head, giving Dr. Crawford a clear shot at the vaccination site. The instant Mickey felt the needle, he released his grip on JoLayne. Dr. Crawford commended her for not losing her temper.

JoLayne said, "Why take it personally. You'd bite, too, if you had a dog's brain. I've seen men with no such excuse do worse things."

Dr. Crawford buttered her thumb with Betadine. JoLayne observed that it looked like steak sauce.

"You want some on that lip?" the doctor asked.

She shook her head, bracing for the next question. *How did that happen?* But all he said was: "A couple sutures wouldn't be a bad idea, either."

"Oh, that's not necessary."

"You don't trust me."

"Nope." With her free hand she patted the bald spot on Doc Crawford's head. "I'll be OK," she told him.

The remainder of JoLayne's workday: cat (Daisy), three kittens (unnamed), German shepherd (Kaiser), parrot (Polly), cat (Spike), beagle (Bilko), Labrador retriever (Contessa), four Labrador puppies (unnamed), and one rhinoceros iguana (Keith). JoLayne received no more bites or scratches, although the iguana relieved itself copiously on her lab coat.

Arriving home, she recognized Tom Krome's blue Honda parked in the driveway. He was sitting in the swing on the porch. JoLayne sat down next to him and pushed off. With a squeak the swing started to move.

JoLayne said, "I guess we've got a deal."

"Yep."

"What'd your boss say?"

"He said, 'Great story, Tom! Go to it!' "

"Really."

"His exact words. Hey, what happened to your coat?"

"Iguana pee. Now ask about my thumb."

"Lemme see."

JoLayne extended her hand. Krome studied the bite mark with mock seriousness.

"Grizzly!" he said.

She smiled. Boy, did it feel good, his touch. Strong and gentle and all that stuff. Which was how it always started, with a warm dumb tingle.

JoLayne hopped out of the swing and said: "We've got an hour before sunset. I want to show you something."

When they got to Simmons Wood, she pointed out the FOR SALE sign. "That's why I can't wait six months for these jerkoffs to get caught. Any day, somebody's going to come along and buy this place."

Tom Krome followed her over the fence, through the pine and palmettos. She stopped to point out bobcat scat, deer tracks and a red-shouldered hawk in the treetops.

"Forty-four acres," JoLayne said.

She was whispering, so Krome whispered back. "How much do they want for it?"

"Three million and change," she said.

Krome asked about the zoning.

"Retail," JoLayne answered, with a grimace.

They stopped on the sandy bluff overlooking the creek. JoLayne sat down and crossed her legs. "A shopping mall and a parking lot," she said, "just like in the Joni Mitchell song."

Tom Krome felt he should be writing down everything she said. His notebook nagged at him from the back pocket of his jeans. As if he still had a newspaper job.

JoLayne, pointing at the tea-colored ribbon of water: "That's where the cooters come from. They're off the logs now, but you should be here when the sun's high."

Still whispering, like she was in church. Which he supposed it was, in a way.

"What do you make of my plan?"

Krome said, "I think it's fantastic."

"You're making fun."

"Not at all—"

"Oh yes. You think I'm nuts." She propped her chin in her hands. "OK, smart guy, what would *you* do with the money?"

Krome started to answer but JoLayne motioned for him to hush. A deer was at the creek; a doe, drinking. They watched it until darkness fell, then they quietly made their way back to the highway, Krome following the whiteness of JoLayne's lab coat weaving through the trees and scrub.

Back at the house, she disappeared into the bedroom to change clothes and check her phone messages. When she came out, he was standing at the aquarium, watching the baby turtles.

"Treasure this," she said. "Chase Bank called. The assholes have already charged a truckload of stuff on my Visa."

Krome spun around. "You didn't tell me they got your credit card."

JoLayne reached for the kitchen phone. "I've got to cancel that number."

Krome grabbed her arm. "No, don't. This is wonderful news: They've got your Visa, plus they seem to be total morons."

"Yeah, I couldn't be happier."

"You wanted to find them, right? Now we've got a trail."

JoLayne was intrigued. She sat down at the kitchen table and opened a box of Goldfish crackers. The salt stung the cut on her lip, made her eyes water.

Krome said: "Here's what you do. Call the bank and find out exactly where the card's been used. Tell them you loaned it to your brother, uncle, something like that. But don't cancel it, JoLayne. Not until we know where these guys are headed."

She did what he told her. The Chase Bank people couldn't have been nicer. She took down the information and handed it to Krome, who said: "Wow."

"No kidding, wow."

"They spent twenty-three hundred dollars at a *gun show*?"

"And two hundred sixty at a Hooters," JoLayne said. "I'm not sure which is scarier."

The gun show was at the War Memorial Auditorium in Fort Lauderdale, the Hooters was in Coconut Grove. The robbers seemed to be traveling south.

"Get packed," Tom Krome said.

"Lord, I forgot about the turtles. You know how hungry they get."

"They're *not* coming with us."

"Course not," JoLayne said.

They stopped at the ATM so she could get some cash. Back in the car, she popped a handful of Goldfish and said: "Drive like the wind, partner. My Visa maxes out at three thousand bucks."

"Then let's pay it off. Put a check in the mail first thing tomorrow—I want these boys to go hog wild."

Sportively JoLayne grabbed a handful of Krome's shirt. "Tom, I've got exactly four hundred and thirty-two dollars left in my checking."

"Relax," he told her. Then, with a sideways glance: "It's time you started thinking like a millionaire."

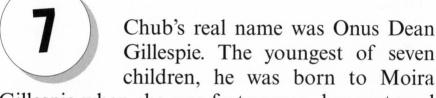

Chub's real name was Onus Dean Gillespie. The youngest of seven children, he was born to Moira Gillespie when she was forty-seven, her maternal stirrings long dormant. Onus's father, Greve, was a blunt-spoken man who regularly reminded the boy that the arc of his life had begun with a faulty diaphragm, and that his appearance in Mrs. Gillespie's womb had been as welcome as "a cockroach on a wedding cake."

Nonetheless, Onus was neither beaten nor deprived as a child. Greve Gillespie made good money as a timber man in northern Georgia and was generous with his family. They lived in a large house with a basketball hoop in the driveway, a secondhand ski boat on a trailer in the garage, and a deluxe set of *World Book* encyclopedias in the basement. All of Onus's siblings made it to Georgia State University, and Onus himself could have gone there, too, had he not by age fifteen already chosen a life of sloth, inebriation and illiteracy.

He moved out of his parents' home and took up with a bad crowd. He got a job in the photo department of a drugstore, where he earned extra money sorting through customers' negatives, swiping the racy ones and peddling the prints to horny kids at the high school. (Even after entering adulthood, Onus Gillespie remained amazed there were women in the world who'd allow their boyfriends or husbands to take pictures of them topless. He dreamed of meeting such a girl, but so far it hadn't happened.)

When he was twenty-four, Onus accidentally landed a well-paying job at a home furnishings warehouse. Thanks to an aggressive union local, he managed to remain employed for six years despite a wretched attendance record, exhaustively documented incompetence and a perilous affinity for carpet glue. Stoned to the gills, Onus one day crashed a forklift into a Snapple machine, a low-speed mishap that he parlayed into an exorbitant claim for worker's compensation.

His extended "convalescence" involved many drunken fishing and hunting excursions. One morning Onus was observed emerging from the woods with a prostitute on one arm and a dead bear cub slung over his shoulders. The man watching him was an investigator for an insurance company, which was able to argue convincingly that Mr. Onus Gillespie was not injured in the least. Only then was he fired from the warehouse. He chose not to appeal.

Moira and Greve wrote one last check to their errant spawn, then disowned him. Onus needed no special encouragement to leave the state. In addition to the pending felony indictments for insurance fraud and game poaching, Onus had received a rather unfriendly letter from the Internal Revenue Service, inquiring why he'd never in his adult life bothered to file a tax return. To emphasize its concern, the IRS sent a flatbed and two disagreeable men to confiscate Onus's customized Ford Econoline van. It was easy to spot. An elaborate mural on the side of the vehicle depicted Kim Basinger as a nude mermaid, riding a narwhal.

Onus had fallen for the beautiful Georgia actress in the movie *9½ Weeks* and conceived the mural as a love tribute.

It was the seizure of his beloved Econoline that turned Onus Gillespie bitterly against the U.S. government (although he was similarly resentful toward his parents, who not only had refused to pay his tax lien but had also tipped off the IRS agents about where to find the van). Before bolting, Onus burned his driver's license and renounced the family name. He began calling himself Chub (which is how his brothers and sisters had referred to him when he was younger and had something of a weight problem). He couldn't make up his mind on a new surname, so he decided to wait until something good popped into his head. He hitchhiked to Miami with only the clothes on his back, seventeen dollars in his wallet and, in a zippered pocket, his only tangible asset— the disabled-parking permit he'd scammed off the company doctor for the workmen's comp claim.

Pure good fortune and a round of free beers led to a friendship with an amateur forger, who entrusted Chub with his printing equipment while he went off to state prison. In no time, Chub was cranking out fake handicapped stickers and selling them for cash to local motorists. His favorite hangout was Miami's federal courthouse, infamous for its dearth of parking spaces. Among Chub's satisfied customers were stenographers, bondsmen, drug lawyers and even a U.S. magistrate or two. Soon his reputation grew, and he became known throughout the county as a reliable supplier of bootleg wheelchair emblems.

That's why he was sought out by Bodean Gazzer, who'd been having a terrible time trying to park downtown. Having recently purchased the Dodge Ram, Bode thought it was foolhardy to leave it three or four blocks away while he went to wrestle the bureaucracy of the corrections department. Those particular neighborhoods weren't such lovely places to go for a stroll; wall-to-wall Haitians and Cubans! He had nightmare visions of his gorgeous new truck stripped to its axles.

Chub felt an instant kinship with Bode, whose global theories and braided explanations struck a comforting chord. For instance, Chub had been stung when his parents scorned him as a tax cheat, but Bode Gazzer made him feel better by enumerating the many sound reasons why no full-blooded white American male should give a nickel to the Infernal Revenue. Chub brightened to learn that what he'd initially regarded as ducking a debt was, in fact, an act of legitimate civil protest.

"Like the Boston Tea Party," Bode had said, invoking his favorite historical reference. "Those boys were against taxation without representation, and that's what you're fightin', too. The white man has lost his voice in this government, so why should he foot the bill?"

It sounded good to Chub. Damn good. And Bode Gazzer was full of such nimble rationalizations.

Some of Chub's acquaintances, especially the war veterans, disapproved of his handicapped-parking racket. Not Bode. "Think about it," he'd said to Chub. "How many wheelchair people you actually see? And look how many thousands of parkin' spaces they got. It don't add up, unless . . ."

" 'Less what?"

"Unless those parkin' spots ain't really for the handicaps," Bode had surmised darkly. "What color's them wheelchair permits?"

"Blue."

"Hmmm-mmm. And what color is the helmets worn by United Nations troops?"

"Fuck if I know. Blue?"

"Yessir!" Bode Gazzer had shaken Chub by the arm. "Don't you see, boy? There's an invasion, who you think's gonna be parked in them blue wheelchair spaces? Soldiers, that's who. UN soldiers!"

"Jesus Willy Christ."

"So in my estimation you're doin' the country a tremendous goddamn service with those imitation handicap stickers. Every one you sell means one less parkin' spot for the enemy. That's how I think of it."

And that's how Chub intended to think of it,

too. He wasn't a crook, he was a patriot! Life was getting better and better.

And now here he was, on the road with his best buddy.

Soon to be multimillionaires.

Spending a long leisurely afternoon at Hooters, eating barbecue chicken wings and slugging down Coronas.

Flirting with the waitresses in them shiny orange shorts, sweet God Almighty, some of the finest young legs Chub had ever seen. And asses shaped just like Golden Delicious apples.

And outside: a pickup truck full of guns.

"A toast," said Bode Gazzer, lifting his mug. "To America."

"Amen!" Chub burped.

"This here is what it's all about."

"For sure."

Said Bode: "No such thing as too much pussy or too much firepower. That's a fact."

They were shitfaced by the time the check came. With a foamy grin, Bode slapped the stolen credit card on the table. Chub vaguely recalled they were supposed to ditch the nigger woman's Visa after the gun show, where they'd used it to purchase a TEC-9, a Cobray M-11, a used AR-15, a canister of pepper spray and several boxes of ammo.

Chub preferred gun shows over gun stores because, thanks to the National Rifle Association, gun shows remained exempt from practically every state and federal firearms regulation. It had been Chub's idea to browse at the one in Fort Lauderdale. However, he'd had strong reservations about paying for such flashy weapons with a stolen credit card, which he thought was risky to the point of stupid.

Again Bode Gazzer had put his friend's mind at ease. He'd explained to Chub that many gun-show dealers were actually undercover ATF agents, and that the use of a phony bank card would send the bully lawmen on a frantic futile search for "J. L. Lucks" and his newly purchased arsenal.

"So they're off on a goose chase," Bode had said, "instead of hassling law-abiding Americans all day long."

His second reason for using a stolen Visa was more pragmatic than political: They had no cash. But Bode had agreed with Chub that they ought to throw away the credit card after the gun show, in case the Chase Bank started checking up.

Chub was about to remind his partner of that plan when an exceptionally long-legged waitress appeared and whisked the Visa card off the table.

Bode rubbed his hands together, reverently. "*That* is what we're fightin' for, my friend. Anytime you start to doubt our cause, think a that young sweet thing and the 'Merica she deserves."

"A-fucking-men," Chub said with a bleary snort.

The waitress reminded him strikingly of his beloved Kim Basinger: fair skin, sinful lips, yellow hair. Chub was electrified. He wondered if the waitress had a boyfriend, and if she let him take topless photos. Chub considered inviting her to sit and have a beer, but then Bode Gazzer loomed into focus, reminding Chub what they both must look like: Bode, in his camo and cowboy boots, his face welted and bitch-bitten; Chub, gouged and puffy, his mangled left eyelid concealed behind a homemade patch.

The girl'd have to be blind or crazy to show an interest. When she returned to the table, Chub boldly asked her name. She said it was Amber.

"OK, Amber, if I might ast—you ever heard a the White Rebel Brotherhood?"

"Sure," the waitress said. "They opened for the Geto Boys last summer."

Bode, who was signing the Visa receipt, glanced up and said: "You are seriously mistaken, sugar."

"I don't think so, sir. I got a T-shirt at the concert."

Bode frowned. Chub twirled his ponytail and whooped. "Ain't that a kick in the nuts!"

Amber picked up the credit-card slip, which included a hundred-dollar tip, and rewarded them with a blush and her very warmest smile, at which time Chub dropped to one knee and begged permission to purchase her orange shorts as a keepsake of the afternoon. Two Hispanic bouncers materialized to escort the militiamen out of the restaurant.

Later, sitting in the truck among their new guns, Chub was chuckling. "So much for your White Rebel Brotherhood."

"Shut up," Bode Gazzer slurred, " 'fore I puke on your shoes."

"Go right ahead, brother. I'm in love."

"Like hell."

"I'm in love, and I got a mission."

"Don't you start!"

"No," Chub said, "don't *you* try and stop me."

To find out if the waitress was right about the militia's name, they stopped at a music store in a Kendall mall. Drowsily Bode pawed through the racks until he came across proof: A compact disc called *Nocturnal Omission,* recorded in Muscle Shoals, Alabama, by the White Rebel Brotherhood. Bode was aghast to see that three of the five band members were Negroes. Even Chub said: "That ain't funny."

Bode shoplifted a half dozen of the CDs, which he shot up good with the TEC-9 after they returned to Chub's trailer. They arranged it like a skeet range, Chub tossing the discs high in the air while Bode blasted away. They quit when the gun jammed. Chub unfolded a pair of frayed lawn chairs and made a fire in a rusty oil drum. Bode complained that his beer buzz was wearing off, so Chub opened a bottle of cheap vodka, which they passed back and forth while the stars came out.

Eventually Chub said, "I b'lieve our militia needs a new name."

"I'm way ahead a you." Bode cocked the bottle to his lips. "The White Clarion Aryans. It just now come to me."

"Well, I like it," said Chub, although he wasn't certain what "clarion" meant. He believed it was mentioned in a Christmas song, perhaps in connection with angels.

"Can we call us the WC . . . ," and then he faltered, trying to recall if Aryan was spelled with an *E* or an *A*.

Bode Gazzer said, "WC*A*. Don't see why not."

"Because otherwise it's kind of a mouthful."

"No more 'n the first one."

"But hey, that's cool," Chub said.

White Clarion Aryans. He sure hoped no smartass rock bands or rappers or other patriot tribes had already thought of the name.

From the lawn chair Bode rose in his rumpled camos and lifted the now-empty vodka bottle to the sky. "Here's to the motherfuckin' WCA. Ready, locked and loaded."

"Damn right," said Chub. "The WCA."

. . .

At that moment the young man called Shiner, glazed by Valium, was admiring the letters *W. R. B.* that were freshly tattooed in Iron Cross–style script across his left biceps. Etched below the initials was a screaming eagle with a blazing rifle locked in its talons.

The tattoo artist worked out of a Harley joint in Vero Beach, Shiner's first stop on his way south to Florida City, where he planned to hook up with his new white brothers. He had quit the Grab N'Go, leaving on a high note—Mr. Singh, the owner, demanding to know why Shiner's Impala was moored in the store's only handicap space. And Shiner, standing tall behind the counter: "I got me a permit."

"Yes, but I do not understand."

"Right there on the rearview. See?"

"Yes, yes, but you are not crippled. The police will come."

Shiner, coughing theatrically: "I got a bad lung."

"You are not crippled."

"Disabled is what I am. They's a difference. From the army is where I hurt my lung."

And Mr. Singh, waving his slender brown arms, hurrying outside to more closely inspect the wheelchair insignia, piping: "Where you get that? How? Tell me right now please."

Shiner beaming, the little man's reaction being a testament to Chub's skill as a forger.

Saying to Mr. Singh: "It's the real deal, boss."

"Yes, yes, but how? You are not crippled or disabled or nothing, and don't lie to me nonsense.
Now move the car."

And Shiner replying: "That's how you treat a
handicap? Then I quit, raghead."

Grabbing three hundred-dollar bills from the
register, then elbowing his way past Mr. Singh,
who was protesting: "You, boy, put the money
back! Put the money back!"

Yammering about the videotape Shiner had
swiped, on Bodean Gazzer's instruction, from the
store's slow-speed security camera—in case (Bode
explained) the cassette hadn't yet rewound and
taped over the surveillance video from November
25, the date JoLayne Lucks bought her lottery
numbers.

Bode Gazzer had emphasized to Shiner the importance of the tape, should the authorities question how they'd come to possess the Grange ticket.
The camera could prove they didn't enter the store
until the day *after* the Lotto drawing.

So, shortly after Chub and Bode had departed,
Shiner obediently removed the incriminating video
from Mr. Singh's recorder and replaced it with a
blank. Shiner wondered, as he gunned the Impala
past the Grange city limits, how Mr. Singh learned
about the switch. Normally the little hump didn't
check the VCR unless there'd been a robbery.

Shiner would have been more properly alarmed

had he known that Mr. Singh had been visited by the same nosy man who'd accompanied JoLayne Lucks to Shiner's house. The man named Tom. He'd persuaded Mr. Singh to check the Grab N'Go's security camera, at which time they'd found that the surveillance tape from the weekend had been swapped for a new one.

Shiner's misgivings about the video theft were fleeting, for soon he was absorbed in the tattooing process. It was performed by a bearded shirtless biker whose nipples were pierced with silver skull pins. When the last indigo turn of the *B* was completed, the biker put down the needle and jerked the cord out of the wall socket. Shiner couldn't stop grinning, even when the biker roughly swabbed his arm with alcohol, which stung like a mother.

What a awesome eagle! Shiner marveled. He couldn't wait to show Bode and Chub.

Pointing at the martial lettering, Shiner asked the biker: "Know what *WRB* stands for?"

"Shit, yeah. I got all their albums."

"No," said Shiner, "not the band."

"Then what?"

"You'll find out pretty soon."

The biker didn't like wise guys. "I can't hardly wait."

Shiner said: "Here's a hint: It's in the Second Amendment."

The biker stood up and casually kicked the tattoo stool into a corner. "I got a hint for you, too, jackoff: Gimme my money and move your cherry white ass down the road."

Demencio was tinkering with the weeping Madonna when the doorbell rang. There stood Jo-Layne Lucks with a tall, clean-cut white man. Jo-Layne carried one end of the aquarium, the white man had the other.

"Evening," she said to Demencio, who could do nothing but invite them in.

"Trish is at the grocery," he said, pointlessly.

They set the aquarium on the floor, next to Demencio's golf clubs. The journey up the steps had tilted all the little turtles to one end of the tank.

JoLayne Lucks said: "Meet my friend Tom Krome. Tom, this is Demencio."

The men shook hands; Krome scrutinizing the decapitated Madonna, Demencio eyeing the agitated cooters.

"Whatcha up to?" JoLayne asked.

"No big deal. One of her eyeholes got clogged." Demencio knew lying would be a waste of energy. It was all there, spread out on the living room carpet for any fool to see—the disassembled statue, the tubes, the rubber pump.

JoLayne said, "So that's how you make her cry."

"That's how we do it."

The man named Tom was curious about the bottle of perfume.

"Korean knockoff," Demencio said, "but a good one. See, I try to make the tears smell nice. Pilgrims go for that."

"That's a fine idea," said JoLayne, though her friend Tom looked doubtful. She told Demencio she had a proposition.

"I need you and Trish to watch over the turtles until I get back. There's a bag of fresh romaine in the car, and I'll leave you money for more."

Demencio said, "Where you goin', JoLayne?"

"I've got some business in Miami."

"Lottery business, I bet."

Tom Krome spoke up: "What've you heard?"

"The ticket got lost, is what I heard," said Demencio.

JoLayne Lucks promised to reveal the whole story when she returned to Grange. "And I sincerely apologize for being so mysterious, but you'll understand when the time comes."

"How long'll you be gone?"

"Truly I don't know," JoLayne said, "but here's what I propose: one thousand dollars to take care of my darlings. Whether it's a day or a month."

Tom Krome looked shocked. Demencio whistled at the number.

JoLayne said, "I'm quite serious."

And quite nuts, thought Demencio. A grand to baby-sit a load of turtles?

"It's more than fair," he remarked, trying to avoid Krome's eye.

"I think so, too," JoLayne said. "Now . . . Trish mentioned you had a cat."

"Screw the cat," said Demencio. "Pardon my French."

"Has it had its shots? I don't remember seeing you folks at Doc Crawford's."

"Just some dumb stray. Trish leaves scraps on the porch."

"All right," JoLayne told him, "but the deal's off if it kills even one of my babies."

"Don't you worry."

"There's forty-five even. I counted."

"Forty-five," Demencio repeated. "I'll keep track."

JoLayne handed him a hundred dollars as an advance, plus twenty for a lettuce fund. She said he'd receive the balance when she returned from the trip.

"What about Trish?" she asked. "How does she get on with reptiles?"

"Oh, she's crazy for 'em. Turtles especially." Demencio could barely keep a straight face.

Krome took out a camera, one of those cardboard disposables. Demencio asked what it was for.

128

"Your Virgin Mary—can I get a picture? It's for a friend."

Demencio said, "I guess. Just give me a second to put her back together."

"That'll be terrific. Put her back together and make her cry."

"Christ, you want tears, too?"

"Please," said Tom Krome, "if it's not too much trouble."

8 It was past midnight when Tom Krome and JoLayne Lucks stopped at a Comfort Inn in South Miami, near the university. Fearing her nasty cuts and bruises would draw stares, JoLayne remained in the car while Krome registered them at the motel. They got separate rooms, adjoining.

Krome fell asleep easily—a wonder, considering he had no job, thirteen hundred dollars in the bank, and an estranged wife who was pretending to be a drug addict while refusing to grant him a divorce. If that wasn't enough to cause brain fever, he'd also been marked for grievous harm by a jealous judge whose wife he'd been screwing for not even a month. All these weighty problems Krome had put aside in order to recklessly endanger himself pursuing two armed psychopaths who'd robbed and assaulted a woman Krome barely knew.

Yet he slept like a puppy. That according to Jo-Layne Lucks, who was sitting in the room when he awoke in bright daylight.

"Not a worry in the world," he heard her say. "That's one of the best things about my job— watching puppies and kittens sleep."

Krome rose up on both elbows. JoLayne was wearing a sports halter and bicycle shorts. Her legs and arms were slender but tautly muscled; he wondered why he hadn't noticed before.

"Babies sleep the same way," she was saying, "but watching babies makes me sad. I'm not sure why."

"Because you know what's in store for them." Krome started to roll out of bed, then remembered he was wearing only underwear.

JoLayne lobbed him a towel. "You are quite the shy one. Want me to turn around?"

"Not necessary." After the bathtub episode, there was nothing to hide.

"Go take a shower," she told him. "I promise not to peek."

When Krome came out, she was asleep on his bed. For several moments he stood there listening to the sibilant rhythms of her breathing. It was alarming how comfortable he felt, considering the lunatic risks that lay ahead. This unfamiliar sense of mission was energizing, and he resolved not to overanalyze it. A woman had been hurt, the men who did it deserved to pay—and Krome had nothing better to do than help. Anyway, chasing gun nuts through South Florida was better than writing brainless newspaper features about Bachelorhood in the Nineties.

He slipped next door to JoLayne's room, so he wouldn't wake her by talking on the telephone. Two hours later she came in, puffy-eyed, to report: "I had quite a dream."

"Bad or good?"

"You were in it."

"Say no more."

"In a hot-air balloon."

"Is that right."

"Canary yellow with an orange stripe."

Krome said, "I'd have preferred to be on a handsome steed."

"White or black?"

"Doesn't matter."

"Yeah, right." JoLayne rolled her eyes.

"As long as it runs," Krome said.

"Maybe next time." She yawned and sat down on the floor, folding her long legs under her bottom. "You've been a busy bee, no?"

He told her he'd lined up some money to finance the chase. Of course she wanted to know where he'd gotten it, but Krome fudged. The newspaper's credit union, unaware of his resignation the day before, had been pleased to make the loan. Jo-Layne Lucks would've raised hell if he'd told her the truth.

"I already wired three thousand toward your Visa bill," he said, "to keep the bastards going."

"Your own money!"

"Not mine, the newspaper's," he said.

"Get outta here."

"Ever heard of an expense account? I get reimbursed for hotels and gas, too."

Krome, sounding like quite the big shot. He wasn't sure if JoLayne Lucks was buying the lie. Her toes were wiggling, which could mean just about anything.

She said, "They must really want this story."

"Hey, that's the business we're in."

"The news biz, huh? Tell me more."

"The men who beat you up," Krome said, "they haven't cashed your Lotto ticket yet. I checked with Tallahassee. They haven't even left their names."

"They're waiting to make sure I don't go to the police. Just like you predicted."

"They'll hold out a week, maybe ten days, before that ticket burns a crater in their pocket."

"That isn't much time."

"I know. We'll need some breaks to find them."

"And then . . . ?"

She'd asked the same thing earlier, and Krome had no answer. Everything depended on who the creeps were, where they lived, what they'd bought at that gun show. That the men had remembered to steal the night videotape from the Grab N'Go showed they weren't as stupid as Krome had first thought.

JoLayne reminded him that her Remington was in the trunk. "The nice thing about shotguns," she said, "is the margin of error."

"Oh, so you've shot people before."

"No, Tom, but I do know the gun. Daddy made sure of that."

Krome handed her the phone. "Call the nice folks at Visa. Let's see what our party boys are up to."

Sinclair had told no one at *The Register* that Tom Krome had resigned, in the hope it was a cheap bluff. Good reporters were temperamental and impulsive; this Sinclair remembered from newspaper management school.

Then the woman who covered the police beat came to Sinclair's office with a xeroxed report he found highly disturbing. The windows of Krome's house had been shot out by persons unknown, and there was no sign of the owner. In the absence of fresh blood or corpses, the cops were treating the incident as a random act of vandalism. Sinclair thought it sounded more serious than that.

He was pondering his options when his sister

Joan phoned from Grange. Excitedly she told Sinclair the latest rumor: The Lotto woman, JoLayne Lucks, left town the night before with a white man, supposedly a newspaper writer.

"Is that your guy?" Joan asked.

Sinclair felt clammy as he fumbled for a pen and paper. Having never worked as a reporter, he had no experience taking notes.

"Start again," he implored his sister, "and go slowly."

But Joan was chattering on with more gossip: The clerk at the Grab N'Go had skipped out, too—the one who'd originally said he sold the winning lottery ticket to JoLayne Lucks and then later changed his mind.

"Whoa," said Sinclair, scribbling spastically. "Run that by me again."

The shaky store clerk was a new twist to the story. Joan briefed her brother on what was known locally about Shiner. Sinclair cut her off when she got to the business about the young man's mother and the Road-Stain Jesus.

"Back up," he said to Joan. "They're traveling together—the clerk, this writer and the Lucks woman? Is that the word?"

His sister said: "Oh, there's all sorts of crazy theories. Bermuda is my personal favorite."

Sinclair solemnly jotted the word "Bermuda" on his notepad. He added a question mark, to denote his own doubts. He thanked Joan for the tip, and she gaily promised to call back if she heard anything new. After hanging up, Sinclair drew the blinds in his office—a signal (although he didn't realize it) to his entire staff that an emergency was in progress.

In solitude, Sinclair grappled with his options. Tom Krome's fate concerned him deeply, if only in a political context. An editor was expected to maintain the illusion of control over his writers, or at least have a sketchy idea of their whereabouts. The situation with Krome was complicated by the fact that he was regarded as a valuable talent by *The Register*'s managing editor, who in his lofty realm was spared the daily anxiety of working with the man. It was Sinclair's cynical theory that Krome had won the managing editor's admiration with a single feature story—a profile of a contro-versial performance artist who abused herself and occasionally audience members with zucchini, yams and frozen squab. With great effort Krome had managed to scavenge minor symbolism from the young woman's histrionics, and his mildly sympathetic piece had inspired the National En-dowment for the Arts to reinstate her annual grant of $14,000. The artist was so grateful she came to the newspaper to thank the reporter (who was, as always, out of town) and ended up chatting in-stead with the managing editor himself (who, of course, asked her out). A week later, Tom Krome was puzzled to find a seventy-five-dollar bonus in his paycheck.

Was life fair? Sinclair knew it didn't matter. He was left to presume his own career would suffer if Krome turned up unexpectedly in a hospital, jail, morgue or scandal. Yet Sinclair was helpless to influence events, because of two crucial mistakes. The first was allowing Krome to quit; the second was not informing anybody else at the newspaper. So as far as Sinclair's bosses were aware, Krome still worked for him.

Which meant Sinclair would be held accountable if Krome died or otherwise got in trouble. Because Sinclair had neither the resourcefulness nor the manpower to find his lost reporter, he energetically set about the task of covering his own ass. He spent two hours crafting a memorandum that recounted his last meeting with Tom Krome, describing at length the severe personal stress with which the man obviously had been burdened. Sinclair's written account culminated with Krome's shrieking that he was quitting, upending Sinclair's desk and stomping from the newsroom. Naturally Sinclair had refused to accept his troubled friend's resignation, and discreetly put him on excused medical leave, with pay. Out of deference to Krome's privacy, Sinclair had chosen to tell no one, not even the managing editor.

Sinclair reread the memorandum half a dozen

times. It was an adroit piece of management sophistry—casting doubt on an employee's mental stability while simultaneously portraying oneself as the loyal, yet deeply worried, supervisor.

Perhaps Sinclair wouldn't need the fable to bail himself out. Perhaps Tom Krome simply would forget about the nutty Lotto woman and return to work at *The Register,* as if nothing had happened.

But Sinclair doubted it. What little he could read of his own wormlike scribbles made his stomach churn.

Bermuda?

Chub couldn't decide where to stash the stolen lottery ticket—few hiding places were as ingenious as Bode Gazzer's condom. At first Chub tucked the prize inside one of his shoes; by nightfall it was sodden with perspiration. Bode warned him that the lottery bureau wouldn't cash the ticket if it was "defaced," a legal term Bode broadly interpreted to include wet and stinky. Dutifully Chub relocated the ticket in the box of hollowpoints that he carried with him at all times. Again Bode Gazzer objected. He pointed out that if Chub got trapped in a fire, the ammunition would explode in his trousers and the Lotto numbers would be destroyed.

The only other idea that occurred to Chub was a trick he'd seen in some foreign prison movie, where the inmate hero kept a secret diary hidden up his butthole. The guy scribbled everything in ant-sized letters on chewing gum wrappers, which he folded into tiny squares and stuck in his ass, so the prison guards wouldn't get wise. Given Bode's low regard for Chub's personal hygiene, Chub was fairly sure his partner would object to the butthole scheme. He was right.

"What if first I wrap it in foil?" Chub offered.

"I don't care if you pack it in fucking kryptonite, that lottery ticket ain't goin' up your ass."

Instead they attached it with a jumbo Band-Aid to Chub's right outer thigh, a hairless quadrant that (Bode conceded) seemed relatively untainted by Chub's potent sweat. Bode firmly counseled Chub to remove the Lotto-ticket bandage when, and if, he ever felt like bathing.

Chub didn't appreciate the insult, and said so. "You don't watch your mouth," he warned Bode Gazzer, "I'm gone do somethin' so awful to your precious truck, you'll need one a them moonsuits to go anywheres near it."

"Jesus, take it easy."

Later they went to the 7-Eleven for their customary breakfast of Orange Crush and Dolly Madisons. Bode swiped a newspaper and searched it for a mention of the Lotto robbery in Grange. He was relieved to find nothing. Chub declared himself in a mood for shooting, so they stopped by Bode's apartment to grab the AR-15 and a case of beer, and headed south down the Eighteen-Mile Stretch. They turned off on a gravel road that led to a small rock-pit lake, not far from a prison camp where Bode had once spent four months. At the rock pit they came upon a group of clean-shaven men wearing holsters and ear protectors. From the type of vehicles at the scene—late-model Cherokees, Explorers, Land Cruisers—and the orderliness with which they'd been parked, Bode concluded the shooters were suburban husbands brushing up on home-defense skills. The men stood side by side, firing pistols and semiautomatics at paper silhouettes just like the ones cops used. Bode was disquieted to observe among the group a Negro, one or two possible Cubans, and a wiry bald fellow who was almost certainly Jewish.

"We gotta go. This place ain't secure." Bode, speaking in his role as militia leader.

Chub said, "You jest watch." He peeled off his eye patch and sauntered to the firing line. There he nonchalantly raised the AR-15 and, in a few deafening seconds, reduced all the paper targets to confetti. Then, for good measure, he opened up on a stray buzzard that was flying no less than a thousand feet straight up in the sky. Without a word, the husbands put away their handguns and departed. A few drove off without removing their ear cups, a sight that gave Bodean Gazzer a good laugh.

Chub went through a half dozen clips before he

got bored and offered the rifle to Bode, who declined to shoot. The blasts of gunfire had reignited the killer migraine from Bode's morning hangover, and now all he craved was silence. He and Chub sat down at the edge of the lake and worked on the beer.

After a while, Chub asked, "So when can we cash out our tickets?"

"Pretty soon. But we gotta be careful."

"That nigger girl, she ain't gonna say a word."

"Probably not," Bode said. Yet, thinking back on the beating, he recalled that the Lucks woman never seemed as scared as she should've been. Mad as a hornet, for sure, and crying like a baby when Chub shot her turtle—but there was no quivering animal panic from the woman, despite all the pain. They'd worked extra hard to make her think they'd return to murder her if she didn't keep quiet. Bode hoped she believed it. He hoped she cared.

Chub said, "Let's tomorrow me and you go straight up to Tal'hassee and git our money."

Bode laughed sourly. "You checked in the mirror lately?"

"Tell 'em we's in a car accident."

"With what—bobcats?"

"Anyways, they gotta pay us no matter how bad we look. We had leprosy, the motherfuckers still gotta pay us."

Patiently Bode Gazzer explained how suspicious it would be for two best friends to claim equal shares of the same Lotto jackpot, with tickets purchased three hundred miles apart.

"It's better," Bode said, "if we don't know each other. We ain't never met, you and me, far as the lottery bureau is concerned."

" 'K."

"Anybody asks, I bought my fourteen-million-dollar ticket in Florida City, you got yours in Grange. And we never once laid eyes on each other before."

"No problem," Chub said.

"And listen here, we can't show up in Tallahassee together. One of us goes on a Tuesday, the other one maybe a week later. Just to play it safe."

"Then afterwards," said Chub, "we put the money all together."

"You got it."

Chub did the arithmetic aloud. "If those first checks is seven hundred grand, times two is like one million four hunnert thousand bucks."

Bodean Gazzer said, "Before taxes, don't forget." It felt like his skull was cleaving down the middle, an agony made worse by his partner's greasy persistence.

"But what I wanna ast," Chub said, "is who goes first. Cashes out, I mean."

"Difference does it make?"

"I guess none."

They got in the truck and headed down the

gravel road toward the Stretch. Chub stared out the window as Bode went on: "I don't like the wait no better'n you. Sooner we get the cash, sooner we get the White Clarion Aryans together. Start serious recruitment. Build us a bomb shelter and whatnot."

Chub lit a cigaret. "So meantime what do we do for money?"

"Good question," Bode Gazzer said. "I wonder if the Negro girl's canceled out her credit card yet."

"Likely so."

"One way to find out."

Chub blew a smoke ring. "I s'pose."

"We're down to a quarter tank," Bode said. "Tell you what. The Shell station up the highway, let's try the self-serve pump. If it spits her Visa, we'll take off."

"Yeah?"

"Yeah. No harm done."

Chub said, "And if it takes the card?"

"Then we're golden for one more day."

"Sounds good to me." Chub dragged contentedly. Already he was daydreaming about barbecued chicken wings and a certain blond-haired beauty in satiny orange shorts.

The bank's computer indicated JoLayne's Visa card hadn't been used since the previous afternoon at Hooters.

"Now what?" she asked, waving the receiver.

"Order a pizza," said Tom Krome, "and wait for them to get stupid again."

"What if they don't?"

"They will," he said. "They can't resist."

The pizza was vegetarian, delivered cold. They ate it anyway. Afterwards JoLayne stretched out on her back, locked her arms behind her neck and bent her knees.

"Sit-ups?" Tom Krome asked.

"Crunches," she said. "Wanna help?"

He knelt on the floor and held her ankles. Jo-Layne winked and said, "You've done this before."

He counted along in his head. After a hundred easy ones, she closed her eyes tight and did a hundred more. He gave her a minute to rest, then said: "That was a little scary."

JoLayne winced as she sat up. She pressed her knuckles to her tummy and said, "Bastards really did a job on me. Normally I can do three-fifty or four."

"I think you should take it easy."

"Your turn," she said.

"JoLayne, please."

Then suddenly Krome was on his back, except she wasn't holding his ankles as a proper sit-up partner would do. Instead she was straddling his chest, pinning his arms.

"Know what I was thinking?" she said. "About

what you said earlier, how white or black doesn't matter."

"Weren't we talking about dreams and horses?"

"Maybe *you* were."

Deliberately Tom Krome went limp. His goal was to minimize the frontal contact, which was indescribably wonderful. He was also trying to think of a distraction, something to make his blood go cold. Sinclair's face was an obvious choice, but Krome couldn't summon it.

JoLayne was saying, "It's important we should have this discussion. . . ."

"Later."

"So it *does* matter. White and black."

"JoLayne?"

Now she was nose-to-nose and pressing her body down harder. "Tom, you tell me the truth."

He turned his head away. Total limpness was no longer sustainable.

"Tom?"

"What."

"Are you mistaking this moment for some kind of clumsy seduction?"

"Call me crazy."

JoLayne pulled away. By the time he sat up, she was perched on the bed, cutting him a look. "Back in the shower for you!"

"I thought we had a professional relationship," he said. "I'm the reporter, you're the story."

"So you're the only one who gets to ask questions? That's really fair."

"Ask away, but no more wrestling." Krome, thinking: What a handful she is.

JoLayne cuffed him. "OK, how many black friends do you have? I mean *friend* friends."

"I don't have many close friends of any color. I am not what you'd call gregarious."

"Ah."

"There's a black guy at work—Daniel, from Editorial. We play tennis every now and then. And Jim and Jeannie, they're lawyers. We get together for dinner."

"That's your answer?"

Krome caved. "OK, the answer is none. Zero black *friend* friends."

"Just like I thought."

"But I'm working on it."

"Yes, you are," said JoLayne. "Let's go for a ride."

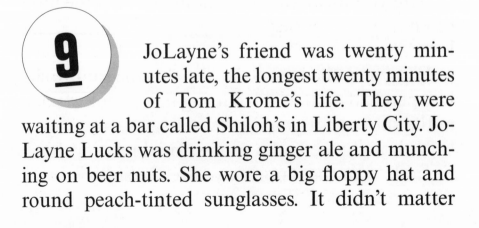

JoLayne's friend was twenty minutes late, the longest twenty minutes of Tom Krome's life. They were waiting at a bar called Shiloh's in Liberty City. JoLayne Lucks was drinking ginger ale and munching on beer nuts. She wore a big floppy hat and round peach-tinted sunglasses. It didn't matter what Tom Krome was wearing; he was the only white person there. Several patrons remarked upon the fact, and not in a welcoming tone.

JoLayne told him to put his notebook on the bar and start writing. "So you look official."

"Good idea," Krome said, "except I left it back in the room."

JoLayne clicked her tongue. "You men, you'd forget your weenies if they weren't glued on."

A gangly transvestite in a fantastic chromium wig approached Krome and offered to blow him for forty dollars.

Krome said, "No, thanks, I've got a date."

"Then I do her fo' free."

"Tempting," said JoLayne, "but I think we'll pass."

With a bony hand, the transvestite gripped one of Krome's legs. "Dolly don't take no for an answer. And Dolly gots a blade in her purse."

JoLayne leaned close to Krome and whispered: "Give him a twenty."

"Not a chance."

"Speak up now," said the Dolly person. Ridiculous fake fingernails dug into Krome's calf. "Come on, big man, let's go out to yo' cah. Bring the fancy lady if you wants."

Krome said, "I like that dress—didn't you used to be on *Shindig*?"

The transvestite gave a bronchial laugh and squeezed harder. "Dolly's gettin' the boy 'cited."

"No, just annoyed."

To unfasten the Dolly person's hand from his knee, Krome twisted the thumb clockwise until it came out of the socket. The popping sound silenced the bar. JoLayne Lucks was impressed. She'd have to find out where he'd learned such a thing.

Dropping to his knees, the transvestite prostitute shrieked and pawed at himself with his crooked digit. Lurching to avenge his honor were two babbling crackheads, each armed with gleaming cutlery. They began to argue about who should get to stab the white boy first, and how many times. It was a superb moment for JoLayne's friend to show up, and his arrival cleared the scene. The Dolly person shed a spiked pump during his scamper out the door.

The name of JoLayne's friend was Moffitt, and he made no inquiries about the crackheads or the yowling robber. Moffitt was built like a middleweight and dressed like an expensive lawyer. His gray suit was finely tailored and his checkered necktie was silk. He wore thin-rimmed eyeglasses with round conservative frames, and carried a small cellular telephone. He greeted JoLayne with a hug but scarcely nodded at Tom Krome.

The bartender brought Moffitt a Diet Coke and a bowl of pitted olives. He popped one in his mouth and asked JoLayne to remove her sunglasses.

After examining her face, he turned to Krome: "She gave me one version over the phone, but I want to hear yours—did you do this to her?"

"No."

"Because if I find out otherwise, you're going on an ambulance ride—"

"I didn't do it."

"—possibly in a bag."

JoLayne said, "Moffitt, it wasn't him."

They moved to a booth. Moffitt asked for a card, and Krome got one from his billfold. Moffitt remarked that he'd never heard of *The Register.* JoLayne told him to lighten up.

Moffitt said, "Sorry. I don't trust anyone in the media."

"Well, I'm stunned," said Krome. "We're so accustomed to being adored and admired."

Moffitt didn't crack a smile. To JoLayne he said: "What's your plan, Jo? What do you need from me?"

"Help. And don't tell me to go to the cops because if I do, I'll never get my Lotto ticket back."

Impassively Moffitt agreed. His cell phone rang. He turned it off. "I'll do what I can," he said.

JoLayne turned to Krome. "We've known each other since kindergarten. He takes a personal interest in my well-being, and I do the same for him."

"Don't lie to the man. I'm lucky to get a Christmas card." Moffitt tapped his knuckles on the table. "Tell me about the guys who did this."

"Rednecks," JoLayne said, "red-to-the-bone rednecks. They called me, among other things, a rotten nigger slut."

"Nice." Moffitt spoke in a tight voice. When he reached for his Coke, Krome noticed the bulge under his left arm.

JoLayne said: "We're following them."

"Following." Moffitt looked skeptical. "How?"

"Her credit card," Krome explained. "They're burning a trail."

Moffitt seemed encouraged. He took out a gold Cross pen and reached for a stack of cocktail napkins. In small precise script he took down the details JoLayne gave him—the purchase of the lottery ticket, how she'd met Tom Krome, the break-in, the beating, the red pickup truck, the missing video from the Grab N'Go. By the time she finished, Moffitt had filled both sides of three napkins, which he folded neatly and tucked into an inside suit pocket.

Tom Krome said, "Now I've got a question."

JoLayne nudged him and said not to bother. Moffitt shifted impatiently.

"Who do you work for?" Krome said. "What do you do?"

"Use your imagination," Moffitt told him. Then, to JoLayne: "Call me in a day or two, but not at the office."

Then he got up and left. The bar stayed quiet; no sign of Dolly or his pals.

Fondly JoLayne said: "Poor Moffitt—I give him fits. And he's such a worrier."

"That would explain the gun," said Krome.

"Oh, that. He works for the government."

"Doing what?"

"I'll let him tell you," JoLayne said, sliding out of the booth. "I'm hungry again, how about you?"

Amber's boyfriend was named Tony. He'd been on her case to quit her job, until she made first alternate for Miss September in the Hooters Girl Calendar. After that Tony came to the restaurant three or four times a week, he was so proud. The more beers he drank, the louder he'd brag on Amber. This, she understood, was his suave way of letting the customers know she was spoken for.

Several months earlier, the Hooters people had asked Amber and three other waitresses to pose for a promotional poster, which was to be given away free to horny college guys on Fort Lauderdale beach. When Amber told Tony about the poster, he immediately joined a gym and began injecting steroids. In ten months he gained thirty-two pounds and developed such an igneous strain of acne across both shoulders that Amber forbade him to wear tank tops.

Initially she'd been flattered by Tony's surprise

appearances at the restaurant, particularly since the other waitresses thought he was so handsome—quite the hunk! Amber never let on that Tony couldn't keep a job, mooched shamelessly off his parents, hadn't finished a book since tenth grade and wasn't all that great in the sack. And ever since he'd started the workout binge, he'd become moody and rough. One time he'd dragged her dripping wet from the shower to the bed, by her hair. She'd considered leaving him, but nothing better had presented itself. Tony *did* look good (at least in a sleeved shirt), and in Amber's world that counted for something.

Yet she wished he'd stop dropping in at work. His presence was not only distracting, it was a drain on her income. Amber had been keeping track: Whenever Tony was there, her tips fell off by as much as a third. Therefore the sight of her hulked-out sweetheart swaggering through the door on this particular Wednesday evening— Wednesday already being a slow night, tipwise— failed to evoke in the alternate Miss September either gladness or affection. The frisky ambience of Hooters brought out Tony's demonstrative side, and at every opportunity he intercepted his tray-laden princess with an indiscreet hug, smooch or pat on the ass. Tony's boisterous possessiveness was meant to discourage other patrons from flirting with Amber, and it did. Unfortunately, it also discouraged excessive gratuities.

Amber's only hope on this night was the icky-looking pair of rednecks at table seven, the same two who yesterday had left her a hundred-dollar tip on a credit card. The shorter man had arrived in a fresh suit of camouflage, while his ponytailed companion—the one who'd tried to buy her shorts—appeared not to have changed clothes or even shaved. Affixed across the orbit of his left eye was a new rubber bicycle patch; Amber tried not to imagine what was behind it. The faces of both men still bore the scabs of savage cuts, as if they'd gone at each other with razors. Amber could not dismiss the possibility.

But for her purposes, the rednecks could not be crude and spooky and disgusting. They were handsome and sexy and sophisticated; Mel Gibson and Tom Cruise, sharing a plate of chicken wings. That's how Amber treated them. It wasn't easy, but a hundred bucks was a hundred bucks.

"Honey," said the ponytailed one, "you's right about the White Rebel Brotherhood. They's a damn rock band."

"You should see 'em live," Amber said. She set two cold Coronas on the table.

The stumpy one in camouflage asked her if the name of the group was some kind of joke. "Considering all the Negroes they got," he added.

Amber said, "I think it's meant to be funny, yeah."

The ponytailed one, lathering his palms with the

condensation from the beer bottle: "Well, Bode don't think it's so funny. Can't say I do, neither."

Amber's poster-quality smile didn't flicker. "The music's killer. That's all I know."

Then she glided away with their empties and an order for more onion rings. Her path to the kitchen took her directly past Tony's table, and of course he snatched her by the elastic waistband of her shorts.

"Not now," she told him.

"Who're those dirtbags?"

"Just customers. Now let me get to work," Amber said.

Tony grunted. "They hit on you? That's what it looked like."

"You're going to get me in trouble with the boss. Let go, OK?"

"First a kiss." With one arm he pulled her close.

"Tony!"

"A kiss for Tony, that's right."

And of course he had to slip her some tongue, right there in the middle of the restaurant. Out of the corner of an eye, Amber noticed the rednecks watching. Tony must have seen them, too, because he was beaming by the time Amber pulled free.

A few minutes later, when she delivered the onion rings to the table, the ponytailed one said: "People ever tell you you look zackly like Kim Basinger."

"Really?" Amber acted flattered, though she'd always seen herself in the Daryl Hannah mold.

"Bode thinks so, too, don'tcha?"

"Dead ringer," said the camouflaged man, "and I'm the better judge. I still got both good eyes."

Amber said, "Well, you're sweet for saying so. Can I get you anything else?"

"Matter a fact, yes you can," the ponytailed man said. "How 'bout one a them red-hot kisses like you give that other guy?"

Amber blushed. With a moist leer the camouflaged man said, "Yeah, I didn't see that on no menu!"

The ponytailed one observed that Amber wasn't too keen on the kissing idea. He cocked his face upward and tapped a dirty fingertip on the bicycle patch. "Mebbe it's me. Mebbe you prejudiced against handicaps."

Amber, sensing (as all good waitresses can) that her tip was in jeopardy: "No, oh no, I can explain. That's my boyfriend."

In unison the men twisted in their chairs to reappraise Tony across the restaurant. He returned their stares with a belligerent sneer.

The ponytailed redneck said, "No shit. The hell is he, Cuban?"

Amber said no, Tony was from Los Angeles. "Sometimes he gets carried away. I'm sorry if it upset you."

Through a mouthful of onions, the one called Bode said: "Meskin, I'll bet. They're all over California is what I heard."

On the way back to the bar station, Amber stopped at Tony's table and curtly related what had happened: "Thanks to you, they think I kiss all the customers. They think it's part of the service. You happy now?"

Tony's eyes darkened. "Those dirtbags—they wanted a kiss?"

"Do us all a favor. Go home," Amber whispered.

"No fuckin' way. Not now."

"Tony, I swear to God . . ."

He was flaring his nostrils, puffing his chest, flexing his arms. All that's missing, Amber thought, is the workout mirror.

Declared Tony: "I'll straighten those shitheads out."

"No you won't," said Amber, bitterly surveying the suddenly empty table. "They're gone."

She hurried back, hoping to find some cash. Nothing—they'd skipped on the tab. *Shit,* she thought. It would come out of her pay.

Suddenly she was enveloped by Tony's cologne, as subtle as paint thinner. She felt him looming behind her. "Goddamn you," she said, retreating to the kitchen. Predictably, Tony stormed out the door.

Two hours later, Amber's redneck customers returned, anchoring themselves at the same table.

She tried not to appear too relieved. "Where'd you fellas run off to?"

"Jest needed some fresh air," said the ponytailed one, lighting a cigaret. "You miss us? Say, where's that kissing-machine boyfriend a yours."

Amber pretended not to hear him. "What can I get for you?"

The camouflaged man ordered four more beers, two apiece, and a fresh heap of wings. "Add it on our bill," he said, flashing the Visa card with two stubby fingers.

Amber was waiting for the drink order when the barmaid handed her the phone. "For you, honey," she said. "Guess who."

Tony, of course. Screaming.

"Slow down," Amber told him. "I can't understand a word."

"My car!" he cried. "Somebody burned up my car!"

"Oh, Tony."

"Right in my fucking driveway! They torched it!"

"When?"

"During wrestling, I guess. It's still on fire, they got like five guys tryin' to put out the flames. . . ."

The barmaid came with the tray of Coronas. Amber told Tony she was really sorry about the car, but she had to get back to work.

"I'll call you on my break," she promised.

"The Miata, Amber!"

"Yes, baby, I heard you."

When she brought the beers and chicken wings to the two rednecks, the one named Bode said: "Sugar, you're our rock 'n' roll expert. Is there a band called the White Clarion Aryans?"

Amber thought for a moment. "Not that I ever heard of."

"Good," Bode said.

"Not jes good," said his ponytailed friend, "fan-fucking-tastic!"

JoLayne Lucks demanded that Tom Krome teach her the thumb-popping trick. "That thing you did with the he-she back at Shiloh's."

When they got to a stoplight, Krome took her left hand to demonstrate.

"Not too hard!" she piped.

Gently he showed her how to disable a person by bending and twisting his thumb in a single motion. JoLayne asked where he'd learned about it.

"One time the newspaper sent me to take a class on self-defense," Krome said, "for a feature story. The instructor was a ninja guy, weighed all of a hundred and twenty pounds. But he knew all sorts of naughty little numbers."

"Yeah?"

"Fingers in the eye sockets is another good one," said Krome. "The scrotal squeeze is a crowd pleaser, too."

"These come in handy in the newspaper biz?"

"Today was the first time."

JoLayne was pleased he didn't let go of her hand until the light turned green and it was time to steer the car. They stopped at a Burger King on Northwest Seventh Avenue and ate in the parking lot with the windows down. The breeze was cool and pleasant, even with the din from the interstate. After lunch they went on a tour of JoLayne's childhood: kindergarten, elementary school, high school. The pet shop where she'd worked in the summers. The appliance store her father once owned. The auto garage where she'd met her first boyfriend.

"He took care of Daddy's Grand Prix," she said. "Good at lube jobs, bad at relationships. Rick was his name."

"Where is he now?"

"Lord, I can't imagine."

While Krome drove, JoLayne found herself spinning through the stories of the significant men in her life. "Aren't you sorry," she said, "you left your notebook at the motel?"

He smiled but didn't take his eyes off the road. "I got a helluva memory." Then, swerving around a county bus: "What about Moffitt—he's not on the List of Six?"

"Friends only." JoLayne wondered if Krome's interest was strictly professional, caught herself hoping it wasn't. "He dated both my sisters, my best friend, a cousin and also my nursing supervisor at Jackson. But not me."

"How come?"

"Mutual agreement."

"Ah," Krome said. He didn't believe it was mutual. He believed Moffitt would go to his grave asking himself why JoLayne Lucks hadn't wanted him.

"We'd been buddies so long," she was saying, "we knew too much about each other. One of those deals."

"Right," Krome said. He pulled to the curb while two police cars and an ambulance sped past. When the wail of sirens faded, JoLayne said, "Plus Moffitt's too serious for me. You saw for yourself. Why I'm telling you this stuff, Lord, I don't know."

"I'm interested."

"But it's not part of the story."

"How do you know?" Krome said.

"Because I'm telling you so. It's *not* part of the story."

He shrugged.

"What in the world was I thinking," JoLayne said, "bringing you in on this. First off, you're a man, and I've got rotten instincts when it comes to men. Second, you're a *reporter,* for heaven's sake. Only a crazy fool would believe a reporter, am I right? And last but not least—"

"I'm awfully white," Krome said.

"Bingo."

"But you trust me anyway."

"Truly it's a mystery." JoLayne removed her floppy hat and flipped it in the back seat. "Can we stop at a pay phone? I need to call Clara before it gets too late."

Clara Markham was the real estate broker who had the listing for Simmons Wood. Clara knew Jo-Layne wanted to buy the property, because Jo-Layne had phoned the night she'd won the lottery. But then, two days later, JoLayne had called back to say something had happened and it might be awhile before she could make a down payment. Clara had promised not to accept any other offers until she spoke to JoLayne again. She was a friend, after all.

Krome spotted a pay phone outside a sub shop on 125th Street. JoLayne got Clara Markham at the realty office.

JoLayne said, "Whatcha up to, working so late."

"Busy, girl."

"How's my pal Kenny?"

Kenny was Clara's obese Persian. Because of its impeccably lush whiskers, Clara had named it after Kenny Rogers, the country singer.

"Much improved," Clara reported. "The hairball crisis is over, you can tell Dr. Crawford. But I'm afraid I've got some other news."

JoLayne sucked in a deep breath. "Damn. Who is it?"

"A union pension fund out of Chicago."

"And they build malls?"

"Girl, they build everything."

"What's the offer?" JoLayne asked gloomily.

"Three even. Twenty percent down."

"Damn. *Goddamn*."

Clara said, "They want an answer in a week."

"I can do better than three million. You wait."

"Jo, I'll stall as long as I can."

"I'd sure appreciate it."

"And be sure and tell Doc Crawford thanks for the ointment. Tell him Kenny says thanks, too."

JoLayne Lucks hung up and sat on the curb. A group of teenagers spilled from the sub shop, nearly tripping over her.

Tom Krome got out of the car. "I take it there's another buyer."

JoLayne nodded disconsolately. "I've got a week, Tom. Seven lousy days to get my Lotto ticket back."

"Then let's go to it." He took her hands and pulled her to her feet.

The place known as Simmons Wood had been owned since 1959 by Lighthorse Simmons, whose father had been an early settler of Grange. Lighthorse maintained the rolling green tract as a private hunting reserve and visited regularly until he'd personally shot nearly every living creature on the property. Then he took up fishing. And although a fly rod could never provide the same hot blood rush as a rifle, Lighthorse Simmons grew to enjoy yanking feisty little bluegills and largemouth bass from the creek. Eventually, as he got older, he even stopped killing them.

Ironically, it was a hunter's bullet that led to the end of Lighthorse's long custodianship of Simmons Wood. The mishap occurred at dusk one evening—Lighthorse was on the creek bank, bending over to cough up a wad of Red Man he'd accidentally swallowed. In the twilight, the old fellow's broad straw hat, tawny suede jacket and downward pose apparently called to mind— at least for one myopic trespasser—the image of a six-point buck, drinking.

The bullet clipped Lighthorse's right kneecap, and after three surgeries he remained unable to hike through Simmons Wood without constant, grating pain. An electric cart was given to him as part of the insurance settlement, but it proved unsuitable for the bumpy terrain. One rainy morning Lighthorse hit a pine stump and the cart overturned. He was pinned for nearly four hours, during which time he was prodigiously befouled by an excitable feral boar—a breed of pig originally introduced to Grange, for sporting purposes, by Lighthorse's own father.

After that incident, Lighthorse never again set foot in Simmons Wood. He went through the legal technicalities of rezoning it from agricultural to commercial, but ultimately he couldn't bring himself to sell. The land remained untrammeled (and the dawn unbroken by gunfire) for such a long time that wild animals finally began to reappear. But when Lighthorse passed away, at age seventy-five, the administrators of his estate put Simmons Wood on the market. The place held no sentimental attachment for the old man's son and daughter, who viewed the potentially immense proceeds from the land sale as several new oil derricks in Venezuela and a winter ski cottage in New Hampshire, respectively.

On the other end of the deal was Bernard Squires, investment manager for the Central Midwest Brotherhood of Grouters, Spacklers and Drywallers International. To Bernard Squires fell the sensitive task of dispensing the union's pension fund in such a way as to conceal the millions of dollars being skimmed annually by organized crime: specifically, the Richard Tarbone family of Chicago.

Bernard Squires' livelihood, and in all probability his very life, depended on his talent for assembling investment portfolios in which vast sums could plausibly disappear. Naturally he had a fondness for real estate developments. Not for a moment did Bernard envision for Simmons Wood a thriving, profitable retail shopping center. Grange was a perfectly ridiculous location for a

major mall—one of the only municipalities in
Florida to have shrunk (according to incredulous
census takers) during the boom years of the eight-
ies and nineties. And while its puny population
was augmented by a modest flow of highway
tourists, the demographics of the average Grange
visitor could most diplomatically be typed, from a
retailer's perspective, as "*low* low end." No major
anchor stores or national chains would dream of
locating there, as Bernard Squires well knew.

His plan, from the beginning, was to create a
very expensive failure. Acting as a bank, the pension fund would finance the purchase of Simmons
Wood and enter into a series of contracts with
construction companies secretly controlled by
Richard Tarbone and his associates. Simmons
Wood would be bulldozed and cleared, a foundation would be poured, and perhaps even a wall or
two would go up.

Then: a run of bad luck. Shortages of labor and
materials. Weather delays. Missed payments on
construction loans. Contractors unexpectedly filing for bankruptcy. And as if that weren't enough,
the leasing agent would dejectedly report that
hardly anyone wanted space in the soon-to-be-
completed Simmons Wood Mall. The project
would sputter and die, and the site would become
a ruin. Florida was full of them.

Whatever true sum was lost in the Simmons
Wood venture would be doubled when it appeared

as red ink on the books of the Central Midwest Brotherhood of Grouters, Spacklers and Drywallers International. That is how Bernard Squires hid the Tarbone family's skimming. If other union officials suspected skulduggery, they were wise enough not to make a peep. Besides, the pension fund made a profit, overall; Squires saw to that. Even the IRS auditors didn't challenge his numbers. Investing in real estate was a crapshoot, as everybody knew. Sometimes you won, sometimes you lost.

Once the write-off had outlived its usefulness, Bernard Squires would contrive to unload Simmons Wood on an insurance conglomerate or maybe the Japanese—somebody with enough capital to finish the stupid mall, or raze it and start over. For now, though, Bernard Squires was eager to lock up the deal.

It was Richard "The Icepick" Tarbone's desire to close on the Grange property as soon as possible. "And don't call me," he had told Squires, "until you got some good fucking news. Do whatever it takes, you understand?"

Bernard understood.

The visitation got off to a rocky start. Once again, Demencio's fiberglass Madonna wasn't weeping properly—this time due to a crimp in the plastic feeder lines between the reservoir bottle and the

eyes. One tear duct was barren while the other
gushed like an artery. A pilgrim from Guatemala,
having been spritzed in the forehead, loudly chal-
lenged the legitimacy of the miracle. Luckily the
tirade was in Spanish and therefore incomprehen-
sible to the other visitors. Trish, who was manning
the Madonna, relayed the details of the plumbing
problem to Demencio at the breakfast table. He
told her to lay off the pump, pronto; no more
crying.

"But we got a bus coming," Trish reminded him.
"The mission bus from West Virginia."

"Aw, shit."

Every week Demencio changed the Madonna's
weeping schedule. It was important to have "dry"
days as well as "wet" days; otherwise there was no
sense of heavenly mystery. Moreover, Demencio
had observed that some pilgrims actually were
glad when the Virgin Mary didn't cry on their first
visit. It gave them a reason to come back to
Grange on a future vacation, just as tourists return
to Yellowstone year after year in the hopes of
spotting a moose.

So Demencio hadn't been alarmed when his
wife told him the Madonna was malfunctioning.
Usually midweek was slow for business, a good
time for an unscheduled dry day. But he'd forgotten about the damn mission bus: sixty-odd Christian pilgrims from Wheeling. The preacher's name
was Mooney or Moody, something like that, and

every other year he roared through Florida with new recruits. Trish would bake a lime pie and Demencio would throw in a bottle of scotch, and in return the preacher would entreat his faithful followers to donate generously at Demencio's shrine. For such a dependable throng, Demencio felt obliged to provide tears.

Thus the Madonna's hydraulic failure was potentially a crisis. Demencio didn't want to interrupt the morning visitation to haul the statue indoors for repairs—to do so would arouse suspicion, even among the most devout. Peering through the curtains, Demencio counted nine victims in the front yard, hovering attentively around the icon.

"Got any ideas?" Trish asked.

"Quiet," said her husband. "Lemme think."

But it wasn't quiet. The sounds of crunching filled the room: JoLayne's cooters, enjoying breakfast.

Demencio's somber gaze settled on the aquarium. Instead of breaking the romaine into bite-sized pieces, he'd dropped the whole head of lettuce into the tank. The sight of it had pitched the baby turtles into a frenzy, and they were now chewing their way up the leafy slopes.

It was, Demencio had to admit, weirdly impressive. Forty-five marauding turtles. He got an idea. "You still got that Bible?" he asked his wife. "The illustrated one?"

"Somewhere, yeah."

"And I'll need some paint," he said, "like they sell for model airplanes at the hobby store."

"We only got two hours before the bus."

"Don't worry, this won't take long." Demencio walked over to the aquarium. He bent down and said: "OK, who wants to be a star?"

10 On the morning of November 28, with rain misting the mountains, Mary Andrea Finley Krome checked out of the Mona Pacifica Mineral Spa and Residential Treatment Center, on the island of Maui. She flew directly to Los Angeles, where the next day she auditioned for a network television commercial for a new home-pregnancy test. Later she flew on to Scottsdale to rejoin the road company for the *Silence of the Lambs* musical, in which she starred as Clarice, the intrepid young FBI agent. Mary Andrea's itinerary was relayed by certain sources to Tom Krome's divorce lawyer, Dick Turnquist, who arranged for a process server to be waiting backstage at the dinner theater in Arizona.

Somehow Mary Andrea got word of the ambush. Midway through the finale, with the entire cast and chorus singing,

"Oh, Hannibal the Cannibal,
How deliciously malicious you are!"

. . . Mary Andrea collapsed, convincingly, in a spastic heap. The process server stood back as paramedics strapped the slack-tongued actress on a stretcher and carried her to an ambulance. By the time Dick Turnquist learned the details, Mary Andrea Finley Krome had miraculously regained consciousness, checked herself out of the Scottsdale hospital, rented a Thunderbird and disappeared into the desert.

Dick Turnquist delivered the bad news to Tom Krome via fax, which Krome retrieved at a Kinko's across the highway from the University of Miami campus. He didn't read it until he and Jo-Layne Lucks were parked under a streetlight on what she called the Big Stakeout.

After scanning the lawyer's report, Krome ripped it into pieces. JoLayne said: "I know what that woman wants."

"Me, too. She wants to be married forever."

"You're wrong, Tom. She'll go for a divorce. It has to be her idea, that's all."

"Thank you, Dr. Brothers." Krome didn't want to think about his future ex-wife because then he would no longer sleep like a puppy. Instead he would awake with marrow-splitting headaches and bleeding gums.

He said, "You don't understand. This is a sport

for Mary Andrea, dodging me and the lawyers. It's like a competition. Feeds her perverse appetite for drama."

"Can I ask how much you send her?"

Krome laughed sulfurously. "*Nada.* Not a damn penny! That's my point, I've tried everything: I cut off the monthly checks, canceled the credit cards, closed the joint accounts, forgot her birthday, forgot our anniversary, insulted her mother, slept with other women, grossly exaggerated how many—and still she won't divorce me. Won't even come to court!"

JoLayne said, "There's one thing you didn't try."

"It's against the law."

"Tell her you're dating a black girl. That usually does the trick."

"Mary Andrea couldn't care less. Hey, check this out." Tom Krome pointed across the parking lot. "Is that the pickup truck?"

"I'm not sure." JoLayne sat forward intently. "Could be."

On the morning the disposable camera arrived in the mail, Katie took it to a one-hour photo studio. Tom had done a pretty good job in Grange: only two pictures of his thumb and several of the Madonna shrine. In the close-ups, the statue's eyes glistened convincingly.

Katie slipped the photographs in her purse and drove downtown for an early lunch with her husband. In keeping with her new policy of marital sharing and complete openness, she placed the snapshots on the table between the bread basket and the pitcher of sangria.

"Tom kept his promise," she said, by way of explanation.

Judge Arthur Battenkill Jr. put down his salad fork and thumbed through the pictures. His dullness of expression and pistonlike mastication reminded Katie of a grazing sheep.

He said, "So what the hell is it?"

"The Virgin Mary. The one that cries."

"Cries."

"See there?" Katie pointed. "They say she cries real tears."

"*Who* says."

"It's a lore, Arthur. That's all."

"A crock is more like it." He handed the photos to his wife. "And your writer boyfriend gave you these?"

Katie said, "I asked him to—and he's not a boyfriend. It's over, as I've told you a dozen times. We're through, OK?"

Her husband took a sip of wine. Then, gnawing on a chunk of Cuban bread: "Let me see if I understand. It's over, but he's still sending you personal photographs."

Katie conveyed her annoyance by pinging a

spoon against the stem of her wineglass. "You don't listen very well," she said, "for a judge."

Her husband snickered. His poor attitude made Katie wonder if this whole honesty thing was a mistake; with someone as jealous as Arthur, maybe it was wiser to keep a few harmless secrets.

If only he'd make an effort, Katie thought. If only he'd open up the way she had. Out of the blue she asked, "So, how's Dana?"

Dana was one of the two secretaries whom Judge Arthur Battenkill Jr. was currently screwing.

"She's just fine," he said, cool as an astronaut.

"And Willow—she still with that ballplayer?"

Willow was the other secretary, Arthur's reserve mistress.

"They're still living together," the judge reported, "but Oscar's out of baseball. Torn rotator cuff, something like that."

"Too bad," said Katie.

"Maybe it was tendinitis. Anyway, he's gone back to get his degree. Restaurant management is what Willow said."

"Good for him," said Katie, thinking: Enough already about Oscar.

The judge looked pleased when his scrod arrived—baked in a bed of pasta, topped with crabmeat and artichokes. Katie was having the garden quiche, which she picked at listlessly. She hadn't seriously expected her husband to confess all his adulteries, but it wouldn't have killed him to admit to one. Willow would've been an encouraging start—she was no prize.

Katie said, "You were tossing and turning last night."

"You noticed."

"Your stomach again?"

"I got up," Arthur said, cheeks full, "and reread that remarkable list of yours."

Uh-oh, thought Katie.

"You and your young man," he said, swallowing emphatically, "every sordid, raunchy, sweaty detail. I can't believe you kept count."

"That's what truthful confessions are. If I went a little overboard, I'm sorry," Katie said.

"Thirteen sexual acts in fourteen days!" Her husband, twirling a pale-green noodle onto his fork. "Including three blow jobs—which, by the way, is two more than you've given me in the last fourteen *months.*"

Talk about keeping count, Katie thought. "Arthur, finish your fish before it gets cold."

"I don't understand you, Katherine. After everything I've done for you, I get a knife in my heart."

She said, "Stop. You're getting worked up over practically nothing."

"Three blow jobs is not 'practically nothing.' "

"You've missed the whole point. The whole darn point." She reached under the table and flicked her husband's hand off her thigh.

"Your young man," he said, "where is he now? Lourdes? Jerusalem? Maybe Turin—getting fitted for the shroud!"

"Arthur, he's not my 'young man.' I don't know where he is. And you, you're just a hypocritical ass."

Neatly the judge buffed a napkin across his lips. "I apologize, Katherine. Tell you what, let's get a room somewhere."

"You go to hell," she said.

"Please?"

"On one condition. You quit obsessing about Tommy."

"It's a deal," said Arthur Battenkill Jr. Jovially he waved at the waiter and asked for the check.

A few hours later, Tom Krome's house blew up.

On the way to breakfast, Bodean Gazzer and Chub stopped to hassle a couple of migrant workers hitchhiking along Highway One. Chub hovered with the .357 while Bode ran through the drill:

Name the fourteenth President of the United States.

Where was the Constitution signed?

Recite the Second Amendment.

Who starred in Red Dawn?

Personally, Chub was glad he didn't have to take the same quiz. Evidently the two Mexicans didn't do so hot, because Bode ordered them in butchered Spanish to show their green cards. Fearfully the men took out their wallets, which Bode emptied in the gravel along the side of the road.

"They legal?" Chub asked.

"They wish."

With the sharp toe of a boot, Bode kicked through the migrants' meager belongings—driver's licenses, farmworker IDs, passport snapshots of children, prayer tabs, postage stamps, bus passes. Chub thought he spotted an immigration card, but Bode ground it to shreds under his heel. Then he removed the cash from the men's wallets and ordered them to get a move on, *muchachos!*

Later, in the truck, Chub asked how much money they'd had.

"Eight bucks between 'em."

"Oh, man."

"Hey, it's eight bucks that rightfully belongs to white 'Mericans like us. Fucking illegals, Chub— guess who pays their doctor bills and food stamps? Me and you, that's who. Billions a dollars every year on aliens."

As usual, Chub saw no reason to doubt his friend's knowledge of such matters.

"And I mean *billions,*" Bode Gazzer went on, "so don't think of it as a robbery, my friend. That was a rebate."

Chub nodded. "You put it that way, sure."

When they returned from the 7-Eleven, they found an unfamiliar car parked crookedly near Chub's trailer. It was a sanded-down Chevrolet Impala; an old one, too. One of Chub's counterfeit handicapped permits hung from the rearview.

"Easy does it," said Chub, pulling the gun from his belt.

The door of the trailer was open, the TV blaring. Bode cupped his hands to his mouth: "Get your ass out here, whoever you are! And keep your goddamn hands in the air!"

Shiner appeared, shirtless and stubbly-bald, in the doorway. He wore the grin of a carefree idiot. "I'm here!" he proclaimed.

At first Bode and Chub didn't recognize him.

"Hey," Shiner said, "it's me—your new white brother. Where's the militia?"

Chub lowered the pistol. "The fuck you do to yourself, boy?"

"Shaved my hair off."

"May I ast why?"

"So I can be a skinhead," Shiner replied.

Bodean Gazzer whistled. "No offense, son, but it ain't your best look."

The problem was with Shiner's scalp: an angry latitudinal scar, shining like a hideous stamp on the pale dome of his head.

Chub asked Shiner if he'd gotten branded by some wild Miami niggers or Cubans.

"Nope. I fell asleep on a crankcase."

Bode crossed his arms. "And this crankcase," he said, "was it still in the car?"

"Yessir, with the engine runnin'." Shiner did his best to explain: The mishap had occurred almost two years earlier on a Saturday afternoon. He'd had a few beers, a couple joints, maybe half a roofie, when he decided to tune the Impala. He'd started the car, opened the hood and promptly passed out headfirst on the engine block.

"Fucker heated up big-time," Shiner said.

Chub couldn't stand it. He went in the trailer to take a shit, turn off the television and hunt down a cold Budweiser. When he came out he saw Bode Gazzer sitting next to Shiner on the front fender of the Chevy.

Bode waved him over. "Hey, our boy done exactly what we told him."

"How's that?"

"The Negro girl come to his house askin' about the Lotto ticket."

"She sure did," Shiner said, "and I said it wasn't her that won it. I said she must of got confused with another Saturday."

Chub said, "Good man. What'd she do next?"

"Got all pissed and run off out the door. She's beat up pretty bad, too. That was you guys, I figgered."

Bode prodded Shiner to finish the story. "Tell about how you quit your job at the store."

"Oh yeah, Mr. Singh, he said I couldn't park with the handicaps even though I got the blue wheelchair dealie on the mirror. So what I done, I grabbed my back pay from the cash register and hauled ass."

Bode added: "Took the security video, too. Just like we told him."

"Yeah, I hid it in the glove box." Shiner jerked his head toward the Impala.

"Slick move," said Chub, winking his good eye. In truth, he wasn't especially impressed by Shiner. Bode Gazzer, too, had doubts. The boy manifested the sort of submissive dimness that foretold a long sad future in minimum-security institutions.

"Look here," Shiner said, flexing his doughy left arm. "Radical new tattoo: *W.R.B.* To make it official."

Over the rim of his beer can, Chub shot Bode a look that said: *You* tell him.

"So how's it look?" Shiner asked brightly. "Seventy-five bucks, 'case you guys want one, too."

Bode slid off the fender and brushed the rust marks off the butt of his camo trousers. "Thing is, we had to change the name."

Shiner quit flexing. "It ain't the White Rebel Brotherhood no more? How come?"

"You was right about the rock band," Bode said.

"Yeah," Chub interjected, "we didn't want no confusion."

"So what's the new name?"

Bode told him. Shiner asked him to repeat it.

"White Clarion Aryans," Bode said, slowly.

Shiner's mouth drew tight. Morosely he stared at the initials burned into his biceps. "So the new ones are . . . W-C-A?"

"Right."

"Shit," said Shiner, under his breath. Looking up, he managed a smile. "Oh well."

There was an uncomfortable silence, during which Shiner rearranged his arms to cover the tattoo. Even Chub felt sorry for him. "But you know what," he said to Shiner, "that's one hell of a eagle you got there."

"Damn right," Bode Gazzer agreed. "That's one mean motherfucker of an eagle. What's he got in them claws, an M16?"

The boy perked up. "Affirmative. M16 is what I told the tattoo man."

"Well, he did you proud. How about a beer?"

Later they all went to the Sports Authority and (using the stolen Visa) purchased tents, sleeping bags, air mattresses, mosquito netting, lantern fuel and other outdoor gear. Bode said they should keep everything packed tight and ready, in case the NATO storm troopers came ashore without warning. Bode was pleased to find out that Shiner, unlike Chub, had a genuine fondness for camouflage sportswear. As a treat Bode bought him a light-

weight Trebark parka—Shiner could hardly wait
to get back to the trailer and try it all on.

While he ran inside to change clothes, Bode said
to Chub: "He's like a kid on Christmas morning."

More like a damn retard, thought Chub. He
said, "You got a spare hat? Because I don't wanna
look at that skinhead's skinned head no more."

In his truck Bode found a soggy Australian-
style bush hat; the mildew blended neatly into the
camo pattern. Shiner wore it proudly, cinching the
strap at his throat.

They spent the afternoon at the rock pit, where
it quickly became evident the young recruit could
not be entrusted with the serious guns. Chub had
illegally converted the AR-15 to fully automatic,
which proved too much, physically and emotion-
ally, for the newest member of the White Clarion
Aryans. Taking the rifle from Chub's hands,
Shiner gave a Comanche-style whoop and began
to shout: "Which way's the Bahamas! Which way's
them cocksuckin' NATO commies!" Then he spun
around and started firing wildly—bullets skipped
across the water, twanged off limestone boulders,
mowed down the cattails and saw grass.

Bode and Chub ducked behind the truck, Bode
muttering: "This ain't no good. Christ, this ain't
no good at all."

Chub cursed harshly. "I need a goddamn
drink."

It took a few minutes for Shiner to relinquish the AR-15, after which he was restricted to harmless plinking with his old Marlin .22. At dusk the three of them, smelling of gunfire and stale beer, returned to Chub's trailer. When Bode Gazzer asked if anybody was hungry, Shiner said he could eat a whole cow.

Chub couldn't tolerate another hour in the hyperactive nitwit's presence. "You gotta stay here," he instructed Shiner, "and stand guard."

"Guard of what?" the kid asked.

"The guns. Plus all the shit we bought today," Chub said. "New man always does guard duty. Ain't that right, Bode?"

"You bet." Bode, too, had grown weary of Shiner's company. He said, "The tents and so forth, that's important survivalist supplies. Can't just leave it here with nobody on watch."

"God, I'm starvin'," Shiner said.

Chub slapped him on the shoulder. "We'll bring you some chicken wings. You like the extry hot?"

According to the bank, JoLayne's credit card had been used two nights consecutively at the same Hooters—a reckless move that Krome found encouraging. The Lotto robbers clearly were not master criminals.

JoLayne figured nobody would be ballsy enough to go there three times in a row, but Krome said it was the best lead they had. Now he and Jo-Layne were outside the restaurant, watching a red pickup truck park in a disabled-only zone.

"Is that them?" Krome asked.

"The guys who came to my house were not crippled. Neither of them," JoLayne said gravely.

Two men—one tall, one short—got out of the truck. They entered the restaurant without the aid of a wheelchair, a crutch, or even a cane.

"Must be a miracle," said Krome.

JoLayne wasn't certain they were the same men who'd attacked her. "We're too far away."

"Then let's get closer."

He went in alone and chose a corner table. A minute later JoLayne came through the door—the floppy hat, Lolita sunglasses. She joined him, sitting with her back to the bar.

"You get the license tag?" she said.

"Yes, ma'am. And how about that bumper sticker? 'Fuhrman for President.'"

"Where are they?" she asked tensely. "Did they look at me?"

"If it's the table I think it is, they didn't notice either of us."

On the other side of the restaurant, two very distinctive customers were chatting with a pretty blond waitress. Her electric smile solved to Krome's satisfaction the mystery of why the shit-kickers returned night after night with a hot credit card: They were smitten. One of the men was outfitted entirely in camouflage, including a cap. His companion wore a dirty ponytail and a vulcanized patch over one eye. Both men, Krome noted, bore deep cuts on their faces.

"You said one was dressed like a hunter."

JoLayne nodded. "That's right."

"Take a peek."

"I'm frightened."

"It's all right," Krome told her.

She turned just enough to catch a quick look. "Lord," she gasped, and turned back.

Tom Krome patted her hand. "We done good, pardner."

JoLayne's expression was unreadable behind the big sunglasses. "Give me the car keys."

"What for?" Krome asked, knowing the answer. She didn't want to open the car; she wanted to open the trunk.

JoLayne said, "Let's wait till they leave—"

"No, not here."

"Tom, we've got the Remington. What could they do?"

"Forget it."

A waitress came, but JoLayne was unresponsive. Krome ordered hamburgers and Cokes for both of them. When they were alone again, he tried to make the case that a busy restaurant parking lot wasn't the ideal place to pull a shotgun on anybody, especially two drunk white-trash psychopaths.

JoLayne said, "I want my damn lottery ticket."

"And you'll get it. We found the bastards, that's the main thing. They can't get away from us now."

Again she peered over her shoulder, shivering at the sight of the ponytailed robber. "That face I'll never forget. But the eye patch I don't remember."

"Maybe you blinded him," Krome said.

JoLayne Lucks smiled faintly. "Lord, I hope so."

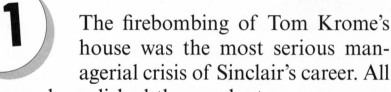 The firebombing of Tom Krome's house was the most serious managerial crisis of Sinclair's career. All afternoon he polished the exculpatory memorandum and awaited a summons from *The Register*'s managing editor. Like Krome's, the managing editor's training was in hard news and he viewed the world darkly. He was an angular, intense man in his mid-forties; prematurely gray, allergy prone, gruff, profane. He was famous for his laserlike glare and his lack of patience.

His last communication with Sinclair had come seven weeks earlier in a terse phone call: No frigging PMS column, you hear me! It had been one of Sinclair's rare brainstorms—a regular feature devoted to coping with PMS. The column would run once a month, of course. The managing editor despised the idea, which Sinclair promptly blamed on one of his subordinates.

Even under the mildest circumstances, direct contact with the managing editor was nerve-racking. So Sinclair whitened when, shortly after six, he was called in to discuss the Tom Krome situation. Upon entering the office, Sinclair was brusquely motioned to a covered armchair. On the other side of a mahogany desk, his boss skimmed a police report, although Sinclair (having never seen one) didn't recognize it as such. What he knew about the burning of Krome's home had come from a gossipy city desk reporter, in a brief conversation at the urinals. Of course Sinclair had been alarmed by the news, but he was more distressed that he hadn't been notified formally, through channels. He was, after all, Krome's immediate supervisor. Didn't anybody believe in E-mail anymore?

With a contemplative snort, the managing editor turned and tossed the police report on a credenza. Sinclair seized the moment to present a crisp copy of the memorandum, which the managing editor crumpled and threw back at him. It landed in Sinclair's lap.

The managing editor said: "I already saw it."

"But . . . when?"

"In all its glorious versions, you schmuck."

"Oh."

Instantly Sinclair realized what had happened.

With the touch of a button on his computer ter-
minal, the managing editor could call up any story
in the newspaper's vast bank of editing queues.
Sinclair had been led to believe his boss paid no attention to what went on in the Features department, but evidently it wasn't true. The managing
editor had electronically been tracking the Krome
memo from the date of its perfidious inception.

Sinclair felt feverish and short of breath. He
plucked the wadded paper from his lap and discreetly shoved it into a pocket.

"What I've found fascinating," the managing
editor was saying, "is the creative process—how
each new draft painted a blacker picture of Tom's
mental state. And the details you added . . . well, I
had to laugh. Maybe you missed your calling, Sinclair. Maybe you should've been a writer." The
managing editor eyed him as if he were a turd on
a carpet. "Would you like some water? Coffee?"

Sinclair, in an anemic murmur: "No, thank
you."

"May we stipulate that your 'memo' is pure
horseshit?"

"Yes."

"OK. Now I have some questions. One: Do you
have any idea why Tom Krome's house was
torched?"

"No, I don't."

"Do you have a clue why anyone would want to
harm him?"

"Not really," Sinclair said.

"Do you know where he is?"

"The rumor is Bermuda."

The managing editor chuckled. "You're not going to Bermuda, Sinclair. You're going to the last place you sent Tom, and you're going to find him. By the way, you look like hell."

"I'm sure I do."

"Another question: Does Tom still work for us?"

"As far as I'm concerned, he does." Sinclair said it with all the conviction he could summon.

The managing editor removed his glasses and began vigorously cleaning the lenses with a tissue. "What about as far as *Tom* is concerned? Any chance he was serious about quitting?"

"I . . . I suppose it's possible."

Woozy with apnea, Sinclair thought he might be on the verge of heart failure. He'd read many articles about critically ill patients who had eerie out-of-body experiences in ambulances and emergency rooms. Sinclair felt that way now—floating above the managing editor's credenza, watching himself being emasculated. The sensation was neither as painless nor as dreamlike as other near-death survivors had described.

"The arson guys are going through the rubble tonight," said the managing editor. "They want to know if the fire could be connected to a story Tom was working on."

"I can't imagine how." Sinclair gulped air like a hippo. Slowly the feeling returned to his fingers and toes.

The managing editor said: "Suppose you tell me exactly what he was writing."

"A quickie feature. Hit and run."

"About what?"

"Just some woman who won the lottery," Sinclair said. Impulsively he added: "A black woman." Just so the boss would know Sinclair was on the lookout for feel-good stories about minorities. Maybe it would help his predicament, maybe not.

The managing editor squinted. "That's it—a lottery feature?"

"That's it," Sinclair asserted.

He didn't want it known that he'd rejected Tom Krome's request to pursue the robbery angle. Sinclair believed the decision would make him appear gutless and shortsighted, particularly if Krome turned up murdered in some ditch.

"Where is this Lotto woman?" asked the managing editor.

"Little town called Grange."

"Straight feature?"

"That's all it was."

The managing editor frowned. "Well, you're lying again, Sinclair. But it's my own damn fault for hiring you." He stood up and removed his suit jacket from the back of his chair. "You'll go to

Grange and you won't come back until you've found Tom."

Sinclair nodded. He'd call his sister. She and Roddy would let him stay in the spare room. They could take him around town, hook him up with their sources.

"Next week they're announcing the Amelias," said the managing editor, slipping into his jacket. "I entered Krome."

"You did?"

Again Sinclair was caught off guard. The "Amelias" were a national writing competition named after the late Amelia J. Lloyd, widely considered the mother superior of the modern newspaper feature. No event was too prosaic or inconsequential to escape Amelia Lloyd's sappy attention. Bake sales, craft shows, charity walka-thons, spelling bees, mall openings, blood drives, Easter egg hunts—Amelia's miraculous prose breathed sweet life into them all. In her short but meteoric career, her byline had graced *The New Orleans Times-Picayune, The St. Louis Post-Dispatch, The Tampa Tribune, The Miami Herald* and *The Cleveland Plain Dealer.* It was in Cleve-land that Amelia J. Lloyd had been tragically killed in the line of duty, struck down by a run-away miniature Duesenberg at a Masonic parade. She was only thirty-one.

All but an elitist handful of newspapers entered

their feature sections in the annual Amelias, because it was the only contest that pretended fluff
was worthwhile journalism. At *The Register,* staff
entries for such awards came, as policy, from the
Assistant Deputy Managing Editor of Features
and Style. Sinclair had chosen not to submit Tom
Krome in the Amelias because his stories invariably showed, in Sinclair's opinion, a hard or sar-
castic edge that the judges might find off-putting.
In addition, Sinclair feared that if by cruel fate
Krome actually won the contest (or even placed),
he would physically attack Sinclair in front of the
staff. Krome had been heard to remark that, even
with its $500 prize, an Amelia was a badge of
shame.

So Sinclair was rattled to learn the managing
editor had, without informing him, replaced Sinclair's handpicked entry with Tom Krome.

"I meant to drop you a note," the managing editor said, not apologetically.

Sinclair measured his response. "Tom's turned
out some super stuff this year. What category did
you pick?"

"Body of work."

"Ah. Good." Sinclair, thinking: Body of work?
The rules called for a minimum of eight stories,
and it was generally assumed they should be upbeat and positive—just like the ones Amelia J.
Lloyd used to write. Sinclair doubted whether

Tom Krome had used eight upbeat *adjectives* in his whole career. And where had the boss found time to cull a year's worth of clips?

"Do you know," said the managing editor, packing his briefcase, "how long it's been since *The Register* won a national award? *Any* national award?"

Sinclair shook his head.

"Eight years," the managing editor said. "Third place, deadline reporting, American Society of Newspaper Editors. Eight fucking years."

Sinclair, sensing it was expected of him, asked: "What was the story?"

"Tornado creamed an elementary school. Two dead, twenty-three injured. Guess who wrote it? Me."

"No kidding?"

"Don't look so shocked." The managing editor snapped the briefcase shut. "Here's another hot flash: We're about to win a first-place Amelia for feature writing. As in 'grand prize.' I expect Tom to be in the newsroom next week when it moves on the wires."

Sinclair's head swum. "How do you know he won?"

"One of the judges told me. An ex-wife, if you're wondering. The only one who still speaks to me. When are you leaving for Grange?"

"First thing tomorrow."

"Try not to embarrass us, OK?"

The managing editor was three steps from the door when Sinclair said, "Do you want me to call you?"

"Every single day, *amigo*. And seriously, don't fuck this up."

Chub believed he was making progress with Amber. Each night she seemed friendlier and more talkative. Bodean Gazzer thought his friend was imagining things—the girl chatted up all her customers.

"Bull," Chub said. "See how she looks at me?"

"Spooked is how she looks. It's that damn patch."

"Fuck yourself," said Chub, though secretly he worried that Bode might be right. Amber might be one of those women who weren't aroused by scars and eye patches and such.

Bode said, "Maybe you oughta take it off."

"I tried."

"Don't tell me."

"It's the tire glue," Chub explained. "It's like goddamn see-ment."

Bode Gazzer said he was glad it was Chub's left eye that was sealed, because the right one was his lead eye for shooting. "But it'd still be better without the patch," he added. "Patch like to give you a blind spot in a firefight."

Chub bit into a chicken bone and noisily

chewed it to a pulp, which he swallowed. "Don't you worry about me when it come to guns. Even my blind spots is twenty-twenty."

When Amber came to collect the empty beer bottles, Chub mischievously inquired about her boyfriend.

"He's not here," she said.

"I can see that, darling."

Chub was tempted to say something about Tony the asshole's sports car catching fire; drop a sly hint that he and Bode had done it, so Amber would know his intentions were serious. But he wasn't sure if she was sharp enough to make the connection, or even if she was the sort of woman who was favorably impressed by arson.

"Another round?" she asked.

Chub said: "Time you get off work?"

"Late."

"How late?"

"Real late."

Bode Gazzer cut in: "Bring us four more."

"Right away," Amber said, gratefully, and dashed off.

"Shit," Chub muttered. Maybe it *was* the patch. He suspected it wouldn't bother her one bit, once she found out he was soon to be a millionaire.

Bode advised him to back off. "Remember what I told you about low profiles. Plus, you're spookin' the girl."

With a thumb and forefinger, Chub deftly extracted a shard of chicken bone from the roof of his mouth. He said, "When's the last time you fucked anything besides the palm a your hand?"

Bode Gazzer said that, being a white man, he had a duty to be extra scrupulous about spreading his seed.

"Your what?" Chub sneered.

"That's what the Bible calls it. Seed."

"Man can't get enough guns and pussy. You said so yourself."

So I did, Bode thought ruefully. The truth was, he didn't want Chub distracted by a Hooters babe or any other woman until they collected the lottery money. Then there'd be plenty of time for wild poon.

Bode tried to improvise: "There's good and bad of everything, Chub. Us white men's got a responsibility—we're an endangered species. Like the unicorn."

Chub didn't fold. He recalled that he once owned a .45 semi, made in Yugoslavia or Romania or some godforsaken place, that misfired every fourth or fifth round. "Now that was a bad *gun*," he said, "but I ain't never had no bad pussy."

They debated until closing time, with Bode holding to the position that militiamen should have carnal relations only with pure white Christian women of European descent, lest the union produce a child. Chub (not wishing to limit his already sparse opportunities) insisted white men

were morally obliged to spread their superior ge-
netics near and far, and therefore should have sex
with any woman who wanted it, regardless of race,
creed or heritage.

"Besides, it's plain to see," he added, "Amber's
white as Ivory Snow."

"Yeah, but her boyfriend's Meskin. That makes
her Meskin by injection," said Bode.

"You can shut up now."

"Point is, we gotta be careful."

The manager flicked the lights twice and the
restaurant began to empty. Bode asked for a box
of chicken wings to go, but a Negro busboy told
him the kitchen had closed. Bode paid the dinner
bill with the stolen Visa, leaving another ludicrous
tip. Afterwards Chub insisted on hanging around
the parking lot, in the remote likelihood Amber
needed a lift. After fifteen minutes she appeared,
brushing her hair as she came out the door. To
Chub she looked almost as beautiful in faded
jeans as she did in her skimpy work shorts. He told
Bode to honk the horn, so she'd see them waiting
in the truck. Bode refused.

Chub was rolling down the window to call her
name when none other than Tony himself drove
up in a new jet-black Mustang convertible. Amber
got in, and the car sped away.

"What the fuck?" said Chub, despairingly.

"Forget about it."

"Asshole must be loaded to 'ford two cars."

Bode Gazzer said, "For Christ's sake, it's probably a rental. Now forget about it."

Half drunk, Bode struggled to back the pickup out of the handicapped slot. He paid no attention to the blue Honda on the other side of the lot, and failed to notice when the same car swung into traffic behind them, southbound on Highway One.

Before the two rednecks broke into her home and attacked her, JoLayne Lucks had in her entire adult life been struck by only two men. One was black, one was white. Both were boyfriends at the time.

The black man was Robert, the police officer. He'd slapped JoLayne across the face when, with ample evidence, she accused him of extorting sex from female motorists. The very next morning Robert found a live pygmy rattlesnake curled up in his underwear drawer, a discovery that impelled him to hop and screech about the bedroom. JoLayne Lucks gingerly collected the snake and released it in a nearby pasture. Later she teased Robert about his girlish reaction, noting that the bite of a pygmy rattler was seldom fatal to humans. That night he slept with his service revolver cocked on the bedstand, a practice he diligently maintained until he and JoLayne parted company.

The white man who hit her was, of all people, Neal the codependent chiropractor. It had happened one night when JoLayne was an hour late getting home from Jackson Memorial Hospital, a delay caused by a short-tempered cocaine importer with personnel problems. Four multiple-gunshot victims had arrived simultaneously in the emergency room, where JoLayne was on duty. Although the shooting spree was the lead story on the eleven o'clock news, Neal the chiropractor remained unconvinced. He preferred to believe Jo-Layne was late because she'd been dallying with a handsome thoracic surgeon, or possibly one of the new anesthesiologists. In a jealous tantrum, Neal threw a wild punch that glanced harmlessly off Jo-Layne's handbag. She was upon him instantly, breaking his nose with two stiff jabs. Soon Neal the chiropractor was sniveling for forgiveness. He rushed out and bought JoLayne a diamond tennis bracelet, which she returned to him in mint condition on the night they broke up.

So she was not accustomed to being struck by men of any color; did not invite it, would not tolerate it, and believed with every fiber in swift, unmitigated retribution. Which is why she couldn't get her mind off the shotgun in the trunk of Tom Krome's Honda.

"You got a plan yet?" she said. "Because I've got one if you don't."

Krome said, "I'm sure you do."

He'd dropped back to put some distance between them and the red pickup truck, which was

weaving slightly and accelerating in unpredictable
bursts. The driver was bombed—even a rookie pa-
trolman could have spotted it. Krome didn't want
the rednecks to crash into anybody, but he also
didn't want them to get pulled over on a DUI.
Who knew what they might do to a cop? And if
they allowed themselves to be tossed in jail, it
might be weeks before they got out, depending on
how many felony warrants were outstanding. Jo-
Layne Lucks didn't have that much time.

Krome's plan was to follow the two men to
where they lived, and to case the place.

"In other words, we're stalking," JoLayne said.

Krome hoped her tone was one of impatience
and not derision. "Correct me if I'm wrong, but I
thought the goal was to retrieve your Lotto ticket.
If you'd rather just shoot these morons and go
home, let me know so I can bail out."

She raised her hands. "I'm sorry, I'm sorry."

"You're angry. I'd be angry, too."

"Furious," she said.

"Stay cool. We're close."

"You memorized the license tag?"

"I told you before. Yes," Krome said.

"Hey, they're speeding up again."

"So I noticed."

"Don't lose 'em."

"JoLayne!"

"Sorry. I'll shut up now."

They tailed the truck all the way to Homestead.

On the way, it stopped three times along the side of the highway, where one or both of the rednecks nonchalantly got out to urinate. Whenever that happened, Krome kept driving. Once he got ahead, he'd quickly pull over in an unlit spot and wait for the pickup to pass by again. Eventually the rednecks turned east off Highway One, then south on a dirt road that bisected a tomato farm. Here there was no other traffic—only a rolling dust cloud kicked up by the truck. The dust smelled faintly of pesticide.

JoLayne poked her head from the car and pretended to drink the air. "Green acres! Men of the soil!" she exclaimed.

Krome slowed and turned off the headlights, so the rednecks wouldn't spot them in the rearview. After a few miles the tomato fields gave way to palmetto scrub and Dade County pines. Gradually the road turned and ran parallel to a wide drainage canal. Across the rippled water, JoLayne was able to make out the shapes of rough shacks, small house trailers and abandoned cars.

A half mile ahead on the dirt road, the pickup's brake lights flashed brightly through the whorls of dust. Krome immediately stopped the Honda and killed the engine. The silence announced that the driver of the truck had done the same.

Krome said, "Nice neighborhood."

"It's not exactly Star Island." JoLayne touched his arm. "Can we please open the trunk now?"

"In a second."

They couldn't see the red truck, but they heard the doors slam. Then came a man's voice, booming down the canal through the darkness.

JoLayne whispered: "What's that all about?"

Before Tom Krome could answer, the night was split open by gunfire.

Alone in the middle of nowhere, Shiner had wigged out. The noises were the same as those in the woods outside Grange—frogs, crickets, raccoons—but here every peep and rustle seemed louder and more ominous. Shiner couldn't stop thinking about all those NATO troops bivouacked in the Bahamas.

Just eighty miles thataway, Bodean Gazzer had said, pointing, *acrost the Gulf Stream.*

Stunted as it was, Shiner's imagination had no difficulty conjuring a specter of blue-helmeted enemy soldiers poised on an advancing flotilla. He became consumed with the idea that the United States of America might be invaded at any minute, while Bode and Chub were off drinking beer.

Acting against orders, Shiner got the AR-15 out of Chub's mobile home and climbed a trellis to the flimsy roof. There, in his moldy bush hat and new camouflage parka, he waited. And while he couldn't see as far as the Bahama Islands, he had an excellent view of the dirt road and the farm canal.

By land or by sea, Shiner thought, let the fuckers try.

The rifle felt grand in his hands; it took the edge off his nerves. He wondered what types of guns the NATO communists were carrying. Russian, Bode Gazzer had speculated, or North Korean. Shiner decided to swipe one off the first soldier he shot, for a souvenir. Maybe he'd chop off an ear, too—he'd heard of such grisly customs during his three weeks in the army, from a drill sergeant who'd been to Nam. Shiner didn't know what he would do with a severed NATO ear, but he'd surely put it someplace where his Ma wouldn't find it. Same with the guns. Ever since she'd found the Road-Stain Jesus, his mother had been down on guns.

After an hour on the roof, Shiner was overcome by a stabbing hunger. Stealthily he climbed down and foraged in Chub's refrigerator, where he located two leathery slices of pepperoni pizza and a tin of boneless sardines. These Shiner carried back to his sentry post. He forced himself to eat slowly and savor each bite—once the invasion began there'd be no more pizza for a long, long time.

On two occasions Shiner fired the AR-15 at suspicious noises. The first turned out to be a clumsy opossum (not an enemy sapper) that knocked over Chub's garbage can, just as the second turned out to be a mud hen (not a scuba-diving commando) splashing in the lily pads.

Better safe than sorry, Shiner thought.

After a while he drifted off, one cheek pressed against the cool stock of the rifle. He dreamed he was back in boot camp, trying to do push-ups while a brawny black sergeant stood over him, calling him a faggot, a pussy, a dickless wonder. In the dream, Shiner wasn't much better at push-ups than he was in real life, so the sergeant's yelling grew louder and louder. Suddenly he drew his sidearm and told Shiner he'd shoot him in the ass if his knees touched the ground once more, which of course happened on the very next push-up. In a rage, the sergeant simultaneously placed a heavy boot on Shiner's back and the gun barrel against Shiner's tremulous buttocks, and fired—

At the concussion, Shiner bolted awake, clutching the AR-15 to his chest. Then he heard it again—not a gunshot but more like a door slamming. He realized it wasn't part of the dream; it was real. Somebody was out there, in the buzzing night. Maybe it was the NATO soldiers. Maybe what Shiner had heard slamming was the turret door of a Soviet tank.

As they stepped toward the trailer, Bodean Gazzer and Chub were startled by the raw, strung-out cry that came from the roof: "Who goes! Who goes there!"

They were about to answer when the darkness

exploded in orange and blue sparks. The spray of automatic rifle fire sent them diving under the pickup truck, where they cursed and cowered and covered their ears until Shiner was done.

Then Chub called out: "It's us, dickface!"

"Us who?" demanded the voice from the roof. "Who goes?"

"Us! *Us!*"

" 'Dentify you selves!"

Bode Gazzer spoke up: "The White Clarion Aryans. Your brothers."

After a significant pause, they heard: "Aw, fuck. Come on out."

Squirming from beneath the truck, Chub said: "What we got here's one brain-dead skinhead."

"Hush," Bode said. "You hear that?"

"Jesus Willy Christ."

Another car on the dirt road—driving away, fast.

Chub groped for his pistol. "What do we do?"

"We chase after the bastards," Bode said, "soon as we get John Wayne Jr. off the roof."

 Tom Krome's chest tightened when the headlights appeared in the rearview. JoLayne Lucks turned to see.

"Just like in the movies," she said.

Krome told her to hang on. Without touching

the brakes, he guided the car off the farm road, over a dirt berm. They jounced and shimmied to a halt in a stand of thin Australian pines.

"Unlock your door," he said, "but don't get out till I tell you."

They ducked in the front seat, their faces inches apart. They heard the pickup truck coming, the rumble of the oversized tires on the packed dirt.

Out of nowhere, JoLayne said, "I wonder what Martha Stewart would do in a spot like this."

Krome thought: OK, she's delirious.

"Seriously," said JoLayne. "There's a woman who'd be completely useless right about now, unless you were in a hurry for a macramé or a flower box. Ever see ole Martha on TV? Planting those bulbs and bakin' them pies."

Krome said, "Get a grip." He lifted his head to peer out.

"Me, I'm all thumbs when it comes to crafts. A total klutz. However, I *can* use a gun—"

"Quiet," Krome told her.

"—which we happen to have in our possession."

"JoLayne, get ready!"

"A perfectly good shotgun."

In the darkness Krome sensed her edging closer. Her cheek touched his, and he astonished himself by kissing her. No big deal; a light brotherly kiss meant only to calm. That's what he told himself.

JoLayne turned her face but said nothing. The pickup truck was approaching rapidly. Krome felt her arm brush his shoulder, as if she were reaching out for him.

She wasn't. She was going for his car keys, which she adroitly plucked from the ignition. In an instant she flung open her door and rolled out.

"No!" Krome shouted, but JoLayne was already at the trunk. By the time he got there, the Remington was in her hands.

Nearby, the roadbed brightened; insects swirled in the white beams of the truck's lights. Hurriedly Krome pulled JoLayne Lucks behind a pine tree. He wrapped his arms around her, pinning the shotgun awkwardly between them.

"Lemme go," she said.

"You got the safety on?"

"Don't be a jerk, Tom."

"Sshhh."

As the pickup passed, they heard the sound of men's voices raised in excitement. Tom Krome didn't relax his hold on JoLayne until the truck was gone and the night was utterly still.

He said, "That was close."

JoLayne laid the shotgun in the trunk, and not gently. "Macramé, my ass," she said.

Demencio was still basking in the praise of the Reverend Joshua Moody, who before departing had turned to his curious flock and proclaimed:

"In thirty-three years of touring miracles, this

is one of the most astounding things I've ever seen!"

He was speaking of the apostolic cooters.

Later, after the Christian pilgrims from West Virginia had keened and swooned and ultimately placed in Trish's wicker collection basket the sum of $211 (not including what was spent on soft drinks, T-shirts, angel food snacks and sunblock), Reverend Moody had pulled Demencio aside: "You gotta tell me exactly where this came from."

"It's like I said."

"Hey, I been doin' this since before you were born." The preacher, arching one of his snowy-white eyebrows. "Come on, son, I won't give it away."

Demencio had coolly stuck to his spiel. "One day the turtles are normal. The next day I look in the aquarium and there's the apostles. All twelve of 'em."

"Sure, sure." With an impatient sigh, Reverend Moody had turned Demencio loose. "Of all the places for a holy apparition—on a cooter's shell, I swear to God, boy."

"Not an apparition," Demencio had said coyly, "just a likeness."

The concept of using turtles is what had intrigued Reverend Moody—how had a mere lay-man such as Demencio dreamed up something so original? The man simply wouldn't say. So, out of professional courtesy, the preacher had backed off. Amiably he'd pumped Demencio's hand and told him: "You are one brilliant bastard." Then he'd shepherded the pilgrims back onto the bus.

Demencio had stood waving on the sidewalk until they were out of sight. With a self-congratulatory smirk he'd turned toward his wife, who was sorting the tear-dampened clumps of cash.

"We did it!" she said elatedly.

"Un-fucking-believable."

"You were right, honey. They'll go for anything."

As a kid, Demencio had seen painted turtles for sale at an outdoor flea market in Hialeah. Some of them had roses or sunflowers lacquered on their shells; others had flags or hearts or Disney characters. Demencio had figured it would be no less absurd to decorate JoLayne's cooters with the faces of religious figures. It had seemed Demencio's only hope for salvaging a profit from Reverend Moody's visitation, since the weeping Madonna was temporarily out of service.

After Trish had brought home the art supplies, Demencio had selected a dozen of the liveliest specimens from JoLayne's big aquarium. The delicate process of painting had been preceded by a brief discussion about how the apostles could be most respectfully portrayed on the carapace of a mud-dwelling reptile. Neither Demencio nor his wife could name even half of the original disciples, so they'd consulted a Bible (which, unfortunately, had not provided a complete set of portraits). Trish then had fished through a box of her late father's belongings and found a Time-Life volume about the world's greatest masterpieces. In it was a photograph of Leonardo's *The Last Supper,* which Trish had torn out and placed on the workbench in front of her husband.

"This is peachy," he'd said, "but who's who?"

Trish, pointing: "I believe that's Judas. Or maybe Andrew."

"Christ."

"Right there," Trish had said helpfully, "in the middle."

Whereupon Demencio had expelled her and settled down with the cooters to paint. There was no sense getting fancy, because the animals' corrugated shells were difficult to work with—as small as silver dollars. Beards was the way to go, he'd told himself. All the big shots in the Bible wore beards.

Soon Demencio had found a rhythm— restraining each baby turtle with his left hand, wielding the brush with his right. He'd been steady and precise, finishing the job in less than three hours. Although every apostle was given lush facial hair, Demencio had tried to make each one distinct.

Beholding the miniature visages, Trish had asked: "Which is which?"

"Beats the hell outta me."

And, as Demencio had expected, it hadn't mattered. One pilgrim's Matthew was another pilgrim's John.

Avidly Reverend Moody's followers had clustered around the cooter corral that Trish had fashioned out of plastic gardening fence. Demencio had called out the names of each apostle as he pointed with deliberate ambiguity among the scrabbling swarm. The pilgrims hadn't merely been persuaded, they'd been overwhelmed. In the center of the small enclosure Demencio had stationed the fiberglass Virgin Mary, who (he'd announced) would not be crying on this special day. The pilgrims had understood completely—the Holy Mother obviously was cheered by the unexpected arrival of her Son's inner circle.

The apostolic turtles proved such a smash that Demencio decided to use them again the next morning. By noon the yard was jammed. Demencio was fixing a sandwich in the kitchen when Trish urgently reported that the cooters were dehydrating in the sun and that the paint on their shells was beginning to flake. Demencio solved the problem by digging a small moat around the fiberglass Madonna and filling it with a garden hose. Later a divinely inspired tourist from South Carolina asked if that was holy water in which the turtles were swimming. When Demencio assured him it was, the man asked to buy a cupful for four dol-

lars. The other visitors rushed to queue up, and before long Demencio had to refill the moat.

He was aglow at his windfall. Turtle worship!
Reverend Moody had been right—it was pure
genius.

The visitation proceeded smoothly until midafternoon, when Dominick Amador showed up to
hustle Demencio's overflow, exhibiting his seeping
stigmata in a most vulgar way. Trish chased him
away with a rake. The altercation took place in
full view of Mayor Jerry Wicks, who made no attempt to intervene on the shameless Dominick's
behalf.

Mayor Wicks had arrived at the shrine in the
company of three persons who definitely weren't
pilgrims. Two of them Demencio recognized from
around town; the third was a stranger. Demencio
acknowledged the group with the air of a busy
man on his way to the bank, which he was.

"Please," the mayor said. "We won't be long."

"You caught me at a bad time." Demencio,
stuffing the last of three fat envelopes.

Jerry Wicks said, "It's about JoLayne Lucks."

"Yeah?" Demencio, thinking: Shit, I knew it was
too good to be true. The damn turtles are probably stolen.

Trish popped her head in the front door: "More
lettuce!"

Demencio locked the bank deposits in a drawer
and headed for the refrigerator. "Have a seat," he

said indifferently to his visitors. "Be with you in a minute."

Roddy and Joan were thrilled to assist Joan's brother on such an important journalistic assignment; in fact, they'd have been ecstatic to help with the weekly crop report. Roddy worked for the state, inspecting gasoline pumps, while Joan taught third grade at the county elementary school. They didn't get much company in Grange so they were delighted when Sinclair asked if he could come over for a few days, to work on the lottery story. Because it had been their tip to the newspaper that had gotten the ball rolling, Roddy and Joan felt duty-bound to help Sinclair locate his star reporter, missing with JoLayne Lucks. The Lotto mystery was the most commotion to sweep Grange in ages, and Roddy and Joan were pleased to be in the thick of it. Sinclair hadn't been in town twenty minutes before they introduced him to the mayor, who listened to Sinclair's account of Tom Krome's disappearance with puzzlement and a trace of dismay.

"Whatever's happened," Jerry Wicks said, "rest assured it wasn't Grangians who are responsible. We are the most hospitable folks in Florida!"

Sinclair balanced the notebook on his knees while writing down every word. Sinclair assumed that's how real reporters worked; like a supercharged stenographer, preserving each article and preposition. He didn't know any better, and was too proud to ask around the newsroom for guidance before he'd left on his trip.

One drawback to Sinclair's exact note-taking technique was the extended silence between the moment a sentence was spoken and the moment Sinclair finished transcribing it. He was an uncommonly slow writer; years at the computer keyboard had left him unaccustomed to the feel of a pen in his hand. To make matters worse, he was a neat freak. Copying every trivial comment wasn't enough; Sinclair painstakingly put in the punctuation, too.

Roddy and Joan loyally remained alert while Joan's brother hunched for what seemed like an eternity over the notebook. The mayor, however, was growing antsy.

"I won't mind," he finally said, "if you want to use a tape recorder."

Sinclair's only response was a fresh burst of scribbling.

Jerry Wicks turned to Roddy: "Why's he writing *that* down?"

"I'm not sure."

"Who cares what I said about the tape recorder—"

"I don't know, Mr. Mayor. He must have a reason."

Sinclair reined himself, midsentence. Sheepishly

he glanced up and capped the pen. Jerry Wicks
seemed relieved. He suggested they all go visit the
last person to see JoLayne Lucks before she left
town. The man's name was Demencio, the mayor
said, and he had a popular religious shrine. Sinclair agreed that he should speak with the man as
soon as possible. He tucked the notebook in his
back pants pocket, like he'd often seen the male reporters at *The Register* do.

Sliding into the back seat of the mayor's car,
Joan murmured to her brother that she kept a
portable Sony at the house.

"Thanks anyway," Sinclair said stiffly, "but I'm
fine."

And upon meeting Demencio, he whipped out
the notebook once again. "Could you spell your
name for me?" he asked, pen poised.

"You a cop?" Demencio turned to the mayor.
"Is he some kinda cop?"

Jerry Wicks explained who Sinclair was and
why he'd come all the way to Grange. They were
seated in Demencio's living room—the mayor,
Roddy, Joan and Sinclair. Demencio was in his favorite TV chair, nervously tossing a head of romaine lettuce from one hand to the other, like a
softball. He was leery of the stranger but he didn't
want to blow a shot at free press coverage for the
shrine.

Sinclair asked, "When's the last time you saw
JoLayne Lucks?"

"Other night," Demencio said, "when she dropped off the cooters."

Roddy and Joan were very curious about the tank of baby turtles, as well as the painted ones in the moat outside, but for some reason Sinclair didn't follow up. Meticulously he wrote down Demencio's answer, then asked:

"Was there a man with Miss Lucks?"

"A white man?"

"Yes. Mid-thirties," Sinclair said. "About six feet tall."

"That's the guy. He took pictures of my Virgin Mary statue. She cries real tears."

Roddy, trying to be helpful: "People come from everywhere to pray at his weeping Madonna."

"There's a visitation every morning," Demencio added. "You oughta stop over."

Sinclair made no response. He was still working frenetically on the first part of Demencio's answer. He'd gotten as far as the word "Virgin" when Roddy's interruption had thrown him off track, causing him to lose the rest of Demencio's quote. Now Sinclair was forced to reconstruct.

"Did you say 'It cries' or 'She cries'?"

"*She* cries," said Demencio, "like a drunken priest."

Neither Roddy nor Joan could imagine seeing such a coarse remark printed in a family newspaper, but Sinclair transcribed it anyway.

"And twelve of my turtles," Demencio said,

"got the apostles on their backs. It's the damnedest thing you ever saw—check out the moat!"

"Slow down," said the frazzled Sinclair. His fingers had begun to cramp. "The man who was with Miss Lucks—they left together?"

"Yeah. In his car."

While Sinclair scribbled, Roddy, Joan and the mayor maintained silence. Any distraction would only slow him down more. Demencio, though, had grown restive. He began to shuck the head of lettuce, arranging the leaves in piles, according to size, on the ottoman. He was worried the newspaperman would ask about his financial arrangement with JoLayne Lucks regarding the turtle-sitting. Demencio had no illusion that one thousand dollars was a customary or reasonable fee, or that the newspaperman would believe it was JoLayne's idea.

But when Sinclair finally looked up from his notes, all he said was: "Did they mention where they were headed?"

"Miami," Demencio answered, in relief.

Joan, her track record as a tipster at stake, piped in: "We heard Bermuda. They say anything about Bermuda?"

"Miami's what they told me. JoLayne said she had some business down that way."

"Slower," Sinclair protested, bent over the pad like a rheumatic jeweler. "Please."

Demencio had run out of hospitality. "It's M-i-a—"

"I *know* how to spell it," Sinclair snapped.

The mayor wedged a knuckle in his mouth, to keep from laughing.

They rode for miles on the farm roads without finding the other car. Bodean Gazzer was too drunk and tired to continue. Chub offered to take the wheel but Bode wouldn't hear of it; nobody else was allowed to drive his new Dodge Ram. He parked on the edge of a tomato field and passed out to the strains of Chub and Shiner bickering about the shooting fiasco at the trailer. At first Bode thought Chub was being too rough on the kid, but his opinion changed at daybreak when he noticed the two ragged bullet holes in the truck's quarter panel.

Bode said to Chub: "Shoot his damn nuts off."

"I didn't know it was you guys!" Shiner protested.

Bode angrily grabbed for the gun in Chub's belt. "Here, gimme that thing."

Chub knocked his hand away. "Somebody'll hear."

"But I thought you was NATO!" Shiner cried. "I said I was sorry, dint I?"

"Look what you done to my truck."

"I'll pay for it, I swear."

"Fucking A you will," snarled Bodean Gazzer.

Shiner was a jittery wreck. "Gimme another chance," he begged.

"Another chance? Shit," Chub said. He'd already concluded the boy was a hopeless fuckup—they had to cut him loose. He and Bode could toss a coin to see who'd break the news.

Chub got out to take a leak, and immediately came upon a rusty aerosol can of spray paint—in the middle of a tomato field! It seemed too wonderful to be true. Because Bode disapproved of sniffing, Chub kept his back to the truck. He knelt in the loamy sand and excitedly shook the can. The rattle soothed him, the beat of an old familiar song. He cupped his hands around the nozzle and pressed down with his chin, but no paint shot out. He held the nozzle beneath his nostrils and sniffed fruitlessly for a trace of fumes; not a whiff. He swore, stood up and hurled the empty can as far as possible.

When he unzipped his pants to pee, a horsefly landed on the tip of his pecker. Chub couldn't imagine feeling less like a millionaire. Despondently he shooed the fly away and finished his business. Then he removed the Colt Python from his belt and tucked it in his left armpit. He groped carefully down his right pants leg until he found the bandage: At least the lottery ticket was safe.

He wondered what his parents would say if they knew he had 14 million bucks taped to his thigh!

When he returned to the pickup truck, he saw that Bodean Gazzer had settled down. Shiner was earnestly inquiring about the pending NATO attack on the United States, wondering if there was something particular he should be watching for; a clear signal it was all right to go for the guns.

"Like helicopters. I heard about them secret black helicopters," he was saying, "from the Internet."

Bode said, "I wouldn't go by the helicopters no more. Hell, they might switch to blimps. All depends."

"Damn," said Shiner.

"Tell you what, I wouldn't be surprised if it happened the dead of night, real quiet. You wake up one morning and the fuckin' mailman's wearing a blue helmet."

Shiner recoiled. "Then what—they kill all us white people, right?"

Chub said, "Not the women. Them they rape. The men is who they'll kill."

"No," Bode Gazzer said. "First thing they do is make us all so dirt poor we can't afford food or medicine or clothes on our back."

"How in the world?" Shiner asked.

"Easy. Suppose they decided all our money's illegal. Everything you saved up, worthless as toilet paper. Meanwhile they print up all new dollars, which they give out by the millions to Negroes and Cubans and such."

Chub sat on the bumper of the truck and tried to massage the hangover from his forehead. He'd already heard Bode's conspiracy theory about U.S. currency replacement. The subject had come up the night before, at Hooters, when Chub again recommended that they get rid of the nigger woman's credit card before it could be traced. Bode had said they ought to hang on to it, in case the New World Tribunal took over all the banks and issued new money. Then everybody's hard-earned American cash would be no good.

What cash? Chub had wondered. They were dead fucking broke.

"And the new money," Bode was telling Shiner, "instead of George Washington and U. S. Grant, it'll have pitchers of Jesse Jackson and Fy-del Castro."

"No shit! Then what do we do?"

"Plastic," Bode replied. "We use plastic. Ain't that right, Chub?"

"For sure." Chub got up, scratching at his crotch. It had been so long since he'd seen a fifty-dollar bill, he couldn't remember whose face was on it. Might as well be James Brown, for all it mattered to Chub.

"Let's get some goddamn food," he said.

On the drive to Florida City, Shiner fell asleep

with his teeth bared, like a mutt. Bode and Chub used the quiet time to discuss the events of the night before. Were they really followed, or was the car they'd heard simply lost in the farmlands?

Bode Gazzer voted for lost. He insisted he would have noticed somebody tailing them from the restaurant.

"Maybe if you was sober," Chub said.

"It was nobody after us, I guarantee. We was just jumpy from all the boy's shootin'."

Chub said, "I ain't so sure."

He had a strong feeling that their luck was going rotten. He became certain after breakfast, at the diner, when the waitress failed to return promptly with the credit card. Chub spotted her consulting with the restaurant manager at the cash register. In one hand the manager was holding the stolen Visa. In his other hand was the telephone.

Chub whispered across the table, "Jig's up."

Bodean Gazzer went rigid. Working his toes back into his cowboy boots, he accidentally kicked Chub in the knee. Irritably Chub glanced under the table and said, "Watch it."

Shiner, bug-eyed, twisting his paper napkin into a knot: "What the hell do we do now!"

"Run, boy. What else?" Chub playfully rapped his knuckles on Shiner's bare marbled scalp. "Run like the fuckin' wind."

13 Bode Gazzer's fondness for stolen credit cards was evident from the double-digit entry on his rap sheet, which also included nine convictions for check kiting, five for welfare fraud, four for stealing electricity, three for looting lobster traps and two for willful destruction of private property (a parking meter and an ATM machine).

All this was revealed to Moffitt soon after Jo-Layne Lucks called to report the license tag of the red pickup truck carrying the men who'd attacked her. The tag number was fed into one computer, which produced the name and birth date of Bodean James Gazzer, and that was fed into another computer, which produced Mr. Gazzer's arrest record. Moffitt was surprised by nothing he found, least of all the fact that despite his many crimes, Bode Gazzer had cumulatively spent less than twenty-three months of his whole worthless life behind bars.

Although the information wasn't available from the computers, it wouldn't have shocked Moffitt to know that Bode Gazzer was an avowed white supremacist and founder of a fledgling right-wing militia. By contrast, Bode Gazzer would have been stunned and appalled to find out that he'd attracted the attention of an agent from the despised

Bureau of Alcohol, Tobacco and Firearms, and that the agent was a damn Negro.

For Moffitt, seeing JoLayne Lucks was simultaneously excruciating and heavenly. She never flirted or strung him along even slightly. It wasn't necessary. All she had to do was laugh, or turn her face, or walk across a room. One of *those* deals.

Moffitt's condition was bad but not pathetic. Sometimes for months he wouldn't think about her. When he did, there was no moon-eyed pining—just a stoic wistfulness he had fine-tuned over the years. He was a realist; he felt what he felt. Whenever she called, he called back. Whenever she needed something, he came through. It made him feel good in a way that nothing else could.

They met at a rib joint on Highway One in South Miami. JoLayne didn't wait half a minute to ask about the man who owned the pickup truck.

"Who is he? Where does he live—out by the tomato farms?"

"No," Moffitt said.

"What's his address?"

"Forget about it."

"Why? What're you going to do?"

"Toss the place," Moffitt said.

JoLayne wasn't sure what he meant.

"Search it," Tom Krome explained, "with extreme prejudice."

Moffitt nodded. "Meantime, cancel your Visa. We got a name now, and that's all we need."

All three of them ordered combo platters and iced tea. JoLayne didn't eat much. She was feeling left out of the hunt.

"When you 'toss' this guy's house—"

"Apartment." Moffitt dabbed a napkin at his mouth.

"OK, but when you do it," said JoLayne, "I'd like to be there."

Moffitt shook his head firmly. "*I* won't even be there. Officially, that is." He took out his ID and set it open on the table, in front of Tom Krome. "Explain to her," Moffitt said, pointing with a sparerib.

When Krome saw the ATF badge, he understood. The agency had been pilloried after the Waco raid. Gun nuts clamored for its abolition and compared its agents to jackbooted Nazis. Congress investigated. Heads rolled at the top; the field staff was put on ultra-low profile.

"A real shitstorm," Krome said to JoLayne.

"I get the papers, Tom. I can read." She gave Moffitt a scalding look. "Don't you be talkin' to me like I'm a child."

The agent said, "No more headlines, that's our orders from Washington. And that's why I'll be doing this burglary alone."

JoLayne Lucks picked at her coleslaw with a plastic fork. She was aching to know who these redneck bastards were, how they lived, and what had possessed them to come after her, of all the lucky people who'd ever won the lottery. Why drive up to Grange to steal a ticket instead of waiting until somebody in Miami or Lauderdale hit the jackpot, which happened all the time.

It made no sense. JoLayne wanted to go with Moffitt and break into the man's home. Dig through his closets, peek under his bed, steam open his mail. JoLayne wanted some answers.

"All I can promise," said Moffitt, "is the ticket. If it's there, I'll find it."

"At least tell me his name."

"Why, Jo—so you can look it up in the phone book and beat me there? No way."

They finished the meal in silence. Krome followed Moffitt to the parking lot while JoLayne stayed to work on a slice of apple pie.

The agent said, "She won't stop with the lottery ticket. You realize that, don't you?"

"She might."

Moffitt smiled. "That girl gets an idea, she'll leave you in the dust. Believe me." He got in his car, a standard government-issue behemoth, and plugged the cell phone into the lighter jack. "Why you doin' this?" he asked Krome. "I hope your reason is better than mine."

"Probably not." Here Krome expected a warning that he'd better take excellent care of JoLayne Lucks, or else.

But instead Moffitt said: "Here's as far as it got between us: Two dates. A movie and a Dolphins game. She hates football."

"What was the movie?"

"Something with Nicholson. We're going back ten, eleven years. The Dolphins got their asses kicked, that much I remember. Anyway, after that it was back to being friends. Her choice, not mine."

Krome said, "I'm not after anything."

Moffitt chuckled. "Man, you're not listening. It's *her* choice. Always." He started the car.

Krome said, "Be careful at the apartment."

"You're the one who needs to be careful." Moffitt winked.

When Krome returned to the restaurant, Jo-Layne reported that the pie was excellent. Then she asked what Moffitt had told him in the parking lot.

"We were talking about football."

"Yeah, I'll bet."

"You realize," Krome said, "he's taking one helluva risk."

"And I appreciate it. I do."

"You've got a funny way of showing it."

JoLayne shifted uneasily. "Look, I've got to be careful what I say with Moffitt. If I sound ungrateful, it's probably because I don't want to sound *too* grateful. I don't want . . . Lord, you know. The man's still got some strong feelings for me."

"The hots is what we call it."

JoLayne lowered her eyes. "Stop." She felt bad about dragging Moffitt into the search. "I know he's supposed to get a warrant, I know he could lose his job if he's caught—"

"Try jail."

"Tom, he wants to help."

"In the worst way. He'd do anything to make you happy. That's the curse of the hopelessly smitten. Here's my question: Do you want your Lotto money, or do you want revenge?"

"Both."

"If you had to choose."

"The money, then." JoLayne was thinking of Simmons Wood. "I'd want the money."

"Good. Then leave it at that. You'll be doing Agent Moffitt a big favor."

And me, too, Krome thought.

Champ Powell was the best law clerk Judge Arthur Battenkill Jr. had ever hired; the most resourceful, the most hardworking, the most ambitious. Arthur Battenkill liked him very much. Champ Powell didn't need to be taught the importance of loyalty, because he'd been a policeman for five years before entering law school: a Gadsden

County sheriff's deputy. Champ understood the rules of the street. The good guys stuck together, helped each other, covered for one another in a jam. That's how you got by, and got ahead.

So Champ Powell was flattered when Judge Battenkill sought his advice about a delicate personal problem—a fellow named Tom Krome, who'd come between the distinguished judge and his lovely wife, Katie. Champ Powell was working late in the law library, researching an obtuse appellate decision on condominium foreclosures, when he felt Arthur Battenkill's hand on his shoulder. The judge sat down and gravely explained the situation with Krome. He asked Champ Powell what *he* would do if it was his wife fooling around with another man. Champ (who'd been on both ends of that nasty equation) said first he'd scare the living shit out of the guy, try to run him out of town. Judge Battenkill said that would be excellent, if only he knew how to do such a thing without getting himself in hot water. Champ Powell said don't worry, I'll handle it personally. The judge was so profusely grateful that Champ Powell could see his future in the law profession turning golden. With one phone call, Arthur Battenkill could get him a job with any firm in the Panhandle.

That very night, the law clerk drove to Tom Krome's house and shot out the windows with a deer rifle. The judge rewarded him the next morning in chambers with a collegial wink and a thumbs-up. Two days later, though, Arthur Battenkill phoned Champ Powell to irately report that Krome was still communicating with Katie, sending her photographs of an occult nature: weeping statuary. Champ was outraged. With the judge's blessing, he left work early so he could get to the hardware store before it closed. There he purchased twelve gallons of turpentine and a mop. Any experienced arsonist could have told Champ Powell that twelve gallons was excessive and that the fumes alone would knock an elephant on its ass.

But the law clerk had no time for expert consultations. With resolve in his heart and a bandanna over his nostrils, Champ Powell vigorously swabbed the turpentine throughout Tom Krome's house, slicking the floors and walls of each room. He was in the kitchen when he finally passed out, collapsing against the gas stove, groping wildly as he keeled. Naturally his hands latched onto a burner knob and unconsciously twisted it to the "on" position. When the explosion came, it was heard half a mile away. The house burned to the foundation in ninety minutes.

Champ Powell's remains were not discovered until many hours after the blaze had died, when firefighters overturned a half-melted refrigerator and found what appeared to be a charred human jaw. Larger bone fragments and clots of jellied tissue were collected from the debris and placed in a

Hefty bag for the medical examiner, who determined that the victim was a white male about six feet tall, in his early thirties. Beyond that, positive identification would be nearly impossible without dental records.

Based on the victim's race, height and approximate age, fire investigators conjectured that the dead body was probably Tom Krome and that he'd been murdered or knocked unconscious when he surprised the arsonist inside his house.

The grisly details of the discovery, and the suspicions surrounding it, were given the following morning to *The Register*'s police reporter, who promptly notified the managing editor. Somberly he assembled the newsroom staff and told them what the arson guys had found. The managing editor asked if anybody knew the name of Tom Krome's dentist, but no one did (though a few staff members remarked upon Krome's outstanding smile, cattily speculating that it had to be the handiwork of a specialist). An intern was assigned the task of phoning every dental clinic in town in search of Krome's X-rays. In the meantime, a feature writer was assigned to work on Krome's obituary, just in case. The managing editor said the newspaper should wait as long as possible before running a story but should prepare for the worst. After the meeting, he hurried back to his office and tried to reach Sinclair in Grange. A woman identifying herself as Sinclair's sister reported he was "at the turtle shrine" but offered to take him a message. The managing editor gave her one: "Tell him to call the goddamn office by noon, or start looking for a new job."

As it happened, Champ Powell and Tom Krome had, in addition to their race and physique, one other characteristic in common: a badly chipped occlusal cusp on the number 27 tooth, the right lower canine. Champ Powell had damaged his while drunkenly gnawing the cap off a bottle of Busch at the 1993 Gator Bowl. Tom Krome's chip had been caused by a flying brick during a street riot he was covering in the Bronx.

One of Krome's second cousins, trying to be helpful, mentioned the broken tooth (and its semi-heroic origin) to a *Register* reporter, who mentioned it to the medical examiner, who dutifully inspected the charred jawbone retrieved from Krome's house. The number 27 canine looked as if it had been busted with a chisel. With confidence, the medical examiner dictated a report that tentatively identified the corpse in the ruins as Tom Krome.

The Register would run the news story and sidebar obituary on the front page, beneath a four-column color photograph of Tom Krome. It would be the picture from his press badge—an underexposed head shot, with Tom's hair windblown and his eyes half closed—but Katie would still fall apart when she saw it, dashing to the bedroom in tears. Judge Arthur Battenkill Jr. would remain at the breakfast table and reread the articles several times. Try as he might, he would not be able to recall the condition of Champ Powell's dentition.

Arriving at the courthouse, he would find that for the second consecutive day his eager law clerk hadn't shown up for work. The secretaries would offer to go to Champ's apartment and check on him, but the judge would say it wasn't necessary. He would pretend to recall that Champ had mentioned driving to Cedar Key, to visit his parents. Later Arthur Battenkill Jr. would go alone into his chambers and shut the door. He would put on his black robe, untie his shoes and sit down to figure out what would be worse for him, from the standpoint of culpability—if the burned body belonged to Champ Powell or to Tom Krome.

Either way meant trouble, the judge would reason, but a live Krome was bound to be more trouble than a dead Champ. Arthur Battenkill Jr. would find himself hoping the newspaper was right, hoping it was Krome's barbecued bones that were found in the house, hoping Champ Powell was lying low somewhere—like the savvy ex-cop he was—waiting for things to cool off. He'd probably contact the judge in a day or two, and together they'd invent a plausible alibi. That's how it would go. In the meantime there was Katie, who (between heaving sobs) would accuse Arthur Battenkill Jr. of arranging the cold-blooded murder of her former lover. The judge wouldn't know what to do about *that,* but he'd find himself wondering whether a new diamond pendant might soothe his wife's anguish.

On his lunch hour he would go out and buy her one.

When they returned to the motel, JoLayne changed to her workout clothes and went for a walk. Tom Krome made some phone calls—to his voice mail at *The Register,* where his insurance agent had left an oddly urgent message regarding Krome's homeowner policy; to his answering machine at home, which apparently was out of order; to Dick Turnquist, who reported a possible sighting (in, of all places, Jackson Hole, Wyoming) of Krome's future ex-wife.

Krome fell asleep watching a European golf tournament on ESPN. He woke up gasping for air, JoLayne Lucks astride him, jabbing his sides with her supernatural-blue fingernails.

"Hey!" she said. "Hey, you, listen up!"

"Get off—"

"Not until you tell me," she said, "what the hell's going on."

"JoLayne, I can't breathe—"

" 'Helluva risk,' that's what you said. But then it dawned on me: Why in the world would a federal lawman tell *you*—a newspaper guy, for Lord's sake!—that he's about to commit a break-in. Talk about risk. Talk about stupid."

"JoLayne!"

She shifted some of her weight to her knees, so that Krome could inhale.

"Thank you," he said.

"Welcome."

She leaned forward until they were nose to nose. "He's a smart man, Moffitt is. He wouldn't blab anything so foolish in front of the press unless he knew there wasn't going to be any story. And there's *not,* is there? That's why you haven't taken out your damn notebook the whole time we've been on the road."

Krome prepared to shield his ribs from a fresh attack. "I told you, I don't write down every little thing."

"Tom Krome, you are full of shit." She planted her butt forcefully on his chest. "Guess what I did? I called Moffitt on his cellular, and guess what he told me. You're not working for the paper now, you're on medical leave. He checked it out."

Krome tried to raise himself up. Medical leave? he thought. That idiot Sinclair—he's managed to muck up a perfectly splendid resignation.

"Why didn't you tell me?" JoLayne demanded. "What's going on with you?"

"OK." He slipped his arms under her knees and gently rolled her off. She stayed on the bed, stretched out, propped on her elbows.

"I'm waiting, Tom."

He kept his eyes on the ceiling. "Here's what really happened. My editor killed the lottery story, so I resigned. The 'medical leave' stuff is news to me—Sinclair probably made it up to tell the boss."

JoLayne Lucks was incredulous. "You quit your job because of me?"

"Not because of you. Because my editor's a useless, dickless incompetent."

"Really. That's the only reason?"

"And also because I promised to help you."

JoLayne scooted closer. "Listen: You can't quit the newspaper. You absolutely cannot, is that understood?"

"It'll all work out. Don't worry."

"You damn men, I can't believe it! I found another crazy one."

"What's so crazy about keeping a promise."

"Lord," said JoLayne. He was perfectly serious. A cornball, this guy. She said, "Don't move, OK? I'm gonna do something irresponsible."

Krome started to turn toward her, but she stopped him, lightly closing his eyes with one hand.

"You deaf? I told you not to move."

"What is this?" he asked.

"I owe you a kiss," she said, "from last night. Now please be still or I'll bite your lips off."

 **14** Tom Krome was caught by surprise.
"Well, say something," JoLayne said.

"Wow."

"Something original."

"You taste like Certs."

She kissed him again. "Spearmint flavored. I think I'm hooked on the darn things."

Krome rolled on his side. He could see she was highly amused by his nervousness. "I'm lousy at this part," he said.

"In other words, you'd rather skip the chitchat and get right to the fucking."

Krome felt his cheeks get hot. "That's not what—"

"I'm teasing."

He sat up quickly. She was too much.

"Tom, you were sweet to quit your job. Misguided, but sweet. I figured you deserved a smooch."

"It was . . . very nice."

"Try to control yourself," JoLayne said. "Here's what you do now: Get in the car and go home. Back to work. Back to your life. You've done more than enough for me."

"No way."

"Look, I'll be fine. Once Moffitt gets my lottery ticket, I'm outta here."

"Yeah, right."

"I swear, Tom. Back to Grange to be a land baroness."

Krome said, "I don't quit on stories."

"Gimme a break."

"What if Moffitt can't find the ticket?"

JoLayne shrugged. "Then it wasn't meant to be. Now start packing."

"Not a chance. Not until you get your money." He fell back on the pillow. "Suppose you wound up on the wet T-shirt circuit again. I couldn't live with myself."

She laid her head on his chest. "What is it you want?"

"One of those mints would be good."

"From all this, I mean. All this wicked craziness."

"A tolerable ending. That's it," Krome said.

"Makes for a better story, right?"

"Just a better night's sleep."

JoLayne groaned. "You're not real. You can't be."

Krome made a cursory stab at sorting his motives. Maybe he didn't want Moffitt to find the stolen Lotto ticket, because then the adventure would be over and he'd have to go home. Or maybe he wanted to recover the ticket himself, in some dramatic flourish, to impress JoLayne Lucks. It probably wasn't anything noble at all; just dumb pride and hormones.

He said, "You want me to go, I'll go."

"Your tummy's growling. You hungry again?"

"JoLayne, you're not listening."

She lifted her head. "Let's stay like this awhile, right here in bed. See what happens."

"OK," Tom Krome said. She was too much.

Chub was gloating about the getaway. He said they wouldn't have made it if Bode's pickup hadn't been parked in the blue zone, steps from the diner's front door. He said the guy at the counter never saw three handicaps move so goddamn fast.

As the truck cruised toward Homestead, Shiner kept looking to see if they were being chased. Bode Gazzer was taut behind the wheel—he'd been expecting the Negro woman to cancel her credit card, but it jarred him anyway. The manager of the diner would be calling the law, no doubt about that.

"We gotta have a meeting," Bode said. "Soon as possible."

"With who?" Shiner asked.

"Us. The White Clarion Aryans." It was time to start acting like a well-regulated militia. Bode said, "Maybe this afternoon we'll hold a meeting."

Chub leaned forward. "What's wrong with right now?"

"Not in the truck. I can't preside and drive at the same time."

"Hell, you can't piss and whistle at the same time." Chub ran a mossy-looking tongue across his front teeth. "We don't need a damn meeting. We need our Lotto money."

Bode said, "No, man, it's too soon."

Chub took out the .357 and placed it on the floorboard at his feet. "Before somethin' else goes wrong," he said.

Wedged between the squabbling criminals in the front seat, Shiner felt inexplicably safe. Chub was the toughest, and not only because of the guns. Bode could be a hardass, too, but he was more of a thinker; the idea man. Shiner liked his suggestion for a real militia meeting, liked his attention to orderliness and strategy. But before the White Clarion Aryans held a meeting, Shiner wanted to get his tattoo fixed. It couldn't be that difficult, changing the *W.R.B.* to *W.C.A.* The screaming eagle was perfect the way it was.

When he inquired about stopping at a tattoo parlor, Chub laughed and said, "Just what you need."

"I'm dead serious."

Bode, stiffening in the driver's seat: "We ain't stoppin' for no such nonsense."

"Please, I got to!"

Chub said, "Aw, look at your damn arm. It's still bruised up from last time, like a rotten banana."

"You don't unnerstand." Shiner's chin dropped as he slid into a sulk.

Not this again, Chub thought. He snatched up the Colt and twisted the barrel into the kid's groin. "Son, you 'bout the whiniest little fuck I ever met."

Shiner's head came up with a jerk. "I'm s-sorry."

"Sorry don't begin to cover it."

Bode told his partner to take it easy. "We're all three of us still jacked up from last night. Tell you what, let's stop over to the trailer and fetch the automatics. Go out by the rock pit and let off some steam."

"Way cool," Shiner said, expectantly.

"Then, after, we'll have a meeting."

Chub said, "Whoop-dee-doo." He put the pistol in his belt. "Fuck the rock pit. I wanna shoot at somethin' that moves. Somethin' bigger 'n' faster than a goddamn turtle."

"Such as?"

"Wait and see," said Chub. "Shoot a Jew, cap a Jap—"

"Pop a wop," Shiner chimed.

"Yeah!"

Bode Gazzer hoped his partner's sinister mood would pass before they broke out the serious toys.

Moffitt wasn't supposed to get mad. He was a pro. He dealt with low-rent shitheads all the time.

But sneaking through the cramped apartment

of Bodean James Gazzer, the agent felt his anger rise.

The wall poster of David Koresh, the Waco wacko himself. Moffitt had lost a friend in that fiasco of a raid.

Then there were the bullet holes in the plaster. Empty ammo clips. Stacks of gun magazines and *Soldier of Fortune.* Porno videos. A paperback book called *The Poacher's Bible.* A pepper mill trimmed with a Nazi armband. A how-to pamphlet on fertilizer bombs. A clipped-out cartoon proposing a humorous aspect to the Holocaust. An assortment of NRA patches and bumper stickers. A closetful of camouflage clothes. Tacked to the peeling wallpaper behind the toilet: a Confederate flag. In the bedroom, a calico cross-stitched portrait of David Duke.

Moffitt thought: These guys must've had a blast, working on JoLayne.

He locked the front door behind him, bracing it with a chair. He opened a back window and punched out the screen, as an escape in case Bodean James Gazzer returned. The fresh air didn't hurt, either—the place smelled of soiled laundry, cigaret ash and stale beer. Methodically, Moffitt began to search. He knew from experience that even the dimmest of thugs occasionally could be brilliant at concealing contraband—and a lottery ticket was easier to hide than an AK-47 or a kilo of hash.

The kitchen was first. One glance at the crusty silverware made Moffitt glad he wore surgical gloves. With a heavy forearm he cleared the cluttered dinette. There he dumped every box and tin from Bodean James Gazzer's cabinets—sugar, flour, instant coffee, Cocoa Krispies, croutons, Quaker Oats.

No Lotto stub.

He took a deep breath before opening the refrigerator, but it wasn't as rancid as he'd feared. The food section was practically empty except for Budweisers, marshmallow-filled cookies, ketchup and a fuzzy chunk of Gouda. Finding nothing hidden there, Moffitt hacked his way into the freezer compartment, a favorite stash of novice dopers and smugglers. A half-gallon container of ancient fudge-ripple ice cream went into a mixing bowl, which went into the stove. When the slop was melted, Moffitt strained it through a colander. Then he emptied the ice trays on the counter and examined each cube.

No ticket.

He grabbed a steak knife and headed for the bedroom, where he eviscerated the pillows, gutted the mattress and box spring, pried up the musty corners of the carpet. Inside Bodean James Gazzer's dresser, Moffitt came across something he'd never before seen: camo-style underwear. There was also a World War II bayonet, a gummy-looking *Penthouse* and a pile of dunning notices from the National Rifle Association for unpaid dues. Moffitt was certain he had hit pay dirt in the bottom drawer, beneath a tangle of frayed socks, where he uncovered five crisp tickets from the Florida Lotto.

But none of the sequences matched JoLayne's winning numbers, and the date of the drawing was wrong: December 2.

That's tomorrow, thought Moffitt. Unbelievable—the $14 million they stole from her wasn't enough. The fuckers want more.

He pocketed the tickets and, with some dread, moved to the bathroom. A colony of plump carpenter ants had taken over the sink, demonstrating a special fondness for Bodean James Gazzer's toothbrush. Moffitt dove into the medicine chest and emptied the pill bottles. Several had been prescribed to persons other than Mr. Gazzer, who'd undoubtedly stolen them or forged the scrips. Moffitt took his time with a dispenser of Crest and a tube of hemorrhoid cream, which he flattened under a shoe and then opened with a wire cutter.

Nothing.

The vanity held an empty box of Trojan nonlubricated condoms, which intrigued Moffitt. Bodean James Gazzer's apartment showed no signs of a woman's presence—certainly no woman who was worried about catching a disease. Maybe Gazzer was gay, the agent thought, although it seemed unlikely, given the homophobic tendencies of gun nuts. Also, the pornographic videos stacked near the TV set bore heterosexually oriented titles.

Maybe the loon wore rubbers when he jacked off. Or maybe he used them with hookers. In any event, he'd been a busy boy.

The answer to the riddle of the Trojans turned up in a plastic trash can: five foil condom wrappers and a razor blade. Moffitt aligned them on the toilet seat. The condoms were inside the packages, and Moffitt cautiously removed them with a tweezers. Each of them bore visible nicks or slices, which presumably was why they'd been discarded.

Moffitt concentrated on the bright wrappers. Clearly they hadn't been torn open in the ordinary haste of lust. Instead they'd painstakingly been cut along one edge, undoubtedly with the razor blade. Even with such care, Bodean James Gazzer had damaged all five rubbers.

The sixth must have been the winner. Moffitt was pretty sure he knew where it was and what was hidden inside it.

"Fucker," he said aloud.

Mr. Gazzer must be quite the optimist, the agent reflected. Why else would he care whether the condom in which he'd concealed the lottery ticket was usable?

On his way out of the apartment, Moffitt encountered a stout rat gorging itself in the mounds of sugar and cereal on the dinette. His first impulse was to shoot it, but then he thought: Why do Gazzer any favors? With luck, the critter was rabid.

By nature Moffitt was not a mischievous person, but he was inspired by the shabby trappings of hate. He had a nagging image of Bodean Gazzer and his sadistic partner—one would be stretched out in his underwear on the futon, the other might be slouched at the dinette. They'd be slugging down Budweisers, laughing about what they'd done to JoLayne Lucks, trying to remember who'd punched her where. The look in her eyes. The sounds she made.

Moffitt simply could not slip away and allow such shitheads to go on with their warped lives, exactly as before. After all, how often did one get the opportunity to make a lasting impression upon paranoid sociopaths?

Not often enough. Moffitt felt morally obligated to fuck with Bodean James Gazzer's head. It took only a few extra minutes, and afterwards even the rat seemed amused.

Sinclair was overcome the instant he touched the cooters: a warm tingle that started preternaturally in his palms and raced up both arms to his spine.

He was sitting cross-legged in Demencio's yard, on the lip of the moat. The daily visitation was over, the pilgrims were gone. Sinclair had never handled a turtle before. Demencio said go ahead, help yourself. They don't bite or nothin'.

Sinclair picked up one of the painted cooters and set it delicately in his lap. The bearded face gazing up from the grooved carapace was purely beatific. And the turtle itself was no less exquisite—bright gemlike eyes, a velvety neck striped in greens, golds and yellows. Sinclair reached into the water and picked up another one, and then another. Before long, he was acrawl with baby turtles—rubbery legs pumping, tiny claws scratching harmlessly on the fabric of his pants. The sensation was hypnotic, almost spiritual. The cooters seemed to emanate a soft, soothing current.

Demencio, who was refilling the moat with "holy" water, asked Sinclair if he felt all right. Sinclair spontaneously began to tremble and hum. Demencio couldn't make out the tune, but it was nothing he was dying to hear on the radio. Turning to Joan and Roddy: "I'd say it's time to take the boy home."

Sinclair didn't want to go. He looked up at Roddy. "Isn't this amazing?" Thrusting both hands high, full of dripping turtles: "Did you see!"

Demencio, sharply: "Be careful with them things. They ain't mine." That's all he'd need, some city dork accidentally smushing one of JoLayne's precious babies. Say *adiós* to a thousand bucks.

Demencio was tempted to turn the hose on the

guy—it had worked like a charm on Trish's tom-cat. Sinclair's face pinched into a mask of concentration. His head began to flop back and forth, as if his neck had gone to rubber.

"Nyyah nurrha nimmy doo-dey," he said.

Roddy glanced at his wife. "What is that—Spanish or somethin'?"

"I don't believe so."

Again Sinclair cried: *"Nyyah nyyah doo-dey!"* It was a mangled regurgitation of a newspaper headline he'd once written, a personal all-time favorite: NERVOUS NUREYEV NIMBLE IN DISNEY DEBUT.

The translation, had Demencio known it, would have failed to put him at ease. "That's it," he said curtly. "Closing time."

At Roddy's urging, Sinclair returned the twelve painted turtles to the water. Roddy led him to the car, and Joan drove home. Roddy began stacking charcoal briquettes in the outdoor grill, but Sinclair said he wasn't hungry and went to bed. He was gone when Joan awoke the next morning. Under the sugar bowl was his journalist's notebook, opened to a fresh page:

I've returned to the shrine.

That's where she found him, rapt and round-eyed.

Demencio took her aside and whispered, "No offense, but I got a business here."

"I understand," said Joan. She walked to the moat and crouched next to her brother. "How we doing?"

"See that?" Sinclair pointed. "She's crying."

Demencio had repaired the Madonna's plumbing; teardrops sparkled on her fiberglass cheeks. Joan felt embarrassed that Sinclair was so affected.

"Your boss called," she told him.

"That's nice."

"It sounded real important."

Sinclair sighed. Cupped in each hand was a cooter. "This is Bartholomew, and I think this one's Simon."

"Yes, they're very cute."

"Joan, please. You're talking about the apostles."

"Honey, you'd better call the newspaper."

Demencio offered to let him use the telephone in the house. Anything to get the goofball away from the shrine before the first Christian tourists arrived.

The managing editor's secretary put Sinclair through immediately. In a monotone he apologized for not calling the day before, as promised.

"Forget about it," said the managing editor. "I've got shitty news: Tom Krome's dead."

"No."

"Looks that way. The arson guys found a body in the house."

"No!" Sinclair insisted. "It's not possible."

"Burned beyond recognition."

"But Tom went to Miami with the lottery woman!"

"Who told you that?"

"The man with the turtles."

"I see," said the managing editor. "What about the man with the giraffes—what did he say? And the bearded lady with penguins—did you ask her?"

Sinclair wobbled and spun, tangling himself in the telephone cord. Joan shoved a chair under his butt. Breathlessly he said: "Tom can't be dead."

"They're working on the DNA," the managing editor said, "but they're ninety-nine percent sure it's him. We're getting a front-page package ready for tomorrow."

"My God," said Sinclair. Was it possible he'd actually lost a reporter?

He heard his boss say: "Don't come home."

"What?"

"Not just yet. Not till we figure out what to say."

"To who?" Sinclair asked.

"The wires. The networks. Reporters don't get murdered much these days," the managing editor explained, "especially feature writers. It's a pretty big deal."

"I suppose, but—"

"There'll be lots of sticky questions: Where'd

you send him? What was he working on? Was it dangerous? It's best if I handle it. That's why they pay me the big bucks, right?"

Sinclair was gripped by a cold fog. "I can't believe this."

"Maybe it had nothing to do with the job. Maybe it was a robbery, or a jealous boyfriend," said the managing editor. "Maybe a fucking casserole exploded—who knows? The point is, Tom's going to end up a hero, regardless. That's what happens when journalists get killed—look at Amelia Lloyd, for Christ's sake. She couldn't write a fucking grocery list, but they went ahead and named a big award after her."

Sinclair said, "I feel sick."

"We all do, believe me. We all do," the managing editor said. "You sit tight for a few days. Take it easy. Have a good visit with your sister. I'll be in touch."

For a time Sinclair remained motionless. Joan took the receiver from his hand and carefully unwrapped the cord from his shoulders and neck. With a tissue she dabbed the perspiration from his forehead. Then she dampened another and wiped a spot of turtle poop from his arm.

"What did he say?" she asked. "What's happened?"

"It's Tom—he's not in Miami, he's dead."

"Oh no. I'm so sorry."

Sinclair stood up. "Now I understand," he said.

Nervously his sister eyed him.

"Finally I understand why I'm here. What brought me to this place," he said. "Before, I wasn't sure. Something fantastic took hold of me when I touched the turtles, but I didn't know what or why. Now I do. Now I know."

Joan said, "Hey, how about a soda?"

Sinclair slapped a hand across his breast. "I was sent here," he said, "to be reborn."

"Reborn."

"There's no other explanation," Sinclair said, and trotted out the door toward the shrine. There he stripped off his clothes and lay down in the silty water among the cooters.

"Nimmy doo-dey, nimmy nyyah!"

Trish, who was setting up the T-shirt display, dropped to one knee. "I believe he's speaking in tongues!"

"Like hell," said Demencio. "Coo-ca-loo-ca-choo."

Balefully he stomped to the garage in search of the tuna gaff.

Krome looked preoccupied. Happy, JoLayne thought, but preoccupied.

She said, "You passed the test."

"The white-guy test?"

"Yep. With flying colors."

Krome broke out laughing. It was nice to hear.

JoLayne wished he'd laugh like that more often, and not only when she made a joke.

He said, "When did you decide this would happen?"

They were under the bedcovers, holding each other. As if it were freezing outdoors, JoLayne thought, instead of seventy-two degrees.

"Pre-kiss or post-kiss?" Krome asked.

"Post," she answered.

"You're kidding."

"Nope. Strictly a spur-of-the-moment deal."

"The sex?"

"Sure," JoLayne said.

Which wasn't exactly true, but why tell him everything? He didn't need to know the precise moment when she'd made up her mind, or why. It amused JoLayne that men were forever trying to figure out how they'd managed to get laid—what devastatingly clever line they'd come up with, what timely expression of sincerity or sensitivity they'd affected. As if the power of seduction were theirs whenever they wanted, if only they knew how to unlock it.

For JoLayne Lucks, there was no deep mystery to what had happened. Krome was a decent guy. He cared about her. He was strong, reliable and not too knuckleheaded. These things counted. He had no earthly clue how much they counted.

Not to mention that she was scared. No denying it. Chasing two vicious robbers through the state—insane is what it was. No wonder they were stressed out, she and Tom. That certainly had something to do with it, too; one reason they were hugging each other like teenagers.

JoLayne retreated to standard pillow talk.

"What are you thinking about?"

"Moffitt," he said.

"Oh, very romantic."

"I was hoping he takes his time searching that guy's place. A week or so would be OK. In the meantime we could stay just like this, the two of us."

"Nice comeback," JoLayne said, pinching his leg. "You think he'll find the ticket?"

"If it's there, yeah. He gives the impression of total competence."

"And what if it's not there?"

"Then I suppose we'll need a plan, and some luck," Krome said.

"Moffitt thinks I'll do something crazy."

"Imagine that."

"Seriously, Tom. He won't even tell me the guy's name."

"I've *got* the name," Krome said, "and an address."

JoLayne sat upright, bursting out of the covers. "What did you say?"

"With all due respect to your friend, it doesn't take Sherlock Holmes to run a license-tag check. All you need is a friend at the highway patrol."

Krome shrugged in mock innocence. "The creep with the pickup truck, his name is Bodean James Gazzer. And we can find him with or without intrepid Agent Moffitt."

"Damn," said JoLayne. The boy was slicker than she'd thought.

"I'd have told you sooner," he said, "but we were preoccupied."

"Don't give me that."

They both jumped when the phone rang. Krome reached for it. JoLayne scooted closer and silently mouthed: "Moffitt?"

Krome shook his head. JoLayne hopped out of bed and headed for the shower. When she came out, he was standing at the window, taking in a grand view of the Metrorail tracks. He didn't seem to notice that she'd repainted her nails a neon green or that she was wearing only the towel on her head.

"So who was it?" she asked.

"My lawyer again."

Uh-oh, she thought, reaching for her robe. "Bad news?"

"Sort of," Tom Krome said. "Apparently I'm dead." When he turned around, he appeared more bemused than upset. "It's going to be on the front page of *The Register* tomorrow."

"Dead." JoLayne pursed her lips. "You sure fooled me."

"Fried to a cinder in my own home. Must be true, if it's in the newspaper."

JoLayne felt entitled to wonder if she really knew enough about this Tom fellow, nice and steady as he might seem. A burning house was something to consider.

She said, "Lord, what are you going to do?"

"Stay dead for a while," Krome replied. "That's what my lawyer says."

 Bodean Gazzer instructed Chub to cease shooting from the truck.

"But it's *him.*"

"It ain't," Bode said. "Now quit."

"Not jest yet."

Shiner cried, "My eardrums!"

"Pussy." Chub continued to fire until the black Mustang skidded off the highway on bare rims. Fuming, Bode braked the pickup and coasted to the shoulder. He was losing his grip on Chub and Shiner; semiautomatics seemed to bring out the worst in them.

Chub hopped from the truck and loped with homicidal intent through the darkness, toward the disabled car. Bode marked his partner's progress by the bobbing orange glow of the cigaret. The man was setting a damn poor example for

Shiner—there was nothing well-regulated about sniping at motorists on the Florida Turnpike.

Shiner said, "Hell we do now?"

"Get out, son." Bode Gazzer grabbed a flashlight from the glove box and hurried after Chub. They found him holding at gunpoint a young Latin man whose misfortune was to vaguely resemble the obnoxious boyfriend of a Hooters waitress, who even more vaguely resembled the actress Kim Basinger.

Bode said: "Nice work, ace."

Chub spat his cigaret butt. It wasn't Tony in the Mustang.

Shiner asked, "Is it the same guy or not?"

"Hell, no, it ain't him. What's your name?" Bode demanded.

"Bob." The young man clutched the meaty part of his right shoulder, where a rifle slug had grazed it.

Chub jabbed at him with the muzzle of the Cobray. "Bob, huh? You don't look like no Bob."

The driver willingly surrendered his license. The name on it made Chub grin: Roberto Lopez.

"Jest like I thought. Goddamn lyin' sumbitch Cuban!" Chub crowed.

The young man was terrified. "No, I am from Colombia."

"Nice try."

"Bob and Roberto, it is the same thing!"

Chub said, "Yeah? On what planet?"

Bodean Gazzer switched off the flashlight. The heavy traffic on the highway made him jumpy; even in Dade County a bullet-riddled automobile could attract notice.

"Gimme some light here." Chub was pawing through the young man's wallet. "I mean, long as we gone to all the trouble and ammo."

Jauntily he held up four one-hundred-dollar bills for Bode to see. Shiner gave a war whoop.

"And lookie here—'Merican Express," Chub said, waggling a gold-colored credit card. "Fuck is the likes a you doin' with *anything* 'Merican?"

Roberto Lopez said, "Take whatever you want. Please don't kill me."

Chub commanded Shiner to search the trunk. Bode Gazzer was a basket case; any second he expected the blue flash of police lights. He knew there would be little chance of satisfactorily explaining a shot Colombian to the Florida Highway Patrol.

"Hurry it up! Goddamn you guys," he growled.

They found a briefcase, a holstered Model 84 Beretta .380 and a new pair of two-tone golf shoes. Shiner said, "Size tens. Same as me."

"Keep 'em!" Roberto Lopez, calling from the front seat.

Bode aimed the flashlight inside the briefcase: bar charts, computer printouts and financial statements. A business card identified Roberto Lopez as a stockbroker with Smith Barney.

Here Chub saw a chance to salvage merit from the crime. Even though the guy had turned out not to be Amber's asshole boyfriend, he was still a damn foreigner with fancy clothes and too much money. Surely Bode would agree that the rifle attack wasn't a total waste of time.

In a tone of solemn indignation, Chub accosted the fearful young Colombian: "You fuckers sneak into this country, steal our jobs and then take over our golf courses. If I might ast, Mister Roberto Stockbroker, what's next? You gone run for President?"

Shiner was so stirred that he patriotically kicked the car, the golf cleats leaving a flawless perforation. Bode Gazzer, however, showed no sign of indignation.

Chub set aside the rifle and seized Roberto Lopez by the collar. "OK, smart-ass," Chub said, recalling Bode's piercing roadside interrogation of the migrant workers, "gimme the fourteenth President of the U.S.A."

Tightly the young Colombian answered, "Franklin Pierce."

"Ha! Frankie who?"

"Pierce." Bode's voice dripped bitterness. "President Franklin Pierce is right. The man got it right."

Deflated, Chub stepped back. "Jesus Willy Christ."

"I'm outta here," Bodean Gazzer said, and

headed toward the pickup truck. Chub vented his disappointment by punching the luckless stockbroker in the nose, while Shiner concentrated his energies on the exterior of the Mustang.

To elude the process servers hired by her estranged husband, Mary Andrea Finley Krome began calling herself "Julie Channing," a weakly veiled homage to her two all-time-favorite Broadway performers. So determined was Mary Andrea to resist divorce court that she went a step further: At a highway rest stop outside Jackson Hole, Wyoming, she cut her bounteous red hair and penciled in new full eyebrows. That same afternoon she drove into town and unsuccessfully auditioned for a ragged but rousing production of *Oliver Twist*.

Back in Brooklyn, the resourceful Dick Turnquist had compiled from the World Wide Web a list of theater promoters in the rural western states. He faxed to each one a recent publicity shot of Mary Andrea Finley Krome, accompanied by a brief inquiry hinting at a family emergency back East—had anyone seen her? The director in Jackson Hole was concerned enough to reply, by telephone. He said the woman in the photograph bore a keen resemblance to an actress who had, only yesterday, read for the parts of both Fagin and the Artful Dodger. And while

Miss Julia Channing's singing voice was perfectly adequate, the director said, her Cockney accent needed work. "She could've handled Richard the Second," the director explained, "but what I needed was a pickpocket."

By the time Dick Turnquist retained and dispatched a local private investigator, Mary Andrea Finley Krome was already gone from the mountain town.

What impressed Turnquist was her perseverance for the stage life. Knowing she was being pursued, Mary Andrea continued to make herself visible. And although changing one's professional name might tax the ego, as subterfuge it was pretty feeble. Mary Andrea could have melted into any city and taken any anonymous job—waitress, receptionist, bartender—with only a negligible decline of income. Yet she chose to keep acting despite the risk of discovery and subpoena. Perhaps she was indomitably committed to her craft, but Turnquist believed there was another explanation: Mary Andrea needed the attention. She craved the limelight, no matter how remote or fleeting.

Well, Turnquist reflected, who didn't.

She could call herself whatever she wanted— Julie Channing, Liza Bacall, it didn't matter. The lawyer knew he would eventually catch up to the future ex–Mrs. Krome and compel her presence in the halls of justice.

He therefore was not at all distressed when *The*

Register called to inform him that Tom Krome had died in a suspicious house fire. Having only an hour earlier chatted with his client, alive and uncharred in a Coral Gables motel, Turnquist realized the newspaper was about to make a humongous mistake. It was about to devote its entire front page to a dead man who wasn't.

Yet the lawyer chose not to edify the young reporter on the end of the line. Turnquist was careful not to lie outright; it wasn't required. Conveniently the young reporter failed to ask Turnquist if he'd spoken to Tom Krome that day, or if he had any reason to believe Tom Krome was not deceased.

Instead the reporter said: "How long had you known each other? What are your fondest memories? How do you think he'd like to be remembered?"

All questions that Dick Turnquist found it easy to answer. He didn't say so, but he was grateful to *The Register* for saving him further aggravation in tracking Mary Andrea Finley Krome. Once she heard the news, she'd naturally assume she could stop running. Tom's dying would get her off the hook, litigation-wise, and she'd have no reason to continue the dodge. Mary Andrea had always been less concerned with saving the marriage than with avoiding the stigma of divorce. The last true Catholic, in her estranged husband's words.

She was also a ham. Dick Turnquist expected

Mary Andrea would get the first plane for Florida, to play the irresistible role of grief-stricken widow—sitting for poignant TV interviews, attending weepy candlelight memorials, stoically announcing journalism scholarships in her martyred spouse's name.

And we'll be waiting for her, thought Dick Turnquist.

On the phone, the reporter from *The Register* was winding up the interview. "Thanks for talking with me at such a difficult time. Just one more question: As Tom's close friend, how do you feel about what's happened?"

The lawyer answered, quite truthfully: "Well, it doesn't seem real."

On the morning of December 2, Bernard Squires telephoned Clara Markham in Grange to inquire if his generous purchase offer had been conveyed to the sellers of Simmons Wood.

"But it's only been three days," the broker said.

"You haven't even spoken to them?"

"I've put in a call," Clara fudged. "They said Mr. Simmons is in Las Vegas. His sister is on holiday down in the islands."

Bernard Squires said, "They have telephones in Las Vegas, I know for a fact."

Normally Bernard was not so impatient, but Richard "The Icepick" Tarbone urgently needed to make a covert withdrawal from the union pension accounts. The nature of the family emergency was not confided to Bernard Squires, and he pointedly exhibited a lack of curiosity on the matter. But since the Florida real estate purchase was crucial to the money laundering, The Icepick had taken a personal interest in expediting the deal. None of this could be frankly communicated by Bernard Squires to Clara Markham, who was saying:

"I'll try to reach them again this morning. I promise."

"And there are no other offers?" Bernard asked.

"Nothing on the table," said Clara, which was strictly the truth.

As soon as the man from Chicago hung up, she dialed the number in Coral Gables that JoLayne had given her. A desk clerk at the motel said Miss Lucks and her friend had checked out.

With heavy reluctance Clara Markham then phoned the attorney handling the estate of the late Lighthorse Simmons. She described the pension fund's offer for the forty-four acres on the outskirts of Grange. The attorney said three million sounded like a fair price. He seemed sure the heirs would leap at it.

Clara was sure, too. She felt bad for her friend, but business was business. Unless JoLayne Lucks found a miracle, Simmons Wood was lost.

An hour later, when Bernard Squires' telephone

rang, he thought it must be Clara Markham calling with the good news. It wasn't. It was Richard
Tarbone.

"I'm sicka this shit," he told Squires. "You get
your ass down to Florida."

And Squires went.

They'd checked out of the Comfort Inn shortly
after Moffitt's visit. The agent had come straight
from the redneck's apartment. His tight-lipped expression told the story: no Lotto ticket.

"Damn," JoLayne had said.

"I think I know where it is."

"Where?"

"He hid it in a rubber. The camo guy."

"A rubber." JoLayne, pressing her knuckles to
her forehead, trying not to get grossed out.

"A Trojan," Moffit had added.

"Thanks. I've got the picture."

"He's carrying it on him somewhere, I'm willing
to bet."

"His wallet," Tom Krome had suggested.

"Yeah, probably." Moffitt matter-of-factly told
them about the search of Bodean James Gazzer's
place—the anti-government posters and bumper
stickers, the gun magazines, the vermin, the condoms in the wastebasket.

"What now? How do we find the ticket?" Krome
had asked.

"Gimme a week."

"No." JoLayne, shaking her head. "I can't. Time's running out."

Moffitt had promised he'd take care of it as soon as he returned from San Juan. He had to go testify in a seizure case—illegal Chinese machine guns, routed through Haiti.

"When I get back, I'll deal with these guys. Do a traffic stop, pat 'em down real hard. Search the pickup, too."

"But what if—"

"If it's not there, then . . . hell, I don't know." Moffitt, working his jaw, stared out the window.

"How long will you be gone?"

"Three days. Four at the most."

Moffitt had handed JoLayne Lucks the lottery tickets from Bodean Gazzer's sock drawer. "For Saturday night," he'd said. "Just in case."

"Very funny."

"Hey, weirder things've happened."

JoLayne had tucked the tickets in her handbag. "By the way, Tom's dead. It'll be in the papers tomorrow."

Moffitt had glanced quizzically at Krome, who'd shrugged and said, "Long story."

"Murdered?"

"Supposedly. I'd prefer to keep it that way for now. You mind?"

"I've never laid eyes on you," Moffitt had said, "and you've never laid eyes on me."

At the door, JoLayne had given the ATF agent a warm hug. "Thanks for everything. I know you stuck your neck out."

"Forget it."

"Nothing happened? You sure?"

"Easy as pie. But the place is trashed—Gazzer'll know it wasn't some chickenshit burglar."

As soon as Moffitt was gone, they'd started to pack. Krome insisted. The robber's address was in Krome's notebook, the one JoLayne said he never used.

The first formal meeting of the White Clarion Aryans was held by lantern light at an empty cock-fighting ring. It began with a dispute over titles; Bode Gazzer said military discipline was impossible without strict designations of rank. He declared that henceforth he should be called "Colonel."

Chub objected. "We's equal partners," he said, " 'cept for him." Meaning the kid, Shiner.

Bode offered Chub the rank of major, which he assured him was on a par with colonel. Chub pondered it between swigs of Jack Daniel's, purchased (along with beer, gas, cigarets, T-bone steaks, onion rings and frozen cheesecake) with the cash stolen from the young Colombian stockbroker.

Major Chub didn't sound particularly distinguished, Chub thought. *Major Gillespie* wasn't

half bad, but Chub wasn't psychologically prepared to revert to the family name.

"Fuck this whole dumb idea," he mumbled.

Shiner raised a hand. "Can I be a sergeant?"

Bode nodded. "Son, you're reading my mind."

Chub raised the liquor bottle. "Can I be a Klin-
gon? Please, Colonel Gazzer, sir. Purty please?"

Bode ignored him. He handed each of the
men a booklet distributed by the First Patriot
Covenant, an infamously disagreeable cell of su-
premacists headquartered in western Montana.
The First Patriot Covenant lived in concrete pillboxes and believed blacks and Jews were the children of Satan; the Pope was either a first or a
second cousin. Simply titled "Starting Up," the
group's booklet contained helpful sections about
organizing militia wings: fund-raising, tax eva-
sion, rules of order, rules of recruitment, dress
codes, press relations and arsenals. Shiner could
hardly wait to read it.

"Page eight," Bode said. " 'Be Discreet.' Everybody understand what that means? It means you
don't go blastin' away with rifles on the goddamn
turnpike."

From Chub came a scornful grunt. "Blow me."

Shiner was startled. This was nothing like the
army. He felt a sticky arm settle around his shoulders. Turning, he got a faceful of whiskey breath.

"Funny thing," Chub said, fingering his ponytail, "how it's fine and dandy for him to roust a

couple beaners for eight lousy bucks, but I swipe four C-notes off poor 'Bob' Lopez and all of a sudden I'm a shitty soldier. You tell the colonel he can blow me, OK?"

An angry cry arose, and the next thing Shiner knew, they were locked together—Bodean Gazzer and Chub—thrashing in the dry dirt of the rooster pit. Shiner wasn't convinced it was a serious fight, since no hard punches were being struck, but he was nevertheless disturbed by the unseemly clawing and hair pulling. The two men on the ground didn't look like battle-ready officers, they looked like barroom drunks. Shiner found himself wondering, with a twinge of shame, whether the White Clarion Aryans had a snowball's chance against crack NATO troops.

Pure fatigue ended the scuffle. Bode got a torn shirt and a bloody nose, Chub lost his eye patch. The colonel announced they were all going to his apartment and cook up the steaks. Shiner was surprised the drive was so peaceful; no one mentioned the fight. Bode talked expansively about the many militias in Montana and Idaho, and said he wouldn't mind moving out there if it weren't for the winters; cold weather aggravated the gout in his elbows. Meanwhile Chub had twisted the rearview mirror to inspect his split eyelid, observing that the whole orb socket had taken on a rank and swampy appearance beneath the airtight bicycle patch. Shiner recommended antibiotics, and

Bode said he had a tube of something orange and powerful in the medicine cabinet at home.

Upon arriving at the apartment building, Bode Gazzer neatly gunned the Dodge Ram into the first handicapped slot. A scolding stare from an insomniac neighbor made no impression. Bode asked his white brothers to mind the guns, while he toted the food inside.

Chub and Shiner were perched on the tailgate, finishing their beers, when they heard it—more a moan than a scream. Yet it was riven with such horror as to raise the fuzz on their necks. They scrambled toward Bode's apartment, Chub drawing the .357 as he ran.

Inside, unaware that the colonel had dropped the groceries, Shiner slipped on an onion ring and went down headfirst. Chub, stepping in cheesecake, skated hard into the television set, which toppled sideways with a crash.

Bodean Gazzer never turned to look. He remained stock-still in the living room. His pale face shone with perspiration. With both hands he clutched his camouflage cap to his belly.

The place had been taken apart from the kitchen to the john; a maliciously thorough job.

Dumbstruck, Chub stuck the Colt in his belt. "Jesus Willy," he gasped. Now he saw what Bode saw. So did Shiner, one cheek smeared with rat shit, peering up from the kitchen tiles.

The intruders had ripped down the posters of

David Koresh and the other patriots. On the bare wall was a message scrawled in red, in letters three feet high. The first line said:

WE KNOW EVERYTHING

The second line said:

FEAR THE BLACK TIDE

It took only fifteen minutes for the White Clarion Aryans to load the pickup—guns, gear, bedding, water, plenty of camo clothes. Wordlessly the men piled into the front, Shiner in the middle as usual. Chub's head lolled against the side window; he was too shaken to ask Bode Gazzer for a theory.

To Shiner it seemed the colonel knew exactly where he was going. He looked determined behind the wheel, taking the truck on a beeline to Highway One, then making a sharp left.

South, by Shiner's reckoning. The Everglades, maybe. Or Key Largo.

Bode flicked on the dome light and said, "There's a map under the seat."

Shiner spread it across his lap.

"Flip it over," Bode told him.

Instead he should've been paying attention to his mirrors. Then he might have noticed the headlights of the compact car that had been following them from the apartment.

Inside the Honda, JoLayne Lucks turned down the radio and asked: "How did you know they'd run?"

Tom Krome said, "Because these are not brave guys. These are guys who beat up women. Running away is second nature."

"Especially with the 'Black Tide' on their tails." JoLayne chuckled to herself. She and Tom had arrived an hour earlier and peeked in the apartment window, to make sure it was the right place. That's when they'd seen Moffitt's menacing valentine on the wall.

Now, pointing at the truck in front of them, JoLayne said: "Think they've got my ticket on 'em?"

"Yep."

"Still no game plan?"

"Nope."

"I like an honest man," JoLayne said.

"Good. Here's more: I'm not feeling so brave myself."

"OK. When we get to Oz, we'll ask the wizard to give you some courage."

Krome said, "Toto, too?"

"Yes, dear. Toto, too."

JoLayne leaned over and put a lemon drop in his mouth. When he started to say something, she deftly popped in another one. Krome was hopelessly puckered. He didn't know where the pickup truck was leading them, but he knew he wasn't turning back. Bachelorhood in the Nineties, he thought. What a headline Sinclair could write:

DEAD MAN DOGS DANGEROUS DESPERADOS

16 The farther they got from Coconut Grove, the stronger grew Chub's conviction that he would never see his treasured Amber again. He was seized by a mournful panic, a talon-like snatch of his heart.

Neither of his companions noticed. Shiner was preoccupied with the mysterious "Black Tide," and Bodean Gazzer was brimming with theories. Both men were shaken by the scene inside the ransacked apartment, and chatting about niggers and communists seemed to steady their nerves. An even flow of conversation also preserved the illusion of a calm orderly flight, when in fact Bode had no plan beyond running like hell. They were being pursued; chased by an unknown evil. Bode's instinct was to hide someplace remote and out of reach, and to get there as fast as possible. Shiner's naive and breathless queries, which otherwise would have provoked the harshest sarcasm, now worked as a tonic by affirming for Bode his role as the militia's undisputed leader. Although he hadn't the foggiest clue who the Black Tide was, Bode gave the full weight of his authority to wild speculation. This kept his mind busy and his spirits up, and Shiner hung on every word. Chub's lack of participation was of small concern, for Bode was accustomed to his partner's nodding off.

He was therefore flabbergasted to feel the gun barrel at the base of his neck. Shiner (who'd detected Chub's arm slipping behind the seat and figured he was just stretching) jerked at a sharp noise near his left ear—the click of the hammer being cocked. He turned only enough to see the Colt Python pointed at the colonel.

"Pull over," Chub said.

"What for?" Bode asked.

"Yer own good."

As soon as his partner stopped the truck, Chub eased down the hammer of the gun. "Son," he said to Shiner, "I got another mission for you. Provided you wanna stay in the brotherhood."

Shiner flinched like a spanked puppy; he'd thought his place in the White Clarion Aryans was solid.

"It's no sweat," Chub was saying. "You'll dig it." He stepped out of the pickup and motioned with the gun for Shiner to do the same.

Being half drunk and exhausted did not affect Bodean Gazzer's low threshold of annoyance. Chain of command obviously meant nothing to Chub; the goon operated on blood impulse and reckless emotion. If it continued, they'd all end up in maximum security at Raiford—not the ideal venue for a white-supremacy crusade.

When Chub reentered the truck, Bode said, "This shit's gotta stop. Where's the boy?"

"I sent him back up the road."

"For what?"

"To finish some bidness. Let's go." Chub, laying the revolver on the front seat between them; Shiner's spot.

"Well, goddamn." Bode could hear the kid's golf spikes clacking on the pavement.

"Jest drive," Chub said.

"Anywheres in particular?"

"Wherever you was goin' is fine. Long as it ain't too fur from Jewfish Creek." Chub launched a brown stream of spit out the window. "Go 'head and ast."

Bode Gazzer said, "OK. How come Jewfish Creek?"

"On account of I like the name."

"Ah." On account of you're a certified moron, Bode thought.

By daybreak they were at a marina in Key Largo, picking out a boat to steal.

Tom Krome's death was announced with an end-of-the-world headline in *The Register,* but the news failed to shake American journalism to its foundations. *The New York Times* didn't carry the story, while the Associated Press condensed *The Register*'s melodramatic front-page spread to eleven sober inches. The AP's rewrite desk circumspectly noted that, while the medical examiner was confident of his preliminary findings, the body found in Tom Krome's burned house had yet to be positively identified. *The Register*'s managing editor seemed certain of the worst—he was quoted as saying Krome was "quite possibly" murdered as the result of a sensitive newspaper assignment. Pressed for details, the managing editor replied he was not at liberty to discuss the investigation.

Many papers across the United States picked up the Associated Press story and reduced it to four or five paragraphs. A slightly longer version appeared in *The Missoulian,* the daily that serves Missoula and other communities in the greater Bitterroot valley of Montana. Fortuitously, it was here Mary Andrea Finley Krome had hooked up with a little-theater production of *The Glass Menagerie.* Although she was not a great fan of Tennessee Williams (and, in any case, preferred musicals over dramas), she needed the work. The prospect of performing in small-town obscurity depressed Mary Andrea, but her mood brightened after she made friends with another actress, a dance major at the state university. Her name was Lorie, or possibly Loretta—Mary Andrea reminded herself to check in the playbill. On Mary Andrea's second morning in town, Lorie or Loretta introduced her to a cozy coffee shop where students and local artists gathered, not far from the new city carousel. The coffee shop featured old stuffed sofas upon which Mary Andrea and her new pal contentedly settled with their cappuccinos and croissants. They spread the newspaper between them.

It was Mary Andrea's habit to begin each morning with an update of entertainment and celebrity happenings, of which several were capsulized in *The Missoulian.* Tom Cruise was being paid $22 million to star in a movie about a narcoleptic heart surgeon who must attempt a six-hour transplant operation on his girlfriend (Mary Andrea wondered which of Hollywood's anorexic blow-job artists had won the part). Also, it was reported that one of Mary Andrea's least-favorite television programs, *Sag Harbor Saga,* was being canceled after a three-year run. (Mary Andrea feared it wasn't the last America would see of Siobhan Davies, the insufferable Irish witch who'd beaten her out for the role of Darien, the predatory textile heiress.) And, finally, a drug-loving actor with whom Mary Andrea once had done Shakespeare in the Park was under arrest in New York after disrobing in the lobby of Trump Tower and, during his flight to escape, head-butting the beefeater at the Fifth Avenue entrance. (Mary Andrea took no joy from the actor's plight, for he had shown her nothing but kindness during *The Merchant of Venice,* when a disoriented june bug had flown into Mary Andrea's right ear and interrupted for several awkward moments Portia's famous peroration on the quality of mercy.)

Having digested, and sagely commented upon, each item in the "People" column, Mary Andrea Finley Krome then turned to the weightier pages of *The Missoulian.* The headline that caught her attention appeared on page three of the front section: NEWS REPORTER BELIEVED DEAD IN MYSTERY BLAZE. It wasn't the slain-journalist angle that grabbed Mary Andrea so much as the phrase "mystery blaze," because Mary Andrea adored a good mystery. The sight of her estranged husband's name in the second paragraph was a complete shock. The newspaper drifted from Mary Andrea's fingertips, and she emitted an oscillating groan that was mistaken by fellow coffee drinkers for a New Age meditative technique.

"Julie, you OK?" asked Lorie, or Loretta.

"Not really," Mary Andrea rasped.

"What is it?"

Mary Andrea pressed her knuckles to her eyes and felt genuine tears.

"You need a doctor?" asked her new friend.

"No," said Mary Andrea. "A travel agent."

. . .

Joan and Roddy got a copy of *The Register* at the Grab N'Go and brought it to Sinclair at the shrine. He refused to read it.

"You're mentioned by name," Joan beseeched, holding up the newspaper for him to see, "as Tom Krome's boss."

Roddy added: "It explains how you're out of town and not available for comment."

"Nyyah nimmy doo-dey!" was Sinclair's response.

The yammering sent a sinusoidal murmur through the Christian tourists gathering along the narrow moat. Some knelt, some stood beneath umbrellas, some perched on folding chairs and Igloo coolers. Sinclair himself lay prone at the feet of the fiberglass Madonna.

Joan was so concerned about her brother's behavior that she considered notifying their parents. She'd read about religious fanatics who fondled snakes, but a turtle fixation seemed borderline deviant. Roddy said he hadn't heard of it either. "But personally," he added, "I'm damn glad it's cooters and not diamondbacks. Otherwise we'd be coffin-shopping."

Sinclair had cloaked himself toga-style in a pale bedsheet, upon which a confetti of fresh lettuce was sprinkled. With surprising swiftness the apostolic turtles scrambled from their sunning stones to ascend the gleaming buffet. Zestfully they traversed Sinclair from head to toe, while he cooed and blinked placidly at the passing clouds. Cameras clicked and video cameras whirred.

Trish and Demencio monitored the visitation from the living room window. She said, "He's really something. You gotta admit."

"Yeah. A fruit basket."

"But aren't you glad we let him stay?"

Demencio said, "A buck's a buck."

"He must've snapped. Stripped a gear."

"Maybe so." Demencio was distracted by a sighting of Dominick Amador, clumping unscrupulously among the pilgrims.

"Sonofabitch. He got him some crutches!"

Trish said, "You know why?"

"I can sure guess."

"Yeah, he finally got his feet drilled. I heard he paid the boy at the muffler shop, like, thirty bucks."

"Psycho," said Demencio.

Then Dominick Amador spotted him in the window and timorously waved a Crisco-filled mitten. Demencio did not return the greeting.

Trish said, "You want me to chase him off?"

Demencio folded his arms. "Now what—who the hell's that?" He pointed at a slender person in a hooded white robe. The person carried a clipboard and moved with clerical efficiency from one tourist to the next.

"The lady from Sebring Street," Trish explained, "the one with the Road-Stain Jesus.

She's working on a petition to the highway department."

"Like hell. She's workin' on my customers!"

"No, honey, the state wants to pave over her shrine—"

"Is that my problem? I got a business going here."

"All right," Trish said, and went outside to have a word with the woman. Demencio had always been leery of his competition—he liked to stay ahead of the pack. It bothered him when Dominick or the others came snooping. Trish understood. The miracle racket was no picnic.

And the queer histrionics of the visiting newspaperman had made Demencio edgier than usual. He could cope with hydraulic malfunctions in a weeping statue; a flesh-and-blood lunatic was something else. For the time being, the recumbent and incoherent Sinclair was drawing plenty of customers. But what if he freaked out? What if his marble-mouthed gibberish turned to violent rant?

Demencio fretted that he might lose control of his shrine. He sat down heavily and contemplated the aquarium, where the unpainted baby turtles eagerly awaited breakfast. JoLayne Lucks had phoned to check on the smelly little buggers, and Demencio reported that all forty-five were healthy and fit. He hadn't told her about the apostle scam. JoLayne had promised she'd be home in a few days to collect her "precious babies."

They're precious to me, too, thought Demencio. I've got to milk 'em for all they're worth.

When Trish returned he said: "Let's do the rest."

"What?"

"*Them.*" He nodded at the tank.

"How come?"

"More painted cooters, more money. Think of how happy Mister Born Again'll be." Demencio cut a glance toward the front window. "Crazy dork can bury himself under the damn things."

Trish said, "But, honey, there's only twelve apostles."

"Who says it's gotta be just apostles? Go find that Bible. All we need is thirty-three more saint types. Most anybody'll do—New Testament, Old Testament."

How could Trish say no? Her husband's instincts on such matters were invariably sound. As she gathered the brushes and paint bottles, she showed Demencio the front page of *The Register,* which had been given to her by Joan and Roddy. "Isn't that the fella went to Miami with JoLayne?"

"Yeah, only he ain't dead." With a forefinger, Demencio derisively flicked the newspaper. "When she called up this morning, this Tom guy was with her. Some phone booth down in the Keys."

"The Keys!"

"Yeah, but don't go tellin' the turtle boy. Not yet."

"I suppose you're right," Trish said.

"He finds out his man's still alive, he might quit prayin'. We don't want that."

"No."

"Or he might stop with them angel voices."

"Tongues. Speaking in tongues," Trish corrected.

"Whatever. I won't lie," Demencio said. "That crazy dork is good for business."

"I won't say a thing. Look here, he's mentioned in the same article."

Demencio skimmed the first few paragraphs while he struggled to uncap a bottle of thinner. "You see this? 'Assistant Deputy Managing Editor of Features and Style.' Hell kinda job is *that*? Ha, no wonder he's rolling in the mud."

Trish handed him a bouquet of paintbrushes. "What do you think about Holy Cooter T-shirts? And maybe key chains."

Her husband looked up. "Yeah," he said, with the first smile of the day.

When Tom Krome got his turn on the pay phone, he called his parents on Long Island to tell them not to believe what they saw in the papers.

"I'm alive."

"As opposed to what?" his father asked.

Newsday had run the story somewhere other

than the sports section, so Krome's old man had missed it.

Tom gave a sketchy explanation of the arson, instructed his folks on fielding future media inquiries, then called Katie. He was genuinely touched to hear she'd been crying.

"You should see the front page, Tommy!"

"Well, it's wrong. I'm fine."

"Thank God," Katie sniffled. "Arthur also insists you're dead. He even bought me a diamond solitaire."

"For the funeral?"

"He thinks I think he had something to do with killing you—which I *did* think, until now."

Krome said, "I'm assuming he's the one who burned down my house."

"Not personally."

"You know what I mean. The dead body in the kitchen must have been his law clerk, faithful but careless."

"Champ Powell. I guess so," Katie said. "Tom, what'm I going to do? I can't stand the sight of Arthur but I honestly don't believe he meant for anyone to get hurt. . . ."

"Pack a bag and go to your mother's."

"And the diamond *is* beautiful. God knows what it cost. So, see, there's a part of him that wants to be true—"

"Katie, I gotta go. Please don't tell anyone you

spoke with me, OK? Keep it a secret for now, it's important."

"I'm so glad you're all right. I prayed so hard."

"Don't stop now," Tom Krome said.

It was a bright and breezy fall morning. The sky was cloudless and full of gulls and terns. The marina stirred but didn't bustle, typical of the dead season between Thanksgiving and New Year's, when the tourists were still up North. For the locals it was a glorious and special time, despite the wane of revenues. Many charter captains didn't even bother to go down to the docks, the chance of walk-ons was so remote.

JoLayne Lucks had dozed off in the car. Krome touched her arm and she opened her eyes. Her mouth was sour, her throat scratchy.

"Yekkk," she said, yawning.

Krome handed her a cup of coffee. "Long night."

"Where are our boys?"

"Still in the truck."

JoLayne said, "What d'you think—they meeting somebody?"

"I don't know. They've been up and down, scoping out the boats."

Squinting at the windshield's glare, JoLayne groped for her sunglasses. She saw the red Dodge pickup at the opposite end of the marina, parked by the front door of the tackle shop.

"Again with the wheelchair zone?"

"Yep."

"Assholes."

They'd decided that the man driving the truck must be Bodean Gazzer, because that was the name on the registration, according to Tom's source at the highway patrol. Bullet holes notwithstanding, the pristine condition of the vehicle suggested an owner who would not casually loan it to fleeing felons. Tom and JoLayne still had no name for Gazzer's partner, the one with the ponytail and the bad eye.

And now a new mystery: a third man, who'd been abruptly put out along the road in the pitch dark of the night—JoLayne and Tom watching from the parking lot of a video store, where they'd pulled over to wait. Something in the bearing of the third man had looked familiar to JoLayne, but in the blue-gray darkness his facial features were indiscernible. The headlights of a passing car had revealed a chubby figure with a disconsolate trudge. Also: An Australian bush hat.

There was no sign of him in the morning, at the marina. Krome didn't know what to make of it.

JoLayne asked if he'd phoned his folks.

"They didn't even know I was dead. Now they're really confused," Krome said. "Whose turn on the radio?"

"Mine." She reached for the dial.

During the long hours in the car, the two of them had encountered a potentially serious divergence of musical tastes. Tom believed that driving in South Florida required constant hard-rock accompaniment, while JoLayne favored songs that were breezy and soothing to the nerves. In the interest of fairness, they'd agreed to alternate control of the radio. If she lucked into a Sade, he got a Tom Petty. If he got the Kinks, she got an Annie Lennox. And so on. Occasionally they found common ground. Van Morrison. Dire Straits. "The Girl with the Faraway Eyes," which they sang together as they rode through Florida City. There were even a few mutual abominations (a Paul McCartney–Michael Jackson duet, for instance) that propelled them to lunge simultaneously for the tuning button.

"Here's what I noticed," said JoLayne, adjusting the volume.

"Who's that?" Krome demanded.

"Céline Dion."

"Geez, it's Saturday morning. Have some mercy."

"You'll get your turn." JoLayne wore a shrewd, schoolteacher smile. "Now, Tom, here's what I noticed: You don't like many black musical artists."

"Oh, bullshit." He was truly stung.

"Name one."

"Marvin Gaye, Jimi Hendrix—"

"A *live* one."

"B.B. King, Al Green, Billy Preston. The Hootie guy, what's his name—"

"You're pushing it," JoLayne said.

"Prince!"

"Oh, come on."

Krome said, "Damn right. 'Little Red Corvette.' "

"I guess it's possible."

"Christ, what if I said something like that to you?"

"You're right," said JoLayne. "I take it all back."

" 'A live one.' Gimme a break."

She eyed him over the rims of her peach-tinted shades. "You're pretty touchy about this stuff, aren't you? I suppose that's the white man's burden. At least the liberal white man."

"Who said I was liberal."

"You're cute when you're on the defensive. Want the rest of my coffee? I gotta pee."

"Not now," Tom Krome said. "Take off your hat and duck."

The red pickup was rolling toward them, in reverse. The driver backed up to a slip where a twenty-foot boat was tied. It had twin outboards, a flecked blue-and-gray finish and a folding Bimini top. From the tackle shop you couldn't have seen it, moored between a towering Hatteras and a boxy houseboat.

Peering over the dashboard, Krome watched a tall, unshaven passenger get out of the truck: the ponytailed man. He carried a bottle of beer and some tools—a screwdriver, a wire cutter, a socket wrench. The man climbed somewhat unsteadily into the boat and disappeared behind the steering console.

"What's going on?" JoLayne, inching up in the seat.

Krome told her to stay down. He saw a puff of blue smoke, then heard the outboards start. The ponytailed man stood up and signaled laconically at the driver of the pickup truck. Then the ponytailed man untied the lines and with both hands pushed the boat away from the pilings.

"They're stealing it," Krome reported.

JoLayne said: "My neck hurts. May I sit up?"

"In a second."

Barely fifty yards from the dock, the ponytailed man shoved forward the throttle of the stolen boat. Momentarily the bow rose upward like a gaily striped missile, then leveled off under a collar of foam as the boat took out across the shallows of Florida Bay. At the same instant, and with a sudden yelp of rubber, the red pickup truck shot toward the marina exit.

"Now?" asked JoLayne.

"All clear," Krome told her.

She rose, glancing first at the departing truck and then at the receding gray speck on the water. "All right, smart guy. Which one's got my ticket?"

"Beats me," Krome said.

 It was Shiner's first kidnapping, and despite a shaky start it came off pretty well.

He had hitchhiked to the Grove, where he'd fallen asleep in Peacock Park. In midafternoon he'd awakened and wandered down Grand Avenue to buy a handgun. His street-corner inquiries had been so poorly received that he'd been chased from the neighborhood by a group of black and Hispanic teenagers. Naturally he'd lost his bush hat and the golf spikes, which were ill-suited for a footrace.

Armed only with a stubby Phillips-head screwdriver he'd found beneath a banyan tree, Shiner arrived at Hooters shortly before five o'clock. Remembering Chub's instructions, he struck up a conversation with the bartender, who was glad to point out Amber among the servers. Shiner scoped her out—hot-looking, like Chub had said, but as a rule most waitresses were hot-looking to Shiner. And while Chub had made a great point of detailing Amber's uncanny resemblance to Kim Basinger, the information was useless to Shiner. He didn't know who Kim Basinger was. While preparing for the crime, Shiner became apprehensive over the possibility of snatching the wrong girl. What if Hooters had more than one Amber? Chub would shoot him dead, that's what.

Hours later, Shiner was crouched behind a hedgerow when the waitress identified by the bartender left work. She slipped behind the wheel of a giant Ford sedan, which momentarily rattled Shiner (who'd been expecting a sports car—in his mind, all hot-looking babes belonged in sports cars). He recovered his composure, flung himself in the passenger side and placed the tip of the screwdriver against Amber's soft and flawless neck.

"Whoa," she said.

Not a scream, but a *whoa*.

"You Amber?"

She nodded carefully.

"The one looks like the actor—Kim something?"

Amber said, "You're the second guy this week who's told me that."

Shiner was flooded with relief. "All right. Now drive."

"That a knife?"

Shiner pulled the screwdriver away from Amber's neck. The grooved tip left a small, stellate impression in her skin; Shiner could see it in the green glow of the dashboard.

Hastily he slipped the tool into his pocket. "Yeah, it's a knife. I got a damn gun, too."

"I believe you," Amber said.

After a few wrong turns, he got her pointed

south. She didn't ask where they were going, but
Shiner was ready if she did. *Base camp,* would
be his answer. Base camp of the White Clarion
Aryans! That'd give her something to think about.

"This your car?" he asked.

"My dad gave it to me. Runs great," Amber
said.

Not the least bit shy. That's cool, Shiner
thought.

"My boyfriend has a Miata," she added. "Well,
had a Miata. Anyhow, I like this better. More
legroom—I've got super-long legs."

Shiner felt his cheeks flush. Up close, Amber
was very beautiful. Whenever headlights passed in
the other direction, he could see glimmers of gold
in her long eyelashes. Plus she smelled absolutely
fantastic for someone who worked with chicken
wings and burgers, not to mention the onions.
Shiner believed Amber smelled about a thousand
times sweeter than the baskets of orange blossoms
his mother would take to the Road-Stain Jesus.
True, they were week-old orange blossoms (purchased in bulk from a turnpike gift shop) but still
they held a fragrance.

Amber said, "What happened to your head?"
She was talking about the crankcase scar.

"I got hurt."

"Car accident?"

"Sort of." Shiner was surprised she noticed it,

since she'd barely taken her eyes off the road since he'd hopped in.

"How about buckling your seat belt," she said.

"No way." Shiner remembered what Bodean Gazzer had said about seat belts being part of the government's secret plot to "neutralize the citizenry." If you're wearing seat belts, Bode had explained, it'll be harder to jump out of the car and escape, once the NATO helicopters start landing on the highways. That's the whole reason they made the seat-belt law, Bode had said, to make sure millions of Americans would be strapped down and helpless when the global attack was launched. As intriguing as Bode's explanation was, Shiner decided the information was too sensitive to share with Amber.

"What's that on your arm?" she asked. She turned on the dome light for a better look at Shiner's tattoo.

"It's a eagle," he said, self-consciously.

"I meant the *W.R.B.* Is that for the White Rebel Brotherhood?"

Shiner said, "Man, it's a long story."

"I saw 'em in concert. They were killer."

"Yeah?"

"The best is 'Nut-Cutting Bitch.' Ever heard it? You like hip-hop?"

"Metal." Shiner gave his decorated biceps a subtle flex; it wasn't often he had a pretty girl's undivided attention.

She said, "Then what's the deal with your
W.R.B.? They are so *not* heavy metal."

Shiner told Amber there'd been a mix-up on his
tattoo. He was pleased to hear her say she could
fix it.

"But only if you let me go," she added.

"No way."

"My best friend worked in a tattoo parlor for
two summers. I hung out there, God, for hours. It's
not as hard as it looks."

Shiner's lips drew tight. Ruefully he said: "I
can't let you free. Not right away."

"Oh." Amber turned off the dome light. For a
long time she didn't speak to him. When two tank-
topped frat boys in a Beemer convertible nearly
sideswiped them, she said: "Fuckheads." But it
was practically a whisper, not intended as conversation. Soon Shiner grew nervous again. He'd
been doing fine while Amber was chatty, but now
his feet were tapping with the jitters. Plus he felt
like a dolt. He felt like he'd blown something.

Finally she said, "You're going to rape me,
aren't you?"

"No way."

"Don't lie. It's better if I know."

"I ain't lyin'!"

"Then what is all this?" Both hands were fixed
on the wheel. Her thin arms were straight and stiff.
"What's going on?"

Shiner said, "It's a favor for a friend."

"I get it. Then *he's* going to rape me."

"Over my dead body!" Shiner was startled by his own vehemence.

It drew a hopeful glance from Amber. "You mean it?"

"Damn straight I do."

"Thanks," she said, turning her attention back to the traffic. "You don't really have a gun, do you?"

"Naw."

"So, what's your name?" Amber asked.

Both of Arthur Battenkill's secretaries knew something was wrong, because he'd stopped pestering them for sex. The women didn't complain; they much preferred typing and filing. The judge's deportment in bed was no different from that in the office—arrogant and abrupt.

Dana and Willow often discussed their respective intimacies with Arthur Battenkill, and this was done with no trace of possessiveness or jealousy. Rather, the conversations served as a source of mutual support—the man was a burden they shared.

Willow reported: "He didn't ask me to stay after work."

"Me, neither," said Dana. "That's two days in a row!"

"What do you think?" Willow said.

"He's upset about Champ quitting."

"Could be."

"If that's what really happened," Dana added, lifting an eyebrow.

Both secretaries were puzzled by the sudden departure of the law clerk, Champ Powell. At first Arthur Battenkill had said he'd gone home for a family emergency. Then the judge had said no, that was merely a cover story. Actually, Champ had been called back to the Gadsden County sheriff's department for a special undercover operation. The project was so secret and dangerous that even his family wasn't told.

Which explained, the judge had said, why Champ's mother kept calling the office, looking for him.

Dana and Willow remained unconvinced. "He didn't seem like the undercover type," Dana remarked. "B'sides, he really loved his job here."

"Plus he idolized the judge," Willow said.

"That he did."

Champ Powell's devotion was almost an unnatural thing, both women agreed. The clerk was so enamored of Arthur Battenkill that initially the secretaries suspected he was gay. In fact they'd privately discussed the possibility of Champ's seducing the judge, which wouldn't have bothered them one bit. Anything to distract the man.

But it hadn't yet happened, at least to their knowledge.

Said Dana: "Whatever's got into Art, let's just leave it be."

"Amen," Willow said.

"Sit back and enjoy the peace."

"Right."

"Hey. Maybe he's found God."

Willow laughed so hard that Diet Pepsi jetted out of her nostrils. Naturally that's when the judge walked in. As Willow grabbled for a box of Kleenex, Arthur Battenkill said, "How elegant."

"Sorry."

"It's like having Princess Grace answering the phones."

With that, the judge disappeared into his chambers, closing the door. Willow was somewhat battered by his first-thing-in-the-morning sarcasm, so Dana took him coffee.

She told the judge he didn't look well.

"It's Saturday," he grumbled. The chief judge had been on Arthur Battenkill's ass about clearing the case backlog, so he'd been putting in hours on weekends.

"You haven't slept." Dana, affecting a motherly tone.

"Pollens. Mold spores." Arthur Battenkill took a sip of coffee. "I sleep fine."

It was the scene at breakfast that had disturbed him—Katie gobbling down four huge buttermilk flapjacks and a bagel, a clear signal she was no longer grieving. Clearing the dishes, she'd exhibited a perkiness that could have at its root only one explanation: She'd come to believe her precious Tommy wasn't dead.

Reluctantly the judge had already reached the same conclusion. The strongest evidence was the uncharacteristic lack of communication from Champ Powell, who by now should have called to seek Arthur Battenkill's praise and gratitude for the arson. Nearly as ominous: Champ's Harley-Davidson motorcycle had been found and towed from a Blockbuster parking lot three blocks from Tom Krome's house. The judge was certain Champ never would have abandoned the bike were he still alive.

The unexpected upswing of Katie's mood had clinched it for Arthur Battenkill. Picking indifferently at his pancakes, he'd recalled hearing the telephone ring while he was in the shower—probably Krome, calling to tell Katie not to worry. The mannerly motherfucker.

Now Dana, arms folded: "You've got that emergency hearing in ten minutes. Would you like me to press your robe?"

"No. Who is it?"

"Mrs. Bensinger."

"God. Let me guess."

Dana dropped her voice. "Another alimony problem."

Arthur Battenkill said, "I hate those horrible people. Thank heaven they never had children."

"Not so loud. She's out in the hall."

"Yeah?" The judge cupped his hands to his mouth: "Greedy freeloading twat!"

Dana looked at him blankly.

The judge said, "Her husband's a thieving shit, too."

"Yes, he is."

"By the way, I've decided to take some time off. I suppose you and Willow will survive without me. I get that impression."

Dana fixed her gaze safely on the coffeepot. "How long will you be gone?"

"I can't say. Mrs. Battenkill and I are going away together." The judge thumbed his appointment book. "See if Judge Beckman will cover for me starting late next week. Can you do that?"

"Certainly."

"And, Dana, this is supposed to be a surprise for my wife, so don't blow it."

Willow buzzed on the speakerphone to report that Mr. Bensinger had arrived and that the atmosphere in the hallway was growing tense.

"Fuck 'em." Arthur Battenkill snorted. "I hope they slaughter each other with blunt objects. Save the taxpayers a few bucks. Dana, isn't it Judge Tigert over in Probate who's got the bungalow in Exuma?"

"The Abacos."

"Whatever. See if it's available."

The notion of the judge taking his wife on a romantic trip to the Bahamas was stupefying. Obviously the man was suffering a breakdown. Dana could hardly wait to share the gossip with Willow.

As she was leaving his chambers, Arthur Battenkill called out: "Dana, darling, you're doing a superb job of concealing your amusement."

"What on earth are you talking about."

"Don't pretend to know everything about me. Don't pretend to have me figured out. I *do* have feelings for Mrs. Battenkill."

"Oh, I believe you," Dana said. "By the way, Art, how'd she like the new necklace?"

The judge's smug expression dissolved. "Send in the goddamn Bensingers," he said.

JoLayne Lucks hadn't been to the Keys since she was a small girl. She was amazed at how much had changed, the homey and congenial tackiness supplanted by franchise fast-food joints, strip malls and high-rise resorts. To take her mind off the riffraff, JoLayne recited for Tom Krome a roster of local birds, resident and migratory: ospreys, snowy egrets, white herons, blue herons, kingfishers, flycatchers, cardinals, grackles, robins, red-tailed hawks, white-crowned pigeons, flickers, roseate spoonbills . . .

"Once there were even flamingos," she informed him. "Guess what happened to them."

Krome didn't respond. He was watching

Bodean James Gazzer strip and clean a large semi-automatic rifle. Even from a distance of a hundred yards, the barrel glinted ominously in the noon sun.

"Tom, you don't even care."

"I like flamingos," he said, "but what we have here is a rare green-breasted shithead. Broad daylight, he's playing with guns."

"Yes, I can see."

Tom had rejected her latest plan, which involved ambushing Bodean Gazzer alone, jamming her twelve-gauge into his groin and demanding under threat of emasculation that he return the stolen lottery ticket.

Not here, Krome had told her. Not yet.

They were parked on a bleached strip of limestone fill, along a rim of lush mangroves. Not far away was a gravel boat ramp, blocked at the moment by Bodean Gazzer's red pickup. The driver's door was open and he stood in full view; neck-to-knees camouflage, cowboy boots, mirrored sunglasses. He had a chamois cloth spread on the hood, the assault rifle in pieces before him.

"Steel balls. I give him that," Krome said.

"No, he's just a fool. A damn fool."

JoLayne feared a cop would drive by and see what Bodean Gazzer was doing. Once the idiot got himself arrested, the chase would be over. The thing would boil down to JoLayne's word against the redneck's, and he'd never produce the ticket.

A small black bird landed in the trees and began to sing. Krome said, "OK, what's that one?"

"Redwing," JoLayne answered stiffly.

"They endangered?"

"Not yet. Don't you find it obscene—their presence in a place like this? They're like . . . *litter.*" She was talking about the two robbers. "They don't deserve this—to feel the sun on their necks and breathe this fine air. It's completely wasted on men like that."

Krome rolled down the car window and took in the cool salt breeze. In a sleepy voice he said, "I could get used to this. Maybe after Alaska."

JoLayne, thinking: How can he act so relaxed? She could no longer distract herself with the island wildlife, so unnerving was the spectacle of Bodean Gazzer toiling ritually at his gun. She couldn't shake the memory of that awful scene in her house—not just the man's punches and kicking, but his voice:

Hey, genius, she can't talk with a gun in her mouth.

Talking to his filthy, ponytailed friend:

You wanna make a impression? Look—here.

Snatching one of the baby turtles from the glass tank, putting it on the wooden floor, coaxing his ponytailed friend to shoot it. That's what Bodean Gazzer had done.

Yet here he was, fit and free in the Florida sunshine. With a $14 million Lotto ticket hidden somewhere, possibly inside a rubber.

JoLayne said to Tom: "I can't just sit here doing nothing."

"You're absolutely right. You should drive to the grocery." Krome took out his wallet. "Then you should stop at one of those motels and rent a boat. I'll give you some money."

JoLayne said she had a better idea. "I'll stay here and keep an eye on the archpatriot. *You* go get the boat."

"Too risky."

"I can handle myself," she insisted.

"JoLayne, there's no doubt in my mind. I was talking about *me*. Dead persons should always keep a low profile—my face has been in *The Herald,* probably even on TV."

She said, "It was a shitty picture, Tom. Nobody'll recognize you."

"I can't take that chance."

"You looked like Pat Sajak on NyQuil."

"The answer is no."

Tom didn't trust her, of course. Didn't trust her not to mess with the redneck. "This is ridiculous," she complained. "I've never driven a boat."

"And I've never fired a shotgun," Krome said, "so we have something new to learn from each other. Just what every romance needs."

"Please."

"Speaking of which." He got out, popped the trunk and removed the Remington. "Just in case."

JoLayne said, "Bad news, Rambo. The shells are in my purse."

"Just as well," he said. "I figure we've got another forty-five minutes, maybe an hour. Ice is priority one. Get as much ice and fresh water as you can carry."

"Forty-five minutes until what?"

"Until our sailor with the ponytail gets here," Krome said.

"Is that so? When were you planning to clue me in?"

"When I was sure."

JoLayne Lucks was determined to appear skeptical. "You think they're going by sea."

"Yup."

"Where?"

"No idea. That's why we need a boat of our own. And a chart would be good, too."

Listen to him, thought JoLayne. Mr. Take-Charge.

She considered holding her ground, telling him off. Then she changed her mind. It did look like a grand day to be out on the bay, especially if the alternative was six more hours in a cramped Honda.

"How big a boat?" JoLayne asked.

Chub was almost at ease on the water. One of the few bearable memories of his childhood was the family ski boat, which the Gillespies had used on weekend outings to Lake Rabun. The young Onus's pudginess had prevented him from developing into a first-rate water-skier, but he'd loved steering the boat.

The thrill returned to him now, at the helm of the *Reel Luv,* which he had hot-wired in the name of the White Clarion Aryans. With its twin Merc 90s, the stolen twenty-footer was much peppier than the boat Chub had captained as a boy. That was fine; he could handle the extra speed. What he couldn't cope with was the irregular layout of Florida Bay, with its shifting hues, snaking channels and treacherous flats. It was nothing like Lake Rabun, which was deep and well-defined and relatively free of immovable obstacles such as mangrove islands. Chub's somewhat rusty navigational skills were further tested by the impaired vision of his wounded left eye (covered by a new rubber patch, purchased for two dollars at an Amoco station) and by his relatively high blood alcohol.

It was only a matter of minutes before he beached the boat. The broad tidal bank was highly visible because of its brown color, which contrasted boldly with the azure and indigo of the deep channels. Also in evidence was a phalanx of wading birds, whose long-legged presence should have signaled the dramatic change of water depth. Chub didn't notice.

The grounding was drawn-out and panoramic,

the big outboards roaring and throwing great gey-
sers of cocoa-colored silt. Chub was hurled hard
against the console, knocking the wind out of him.
The egrets and herons took flight in unison, wheeling once over the noisy scene before stringing out
westbound in the porcelain morning sky. When
the spewing engines finally died, the *Reel Luv* was
at rest in approximately seven inches of water. The
hull drew exactly eight.

As soon as Chub regained his breath, he got up
and saw there was but one way off the shallows:
Get out and push. Swearing bitterly, he pulled off
his shoes and slipped overboard. Immediately he
sank to his nuts in the clammy marl. With great
thrashing he managed to position himself at the
stern and lean his weight against the transom.

The boat actually moved. Not much, but Chub
felt somewhat encouraged.

Every sloppy inch of progress was muscle-
sapping, like trying to march in wet cement. The
mud sucked at Chub's legs, and his bare skin stung
from the sea lice. Fastening to his arms and belly
were tiny purple leeches, no larger than rice ker-
nels, which he swatted away savagely. Additional
concern was generated by an unfamiliar tingle in
his crotch, and it occurred to Chub that some
exotic parasite might have entered his body by
swimming into the hole of his pecker. No other
millionaire in the entire world, he thought ran-
corously, had these kinds of problems. He was

thankful Amber wasn't there to witness the degrading scene.

Finally the stolen boat came free of the grassy bank. Chub boosted himself aboard and manically stripped off his pants to attend to the stinging.

That's when he remembered it.

The ticket.

"Jesus!" he cried hoarsely. "Jesus Willy Christ!"

His right thigh was bare and dripping wet. The jumbo Band-Aid had fallen off. The Lotto ticket was gone.

Chub uttered an inhuman croak and sorrowfully toppled back into the water.

18 Bodean Gazzer was obsessed with the specter of the Black Tide. He could recall no mention of the group in the stacks of white-supremacist pamphlets he'd collected.

Black Panthers, MOVE, Nation of Islam, NAACP—Bode had read extensively about them. But nothing called the Black Tide.

Whoever they were, they'd been through his apartment. Negroes, almost certainly! Bode thought he knew why he'd been singled out: They'd learned about the White Clarion Aryans.

But how? he asked himself. The WCA had been

together scarcely one week—he hadn't even composed a manifesto yet. His pulse fluttered as he mulled the only two possible explanations: Either the Negro force possessed a sophisticated intelligence-gathering apparatus, or there was a serious leak within the WCA. Bode Gazzer regarded the latter as almost inconceivable.

Instead he would proceed on the assumption that the Black Tide was exceptionally cunning and resourceful, probably connected to a government agency. He would also presume that no matter where the White Clarion Aryans took up hiding, the devious Negroes would eventually track them down.

That's all right, Bode thought. He'd have his militia ready when the time came.

Meanwhile, where was that fucking Chub with the boat?

Panic nibbled at Bode Gazzer's gut. The idea of deserting his trigger-happy partner began to make some sense. Bode had, after all, fourteen million bucks tucked in a condom. Once he cashed the lottery ticket, he could go anywhere, do anything— build himself a fortress in Idaho, with the mother of all hot tubs!

Lately Bode had been thinking a lot about Idaho, lousy winters and all. From what he'd heard, the mountains and forests were full of straight-thinking white Christians. Recruiting for the WCA would be so much easier in a place like

that. Bode was thoroughly fed up with Miami—
everywhere you turned were goddamn foreigners.
And when you finally came across a real English-
speaking white person, there was a better than
even chance he'd turn out to be a Jew or some ul-
traliberal screamer. Bode was sick and tired of
walking on eggshells, whispering his true righteous beliefs instead of declaring them loud and
proud in public. In Miami you always had to be so
damn careful—God forbid you accidentally insulted somebody, because they'd get right in your
face. And not just the Cubans, either.

Bodean Gazzer felt sure the minorities out West
were more docile and easily intimidated. He decided it might be a good move, providing he could
adjust to the cold weather. Even in summer camos,
Bode Gazzer thought he could fit right in.

As for Chub, he probably wouldn't go over big
in Idaho. He'd probably spook even decent white
people away from the Aryan cause. No, Bode
thought, Chub belonged in the South.

And it wasn't as if Bode would be leaving the
man high and dry. Chub still held the other Lotto
ticket, the one they'd taken off the Negro woman
in Grange. Hell, he'd be rich enough to start his
own militia if he wanted. Be his own colonel.

Bode checked his wristwatch. If he left now, he
could make Tallahassee before midnight. This
time tomorrow, he'd have his first Lotto check.

Unless they got to him first—the vicious bastards who'd ransacked his apartment.

Ironically, that's when a crazy stoner like Chub
was most useful—in the face of violence. He didn't
spook easily, and he'd do just about anything you
told him. He'd be damn handy to have around if
shooting started. It was something to consider,
something to mark on the positive side of the
Chub ledger. An argument could be made for
keeping the man nearby.

Pacing the boat ramp, Bode sweated through his
Timber Ghost jumpsuit. The weekend road traffic
zipped past, Bode feeling the curious eyes of the
travelers on his neck—not all were tourists and
fishermen, he felt certain. Undoubtedly the Black
Tide enlisted many watchers, and they'd be scouting for a red Dodge Ram pickup with a FUHRMAN
FOR PRESIDENT sticker (which Bode Gazzer had
tried unsuccessfully to scrape off the bumper with
a penknife).

That's when he'd decided to haul out the AR-15.
Let the fuckers see what they're up against.

He laid a chamois across the hood of the truck
and disassembled the semiautomatic exactly as
Chub had taught him. He hoped the Black Tide
was catching all this. He hoped they'd come to the
conclusion he was mentally deranged, displaying
an assault rifle in broad daylight along a U.S. government highway.

When it was time to put the AR-15 back together, Bodean Gazzer ran into difficulty. Some parts fit together, some didn't. He wondered if he'd accidentally misplaced a screw or two. The pieces of the gun were slick and oily, and Bode's fingers were moist with perspiration. He began dropping little things in the gravel.

In exasperation, he thought: *How hard can this be? Chub can do it when he's drunk!*

After half an hour, Bode angrily gave up. He folded the chamois cloth around the loose components of the rifle and set the bundle in the bed of the pickup truck. He tried to act nonchalant, for the benefit of the spying Negroes.

He got behind the wheel and cranked the AC up full blast. He scanned the bottle-green water in all directions. A low-riding fishing skiff crossed his view. So did a pretty girl, cutting angles on a sailboard. Then came two hairy fat guys on Jet Skis, jumping each other's wakes.

But there was no sign of Chub in the stolen boat. Sourly Bode thought: Maybe the dickhead's not coming. Maybe he's ditching *me.*

Five more minutes, he told himself. Then I'm gone.

On the highway, cars streamed southbound as if loaded on a conveyor belt. Staring at them made Bode drowsy. He'd been up for almost two days and in truth was physically incapable of driving to Cutler Ridge, much less Tallahassee. He would've loved to take a nap, but that would be suicide. That's when they'd make their move—the Black Tide, whatever and whoever it was.

When Bode closed his eyes, a question popped belatedly into his brain: What the hell do they want?

He was not too exhausted to figure it out. They seemed to know everything, didn't they? Who he was, where he lived. They knew about the White Clarion Aryans, too.

So surely they also knew about one, if not both, of the lottery tickets. That's what the greedy bastards had been searching for inside his apartment!

Bodean Gazzer was snapped alert by the icy realization that the only stroke of good fortune he'd ever experienced was in danger of being ripped from his grasp. Alone on the road, with the AR-15 in pieces, he was a sitting duck.

Impulsively Bode dug into his pants for his wallet, took out the Trojan packet, peeked inside. The Lotto coupon was safe. He put it away. He didn't need to look at his watch to know five minutes was up. Maybe Chub had bailed. Or got busted by the marine patrol. Or found some fiberglass resin to sniff, fell off the boat and drowned.

Adiós, muchacho.

Bode's heart was hammering like a rabbit's. Recklessly he gunned the truck across Highway One and fishtailed into the northbound lane. With trembling fingers he adjusted the rearview mirror, something he should've done the night before. With only a Molson truck on his bumper, Bode was breathing easier by the time he reached Whale Harbor. Crossing the bridge, he glanced along a broad tree-lined channel to the west. As if seized by a cramp, his foot sprang off the accelerator.

A blue-and-gray speedboat was snaking down the waterway. The driver's ponytail flapped like a gray rag in the breeze.

"Aw, hell," Bodean Gazzer said. He made a noisy U-turn at the Holiday Isle charter docks and hauled ass back to the ramp.

The grocery store was a treat; everyone friendly, helpful. Not so at the motel marina. The man in charge of the boats—old fart, pinched gray face with a yellow three-day stubble—was clumsy with edginess and indecision. Clearly he'd never done business with a solitary black woman, and the prospect had afflicted him with the yips.

"Is there a problem?" JoLayne Lucks inquired, knowing full well there was. She drummed her daunting fingernails on the cracked countertop.

The dock guy coughed. "I'll need your driver's license."

"Fine."

"And a cash deposit." More coughing.

"Certainly."

The dock guy gnawed his lower lip. "You done

this before? Mebbe you wanna try a water bike
'stead."

"Lord, no." JoLayne laughed. She spotted a calico cat curled beside the soda cooler. She scooped
it off the floor and began stroking its chin. "Poor
lil princess got ear mites, don't ya?" Then, addressing the dock guy: "Chlorhexidine drops. Any
veterinarian carries them."

The old man fumbled his pen. "Ma'am, is the
boat fer fishin' or divin' or what azackly? How fur
you gone take it?"

JoLayne said, "I was thinking Borneo."

"Now, don't you get huffy. It's jest the boss
owner makes me do all this shit paperwork."

"I understand." Tacked to a wall of the shack
was a marine chart of Florida Bay. JoLayne sur-
reptitiously scanned it and said: "Cotton Key.
That's as far as I'm going."

The dock guy looked disappointed as he wrote
it down on the rental form. "They's a grouper hole
out there. I guess the whole damn world knows."

JoLayne said, "Well, they won't hear it from
me." The cat jumped from her arms. She opened
her purse. "How about a tide table," she asked,
"and one of those maps?"

The dock guy seemed pleasantly surprised by
the request, as if most yahoo tourists never
thought to ask. JoLayne could see his estimation
of her rise meteorically. In his scarlet-rimmed eyes
appeared a glimmer of hope that the motel's pre-

cious sixteen-foot skiff might actually be returned in one piece.

"Here go, young lady." He handed her the chart and the tide card.

"Hey, thanks. Could you warm up the boat for me? I'll be there in a jiff—I've got ice and food out in the car."

The dock guy said OK, which was a good thing because JoLayne didn't know how to start a cold outboard. The old man had it purring by the time she stepped aboard with the grocery bags. He even held the lid of the cooler while she stocked it. Then he said, " 'Member. Back by sunset."

"Gotcha." JoLayne examined the controls, trying to recall what Tom had told her about working the throttle. The old guy hobbled out of the boat and, with a creaky grunt, pushed it away from the pilings. JoLayne levered the stick forward.

The man stood on the dock, eyeing her like a bony old stork. "Sunset!" he called out.

JoLayne gave him the thumbs-up as she motored slowly away, aiming the bow down a marked channel. She heard the dock guy call to her once more. A funereal droop had come to his shoulders.

"Hey!" he cried.

JoLayne waved; the robotic sort of wave you got from the girl on the homecoming float.

"Hey, what about some b-bait!"

JoLayne waved some more.

"The hell you gone catch fish without no bait?"

he shouted at her. "Or even a damn rod and reel?"

She smiled and tapped a forefinger to her temple. The old guy sucked in his liver-colored cheeks and stomped into the shack. JoLayne accelerated as much as she dared in the bumpy chop and then concentrated on not crashing. The chief hazards were other recreational vessels, a large percentage of which seemed to be piloted by lobotomized young men holding beer cans. They regarded JoLayne as if she were an exotic squid, causing her to conclude that not many African-American women were seen alone on the waters of the Florida Keys. One witty lad even sang out: "Are you lost? Nassau's *that*away!" JoLayne congratulated herself for not flipping him the finger.

To avoid being noticed by Bodean Gazzer, Tom had arranged to meet a safe distance from the gravel ramp where the pickup truck was parked. He'd pointed out a break in the mangroves, a bare gash of rocky shoreline on the ocean side of the highway. A deepwater cut strung with red-and-blue lobster buoys would help JoLayne locate the place.

She navigated with excessive precision, cleaving two of the bright Styrofoam balls on her way in. Krome was waiting by the water's edge, to catch the bow. After patiently untangling the trap ropes from the skeg, he climbed in the boat and said, "OK, Ahab, scoot over. They've got a ten-minute head start."

"Aren't you forgetting something?"

"JoLayne, come on."

She said, "The shotgun." Expecting another argument.

But Tom said, "Oh yeah." He jumped out and dashed across the road. In a minute he'd returned with her Remington, concealed in a plastic garbage bag. "I really *did* forget," he said.

JoLayne believed him. She had one arm around his shoulders as they headed across the water.

According to Chub's orders, Shiner wasn't supposed to talk to Amber except to give directions. He found this to be impossible. The longest and closest he'd ever been with such a beautiful girl was a thirty-second elevator ride with an oblivious stenographer at the Osceola County Courthouse. Shiner burned to hear everything Amber had to say—what stories she must have! Also, he felt crummy about poking her with the screwdriver. He longed to reassure her that he wasn't some bloodthirsty criminal.

"I'm in junior college," she volunteered, sending his heart airborne.

"Really?"

"Prelaw, but leaning toward cosmetology. Any advice?"

Now, what was he supposed to do? For all his crude faults, Shiner was essentially a polite young fellow. This was because his mother had flogged the rudeness out of him at an early age.

And it was rude, his mother always said, not to speak when one was spoken to.

So Shiner said to Amber: "Cosmetology—is that where they teach you to be a astronaut?"

She laughed so hard she nearly upended her bowl of minestrone. Shiner perceived that he'd said something monumentally stupid, but he wasn't embarrassed. Amber had a glorious laugh. He'd have gladly continued to say dumb things all night long, just to listen to that laughter.

They'd stopped at a twenty-four-hour sub shop on the mainland, Shiner being in no hurry to get down to Jewfish Creek. It was possible his white brethren were already waiting there, but he wasn't concerned. He wanted nothing to spoil these magical moments with Amber. In her skimpy Hooters uniform she was drawing avid stares from the dining public. Shiner despaired at the thought of turning her over to Chub.

She said, "What about you, Shiner? What do you do?"

"I'm in a militia," he replied without hesitation.

"Oh wow."

"Saving America from certain doom. They's NATO troops gonna attack any day from the Bahamas. It's what they call a international conspiracy."

Amber asked who was behind it. Shiner said

communists and Jews for sure, and possibly blacks and homos.

"Where'd you come up with this?" she said.

"You'll find out."

"So how big is this militia?"

"I ain't allowed to say. But I'm a sergeant!"

"That's cool. You guys have a name?"

Shiner said, "Yes, ma'am. The White Clarion Aryans."

Amber repeated it out loud. "There's, like, a little rhyme."

"I think it's on purpose. Hey, remember what you said about fixin' my tattoo? What I need is somebody knows how to make the *W.R.B.* into a *W.C.A.*"

She said, "I'd like to help. Really I would, but first you've got to promise to let me go."

Not this again, Shiner thought. Nervously he rolled the screwdriver between his palms. "How 'bout if I pay ya instead?"

"Pay me what?" Amber said, skeptically.

Shiner saw her cast a glance at his dirty bare feet. Quickly he said: "The militia's got a shitload a money. Not right now, but any day."

Amber leisurely finished her soup before she got around to asking how much they had coming. Fourteen million, Shiner answered. Yes, dollars.

What a laugh *that* brought! This time he felt compelled to interject: "It's no lie. I know for a fact."

"Oh yeah?"

Decisively he lit a cigaret. Then, in a tough voice: "I helped 'em steal it m'self."

Amber was quiet for a while, watching a long white yacht glide under the drawbridge. Shiner worried that he'd said too much and now she didn't believe any of it. Desperately he blurted, "It's the God's truth!"

"OK," said Amber. "But where do I fit in?"

Shiner thought: I wish I knew. Then he got an idea. "You believe in the white man?"

"Honey, I'll believe in Kermit the Frog if he leaves twenty percent on the table." She reached over and took hold of Shiner's left arm, causing him to tremble with enchantment. "Let's have a look at that tattoo," she said.

Chub was in no mood to hear whining about the pickup truck.

"Leave it," he snapped at Bode Gazzer.

"Here? Right by the water?"

"Won't nobody fuck with it, you got the handicap deal on there."

"Yeah, like *they* care."

"They who?"

"The Black Tide."

"Look here," Chub said, "the boat thing was your idea, so don't go chickenshit on me now. Not after the motherfucker of a day I've had."

"But—"

"Leave the goddamn truck! Jesus Willy, we got twenty-eight million bucks. Buy a whole Dodge dealership, you want."

Sullenly Bode Gazzer joined Chub in loading the stolen boat. The last thing to come out of the pickup was the rolled-up chamois.

"The hell's in there?" Chub said. "Or shouldn't I ast. Sounds like a bag a Budweiser cans."

Bode said, "The AR-15. I took it apart to clean."

"God help us. Let's go."

Bode knew better than to ask for the wheel; he could see there'd been problems on the boat. Chub's clothing was soaked, and his ponytail was garnished with a strand of cinnamon-colored seaweed. The deck and vinyl bucket seats were littered with small broken pieces of what appeared to be bluish ceramic, as if Chub had smashed a plate.

As they idled away from the ramp, Bode turned for one last look at his red Ram truck, which he fully expected to be stripped or stolen outright by dusk. He noticed a man standing a short distance up the shore, at the fringe of some mangroves. It was a white man, so Bode Gazzer wasn't alarmed; probably just a fisherman.

As the boat labored to gain speed, Bode shouted: "How's she run?"

"Like a one-legged whore."

"What's all the mud and shit in here?"

"I can't hear you," Chub yelled back.

Given the slop on deck and the halting performance of the outboards, it was pointless for Chub to deny that he'd run the thing aground. He saw no reason, however, to tell Bodean Gazzer how close he'd come to losing half the lottery jackpot.

Bravely kicking back to the shallows.

Flailing and groping in the marl and grasses until he'd found it in eighteen inches of water: the Lotto ticket, waving in the current like a small miracle.

Naturally it was in the claws of a blue crab. The nasty fucker had staked a claim to the moldy Band-Aid on which the ticket was stuck. The delirious Chub hadn't hesitated to leap upon the feisty scavenger, which gouged him mercilessly with one claw while clinging with the other to its sodden prize. With the crab fastened intractably to his right hand, Chub had clambered over the transom and thrashed the little bastard to pieces against the gunwale. In this manner he had reclaimed the Lotto ticket, but victory came with a price. The only intact segment of the defunct crab was the cream-blue pincers that hung from the web of skin between his thumb and forefinger; a macabre broach.

Bodean Gazzer noticed it immediately, but decided not to say a word. Thinking: *I shoulda kept drivin' straight to Tall'hassee. I shoulda never turnt around.*

"I got a map," he shouted over the hack of the mud-choked Mercurys.

No audible response from Chub.

"I picked out a island, too."

Chub seemed to nod.

"Pearl Key!" Bode shouted. "We'll be safe there."

Chub launched a gooey hawker over the windshield. "First we gotta make a stop."

"I know, I know." Bode Gazzer let the engines drown his words. "Jewfish goddamn Creek."

19 Demencio spent all day painting the rest of JoLayne's cooters. Without a reliable biblical archive, it was difficult to find thirty-three separate portraits for duplication on turtle shells. In the interest of time Demencio chose a generic saintly countenance, varying the details only slightly from cooter to cooter.

While the reptiles were drying, Trish burst into the house and exclaimed: "Four hundred and twenty bucks!"

Demencio's eyebrows danced—it was a gangbuster of a visitation.

"They flat-out love this guy," said his wife.

"Sinclair? My theory, it's more the apostles."

"Honey, it's the whole package. Him, the weeping Mary, the cooters . . . There's a little something for everybody."

It was true; Demencio had never seen a group of pilgrims so enthralled.

Trish said, "Just think what we could clear, Christmas week. When did JoLayne say she'll be back?"

"Any day." Demencio began capping the paint bottles.

"I bet she'd loan us the cooters over the holidays!"

One thing about Trish, she had a ton of faith in human nature. "Loan or *rent*?" said Demencio. "And even if she did, what about him?"

"Sinclair?"

"He ain't wrapped for the long haul. By tomorrow he's liable to be flashin' his weenie at old ladies."

Trish said, "You should go have a talk."

Demencio reminded her that he couldn't understand very much Sinclair said. "It's like his tongue come off the hinges."

"Well, Mister Dominick Amador doesn't seem to have any trouble communicating." Trish stood at the front window, parting the drapes to get a view of the shrine.

Demencio jumped up. "Sonofabitch!"

He hurried outside and chased Dominick from the property. In retreat the stigmata man hastily discarded his new crutches, slick with Crisco, which Demencio snatched up and beat to pieces against a concrete utility pole. Demencio meant the outburst to serve as a warning. He scanned the distant ficus hedge into which Dominick Amador had disappeared, and hoped the pesky con artist was watching.

To Sinclair he admonished: "That guy's bad news."

Sinclair sat Buddha-style among the apostolic turtles. The white sheet he wore was bunched and soiled, crisscrossed with diminutive muddy tracks.

Demencio said, "What'd that asshole want? Did he ask you to work with him?"

Sinclair's expression was quizzical and remote, an accurate reflection of his state of mind.

"Did he show you his hands?" Demencio demanded.

"Yes. His feet, too," Sinclair said.

"Ha! Now here's a bulletin: He did that to *himself*. Bloody holes and all. That Dominick, he's one twisted sonofabitch."

Demencio felt he could speak freely, since the tourists were gone. "He bothers you again, let me know," he said.

"Oh, I'm fine," said Sinclair, which was the truth. Never had he felt such spiritual peace. Watching the clouds was as good as floating: cool and weightless, free from earthly burdens. Except for lemonade breaks, he'd scarcely moved a muscle all day. Meanwhile the turtles had explored him—

up one arm, down one leg, back and forth across his chest. The march of miniature toenails tickled and soothed Sinclair. One of the cooters—was it Simon?—had made it up the steep slope of Sinclair's skull and settled on his vast unlined forehead, where it sunned itself contentedly for hours. The sensation had put Sinclair into a Zen-like trance; he lolled among the tiny creatures like a Gulliver, without the ropes. The crushing guilt of sending Tom Krome to his death evaporated like a gray mist. *The Register's* frenetic newsroom and the job that Sinclair had once taken so seriously receded into the vaguest of recollections, appearing to him in cacophonous and incoherent flashes. Every so often, all the headlines he'd ever composed would scroll through his consciousness one after another, like a demonic Dow Jones ticker, causing Sinclair to yodel alliteratively. He understood these eruptions to mean he was forever finished with daily journalism, a revelation that contributed in no small way to his serenity.

Demencio dropped to a crouch, to secure better eye contact with the dreamy turtle boy. "Can I get you anything—soda? Half a sandwich?"

"Nuh-uh," Sinclair said.

"You wanna stay for supper? Trish is doing one of her angel foods for dessert."

"Sure," said Sinclair. He was too drowsy for the walk to Roddy and Joan's house.

"Sleep over, if you like. There's a daybed in the

spare room," Demencio offered, "and plenty of clean sheets to wear, in case you wanna hang around tomorrow."

Sinclair had given no thought whatsoever to the future, but for the moment he couldn't imagine parting with the holy cooters.

Demencio said, "Plus I got a surprise for you."

"Ah."

"But you gotta promise not to faint or nothin', OK?"

Demencio ran into the house and came out lugging the aquarium, which he placed at Sinclair's feet. In breathless reverence Sinclair gazed at the freshly painted turtles; he reached out, tenuously fingering the air, like a child trying to touch a hologram.

Demencio said, "Here you go. Enjoy!"

When he tipped the tank on one side, thirty-three newly sanctified cooters swarmed forth to join the others in the moat. Sinclair joyfully scooped up several and held them aloft. He tossed back his chin and began to croon, *"Muugghhh meeechy makk-a-mamma,"* a subconscious rendition of the classic MUGGER MEETS MATCH AGAINST MARTIAL-ARTS MOM.

Demencio edged away from the ranting turtle boy and returned to the house. Trish was in the kitchen with the cake mix. "Did you ask about the T-shirts? Will he give us permission?"

Her husband said, "The guy's so far gone, he'd let us yank out his kidneys if we wanted."

"So I should fix up the guest room?"

"Yeah. Where are the car keys?" Demencio patted his pockets. "I gotta make a lettuce run."

Also disengaging from the newspaper business was Tom Krome, though in the opposite manner of his editor and without the mystic balm of reptiles. While Sinclair escaped transcendentally from the headlines, Krome had become one of them. He'd hurled himself into a tricky cascade of events in which he was a central participant, not a mere chronicler.

He'd become a news story. Off the sidelines and into the big game!

Joining JoLayne Lucks meant Krome couldn't write about her mission; not if he still cared about the tenets of journalism, which he did. Honest reporters could always make a good-faith stab at objectivity, or at least professional detachment. That was now impossible regarding the robbery and beating of a black woman in Grange, Florida. Too much was happening in which Tom Krome had sway, and there was more to come. Absolved of his writerly duties, he felt liberated and galvanized. It was an especially good buzz for someone who'd been declared dead on the front page.

Yet Krome still caught himself reaching for the spiral notebook he no longer carried. Sometimes he could still feel its stiff, rectangular shape in his back pocket; a phantom limb.

Like now, for instance. Watching the bad guys.

Ordinarily Krome would've had the notebook opened on his lap. Hastily jotting in what Mary Andrea once described as his "serial killer's scrawl."

> *3:35 pm Jewfish Crk.*
> *Camo, Ponytail fueling boat.*
> *Arguing—about what?*
> *Buying beer, food, etc.*
> *Joined by 2 people, unidentif. m and f. He bald and*
>   *barefoot. She blond w/orange shorts.*
> *Who?*

These observations compiled automatically in Tom Krome's brain as he sat with JoLayne in the scuffed old Boston Whaler she'd rented. Both of them were stiff and tired from a long night aboard the cramped skiff. They'd closed the gap on the rednecks, only to watch the stolen ski boat plow sensationally into a shallow grass bank. It was the first of several detours, as the robbers would spend hours pinballing from one nautical obstruction to another. Tom and JoLayne, astounded at their quarry's incompetence, followed at a prudent distance.

Now their skiff was tied to a PVC stake at the

mouth of a shallow inlet. The makeshift mooring afforded a partially obstructed view of the busy docks at Jewfish Creek, where the rednecks finally had managed an uneventful landing.

Krome grumbling, for the second time: "I should've got some binoculars."

JoLayne Lucks saying she didn't need any. "It's the kid. I'm sure of it."

"What kid?"

"Shiner. From the Grab N'Go."

"Hey . . . you might be right." Krome, cupping both hands at his eyes to cut the glare.

JoLayne said, "The rotten little shit. That explains why he lied about my Lotto ticket. They gave him a piece of the action."

All things considered, Krome thought, she's taking it well.

"Guess what else," she said. "The girl in the shorts and T-shirt?—it looks like the Hooters babe."

Krome broke into a grin. "The one they were hitting on the other night. Yes!" He could see them boarding the stolen boat: Bodean Gazzer first, followed by the skinhead Shiner, then the ponytailed man, tugging the blond woman behind him.

Pensively JoLayne said, "That's four of them and two of us."

"No, it's fantastic!" Krome kissed her on the forehead. "It's the very best thing that could happen."

"Are you nuts?"

"I'm talking about the babe. Her being there changes everything."

"The babe."

"*Yes.* Whatever grand plan these guys had, it's in tatters as of this moment!"

JoLayne had never seen him so excited. "In one small boat," he said, "we've got three smitten morons and one beautiful woman. Honey, there's an incredible shitstorm on the horizon."

She said, "I'm inclined to be insulted by what you just said. On behalf of all womanhood."

"Not at all." He untied the Whaler from the trees. "It's men I'm talking about. The way we are. Look at those googans and tell me they know how to cope with a girl like that."

JoLayne realized he was right: The stolen boat had become a time bomb. Any kind of a dispute would set the men off—over cigarets, the last cold beer . . . or a stolen lottery ticket.

Krome said, "We needed these boys to be distracted. I would say our prayers have been answered."

"Then God bless Hooters." JoLayne jerked her chin toward the docks. "Tom, they're heading back this way."

"So they are."

"Shouldn't we duck?"

"Naw," Krome said. "Just stay cool until they go past. Turn toward me, OK?"

"Hold on a second. Is this another kiss?"

"A long romantic one. To make sure they don't see our faces."

"Aye, aye, captain."

Judge Arthur Battenkill Jr. was an intelligent man. He knew Champ Powell's remains would eventually be identified. A medium-rare lump of tissue was already on its way to the FBI for DNA screening, or so the judge had heard.

A dead law clerk in the torched house of your wife's lover was not easy to explain, especially if the lover was to return and make an issue of the arson. Which that bastard Tom Krome likely would.

Arthur Battenkill knew his judicial career would soon end in scandal if he didn't take the bull by the horns. So, being as practical as he was smart, he began making plans to quit the bench and leave the country.

Starting over would be expensive. As a matter of convenience, the judge decided that the insurance carrier for Save King Supermarkets should pay for his new life in the Bahamas, or wherever he and Katie chose to relocate. This meant placing a call to Emil LaGort's lawyer.

Emil LaGort was a plaintiff in a civil lawsuit filed in Arthur Battenkill's court. In fact, Emil LaGort was a plaintiff in numerous lawsuits from

Apalachicola to Key West—a habitual fraud, a renowned slip-and-fall artist. He was also seventy-four years old, which meant that one of these days he would *really* slip and fall.

Why not now? mused Arthur Battenkill. Why not in the aisle of a Save King Supermarket?

Emil LaGort was suing the store for $5 million, but he gladly would've settled out of court for fifty grand and costs. He did it all the time. Therefore his attorney was greatly surprised to receive a phone call, at home, from Judge Arthur Battenkill Jr.

As a rule, Emil LaGort shied from judges—if a deal couldn't be cut, he'd quietly drop the case. Going to trial was a time-consuming inconvenience that Emil LaGort simply could not afford, what with so many irons in the fire. He had a good thing going with the quickie settlements. Most insurance companies were pushovers when it came to frail senior citizens who claimed to have fallen on their policyholders' premises. Most insurance companies wished to spare jurors the sight of Emil LaGort, enfeebled in a neck brace and a wheelchair. So he got paid to go away.

The complaint scheduled to be heard in Arthur Battenkill's court was fairly typical. It alleged that, while shopping one morning at the Save King, Emil LaGort had slipped and fallen, causing irreparable harm to his neck, spine and extremities; furthermore, that the accident was due to the gross negligence of the store, whereas an extra-large tube of discount hemorrhoid ointment was left lying on the floor of the health-care-and-hygiene aisle, where it subsequently was run over by one or possibly more steel-framed shopping carts, thus distributing the slippery contents of the broken tube in a reckless and hazardous manner; and furthermore, that no timely efforts were made by Save King or its employees to remove said hazardous ointment, or to warn customers of the imminent danger, such negligence resulting directly in the grave and permanent injury to Emil LaGort.

Emil LaGort's attorney figured that Judge Arthur Battenkill Jr., like everyone else familiar with the case, knew that Emil had purposely knocked the tube of goop off the shelf, stomped it with both feet and then laid himself very gingerly on the floor of the health-care-and-hygiene aisle. The attorney certainly was not expecting the judge to call him at home on a Sunday morning and say:

"Lenny, it would be in your client's interest to hang tough."

"But, Your Honor, we were preparing to settle."

"That would be precipitous."

"A hundred even was the offer."

"You can do better, Lenny. Trust me."

The attorney tried to stay cool. "But I'm not ready for a trial!"

"Put on a little show," Arthur Battenkill said, needling. "That snotty bone guy you always use as an expert witness, the one with the ratty toupee. Or that lying dipshit of a so-called neurologist from Lauderdale. Surely you can manage."

"Yeah, I suppose." The attorney was beginning to get the picture.

The judge said, "Let me ask you something. Do you think Mr. LaGort would be satisfied with, say, $250,000?"

"Your Honor, Mr. LaGort would be fucking jubilant." And I would, too, the attorney thought. Me and my thirty-five percent.

"All right, Lenny, then I'll tell you what. Let's see if we can save the taxpayers some dough. First thing tomorrow we'll all meet in chambers, after which I anticipate the defendants will be motivated to settle."

"For two fifty."

"No, for half a million. Are you following me?" said Arthur Battenkill.

There was an uncomfortable pause on the other end. The attorney said, "Maybe we should have this conversation in person."

"The phones are clean, Lenny."

"If you say so."

"Five hundred is a smart number," the judge continued, "because Save King's insurance company can live with it. A trial is too risky, especially if you get a couple old geezers on the jury. Then you're looking at seven figures, automatic."

The attorney said, "Amen."

"Next question: Can Mr. LaGort be persuaded that the court's costs are unusually high in this case?"

"For the kind of money he's getting, Your Honor, Mr. LaGort can be persuaded that cows shit gumdrops."

"Good," said Arthur Battenkill. "Then you know what to do with the other two fifty."

"Do I?"

"Escrow, Lenny. You do have an escrow account?"

"Of course."

"That's the first place it goes. Then it's wired overseas. I'll give you the account number when I get one."

"Oh."

"What's the matter now?"

The attorney said, "It's just . . . I've never done it this way before."

"Lenny, do I strike you as a brown-bag-in-the-alley sort of fellow? Do you see me as some kind of low-class bumpkin?"

"No, Your Honor."

"I hope not," Arthur Battenkill said. "By the way, next week there will be an announcement of my pending retirement, for unspecified health reasons. Tell Mr. LaGort not to be alarmed."

The attorney endeavored to sound genuinely concerned. "I'm sorry to hear that. I didn't know you'd been ill."

The judge laughed acidulously. "Lenny, you're not too swift, are you?"

"I guess not, Your Honor."

Not for a moment did it occur to Mary Andrea Finley Krome that the newspapers might be wrong and that her husband was still alive. She departed Missoula on an upswelling of sympathy from Loretta (or was it Lorie?) and her other new acquaintances among the *Menagerie* cast, and with the director's personal assurance that the role of Laura Wingfield would be waiting when she returned.

Which, of course, Mary Andrea had no intention of doing. She believed that being a famous widow would open new doors, careerwise.

The long flight to Florida gave Mary Andrea time to prepare for the bustle of attention that awaited. Knowing she'd be asked by interviewers, she tried to reconstruct the last time she'd seen Tom. Incredibly, she could not. Probably it was at the apartment in Brooklyn, probably in the kitchen over breakfast. That was usually when he'd tried to initiate the so-called serious discussions about their marriage. And probably she'd gotten up from the table and moseyed into the bathroom to pluck her eyebrows, her customary response to the subject of divorce.

All Mary Andrea could remember with certainty was that one morning, four years ago, he hadn't been there. Poof.

The previous night, she'd come home from rehearsals very late and fallen asleep on the sofa. She expected to be awakened, as she had so many days, by the sound of Tom munching on his cereal. He was partial to Grape-Nuts, which had the consistency of blasted granite.

What Mary Andrea recalled most distinctly from that morning was the silence in the apartment. And of course the brief note, which (because it had been Scotch-taped to the cereal box) had been impossible to take seriously:

If you won't leave me, I'll find somebody who will.

Only later did Mary Andrea discover that Tom had lifted the line from a Warren Zevon song, an irritating detail that merely fortified her resolve to stay married.

As for the last time she'd actually laid eyes on her husband, what he'd said to her, his mood, the clothes he'd been wearing—none of this could Mary Andrea remember.

She did recall what she'd been doing on the afternoon the lawyer phoned, that asshole Turnquist. She'd been reading *Daily Variety* and running through her vocal exercises; octaves and whatnot. She remembered Turnquist saying Tom wanted to give her one more chance to sit down and work out the details, before he filed the papers. She remembered manufacturing a giggle and telling the lawyer he'd been the victim of an elaborate practical joke her husband arranged every year, on their anniversary. And she remembered hanging up the telephone and breaking into tears and wolfing three Dove bars.

Compared to other newsworthy breakups it seemed mundane, and Mary Andrea saw no benefit in launching her public widowhood by boring the media. So, gazing from the window of the plane at the scooped-out cliffs of the Rocky Mountains, she invented a suitable parting scene that she could share with the press. It had happened, say, six months ago. Tom had surprised her in, say, Lansing, where she'd landed a small part in a road tour of *Sunset Boulevard.* He'd slipped in late and sat in the rear of the theater, and surprised her with pink roses backstage after the show. He'd said he missed her and was having second thoughts about the separation. They'd even made plans to get together for dinner, say, next month, when she was scheduled to come back east with the production of *Lambs.*

Sounds pretty good, Mary Andrea thought. And who's to say it didn't happen? Or wouldn't have happened, if Tom hadn't died.

As the flight attendant freshened her Diet Coke, Mary Andrea thought: Crying won't be a problem. When the cameras show up, I'll have gallons of tears. Heck, I could cry right now.

Because it *was* terribly sad, the senseless death of a young and moderately talented and basically goodhearted man.

So what if she didn't lie awake at nights, missing him. She'd really never known him well enough to miss him. That was sort of sad, too. Imagining the intimacy and caring that might have been; the kind of closeness only years of separation could bring.

Mary Andrea Finley Krome dug through her handbag until she located the rosary beads she'd found at a Catholic thrift shop in Missoula. She would clutch them in her left hand as she got off the plane in Orlando, and mention in a choked voice that they'd been a gift from Tom.

Which they might have been, someday, if the poor guy hadn't been murdered.

 JoLayne Lucks sat up so abruptly she made the boat rock.

"Lord, what an awful dream."

Krome put a finger to his lips. He'd killed the engine, and they were drifting in the dark toward the island.

"Get this," she said. "We're in the hot-air balloon, the yellow one from before, and all of a sudden you ask for half the lottery money."

"Only half?"

"This is after we get the stolen ticket back. Out of nowhere you're demanding a fifty-fifty split!"

Krome said: "Thank you, Agent Moffitt, wherever you are."

"What?"

"He put that idea in your head."

"No, Tom. As a matter of fact, he said you didn't strike him as a typical moneygrubbing scumbag."

"Stop. I'm blushing."

It was a windy night, wispy clouds skating overhead. A cold front was moving in from the north. The starlight came and went in patches. They'd approached the island on a wide arc. The tree-lined shore looked black and lifeless—the robbers were nowhere in sight, having disappeared up a creek on the lee side. Krome surmised it was too soon for the group to send a lookout; the men would be busy unloading their gear.

JoLayne said, "You're sure they didn't see us following them?"

"I'm not sure of anything."

She thought: That makes two of us.

Evidently Tom was sticking with her, shotgun and all. She couldn't help but wonder why, a riddle she'd been avoiding since the first day. Why was he

doing this? What was in it for him? Krome had
said nothing in particular to trigger these doubts
in JoLayne; it was only the backwash from a lifetime of being let down by men she trusted.

As the skiff floated closer to the mangroves, she
heard Tom say: "Hang on." Then they were tilting,
and she saw he was over the side and wading for
shore. He held the bow rope in one fist, pulling the
Whaler quietly across the flat toward the tree line.

JoLayne sat forward. "You be careful," she
whispered.

"Water's nice."

"Skeeters?"

Krome, keeping his voice low: "Not too bad."

It's the breeze, JoLayne thought. Mosquitoes
like hot still nights. If this were August, they'd be
devouring us.

"See any place to tie off?" she asked. "What
about over there?"

"That's where I'm headed."

The opening wasn't much wider than the skiff itself. Krome advised JoLayne to lie flat and cover
her face as he led them through a latticework of
mangroves. The branches raked at her bare arms,
and a gossamer fragment of a spider's web caught
in her hair. She was more alarmed by the sound of
the roots screaking along the hull, but Tom
seemed unconcerned. He hauled the skiff to the
bank and helped her step out.

In fifteen minutes they had the gear unpacked and sorted. By flashlight they wiped down the Remington and loaded two shells. It was the first time since sunset that JoLayne had been able to see Tom's face, and it made her feel better.

She said, "How about a fire?"

"Not just yet." He stood the gun against a tree and clicked off the light. "Let's just sit and listen."

The vibrant quiet was a comfort; nothing but the hum of insects and the whisk of wavelets against the shore. The peacefulness reminded Jo-Layne of the evening at Simmons Wood when she and Tom had stopped to watch the deer.

Except this time he was squeezing her hand. He was tense.

She told him: "This is a good place you found. We'll be safe here."

"I keep hearing noises."

"It's just the wind in the trees."

"I don't know."

"It's the wind, Tom." She could tell he hadn't spent much time in the outdoors. "Let's have a fire."

"They'll smell the smoke."

"Not if they've got one burning, too," she said, "and I'll bet you five bucks they do. I'll bet that cute little waitress is freezing her buns in those shorts."

Tom broke up some driftwood while JoLayne

dug out a small pit in the sand. For tinder they used handfuls of the crispy, dried-out seaweed that ringed the shore. It didn't take long for a spark to catch. JoLayne stood close, enjoying the heat on her bare arms. Tom unsnapped the faded blue canvas from the skiff's Bimini top and spread it on the ground. JoLayne tactfully suggested he should move it to the upwind side of the fire, so the smoke wouldn't blow in their eyes.

"Good thinking," he said tightly.

They sat close to the flames—Tom with a Coke and a granola bar; JoLayne with a Canada Dry, a box of Goldfish crackers and the Remington.

She said, "All the comforts of home."

"Yeah."

"Except a radio. Wouldn't Whitney hit the spot right now?" JoLayne, trying to loosen him up, singing in a tinny voice: "Aaahheeeayyyyy will all-ways love you-aaaoooooo . . ."

A small laugh; not much. "Something wrong?" she asked.

"I guess I'm just tired."

"Well, it's about time."

"We should do some scouting at dawn, while they're still asleep."

"They might be up early."

"I doubt it. They bought a shitload of beer," Tom said.

"Dawn it is. Then what?"

"We get as close as possible to their camp—close enough to see and hear what's going on. That way we'll know when things go sour."

JoLayne said, "I sure hope you're right about that. OK, then what happens?"

"We get them one by one."

"You serious?"

"Not with the shotgun, JoLayne. Not unless they leave us no choice."

"I see."

Tom opened a can of tuna fish and forked it onto a paper plate. JoLayne waved it off before he could offer.

"I was thinking about your dream," he said.

"Uh-oh."

"I don't blame you for being suspicious of me. Only a fool wouldn't be—"

"That's not the right word—"

"Look," he said, "if I were reporting this story instead of participating, that's the first thing I'd ask: 'How do you know that guy isn't after your Lotto money, too?' And all I can say is, I'm not. The idea never crossed my mind, that's the truth. Which raises the obvious question: What in the hell's wrong with me? Why risk my neck for a woman I've only known a week?"

"Because I'm extra-special?" JoLayne, through a mouthful of Goldfish crackers.

"Hey. I'm trying to be serious."

"Wild," she said. "You really can't explain why

you're here. You, who are in the profession of putting words together. An intelligent, successful guy who doesn't hesitate to drop everything, to walk away from a whole other life."

"Unbelievable, I know. I *do* know." He stared beyond the flames. "It just seemed . . . necessary."

JoLayne took a slug of ginger ale. "All right, Mister Krome. Since neither of us can figure out your motives, let's look at the possibilities."

"The fire's dying."

"Sit your ass down," JoLayne said. "Let's start with sex."

"Sex."

"Yes. That thing we were doing last night in the motel. Remember? We take off all our clothes and one of us climbs on top—"

"You're suggesting that I'd risk being massacred by vicious psychopaths just to charm you into the sack?"

"Some men'll do anything."

"No offense," Tom said, "but I'm not quite that starved for affection."

"Oh really? Before last night, when was the last time you made love to a woman."

"A week ago."

"Yipes," said JoLayne, with a blink.

"The wife of a judge." Krome got up to toss more driftwood on the embers. "Apparently she kept a scorecard. I could probably get a copy, if you want."

JoLayne recovered admirably. "So we've ruled out money and nooky. What about valor?"

Tom chuckled mirthlessly. "Oh, how I wish."

"White man's guilt?"

"That's possible."

"Or how about this: You're just trying to prove something to yourself."

"Now we're getting somewhere." He lay back, entwining his hands behind his head. In the firelight JoLayne could see he was exhausted.

He said, "Hey, we missed the lottery."

"Lord, that's right—it was last night, wasn't it? I believe we were distracted." In her handbag she found the Lotto coupons Moffitt had confiscated from Bodean Gazzer's apartment. She fanned them, like a royal flush, for Tom to see.

"You feeling lucky?"

"Very," he said.

"Me, too." She leaned forward and dropped the tickets, one by one, into the flames.

By the time they reached Pearl Key, Bodean Gazzer and Chub were hardly speaking. At issue was the newly purchased marine chart of Florida Bay, which neither of them was able to decipher. Chub blamed Bode, and Bode blamed the mapmakers from the National Oceanic and Atmospheric Administration, who (he insisted) had purposely mislabeled the backcountry channels to thwart the flight of survivalists such as the White Clarion Aryans. This time Chub wasn't buying it.

The inability of either man to make sense of the navigational markers resulted in a succession of high-speed groundings that seriously eroded the aluminum propellers. The ski boat was shaking like a blender long before the militiamen got to the island.

Chub seethed—he had so hoped to impress Amber with his nautical skills. Yet, during their third mishap after departing Jewfish Creek, he'd heard her say: "This is a joke, right?"

At the time he was waist-deep in water, fighting the tide, pushing against the transom with all his strength. Bode Gazzer sloshed next to him in the shallows, working on the starboard side. Amber was in the boat with Shiner.

This is a joke, right?

And Chub had heard Shiner say, "If only."

The snotty fuck.

Panting in the marl, Chub found his worries turning to the lottery tickets. Both were hidden in the steering console—the stolen one still damp from the previous near disaster; the one in Bode's wallet relocated when Chub made him go overboard to push.

The console had cheap plastic doors that didn't lock. Chub resolved to shoot Shiner in the kneecaps if he went anywhere near it.

Night had fallen before they beached at Pearl

Key. Bode Gazzer used liquid charcoal lighter to get a fire going. Chub stripped down and hung his sopping clothes in the mangroves. Shiner was ordered to unload the boat. He couldn't believe Chub was sauntering around camp in his underwear, right in front of Amber.

"Want some bug spray?" Chub asked her.

"I'm cold," she said.

In an instant Shiner was there with an army blanket. Chub snatched it and wrapped Amber's shoulders. He handed her an aerosol can of insect repellent and said: "Squirt a lil on my legs, wouldya?"

She did as she was told, her expression concealed by Chub's lanky shadow. Bode Gazzer glanced up from the campfire—it was foolishness; such a girl had no place in a paramilitary unit. Shiner was equally dismayed, but for different reasons.

He piped, "They's some dry camos in the duffel."

Chub ignored him. He seemed entirely relaxed in mud-splattered Jockey shorts.

"So, Amber," he said, "where'd y'all sleep last night?"

"The car."

Chub cut a hard look at Shiner, who said: "By the side of the road."

"Is that right."

"Whatsa big damn deal?" Shiner didn't appreciate how Chub was putting him on the spot: giving him the eye, acting like Shiner was holding something back.

Amber came to his defense. "It's a Crown Victoria. You can fit a football team in there," she said. "I slept in the back seat, Shiner slept in front. Anything else you want to know?"

Chub got red and flustered. The last thing he'd wanted to do was piss her off—hell, some girls were flattered when you got jealous. He offered Amber a Budweiser.

"No, thanks."

"Some jerky?"

"I think I'll pass."

Bodean Gazzer said, "We got to have a meeting. Sugar, can you leave us men alone for 'bout thirty minutes."

Amber looked out toward the gray woods, then turned back to Bode. "Where exactly am I supposed to go?"

Shiner cut in, saying it was all right for her to stay. "She knows who we are, and she's a hundred percent with the program."

Now it was the colonel's turn to shoot him the evil eye. Shiner didn't cave. "She's even gonna fix my tattoo!"

"Too bad she can't fix your fuckin' brain." Chub, picking at his eye patch as if it were a scab.

Bodean Gazzer sensed that his hold on the newborn militia was slipping. Amber would have to shut up and behave, that's all. Her presence was disrupting the group; the scent of her in particular. While Bode was grateful for any fragrance potent enough to neutralize the stink of Chub's perspiration, he felt throttled by Amber's perfume. It fogged his brain with impure thoughts, some of them jarringly explicit. Bode was angry at himself for entertaining base fantasies when he should be concentrating totally on survival.

He spread an oilskin tarpaulin and called the meeting to order. Amber sat cross-legged in the center of the tarp, with Shiner and Chub on each side.

"As you know," Bode began, "we're here on this island because something—somebody—calls themselves the Black Tide is out to destroy us. I got no doubt it's a Negro operation, a pretty slick one, and I expect they'll find us eventually. We come all the way out here to regroup, get our weapons in tiptop shape and make a stand.

"Now, I believe with all my Christian heart we're gonna prevail. But to whip these black bastards we gotta be prepared, and we gotta be a team: armed, disciplined and well-regulated. Pretty soon 'Merica's gonna come under attack— I don't need to tell you about that. The New World Tribunal, the communists, NATO and so forth. But this here's our first big test, this Black Tide . . . now what?"

The Hooters girl had raised her hand.

"You got a question?" Bode Gazzer said, perturbed.

"Yeah. Where do you guys see this going?"

"Pardon?"

"The plan," Amber said. "What's the long-range plan?"

"We are the White Clarion Aryans. We believe in the purity and supremacy of the Euro-Caucasian people. We believe our Christian values been betrayed and forsaken by the United States government. . . ."

As he spoke, Bodean Gazzer glowered at Chub. How were they going to win a race war with a damn waitress hanging around?

Chub wasn't annoyed by Amber's interruption; he was too busy trying to cop a peek up her shorts. Shiner, by contrast, was painfully attentive. Taking Amber's lead, he raised his right arm and waved at Bode.

"What!"

"Colonel, you said Euro something . . ."

"Euro-Caucasian."

"Could you 'xplain what that is?" Shiner asked.

"White people," Bode Gazzer snapped. "White people whose folks come from, like, England or Germany. Places such as that."

"Ireland?" asked Amber.

"Yeah, sure. Denmark, Canada . . . you get

the goddamn idea." He couldn't believe these nimrods—the concept of ethnic purity wasn't that complicated.

Then Shiner said: "They got white people in Mexico."

"Bullshit."

"Guy used to work days at the Grab N'Go. Billy was his name. He looked awful white, Colonel."

Bode was steaming. He walked over to Shiner and kicked him in the side of the head. Shiner cried out and toppled across Amber's lap. Chub looked on, abject with envy.

Leaning over, Bode took Shiner by the chin. "Listen, you pimple-faced little shitweasel. Ain't no such thing on God's earth as a white Meskin named Billy or Hay-zoos or any other damn thing. They's no white Cubans or Spaniards, neither."

"But Spain *is* in Europe." Amber, calm as you please, stroking Shiner's bestubbled scalp.

Chub, who was tired of being left out, declared: "She got a point there." Then, turning with a smirk toward the girl: "And here's a man won't even say the word 'nigger.' "

Bodean Gazzer took a deep breath and walked a slow circle around the campfire. He had to cool off; he had to be the calm, clear-thinking one.

"When I talk about Euro-Caucasians," he said, "I'm referrin' to *white* white people, all right? That's the easiest way to explain it. I'm talkin' about Aryan ancestry, which is something all four of us share."

Impatiently Chub said, "Get on with it." To his immense relief, Shiner sat up, uncluttering Amber's thighs. The glow of the flames gave a delicious sheen to her nylon stockings; it was all Chub could do to restrain himself from stroking them. It was, in fact, only a matter of moments before he tried.

When he did, Amber whacked him in the face. "Look what you did!" she exclaimed.

The aborted grope had snagged Chub's hand in her hose. It was the crab claw, he was disheartened to see.

"What's the matter with you!" Amber said, and took another swipe. She wanted the kidnappers to know she was a fighter and that every touch would cost them dearly. It was a cardinal rule of waitressing: Defend your dignity.

Chub knocked over his beer as he fumbled to disentangle himself. "*I'll* do it," Amber snapped.

In disgust Bode Gazzer spit a chunk of jerky into the campfire. Shiner was stunned by the scene. Amber's fear of a rape no longer seemed farfetched; the same could not be said of Shiner's gallant vow to protect her. Chub was so much stronger and meaner; short of killing him in his sleep, Shiner's options were limited.

The crab pincers left a ragged hole in Amber's nylons.

"Damn," she muttered. Then to Chub: "Hope you're happy, Romeo." It was the sort of asshole stunt that boyfriend Tony might pull, pawing at her crotch in public.

Chub told her to chill. He dug in the cooler for another beer. Then he opened the chamois and tackled (with a scathing cackle) the reassembly of the AR-15. Bode pretended not to pay attention.

Amber picked up a flashlight and went into the woods to change clothes. She came out wearing one of Bode Gazzer's camouflage jumpsuits; Mossy Oak.

Instantly a gloom settled over Chub. He pined for the cutoff T-shirt and the silky shorts. He tried to imagine Kim Basinger as a bear hunter and could not. Bodean Gazzer, however, found himself helplessly intoxicated by the flickering vision in mottled camos. *His* camos. The dainty white Keds added a devastating element.

"Meeting's over," he said, and sat down heavily.

Amber, who was soundly apprehensive, resolved not to let it show. She walked forthrightly up to Chub and said: "We need to talk."

"Gimme a minute with this rifle."

"No. Right now."

She took his hand—the claw-hobbled hand!—and led him into the shadows of the mangroves. Shiner was dumbfounded. Was the girl crazy?

Bode Gazzer didn't like it, either. He caught himself grinding his molars; the only thing that could make him do that was a woman. Don't get stupid, he warned himself. It's no time to grow horns. Yet he couldn't stop thinking about her; about what the Mossy Oak jumpsuit would smell like after she removed it. Or after Chub tore it off, in which case Bode might have to blow the man's brains out. Purely for the sake of maintaining discipline.

Twenty yards into the woods, Amber turned and put the flashlight on Chub's face. She said, "I know what you want."

"It don't take a genius."

"Well, this can go two ways," she told him. "You can be a pig and rape me, and I'll hate your guts forever. Or we can get to know each other and see what happens."

With his good eye Chub squinted against the spear of light, trying to read Amber's expression. He said, "I thought you already liked me jest fine. Seemed that way at the resty-rant."

"Let me explain something: Just because I smile at a customer doesn't mean I want to fuck him."

The word rocked Chub on his heels.

"And if you rape me," Amber said, "it will be the worst time you ever had with a woman. The *worst.*"

"Wh-why?"

"Because I'm not moving a muscle, I'm not making a sound. I'm going to lie there like a cold sack of mud, bored out of my mind. I might even *time* you." She held up her wrist, so he could get a glimpse of her watch.

Chub said, "Jesus Willy." Feeling himself wither, he now wished he'd put on some pants.

"Or we can try to be friends," Amber said. "Think you can handle that?"

"Sure." His ears were buzzing. He slapped at them.

"Bugs," Amber said. She shooed them away.

"Thanks."

"We got a deal?" She held out her hand. Chub took it. Briefly he considered throwing her down and sticking it to her right there, but he decided against it. Fucking a cold sack of mud didn't sound like much fun, even if the sack looked like a movie star. He thought: Hell, at least hookers *acted* like they were having a good time.

"What kinda guys you go for?" he asked. "Your boyfriend don't seem all too polite, neither."

Amber said, "Sometimes he's not."

"Then how come you stay with him? He rich?"

"He does all right." A big fat lie.

"I bet I'm richer," Chub said.

"Oh, sure."

"How does fourteen million damn dollars sound?"

The flashlight clicked off. In the shadows he heard Amber say, "You're kidding." The smell of perfume was stronger than before, as if she'd moved closer.

"No, I ain't kidding. Fourteen million."

Amber said, "I want to hear all about it."

There was a break in the rolling clouds, and for a few moments Chub could see her eyes by the light of the stars. He felt himself twitching back to life; inadvertently his claw hand went to his groin.

She said, "Maybe tomorrow we can go for a walk. Just the two of us."

"Fine by me." The excitement made him light-headed.

The next time Amber spoke, it was a whisper: "Oh, I've got something for you." She took his unwounded hand—the one clenched at his side—opened it gently and pressed something soft into the palm.

Even in the blackness Chub knew what it was.

Her orange Hooters shorts.

"A little token of our friendship," she said.

Cold rain fell after midnight, slapping at the leaves. Bodean Gazzer was curled up beside the hissing embers, where he'd passed out from exhaustion. Chub was splayed in the cockpit of the *Reel Luv*. To his chest he clutched Amber's waitress shorts, a beer bottle and a tube of polyurethane marine adhesive he'd come across while rifling a hatch. He had gnawed off the plastic nipple and placed the glue inside a paper grocery bag, leaving space for his head. Amber doubted if the storm would rouse him; his snoring sounded like a locomotive.

Shiner was pulling guard duty, sopping and forlorn. Amber shook out the oilskin tarpaulin and draped it across the mangroves, for a lean-to. She tugged Shiner out of the rain and said: "You're going to catch your death."

"No, I can't sit down."

"Don't be ridiculous."

"But the colonel put me on perimeter."

"The colonel's out like a light. Relax," Amber said. "What kind of gun is that? It's ugly."

"TEC-9," said Shiner.

"I'd be scared to even hold it."

"Piece a crap."

"Sure beats the screwdriver."

Shiner said, "I like the AR-15 better." The wind snapped the corners of the tarp. "God, this weather sucks. You hear that?"

"It's just the waves."

"I hope." Through the trees he could make out the shape of the boat at the waterline. Chub had anchored it in a skinny channel that ran along the shore of the island.

"It's, like, zero visibility," Shiner remarked.

Amber blinked the flashlight in his face. "Just in case," she said.

"Don't tell me you gonna make a run for it."

She laughed emptily. "Where?"

"I'd have to stop you. That's my orders."

Amber said, "I'm not going anywhere. Tell me about the money."

Shiner fell silent for a short while. Then he thought he heard a helicopter. "The NATO troops got Blackhawks. They's lined up on the beach at Andros Island, is what Colonel Bode says."

Water streamed off the tarp in sheets. Amber said, "There are no helicopters coming tonight, all right? Not in this shitty storm. Maybe submarines, but no helicopters."

"You think this is funny?"

"Oh yeah. Getting kidnapped, that really cracks me up."

Shiner asked, "What'd Chub want? Before, when you guys went in the woods."

"What do you think."

"He dint try nothin', did he?"

"Yeah, he tried something. He tried to tell me he was a millionaire."

"The brotherhood, he means."

"No. Him personally," said Amber.

"I don't think so." Shiner looked troubled.

"Fourteen million dollars is what he said. That's the same money you helped to steal, right?" Amber poked his arm. "Well?"

Again Shiner turned away, toward the boat. "Did he take your pants? He said he took your pants."

She could scarcely hear him above the wind and the shake of the trees.

Shiner said, "He showed 'em to us. Them orange ones."

"He didn't *take* anything. I gave him the damn shorts." Amber put the light on his face. "Don't worry, it's all right."

"You say so."

"I'm a big girl."

"Yeah, but he's crazy," Shiner said.

A string of cold drops landed on Amber's forehead. Glancing up, she noticed a shiny bulge in the skin of the tarpaulin, where the water had puddled on the other side.

She told Shiner: "Watch out, it's dripping on your Tex." Turning the flashlight on the gun.

"It's T-e-c, not T-e-x." He dried the stubby barrel on one of his sleeves.

"You still worried about helicopters?"

"Naw," Shiner said.

"The money?"

"Right." He sniffed sarcastically.

"Where'd you guys get so much?" Amber asked. "Rob Fort Knox or something?"

"Try a lottery ticket."

"You're kidding."

"It was easy."

"Well, tell me about it," Amber said.

And Shiner did.

. . .

Tom Krome couldn't get to sleep in the slashing storm. The shadows swayed in the wind, and it got chilly without a fire. He and JoLayne bundled beneath the boat canvas, raindrops popping on the stiff fabric.

"I'm freezing," she said.

"This is nothing."

JoLayne briskly rubbed her hands on the knees of her jeans.

Tom said, "Incredible. It was sunny all day."

"Florida," she said.

"You like it down here?"

"I like what's left."

"Ever been to Alaska?"

"Nope," she said. "They got black folks up there?"

"I'm not sure. Let me get back to you on that."

They took out the marine chart and tried to figure out where they were. Tom guessed it was one of three keys in the middle of Florida Bay—Calusa, Spy or Pearl. They wouldn't know for sure until they got enough daylight to see the horizon.

"Not that it really matters. They're all uninhabited," Tom said.

JoLayne nudged him. A tall, long-necked bird was perched regally on the stern of the Whaler. It cocked its head and studied them with blazing yellow eyes. Rain dripped off the tip of its lancelike beak.

"Great blue," JoLayne whispered.

The bird was really something. Tom said, "Hey, big guy. What's up?"

The heron took off, croaking and bellowing across the treetops.

JoLayne said, "He's pissed. We must be in his spot."

"That, or something spooked him."

They listened for movement in the mangrove. The shotgun was positioned under the canvas at JoLayne's feet.

She said, "I don't hear a thing."

"Me, neither."

"They're not exactly Green Berets, these guys. They won't be sneaking around in this weather."

"You're right," said Tom.

To pass the time until the skies cleared, they compared futures. He told her his plan to move to Alaska and write a novel about a man whose wife wouldn't divorce him, no matter what he did. Jo-Layne said she liked the premise.

"It could be very funny."

"Funny wasn't the direction I was going," Tom said.

"Oh."

"I had a darker tone in mind."

"I see. More Cheever than Roth."

"Neither," he said, "I was thinking along the lines of Stephen King."

"A horror story?"

"Sure. *The Estrangement.* What do you think?"

JoLayne said, "Scary."

She told him her idea to make a nature preserve of Simmons Wood. She intended to speak to a lawyer about inserting a conservation easement in her deed, so the property could never be developed.

"Even after I'm dead," she said. "That'll fix the greedy bastards."

"Will you stay in Grange?"

"Depends."

"On what?"

"On whether there's any other black folks in Alaska," she said. "Doesn't have to be many—one would be fine, as long as it's Luther Vandross."

"Might as well aim high," Tom said.

"Hey, I'm inviting myself, in case you hadn't noticed."

He wondered if she was serious. It sounded like it.

"Try to control yourself, Tom."

"I was just thinking it's too good to be true." He slipped an arm around her.

"You mean it?"

"I was about to ask you the same thing."

"Let's say I do. Say we both mean it," JoLayne

said. "What happens if we don't find the lottery ticket? If we're broke and bummed out."

"We'll go anyway. Don't you want to see a grizzly before they're all gone?"

JoLayne loved the thought of a northern wilderness, but she wondered about the redneck quotient. Alaska was almost as famous for its shit-kickers as for its wildlife.

Tom said, "And the place is loaded with eagles, according to what I've read."

"That would be something."

She fell asleep with her head against his shoulder. He remained awake, listening for intruders. With his free arm he moved the Remington closer. A cool gust made him shiver. Sixty-three degrees, he thought, and already my bones are cold. Perhaps the Kodiak scenario needed more thought. Also, he'd gotten the impression JoLayne wasn't bowled over by his idea for the divorce novel. He had a feeling she was humoring him.

He was tinkering with the plot when he was startled by flapping behind him—the stately heron, returning. This time it stood on the bow of the boat. Tom Krome saluted. The bird paid no attention; a small silvery fish wriggled in its beak.

Nice work, Krome thought, especially in a deluge.

Then the heron did something unexpected. It let go of the fish, which bounced off the slick deck and landed on the grass-covered beach. The bird made no move to retrieve its meal. Instead it froze like an iron weather vane, its head erect and its snakelike neck extended.

Uh-oh, Krome said to himself. What does it hear?

He didn't have to wait long. Between the stutter of the gunshots and the woman's scream, the great blue flared its wings and took off. This time it flew away from the island, into the teeth of the squall, and this time it made no sound.

Amber had never witnessed gunfire.

She'd heard it before, of course; everyone who lived in Dade County knew the sound of a semi-automatic. Yet she'd never actually seen a flame-blue muzzle flash until Shiner cut loose with the TEC-9. Her shriek was involuntary but hair-raising, cutting like a sickle through the respective stupors of Bodean Gazzer and Chub. Spewing curses, they lumbered bleary-eyed into the clearing—first Bodean Gazzer, brandishing the .380 stolen off the Colombian motorist; then Chub, in his droopy underwear, stoned and waving the Colt.

Shiner met them at the edge of the clearing. "I seen somebody! I did!" He radiated uncertainty and shame.

Bode snatched the TEC-9 and turned to Amber. "Tell the damn truth," he said.

"There *was* something out there. I heard it."

"A man? A critter?"

"I couldn't say—it's too dark."

Chub said, "Un-fucking-believable." He coughed up something that landed near Shiner's feet.

The kid knew he was in trouble. After the earlier fiasco at the trailer, the colonel had given him a stern lecture about wasting ammo. "It was a human bean," Shiner insisted in a mumble. "A nigger is what it looked like, a small un."

Impatiently Bode Gazzer motioned for the flashlight. Amber handed it to him. He ordered everyone to stay put and stalked into the trees. Ten minutes later he returned to report finding no signs of a human prowler, Negro or otherwise.

"Figgers." It was Chub growling. With a difficulty born of distaste and insobriety, he was attempting to insert his legs and arms into a set of Bode's camos. His own clothes were soaked by the rain, and he was freezing his ass off in the Jockey shorts.

Amber saw Shiner's stock sliding and tried to help. "It was making all kinds of noise. Right over there." Pointing where Shiner had fired.

"Yeah, I bet it did," said Bode Gazzer. From the pocket of his parka he produced a bloodied tuft of brown fur. "Got this off a leaf."

Amber declined an offer to inspect the evidence. Shiner shrunk away in embarrassment.

"You shot a mean ole bunny rabbit." Chub, with a sneer. "Or maybe a killer mouse."

Amber rose. Chub asked where she was going.

"To get some sleep. You mind?" She walked to the lean-to and lay down beneath the tarp.

Chub said, "We got us a Girl Scout. She made her own tent."

Bode told Shiner to go back out in the boat. "I need to talk to Major Chub alone."

"Don't call me that," Chub grumped. The camos looked absurd; the cuffs were six inches short, and the seat was about to rip out of the trousers. Yet he couldn't work up much indignation, he was still so high from the marine glue. He announced he was beat and headed for the lean-to to join his dream girl.

Bode intercepted him. "Not right now." Then, under his breath: "You got the tickets, right?"

"Yeah. Somewheres." Chub gingerly probed at his nose, which felt scalded on the inside. "I think they's still in the boat."

"You *think*." Bode wheeled and called to Shiner: "Hey, sergeant, change of plans!" Motioning toward the tarp. "You go ahead and sleep there. Chub and me'll take the perimeter."

Wordlessly Shiner did what he was told. He stretched out next to Amber, whose lovely eyes were closed. The wind had dropped off noticeably, and the rain had waned to an irregular drizzle that made whispers on the oilskin. Shiner was half dozing when he heard Amber's voice:

"It's going to be OK."

"I don't think so."

"Don't underestimate yourself," she told him.

Nothing could have puzzled Shiner more.

They waited until the kid and the waitress were asleep before checking the *Reel Luv*. The lottery tickets were safe in the console. Bodean Gazzer returned the precious condom to his wallet. Chub rolled up the other ticket, the stolen one, and slipped it into an empty bullet chamber in the .357. He laughed dopily at his own cleverness.

"Bang bang," he said.

Bode was buoyed by the sight of Chub in camouflage, even if it wasn't a tailored fit. At least they were finally dressed like an honest-to-God militia; Bode, Chub, Amber and Shiner.

Shiner, God Almighty . . .

They'd lucked out again. Thanks to the heavy weather, nobody seemed to have heard the kid's reckless shooting or the girl's scream. No planes or boats had come out to the island to investigate. The group's secret position seemed safe, for now.

Bode said to Chub: "The dumb fuckup, he's gonna get us killed."

"No shit."

"I say we cut him loose."

"You got my vote."

They agreed Shiner had outlived his usefulness to the White Clarion Aryans. While he'd faithfully backed up their story for the Lotto scam and delivered Amber to Jewfish Creek as ordered, he had become a security risk. It was only a matter of time before he'd blow away one of them by mistake.

"Maybe even the girl," Chub said, though in truth he was more worried about Shiner putting the moves on Amber than shooting her. Not that she'd ever sleep with a zit-faced skinhead, but she did seem awful protective of the kid. Chub didn't go for that one bit.

He said, "We kick him out, he's like to rat on us. How 'bout we kill him."

Bode flatly said no. "I'll never shoot no Christian white man, I can help it."

"Then let's pay the fucker off."

"How much?"

"I dunno. A grand?" Glue fumes always made Chub generous.

Bode Gazzer said, "You gotta be jokin.' "

A thousand dollars wouldn't put a ding in the $28 million, but it was still too much money for a half-wit. Especially since Bode still suspected Shiner as a possible leak in the organization. What if the kid was working undercover for the Black Tide? What if the nutball shooting sprees were an act and he was actually using the guns to signal the Negroes? Bode had no proof, but the doubts nagged at him like an itch.

He said, "How about this: A thousand bucks, less what it costs for a new quarter panel on my pickup. On account a the bullet holes he made."

"Fair by me. Tell him he gets his money soon as we get ours," Chub said, "long as he keeps his trap shut."

The decision was made to inform Shiner of his expulsion first thing in the morning. Chub would transport him by boat to the Overseas Highway, where he could hitch a ride up to Homestead and retrieve his car.

"Meanwhiles I can pick up s'more beer," Chub said.

"Cigarets, too. And ice."

"And A.1 sauce for my scrambly eggs."

Bode Gazzer said, "I better make a list."

"You do that now."

Chub took out the grocery bag containing the tube of marine adhesive. He squeezed out a moist curlicue and offered a hit to Bode, who declined. Chub buried his face in the bag and luxuriantly sucked in the vapors.

Bode said, "Easy."

Chub whooped. He had a rubber patch stuck on one eye and a rotting crab claw poking through one hand, and still he felt fucking wonderful. He wasn't the least tiny bit worried about the Black

Tide or NATO or the Tri-fucking-Lateral Commission, no siree. Nobody was gonna find 'em out
here on this faraway island, not even the trickiest
niggers. It was OK to get wasted tonight because
him and Bode was white and free and well-armed,
and best of all they was goddamn m-millionaires.

"You imagine?" Chub wheezed with glee.

Bode refrained from reminding him that the lottery proceeds were to be used strictly for militia
building. There would be a better time for that
conversation.

"Little Amber," Chub was saying. "You shoulda
seed her face when I tole her about the money. All
of a sudden she wants to go for a walk in the
woods tomorrow, just her and me."

"Aw, shit," Bode said. He should've seen it coming. "What all did you tell her?"

"Only that I's worth fourteen million dollars.
You might say it changed her opinion a me."

So would a bath, Bode thought.

"That look she give me," Chub went on dream-
ily, "like she could suck a golf ball through a garden hose."

"Careful what you say to her. Understand?"

With a hiccup Chub thrust the paper bag to his
face.

"Knock that shit off!" Bode said. "Now listen:
Pussy's fine, but there's a time and a place. Right
now we're in a battle for the heart and soul of
America!"

Chub made a noise like a tire going flat. "Hilton Head," he rasped euphorically.

"What?"

"I wanna buy Amber and me a condo up at Hilton Head. That's a island, too, and it beats the hell outta *this* one."

"You serious?"

But later, after Chub had nodded off, Bode Gazzer caught himself warming to his partner's fantasy. Strolling a sunny Carolina beach with a half-naked Hooters girl on your arm sounded much more appealing than sharing a frigid concrete pillbox with a bunch of hairy white guys in Idaho.

Bode couldn't help wondering what Amber's attitude toward him might be if she knew that he, too, was about to become a tycoon.

When JoLayne Lucks woke up, Tom Krome was sighting the shotgun across his kneecaps. That's when she realized the screaming wasn't part of a dream.

"What do you see?" she asked in a low voice. "Honey, don't forget the safety."

"It's off." He squinted down the barrel, waiting. "Did you hear the shots?"

"How many?"

"Five or six. Like a machine gun."

JoLayne wondered if the rednecks shot the

waitress. Or possibly they shot each other while fighting *over* the waitress.

As long as the waitress didn't shoot *them*. Not until I get my Lotto ticket back, JoLayne thought.

Tom said, "Listen!"

His shoulders tightened; he moved his finger on the trigger.

JoLayne heard it, too—in the woods, something running.

"Wait, it's small." She touched Tom's elbow. "Don't fire."

The rustling got closer, changed direction. Krome followed the noise with the barrel of the Remington. The movement came to a halt behind an ancient buttonwood trunk.

JoLayne grabbed the flashlight and crawled out of the makeshift blanket. She said, "Don't you go shooting me by accident. I blend in pretty good with the night."

There was no stopping her. Tom lowered the gun and watched her sneak up to the tree. She was met by an unearthly, high-pitched chittering that descended to a low snarl. Tom got goose bumps.

He heard JoLayne saying: "Now hush and behave." As if talking to a child.

She came back holding a runty-looking raccoon. There was a smear of blood on the breast of her sweatshirt; one of the animal's front paws had been grazed by a bullet.

"Assholes," said JoLayne. With the flashlight

she showed Tom what had happened. When she touched the coon, it growled and bared its teeth. Krome believed the animal was well-equipped to rip open his throat.

He said, "JoLayne—"

"Could you get me the first-aid kit?"

She'd bought a ten-dollar cheapo at the grocery store before renting the boat.

"You're going to get bit," Tom said. "We're *both* going to get bit."

"She's just frightened, that's all. She'll settle down."

"She?"

"Could you find the bandages, please?"

They worked on the raccoon's leg until nearly daybreak. They both got bit.

JoLayne beamed when the animal scurried away, feisty and muttering. As Tom dressed a punctured thumb, he said, "What if she gave us rabies?"

"Then we find ourselves somebody to chew on," JoLayne replied. "I know just the guys."

They tried to light another fire but the rain swept in, harder than before, though not as chilly. Huddling beneath the boat canvas, they worked to keep the food and the shotgun shells dry. Soon after the downfall stopped, the damp blue-gray darkness faded to light. JoLayne lay down and did two hundred crunches, Tom holding her ankles. The eastern rim of sky went pink and gold, ahead of the sun. They snacked on corn chips and gra-nola bars—everything tasted salty. In the dawn they moved the Whaler out of the mangroves to a spit of open shore, for an easier getaway. From camp they gathered what they needed and began making their way to the other end of the island.

22 When Mary Andrea Finley Krome stepped off the plane, she thought she was at the wrong airport. There were no news photographers, no TV lights, no re-porters. She was greeted only by a brisk, sharp-featured man with prematurely graying hair. He introduced himself as the managing editor of *The Register.*

Mary Andrea said, "Where's everybody else?"

"Who?"

"The reporters. I was expecting a throng."

The managing editor said, "Consider me a throng of one."

He picked up Mary Andrea's bag. She followed him outside to the car.

"We're going to the newspaper office?"

"That's right."

"Will the media be there?" Mary Andrea, peev-ishly twirling her rosary beads.

"Mrs. Krome, we *are* the media."

"You know what I mean. Television."

The managing editor informed Mary Andrea that the interest in her husband's tragic death was somewhat less avid than anticipated.

She said, "I don't understand. A journalist gets burned to smithereens—"

"Tell me about it."

The managing editor drove at excessive speed with one hand on the wheel. With the other he poked irritably at the radio buttons, switching between classical music stations. Mary Andrea wished he'd settle on something.

"I know it's made the papers," she persisted, "all the way out to Montana."

"Oh yes. Even television," said the managing editor, "briefly."

"What happened?"

"I would describe the public reaction," he said, "as a mild but fleeting curiosity."

Mary Andrea was floored. A despondency settled upon her; it might have been mistaken for authentic grief, although not by those aware of Mary Andrea's background as an actress.

The managing editor said: "Don't take it personally. It's been a humbling experience for all of us."

"But they should make Tom a hero," she protested.

The managing editor explained that the job of newspaper reporter no longer carried the stature it had in the days of Watergate. The nineties had brought a boom in celebrity journalism, a decline in serious investigative reporting and a deliberate "softening of the product" by publishers. The result, he said, was that daily papers seldom caused a ripple in their communities, and people paid less and less attention to them.

"So your husband's death," said the managing editor, "didn't exactly generate an uproar."

Gloomily Mary Andrea stared out the car window. If only Tom had made it to *The New York Times* or *The Washington Post,* then you'd have seen a damn uproar.

"Was he working on something big?" she asked hopefully.

"Not at all. That's part of the problem—it was just a routine feature story."

"About what?"

"Some woman who won the lottery."

"And for that he got blown up?"

"The police are skeptical. And as I said, that's part of our problem. It's far from certain Tom was killed in the line of duty. It could have been a robbery, it could have been . . . something more personal."

Mary Andrea gave him a sour look. "Don't tell me he was doing somebody's wife."

"Just a rumor, Mrs. Krome. But I'm afraid it was enough to spook Ted Koppel."

"Shit," Mary Andrea said. She would've gargled battery acid to get on *Nightline.*

The managing editor went on: "We gave it our best shot, but they wanted it to be a mob hit or some cocaine kingpin's revenge for a front-page exposé. They were disappointed to find out Tom was just a feature writer. And after the adultery rumor, well, they quit returning our calls."

Mary Andrea slumped against the door. It was like skidding into a bad dream. That the media had already lost interest in Tom Krome's murder meant vastly reduced exposure for his bereft wife—and a wasted plane fare, Mary Andrea thought bitterly. Worse, she'd put herself in position to be humiliated if the fatal "mystery blaze" was traced to a jealous husband instead of a vengeful drug lord.

Damn you, Tom, she thought. This is my career on the line.

"How's the hotel?" she asked glumly.

"We got you a nonsmoking room, like you requested." Now the managing editor was chewing on a toothpick.

"And there's a gym with a StairMaster?"

He said: "No gym. No StairMaster. Sorry."

"Oh, that's great."

"It's a HoJo's, Mrs. Krome. We put up everybody at the HoJo's."

After a ten-minute sulk, Mary Andrea announced she'd changed her mind; she wished to return to the airport immediately. She said she was too grief-stricken to appear at the newspaper to accept the writing award Tom had won.

"What's it called again—the 'Emilio'?"

"Amelia," said the managing editor, "and it's quite a big deal. Tom's the first journalist to win it posthumously. It would mean a lot if you could be there in his place."

Mary Andrea sniffed. "Mean a lot to who?"

"Me. The staff. His colleagues." The managing editor rolled the toothpick with his tongue. "And possibly your future."

"Come on, you just told me—"

"We've got a press conference scheduled."

Mary Andrea Finley Krome drilled him with a stare. "A *real* press conference?"

"The TV folks will be there, if that's what you mean."

"How do you know for sure?"

"Because it's a safe story."

"Safe?"

"Fluff. Human interest," the managing editor explained. "They don't want to get into the murky details of the murder, but they're thrilled to do twenty seconds on a pretty young widow receiving a plaque for her slain husband."

"I see."

"And I'd be less than frank," the managing editor added, "if I didn't admit my paper could use the publicity, too. This is a big award, and we don't win all that many."

"When you say TV, are we talking network?"

"Affiliates, sure. CBS, ABC and Fox."

"Oh. Fox, too?" Mary Andrea, thinking: I'll definitely need a new dress, something shorter.

"Will you do it?" the managing editor asked.

"I suppose I could pull myself together," she said.

Thinking: Twenty seconds of airtime, my ass.

Katie Battenkill made a list of things for which she had forgiven Arthur, or overlooked, because he was a judge and being married to a judge was important. The inventory included his annoying table manners, his curtness to her friends and relatives, his disrespect for her religion, his violent jealousy, his cheap and repeated adulteries, his habit of premature ejaculation and of course his rancid choice of cologne.

These Katie weighed against the benefits of being Mrs. Arthur Battenkill Jr., which included a fine late-model car, a large house, invitations to all society events, an annual trip to Bermuda with the local bar association, and the occasional extravagant gift, such as the diamond pendant Katie was now admiring in the vanity mirror.

She hadn't thought of herself as a shallow or materialistic woman, but the possibility dawned upon her. Art was quite the unrepentant sinner, yet for eight years Katie had put up with it. She'd spent little time trying to change him, but allowed herself to be intimidated by his caustic tongue and mollified by presents. Ignoring what he did became easier than arguing about it. Katie told herself it wasn't a completely loveless marriage, inasmuch as she honestly loved being the wife of a circuit court judge; it was Arthur himself for whom she had no deep feelings.

Many Sundays she'd gone to church and asked God what to do, and at no time had He specifically counseled her to start an illicit affair with an itinerant newspaperman. But that's what had happened. It had caught Katie Battenkill totally by surprise and left her powerless to resist—like one of her uncontrollable cravings for Godiva chocolate, only a hundred times stronger. The moment she'd laid eyes on Tom Krome, she knew what would happen. . . .

She was in a walkathon for attention-deficit children when all of a sudden this good-looking guy came jogging down James Street in the opposite direction, weaving through the phalanx of T-shirted marchers. As he approached Katie, he slowed his pace just enough to smile and press a five-dollar bill in her palm. For the kids, he'd said, and kept running. And Katie, to her astonishment, immediately turned and ran after him.

Tom Krome was the first man she'd ever seduced, if that's what you call a hummer in the front seat.

Now, looking back on those wild and guilt-ridden weeks, Katie understood the purpose.

Everything happens for a reason—a divine force had brought Tommy jogging into her life. God was trying to tell her something: that there were good men out there, decent and caring men whom Katie could trust. And while He probably didn't intend for her to have torrid reckless sex with the first one she met, Katie hoped He would understand.

The important thing was that Tom Krome made her realize she could get by without Arthur, the lying snake. All she needed was some self-confidence, a reordering of priorities and the courage to be honest about the empty relationship with her husband. There hadn't been enough time to fall in love with Tommy, but she certainly *liked* him better than she liked Arthur. The way Tom had apologized for forgetting to call that night from Grange—Katie couldn't remember hearing Arthur say he was sorry for anything. Tom Krome wasn't special or outstanding; he was just a kind, affectionate guy. That's all it took. The fact that Katie Battenkill was so easily drawn astray portended a dim future for the marriage. She decided she had to get out.

Katie recalled a line from an Easter sermon: "To tolerate sin is to abet it, and to share in the sinning." She thought of Arthur's many sins, including Dana, Willow and others whose names she never knew. That was bad enough, the adultery, but now the judge had commissioned an arson and a man was dead.

Not an innocent man, to be sure; an evil little shit. Yet still precious in the eyes of a benevolent God.

That was a sin Katie could not tolerate, if she hoped to save herself. What to do now?

In the mirror the diamond necklace glinted like a tiny star among her many freckles. Of course it was nothing but a bribe to ensure her silence, but dear God, was it gorgeous.

The bathroom door opened and out came her husband with *The Register* folded under one arm.

"Art, we need to talk."

"Yes, we do. Let's go to the kitchen."

Katie was relieved. The bedroom was no place to drop the bomb.

She noticed her hands fluttering as she filled the coffeemaker. Over her shoulder she heard Arthur say, "Katherine, I've decided to retire from the bench. How would you like to live in the islands?"

Slowly she turned. "What?"

"I've had enough. The job is killing me," he said. "I'm up for reelection next year but I don't have the stomach for another campaign. I'm burned out, Katie."

All she could think to say was: "We can't afford to retire, Art."

"Thank you, Ms. Dean Witter, but I beg to differ."

In that acid tone of voice that Katie had come to despise.

"Shocking as it may seem," the judge went on, "I made a few modest investments without consulting you. One of them's paid off very handsomely, to the tune of a quarter-million dollars."

Katie gave no outward sign of being impressed, but it was a struggle to remain composed. "What kind of investment?"

"A unit trust. It's a bit complicated to explain."

"I bet."

"Real estate, Katherine."

She made the coffee and poured a cup for Arthur.

"You're forty-three years old and ready to retire."

"The American dream," said the judge, smacking his lips.

"Why the islands? And which islands?" Katie, thinking: I can't even get him to take me to the beach.

Arthur Battenkill said, "Roy Tigert has offered to loan us his bungalow in the Bahamas. At Marsh Harbour, just to see if we like it. If we don't, we'll try someplace else—the Caymans or Saint Thomas."

Katie was speechless. Bungalow in the Bahamas—it sounded like a vaudeville song.

Awkwardly her husband reached across the table and stroked her cheek. "I know things haven't been perfect around here—we need to make a change, Katherine, to save what we've got.

We'll go away and start over, you and me, with no-body else to worry about."

Meaning Tom Krome—or Art's secretaries?

Katie asked, "When?"

"Right away."

"Oh."

"Remember how much you liked Nassau?"

"I've never been there, Arthur. That must've been Willow."

The judge sucked desperately at his coffee.

Katie said, "This isn't about saving our marriage, it's about Tommy's house burning down with a dead body inside. You're scared shitless because it's your fault."

Arthur Battenkill Jr. stared blankly into his cup. "You've developed quite an imagination, Katherine."

"You're running away. Admit it, Arthur. You stole some getaway money, and now you want to leave the country. Do you think I'm stupid?"

"No," said the judge, "I think you're practical."

On that same Monday morning, the fourth of December, the real estate office of Clara Markham received an unexpected visitor: Bernard Squires, investment manager for the Central Midwest Brotherhood of Grouters, Spacklers and Dry-wallers International. He'd flown to Florida on a private Gulfstream jet, chartered for him by

Richard "The Icepick" Tarbone. The mission of Bernard Squires was to place a large deposit on the Simmons Wood property, thereby locking it up for the union pension fund from which the Tarbone crime family regularly stole. After driving through Grange, Bernard Squires felt more confident than ever that the shopping mall planned for Simmons Wood could be devised to fail both plausibly and exorbitantly.

"We spoke on the phone," he said to Clara Markham.

"Yes, of course" she said, "but I'm afraid I've got nothing new to report."

"That's why I'm here."

Clara Markham asked if Squires could come back later, as she had an important closing to attend.

Squires was courteous but insistent. "I doubt it's as important as this," he said, and positioned a black eelskin briefcase on her desk.

The real estate agent had never seen so much cash; neat, tight bundles of fifties and hundreds. Somewhere among the sweet-smelling stacks, Clara knew, was her commission; probably the largest she'd ever see.

"This is to show how serious we are about acquiring the property," Squires explained, "and to expedite the negotiations. The people I represent are eager to get started immediately."

Clara Markham was in a bind. She'd heard

nothing over the weekend from JoLayne Lucks. Their friendship was close—and JoLayne was an absolute saint with Kenny, Clara's beloved Persian—but the real estate agent couldn't permit her personal feelings to jeopardize such a huge deal.

She waved a hand above the cash and said, "This is very impressive, Mr. Squires, but I must tell you I'm expecting a counteroffer."

"Really?"

"There's nothing in writing yet, but I've been assured it's on the way."

Squires seemed amused. "All right." With a well-practiced motion he quietly closed the briefcase. "We're prepared to match any reasonable counteroffer. In the meantime, I'd ask that you contact your clients and let them know how committed we are to this project."

Clara Markham said, "Absolutely. First thing after lunch."

"What's wrong with right now?"

"I . . . I'm not sure I can reach them."

"Let's try," said Bernard Squires.

Clara Markham saw that stalling was fruitless; the man wouldn't return to Chicago without an answer. Bernard Squires settled crisply into a chair while she telephoned the attorney for the estate of Lighthorse Simmons. Five minutes later the attorney called back, having patched together a conference call with Lighthorse's two profligate heirs—his son, Leander Simmons, and his daughter, Janine Simmons Robinson. Leander dabbled in fossil fuels and Thoroughbreds; Janine spent her money on exotic surgeries and renovating vacation houses.

Leaning close to the speakerphone, Clara Markham carefully summarized the union's offer for Simmons Wood, the key detail being the figure of $3 million.

"In addition," she concluded, "Mr. Squires has delivered to my office a substantial cash deposit."

On the other end, Leander Simmons piped, "How much?" He whistled when the real estate agent told him.

An old pro at conference calls, Bernard Squires raised his voice just enough to be heard: "We wanted everyone to know how serious we are."

"Well, you got *my* attention," said Janine Simmons Robinson.

"Me, too," her brother said.

On behalf of JoLayne Lucks and the doomed wildlife of Simmons Wood, Clara Markham felt compelled to say: "Mr. Squires and his group want to build a shopping mall on your father's land."

"With a playground in the atrium," Squires added coolly.

"And a Mediterranean fountain in front," the attorney chimed, "with real ducks and geese. It'll be a terrific attraction for your little town."

From the speakerphone came the instant reaction of Leander Simmons: "Personally, I don't give a shit if you guys want to dig a coal mine. How about you, Sis?"

Said Janine: "Hey, three million bucks is three million bucks."

"Exactly. So what the hell are we waiting for?" Leander demanded. "Just do it."

Bernard Squires said, "We're ready to go. However, Ms. Markham informs me there may be another offer."

"From who?" asked Janine Simmons Robinson.

"How much?" asked her brother.

Clara Markham said, "It's a local investor. I intended to call you as soon as I received the papers, but they haven't arrived."

"Then screw it," said the attorney. "Let's go with Squires."

"Whatever you wish."

"Now just hold on a second." It was Leander Simmons. "What's the big rush?"

He smelled more money. Bernard Squires' expression blackened at the prospect of a bidding duel. Clara Markham noticed some fresh veins pulsing in his neck.

As it happened, Janine Simmons Robinson was on the same opportunistic wavelength as her brother. "What's the harm in waiting a couple three days?" she said. "See what these other folks have in mind."

"It's your call," said their attorney. Then: "Ms. Markham, will you get back to us as soon as you hear something—say, no later than Wednesday?"

"How about tomorrow," said Bernard Squires.

"Wednesday," said Leander Simmons and his sister in unison.

There was a series of clicks, then the speaker box went silent. Clara Markham looked apologetically first at Bernard Squires, then at the eelskin briefcase on her desk. "I'll deposit this in our escrow account," she said, "right away."

Gravely Squires rose from the chair.

"You don't strike me as a deceitful person," he said, "the sort who'd try to jack up her commission by cooking up phony counteroffers."

"I'm not a sneak," said Clara Markham, "nor am I an imbecile. Simmons Wood will be my biggest deal of the year, Mr. Squires. I wouldn't risk blowing the whole enchilada for a few extra bucks."

He believed her. He'd seen the town; it was a miracle she hadn't starved to death.

"A local investor, you said."

"That's right."

"I don't suppose you'd be kind enough to tell me the name."

"I'm afraid I can't, Mister Squires."

"But you're confident they've got some resources."

"They do," said Clara Markham, thinking: Last I heard.

Shiner's mother overslept. The road machines woke her.

Hurriedly she squeezed into the bridal gown, snatched her parasol and sailed out the door. By the time she reached the intersection of Sebring Street and the highway, it was too late. The Department of Transportation was ready to pave the Road-Stain Jesus.

Shiner's mother shrieked and hopped about like a costumed circus monkey. She spat in the face of the crew foreman and used her parasol to stab ineffectively at the driver of the steamroller. Ultimately she flung herself facedown upon the holy splotch and refused to budge for the machines.

"Pave me, too, you godless bastards!" she cried. "Let me be one with my Savior!"

The crew foreman wiped off his cheek and signaled for his men to halt work. He telephoned the sheriff's office and said: "There's a crazy witch in a wedding dress out here humping the road. What do I do?"

Two deputies arrived, followed later by a television truck.

Shiner's mother was kissing the pavement, on the place she imagined to be Jesus' forehead.

"Don't you worry, Son of God," she kept saying. "I'm right here. I'm not goin' nowheres!" Her devotion to the stain was remarkable, considering its downwind proximity to a flattened opossum.

A vanload of worried-looking pilgrims arrived, but the deputies ordered them to stay out of the right-of-way. Shiner's mother raised her head and said: "That's the collection box on top of the cooler. Help yourselves to a Sprite!"

By now traffic was blocked in both directions. The crew foreman, who was from Tampa and unfamiliar with the local lore, asked the deputies if there was a mental institution in town.

"Naw, but we're overdue," said one of them.

They each grabbed an arm and hoisted Shiner's mother off the highway. "He's watching! He sees you!" she screamed.

The deputies deposited her in the cage of a patrol car and chased the curious tourists away. Before continuing with the paving job, the crew foreman and his men assembled in a loose semicircle at the center line. They were trying to figure out what the lunatic biddy was ranting about.

Bending over the stain, the foreman said, "If that's Jesus Christ, I'm Long Dong Silver."

"Hell, it's fuckin' brake fluid," declared one of his men, a mechanic.

"Oil," asserted another.

Then the driver of the steamroller said: "From

here it kinda looks like a woman. If you close one eye, a naked woman on a camel."

That was it for the foreman. "Back to work," he snapped.

The TV crew stayed for the paving. They got an excellent close-up of the Road-Stain Jesus disappearing beneath a rolling black crust of hot asphalt. The scene was deftly crosscut with a shot of a young pilgrim sniffling into a Kleenex as if grieving. In reality she was merely trying to stave off dead-opossum fumes.

The story ran on the noon news out of Orlando. It opened with videotape of Shiner's mother, tenderly smooching the sacred smudge. Joan anxiously phoned Roddy at work. "There's TV people in town. What if they hear about the turtle shrine?"

"Pretend we don't know him," Roddy said.

"But he's my brother."

"Fine. Then you do the interviews."

Shiner's mother was booked for disturbing the peace and after three hours was released without bail. Immediately she took a cab to the intersection of Sebring and the highway. The asphalt had hardened, dry to the touch; Shiner's mother wasn't even positive where the stain had been. She observed that somebody had stolen her collection box and most of the cold sodas. She was officially out of business.

She made her way to Demencio's house and set her empty cooler in the shade of an oak tree, away from Sinclair's crowd. Trish noticed her sitting there and brought a lemonade.

"I heard what happened. I'm so sorry."

"Pigs tore my gown," Shiner's mother said.

"We can mend that in no time," said Trish.

"What about my shrine. Who's gonna fix *that*?"

"Just you wait. There'll be new stains on the highway."

Shiner's mother said, "Ha."

Trish glanced at the front window of the house, in case Demencio was watching; he'd be miffed if he spotted the old lady on the premises. Her ice-blue parasol stood out like a pup tent.

"You should go home and get some rest," Trish said.

"Not after I've lost the two things in the world I care about most—the Road-Stain Jesus, and my only son."

"Oh, Shiner will be back." Trish, thinking: As soon as he needs money.

"But he won't never be the same. I got a feeling he is bein' corrupted by the forces of Satan." Shiner's mother drained the glass of lemonade. "How about some of that angel food?"

"I'm afraid it's all gone. Need a lift home?"

"Maybe later," Shiner's mother said. "First I got to talk to the turtle boy. My heart's been steam-rolled, I need some spiritual healing."

"Poor thing." Trish excused herself and hurried inside to warn Demencio. Shiner's mother lit a cigaret and waited for the line around the moat to dwindle.

23 The Everglades empties off the Florida peninsula into a shimmering panorama of tidal flats, serpentine channels and bright-green mangrove islets. The balance of life there depends upon a seasonal infusion of freshwater from the mainland. Once it was a certainty of nature, but no more. The drones who in the 1940s carved levees and gouged canals throughout the upper Everglades gave absolutely no thought to what would happen downstream to the fish and birds, not to mention the Indians. For the engineers, the holy mission was to ensure the comfort and prosperity of non-native humans. In the dry season the state drained water off the Everglades for immediate delivery to cities and farms. In the wet season it pumped millions of gallons seaward to prevent flooding of subdivisions, pastures and crops.

Over time, less and less freshwater reached Florida Bay, and what ultimately got there wasn't so pure. When the inevitable drought came, the parched bay changed drastically. Sea grasses began to die off by the acre. The bottom turned to mud. Pea-green algae blooms erupted to blanket hundreds of square miles, a stain so large as to be visible from NASA satellites. Starved for sunlight, sponges died and floated to the surface in rotting clumps.

The collapse of the famous estuary produced the predictable dull-eyed bafflement among bureaucrats. Faced with a public-relations disaster and a cataclysmic threat to the tourism industry, the same people who by their ignorance had managed to starve Florida Bay now began scrambling for a way to revive it. This would be difficult without antagonizing the same farmers and developers for whom the marshlands had been so expensively replumbed. Politicians were caught in a bind. Those who'd never lost a moment's sleep over the fate of the white heron now waxed lyrical about its delicate grace. Privately, meanwhile, they reassured campaign donors that—screw the birds—Big Agriculture would still get first crack at the precious water.

For anyone seeking election to office in South Florida, restoring the Everglades became not only a pledge but a mantra. Speeches were given, grandiose promises made, blue-ribbon task forces assembled, research grants awarded, scientific symposiums convened . . . and not much changed. The state continued to siphon gluttonously what should have been allowed to flow naturally toward Florida Bay. In the driest years the bay struggled;

turned to a briny soup. In the rainiest years it re-
bounded with life.

The condition of the place could be assessed
best at remote islands such as Pearl Key. When the
mangroves were spangled with pelicans and egrets,
when the sky held ospreys and frigate birds, when
the shallows boiled with mullet and snook—that
meant plenty of good water was spilling from the
'Glades; enough for a reprieve from the larceny
perpetrated upstream.

It was Chub's misfortune to have arrived at
Pearl Key after an exceptionally generous rainy
season, when the island was lush and teeming.
Scarcely two months later the flats would be as
murky as chocolate milk, the game fish and wading birds would have fled, and in the water would
swim few creatures of serious concern to a glue-
sniffing kidnapper, passed out with one hand
dangling.

His wounded hand, as it happened; swollen and
gray, still adorned with a severed crab claw.

As fishermen know, the scent of bait is diffused
swiftly and efficiently in saltwater, attracting scavengers of all sizes. Chub knew this, too, although
the information currently was stored beyond his
grasp. Not even a doctorate in marine biology
would've mitigated the stupefying volume of
polyurethane fumes he'd inhaled from the tube of
boat glue. He was completely unaware that his
wounded mitt hung so tantalizingly in the water,

just as he was unaware of the cannibalistic pro-
clivities of *Callinectes sapidus,* the common blue
crab.

In fact, Chub was so blitzed that the sensation
of extreme pain—which ordinarily would have
reached his brain stem in a nanosecond—instead
meandered from one befogged synapse to another.
By the time his subconscious registered the feeling,
something horrible was well under way.

His screams ruined an otherwise golden
morning.

The other three had been awake for hours. Bodean
Gazzer was patrolling the woods not far from the
campsite. Amber was attempting to revise Shiner's
tattoo, using a honed fishhook and a dollop of violet mascara. Before starting she'd numbed his
upper arm with ice, but the pricking still stung like
hell. Shiner hoped the procedure would be brief,
since only two of the three initials required alter-
ing. Amber warned him it wasn't an easy job,
changing the letters from *W.R.B.* to *W.C.A.*

"The *B* won't be bad. I'll just add legs to make
it look like a capital *A*. But the *R* is tricky," she
said, frowning. "I can't promise it'll ever pass for
a *C.*"

Shiner, through clenched teeth: "Do your
best, 'K?"

He turned away, so he wouldn't see the punctures. Occasionally he'd let out a grunt, which was Amber's cue to apply more ice. Despite the discomfort, Shiner found himself enjoying being the focus of her concentration. He liked the way she'd rolled up the sleeves of the camouflage jumpsuit and pinned her hair in a ponytail; all business. And her touch—clinical as it was—sent a pleasurable tickle all the way to his groin.

"I had a friend," she was saying, "he was paranoid about dying in a plane crash. So he got his initials tattooed on his arms and his legs, his shoulders, the soles of his feet, both cheeks of his butt. See, because he'd read where that's one way they can identify the body parts, if there's tattoos."

Shiner said, "That's pretty smart."

"Yeah, but it didn't help. He was, like, a smuggler."

"Oh."

"His plane went down off the Bahamas. Sharks got him."

"There wasn't nothin' left?"

"One of his Reeboks is all they found," Amber said. "Inside was something that looked like a toe. Of course, it wasn't tattooed."

"Damn."

To Shiner's surprise, Amber began to sing as she went at him with the fishhook:

> *"Smile like a princess but bite like a snake—*
> *Got ice in her veins and a heart that don't ache.*

She a nut-cutting bitch and that's no lie,
Hack 'em both off with a gleam in her eye . . ."

Shiner said, "You got a nice voice."

"White Rebel Brotherhood," said Amber, "the song I told you about. It's killer." As she worked on the tattoo, her face was so close he could feel the soft breath on his skin.

He said, "Maybe I'll check out the CD."

"They do it more hip-hop."

"Yeah, I figgered."

"Am I hurting you?"

"Naw," Shiner lied. "Matter a fact, I was wonderin' if mebbe you could add somethin' extry. Under the eagle."

"Such as?"

"A swatch ticker," said Shiner.

"A what?"

"You know—a swatch ticker. Like the Nazis had."

Amber glanced up sharply. "Swastika, you mean."

"Yeah!" He practiced the proper pronunciation. "That'd be cool, don'tcha think?"

"I don't know how to draw one. Sorry."

Shiner mulled it over, wincing every so often at the stabs of the fishhook. "I seen some good ones at the colonel's place," he said eventually, "if I can only 'member how they went. Look here. . . ."

He cleared a place in the sand and, using a forefinger, drew his version of the infamous German cross.

Amber shook her head. "That's not right."

"You sure?"

"You made it look like . . . like something from the Chinese alphabet."

"Now hold on," said Shiner, but he was stumped. Just then Bodean Gazzer came stomping out of the mangroves. He sat near the fire and began wiping dew from his rifle. Shiner called him over.

"Colonel, can you do a swatch ticker?"

"No problem." Bode saw an opportunity to impress Amber at the kid's expense. He put down the gun and joined them under the tarp. With a sweep of a hand he erased Shiner's chicken-scratch swastika. In broad, sure strokes he sketched his own.

Amber briefly scrutinized the design before declaring it had "too many thingies." She was referring to the tiny stems that Bode had drawn on the ends of the secondary legs.

"You're wrong, sweetheart," he told her. "That's exactly how the Nasties done it."

Amber didn't argue, but she thought: Any serious white supremacist and Jew-hater would know how to make a swastika. Bode and Shiner's confusion on the topic reaffirmed her suspicions that the White Clarion Aryans were a pretty lame operation.

"OK, you're the expert," she said to Bode, and

began reheating the point of the fishhook with a cigaret lighter.

Shiner felt his stomach jump. He had a hunch Amber was right—the colonel's swastika was odd-looking; too many angles, and the lines seemed to point in the wrong directions. The damn thing was either upside down or inside out, Shiner couldn't tell which.

"Where you gone put it?" Bode asked.

"Under the bird." Amber tapped the designated location on Shiner's left biceps.

Bode said, "Perfect."

Shiner didn't know what to do. He didn't want to offend his commanding officer but he sure as hell didn't want another defective tattoo. And a fucked-up swastika would be difficult to fix, Shiner knew; difficult and painful.

Amber pressed a fresh batch of ice cubes against his arm. "Let me know when you can't feel the cold."

Bode Gazzer edged closer. "I wanna watch."

Shiner fixed his gaze on the blackened barb of the fishhook and instantly became dizzy.

"Ready?" asked Amber.

Shiner sucked in a deep breath—he'd made up his mind. He'd do it for the brotherhood.

"Anytime," he said thickly, and locked his eyes shut.

At first he believed the screams he heard were his own. Then, as the animal howling tapered to a stream of profanity, Shiner recognized the timbre of Chub's voice.

Then Amber saying: "Oh my God."

And Bodean Gazzer: "What the hell!"

Shiner looked up to see Chub, nude except for Amber's orange shorts, which he wore upon his head. The shorts were pulled down as snugly as a skullcap, fitted at an angle to hide Chub's eye patch.

But that's not what made the others stare.

It was fastened to the end of Chub's right arm, which hung limp and heavy at his side. Where once there was only a pair of dead crab pincers there was now a complete live crab; one of the largest crabs Amber had ever seen, outside the Seaquarium.

"What do I do?" Chub pleaded. "Jesus Willy, what the fuck do I do?" Gummy-eyed from either sleep or glue, he displayed his other hand— his functional hand—for them to see. The knuckles were bloody knobs, from beating on the crustacean.

Amber cast her eyes at Shiner, who had not much experience with marine life and, thus, no counterstrategy. Despite his white brother's awful predicament, he couldn't help feeling a sense of reprieve. While the others stood transfixed by the sight of Chub, Shiner discreetly scuffed his feet across the dirt until he'd obscured Bode Gazzer's dubious swastika sketch.

"The crab!" Chub was bellowing. "The crab, it's after that g-g-goddamn claw!"

Gravely Bode surmised: "It's either trying to eat it or fuck it."

In its bloated and discolored state, Chub's hand could have been mistaken by a farsighted crab for another member of its species; that was Bode's hypothesis. Amber had nothing more plausible to offer.

Shiner asked, "How come he got your pants on his head?"

"God only knows," she said with a sigh.

Chub bolted toward the water. When the others caught up, they found him madly slinging his lifeless crab arm against the stump of an ancient buttonwood.

Shiner stepped forward. "I'll take care a that goddamn thing."

Bode was alarmed to see the Beretta glinting in the kid's paw. "Oh, no you don't," he said, snatching it away. "I'll do the honors, son."

"Do what?" Amber asked.

She felt Shiner's hand on her shoulder. "Better stand back," he advised.

Although he was unaware of it, Bodean Gazzer almost hadn't made it back to camp. Tom Krome and JoLayne Lucks almost caught him alone.

They'd spotted him from about a hundred

yards, moving across a salt flat on the crown of the island. The flat was wide and oval-shaped, ringed by mangroves and hurricane deadfall. Normally it filled up as a lagoon during the big autumn tides, but two days of heavy winds had blown out much of the water. Assault rifle in hand, Bode had scattered groups of stilt-legged birds as he clomped through the custardlike marl.

JoLayne and Tom had emerged from the tree line no more than two minutes behind him. They couldn't risk following the same path across the flat because there was no cover. So they kept low to the ground and skirted the fringe, picking their way through the stubborn mangroves. It was slow going; Tom leading the way, holding the springy branches until JoLayne could squeeze past with the Remington. When they reached the place where the stumpy redneck had reentered the woods, they could make out his heavy-footed crackles and crunches ahead of them. They moved forward carefully, baby-stepping, so he wouldn't hear.

Then the twig-snapping stopped. JoLayne tugged Tom's sleeve and motioned him to be still. She came up beside him and whispered: "I smell wood smoke."

The sound of conversation confirmed it. They were very near the robbers' camp; possibly too near. Quietly JoLayne and Tom backed off, concealing themselves in a tangled canopy. All around them, the tree limbs were necklaced with freshly spun spiderwebs. Tom leaned back, dazzled.

"Golden-orbed weaver," JoLayne said.

"It's gorgeous."

"Sure is." She found it interesting that he was so calm, almost relaxed, as long as they were on the chase. It was doing nothing that seemed to unsettle him, the sitting and waiting.

When JoLayne mentioned it, Tom said, "That's because I'd rather be the hunter than the hunted. Wouldn't you?"

"Well, we got pretty close to the bastard."

"Yeah. You're good at this."

"For a black girl, you mean?"

"JoLayne, don't start with that."

"Not all of us hang out on street corners. Some of us actually know our way around the woods . . . or maybe were you referring to women in general."

"Actually, I was." Tom decided it was better to be thought a chauvinist than a racist—assuming JoLayne was half serious.

She said, "Are you saying your wife never took you stalking?"

"Not that I can recall."

"And none of your girlfriends?" Now JoLayne was smiling. Obviously she enjoyed giving him a start now and then.

Kissing his neck sweetly: "I'm sorry to be jerking your chain, but it's more fun than I can stand.

You don't know how long it's been since I've had a guilt-ridden white boy all to myself."

"That's me."

"We should've made love again," she said, suddenly pensive. "Last night—to hell with the rain and cold, we should've done it."

Tom thought it an odd moment to raise the subject, what with a gang of heavily armed lunatics three hundred feet away.

"I decided a long time ago," she said, "that if I knew exactly when I was going to die, I'd make a point of screwing my brains out the night before."

"Good plan."

"And we *could* die out here on this island. I mean, these are very bad guys we're chasing."

Tom said he preferred to think positive thoughts.

"But you do agree," JoLayne said, "there's a chance they'll kill us."

"Hell, yes, there's a chance."

"That's all I'm saying. That's why I wish we'd made love."

"Oh, I think we'll get another shot." Tom, trying to stay upbeat.

JoLayne Lucks closed her eyes and rolled her head back. "Mortal fear makes for great sex—I read that someplace."

"Mortal fear."

"It wasn't *Cosmo,* either. I'm sorry for babbling, Tom, I'm just really—"

"Nervous. Me, too," he said. "Let's concentrate on what to do about these assholes who stole your lottery ticket."

The dreamy expression passed from JoLayne's face. "That wasn't all they did."

"I know."

"But still I'm not sure if I can make myself pull the trigger."

"Maybe it won't come to that," he said.

JoLayne pointed up in the mangrove branches. A tiny barrel-shaped beetle had become trapped in one of the gossamer webs. Slowly, almost casually, the spider was crossing the intricate net toward the struggling insect.

"That's what we need. A web," JoLayne said.

They watched the stalking until a drawn-out cry broke the stillness; not a woman's cry, this time, but a man's. It was no less harrowing.

JoLayne shuddered and rose to her knees. "Damn. What now?"

Tom Krome got up quickly. "Well, I'd rather have them screaming than singing campfire songs." He held out his hand. "Come on. Let's go see."

Chub didn't trust either Bode or Shiner to shoot the crab safely off his hand. He didn't even trust himself.

"I feel like dogshit," he admitted.

They persuaded him to lie down, and the panic passed after a few minutes. The piercing pain subsided into a dead throbbing weight. Bode brought a lukewarm Budweiser and Shiner offered a stick of beef jerky. From Amber, nothing; not a peep of sympathy.

"I'm cold," Chub complained. "I got the shakes."

Bode told him the wound was badly infected. "What I can see of it," he added. The crab had quite a mouthful.

"Is the fucker dead or alive?" Chub, squinting fretfully.

Shiner said, "Dead."

Bode said, "Alive."

Chub looked to Amber for the tiebreaker. "I can't honestly tell," she said.

"God, I'm freezin'. My skin's on fire but the rest a me is freezin' cold."

Amber pulled the tarpaulin off the tree and blanketed Chub, up to his neck. He was thrilled by what he perceived, incorrectly, as an act of comfort and affection. Amber's true intent was selfish: to conceal from plain view Chub's stringy nakedness, as well as the ghastly crab.

He said, "Thank you, darling. Later we'll go on that walk you promised."

"You're in no shape to walk anywhere."

Shiner said, "Amen, that's a fact." Dreading the thought of the two of them alone.

Bodean Gazzer warmed a pot of coffee on the fire. Chub began to doze. Amber furtively tried to retrieve her waitress shorts but they caught on Chub's ponytail, which snapped him awake. "No, don't you dare! They're mine, goddammit, you gave 'em to me!" Twisting and shaking his head.

"OK, OK." Amber backed off.

From beneath the tarp emerged Chub's good hand. It readjusted the shiny pants across his nose and mouth, leaving his unpatched eye exposed through one of the leg holes.

Shiner, his back turned to Chub, mouthed the words: "He's crazy."

"Thanks for the news flash," said Amber.

They drank the coffee while Bodean Gazzer read aloud from the writings of the First Patriot Covenant. When he got to the part about Negroes and Jews being descended from the devil, Amber waved a hand. "Where does it say *that* in the Scriptures?"

"Oh, it's in there. 'Those who lay down with Satan will bring forth from his demon seed only children of darkness and deceit.' " Bode was winging it. He hadn't cracked a Bible since junior high.

Amber remained skeptical, but Shiner chirped: "If the colonel says it's in there, it's in there." Though Shiner couldn't recall his fanatically reborn mother invoking such a potent verse. It seemed like something she would've mentioned, too; demon seeds!

Chub lifted his head and requested his sack of marine glue. Angrily Bode said, "You're done with that shit."

"I ain't, either." Whenever Chub spoke, the satiny fabric of Amber's shorts puckered around his mouth. Amber expected she would carry the freaky vision to her grave.

Bodean Gazzer was saying, "Christ, you already got a fucked-up eye, a fucked-up hand—last thing you need is a fucked-up brain. You're a soldier, remember? A major."

"My ass." Chub, glowering through the pants.

Bode resumed reading, but only Shiner remained attentive. His questions mostly concerned the living accommodations provided in Montana by the First Patriot Covenant. Did the pillboxes have central heating? Was there cable TV, or a dish?

Chub, who'd nodded off again, suddenly sprung to a sitting position. "My gun! Where's it at?"

"Probably in the boat," Bode said disapprovingly, "with your camos."

"Go find it!"

"I'm busy."

"Now! I ast for my goddamn gun!" Chub had remembered the lottery ticket, hidden in one of the chambers.

Shiner said, "I'll go."

"Like hell," Chub snarled. His eye fell upon Amber. She was on the other side of the campfire, sitting beside the kid; real close, too. *Touching him*—touching his pudgy arm!

Chub didn't realize she was icing the tattoo, but it likely wouldn't have mattered. To Bode Gazzer he said: "Time for a meetin'."

"What?"

"Of the WCA. We got 'portant bidness, remember?"

"Oh yeah," said Bode. He'd have preferred to wait until the crab crisis was resolved. Encumbered as he was, Chub had lost some of the menacing presence that was so useful in tight confrontations.

Bode called the meeting to order with such a lack of enthusiasm that it put Amber on alert. She gave Shiner a quick jab with an elbow, to let him know it was coming; what they'd debated privately in the hours before dawn. Shiner looked crushed, like a kid who just found there was no such thing as Santa Claus.

"Son," Bode Gazzer began, "first I want you to know how much we 'preciate all you done for the militia. We ain't gonna forget it, neither. Down the road we intend to settle up fair and square. But the thing is, it's not workin' out so good. Particularly with the weapons, son—you're just too damn excitable."

Chub cut in: "You like to get ever' one of us kilt, shootin' at birds and bunny rabbits. Jesus!"

"I said I'm sorry," Shiner reminded them. "And, Colonel, didn't I promise to pay for them holes in your truck?"

"You did, you will, and I respect that. Truly I do. But we're in a high-risk scenario here. We got the Black Tide on our asses, not to mention the NATO problem over in the Bahamas. That's wall-to-wall Negroes, son. We can't afford no mistakes."

Chub said: "Life or death. This ain't a game."

"And that's how come we got to let you go," said Bode Gazzer. "Go on home and watch over your momma. Ain't no shame in that."

Shiner surprised them both. He stood up and said, "No way." He glanced at Amber, who gave a nod of support. "You can't kick me out. You can't." He pointed at the bruised and scabby tattoo. "See there? *W.C.A.* I'm in for life."

"Son, I'm sorry, but it's no good." Bode understood it was up to him to reason with the boy, because Chub had no tolerance for argument. "All we can say is thanks for everything, and so long. Also, we're gonna give you a thousand bucks for all your loyalty."

Amber chuckled sarcastically. These guys were unbelievable.

Emboldened, Shiner said, "A thousand dollars is a goddamn joke."

Bode asked him what he wanted.

"To stay in the militia," Shiner answered briskly, "plus I want one-third of the lottery money. I earned it."

Chub hurled the tarpaulin aside and lurched to his feet. "Shoot the motherfucker," he said to Bode.

"Just hold on."

"If you don't, I will."

Bode Gazzer scowled at Shiner. "Goddammit, son." He took the stolen .380 out of his belt. "Why'd you put me in this posture?"

Amber saw that Shiner was scared out of his mind. She said: "Colonel, there's something you ought to know. Tell him, Shiner. Tell them what you did at Jewfish Creek."

Here was the big bluff. Shiner struggled to remember what Amber had coached him to say, exactly the way she'd said it last night. But he couldn't quite piece it all together—the sight of the Beretta had unnerved him.

"About the videotape," Amber prodded.

"Oh . . . yeah."

"The phone call you made," she said.

Bode asked, "What phone call?"

"That's right," Shiner said. "The store video, 'member? You guys had me swipe it from the Grab N'Go. On account of it proves you didn't win the Lotto—"

"Shut the fuck up," Chub barked.

"—because you didn't even show up in Grange till the day after. It's all on the tape."

Bode, tapping the .380 against his thigh. "*What* phone call?"

"Tell him," Amber said to Shiner.

"To my Ma," Shiner lied. "The tape's hid in my car and the car's at Major Chub's trailer. I called my Ma and told her come down get it, she don't hear from me by Thursday—"

"Tuesday," Amber interjected.

"Right, Tuesday. I told her come get the car."

"Then what?" Bodean Gazzer's throat was like chalk.

Shiner said, "I told her to give the video to the black girl. JoLayne. She'll know what to do."

"You're full a shit," Bode said, without conviction.

"I ain't."

"I heard him make the phone call," said Amber.

"Then goddamn the both a you."

Amber announced she was going for a swim, alone. Shiner was relieved, because he'd been waiting to take a world-record leak.

Chub and Bode withdrew to the *Reel Luv* for an urgent conference. Even in his dazed and febrile condition, Chub comprehended what the kid had done; gotten hisself some insurance. "Does this mean we can't kill the fucker?"

"I don't see how," Bode said.

"And what's all this about the money?"

"He wants a cut, we gotta give it to him," Bode said. "Thank God he only knows about one a them lottery tickets. So, like . . . what's a third of fourteen million?"

Chub strained to do the division in his head. "Four something. Four point five, four point six."

"So that'll be his share. Long as he don't find out about the other goddamn ticket."

Chub felt like puking. Four and a half million bucks for that dumb dork! It wasn't right. Sinful was what it was.

"Blackmail," Bode said morosely. There was no denying the gravity of their predicament. Saving white America would have to wait; first they had to save themselves.

"Tell you what else," he said to Chub. "Your pretty blond sweetheart's in on the deal."

"Not Amber. Ain't no way."

"You think Shiner's smart enough to dream this shit up? Kid can't find his own dick with a pair of salad tongs."

"But still." Chub didn't want to believe Amber had hooked up with Shiner. Why would she be with him, he wondered, when she could have me?

Bode Gazzer told him to put on some clothes. "Before your pecker gets fried."

"But I'm burnin' up. Feel how hot." He flopped his tumescent crab arm on the deck of the boat.

"No, thanks," Bode said, stepping away. A notion had come to him. "Today's Monday, right?"

"Don't ask me."

Bode drummed his fingers on the gunwale.

"That gives us a whole day until Shiner's momma hits the launchpad. Say we leave right now—run this puppy back to the highway, hop in the truck and haul ass. We could make Tall'hassee by lunchtime tomorrow."

Chub peeped ferretlike from inside Amber's orange shorts. "What about the video?"

"We stop at the trailer on the way north. Find the damn tape and burn it. Burn the whole car if we got to, just like we done to that asshole's Miata."

"Fan-fucking-tastic." Chub's laugh came out as a dry rattle. He couldn't wait to get off that miserable island. "Leave the sneaky bastard out here to rot. I love it, man."

"Her, too."

"Aw, no!"

Bode Gazzer said, "We better."

"But I haven't got to fuck her yet. Not even a b.j."

"Come on. Let's load the boat."

Chub said, "We got time, man, if we hurry. Time for both of us to get a piece."

Bode should've short-circuited the idea, but instead he allowed it to float around his imagination. He was beset by a vision of Amber nude, on her knees.

"We tie up the skinhead," Chub proposed, "we each take a turn with the girl and then we split."

"Will she go for it?" Bode didn't feel right about

raping a white woman. More important, it was a big-time felony.

Chub said, "S'pose it was her only way off the island. Then she'd go for it, you bet she would."

"Good point," Bode said.

It was a historic moment, Chub with an actual brainstorm. He climbed into the *Reel Luv* to search for his bag of glue.

Bode heard footsteps and wheeled around. He should've been ready with the Beretta, but he wasn't.

Amber stood there in the camo jumpsuit, the top half open, her hair slick and shining from her swim. "I can't find Shiner," she said.

"Ain't that a shame." Chub, leering through the crotch of her waitress shorts.

Bode Gazzer matter-of-factly told Amber the plan, told her the price of the boat ride back to the Keys. She didn't sob, didn't run, didn't get mad. Her expression was totally neutral, giving both men a misplaced sense of expectation. Chub had a bounce in his step as he got out of the boat.

Amber said, "Take those ridiculous pants off your face."

Bode was momentarily distracted by the crab attached to Chub's hand; he thought he detected movement.

Amber repeated her demand. "Take 'em off. You look like a pervert."

"Listen to you," Chub said, and made a step

toward her. That's when he saw the Colt Python .357. *His* Colt. His Lotto ticket, his life's fortune, his entire mortal future—all in the hands of a pissed-off Hooters babe.

"Jesus Willy," he said.

Bodean Gazzer was amazed at how fast it was unraveling, all because of rotten luck, blind lust and stupidity.

"Have some more glue," he told his partner. "See what else you can fuck up."

Amber fired the pistol at Chub's feet. The bullet kicked sand on his shins and ankles. He yanked the orange pants off his head and tossed them.

"Thank you," Amber said. "Now, what did you guys do with Shiner?"

"Nothin'," they answered, Bode first and then Chub.

None of them could know that Shiner was exactly one hundred and twenty-seven paces away, wetting himself in stark terror.

 As he pointed the shotgun, Tom Krome wrote the lead of the story in his head:

An unidentified convenience store clerk was shot to death Monday in a bizarre attack on a remote island off the Florida Keys.

> *Police said the victim apparently was stalked and ambushed while relieving himself in a mangrove thicket. Arrested for first-degree murder was Thomas Paine Krome, 35, a newspaper reporter who had been missing and believed dead.*
>
> *Coworkers described Krome as a moody and volatile "loner." One of his former editors said he wasn't "the least bit surprised" by the homicide charge.*

Krome made Shiner put up his hands. JoLayne Lucks instructed him not to move a muscle.

"But I peed on myself," the kid said.

"I expect it'll be the high point of your day."

Shiner blinked wildly.

Krome said, "OK, Goober, where's the Lotto ticket?"

"I d-don't got it." Shiner's eyes jumped from the Remington to the dark crescent radiating across his trousers. "Can I least tuck myself in?"

"No, you cannot," JoLayne said sternly. "I want your little white wacker right where it is, hangin' in the fresh air so we can shoot it off if necessary."

The clerk looked as if he would weep.

"But, JoLayne, I don't got your ticket. I don't know what they done with it, I swear up to God."

JoLayne turned to Tom Krome. "Give me my gun."

"Stay cool."

"Tom, don't be difficult."

With a mix of dread and relief, Krome passed

her the shotgun. Immediately Shiner began mewling. He saw that he'd shrunk entirely into his pants. JoLayne Lucks poked the barrel inside his zipper.

"Anybody home?" Her voice was so cheery that it gave Shiner an arctic chill.

"Please don't," he squeaked.

"Then tell me where the ticket is."

Krome tapped the face of his watch. "Hurry up, son." He didn't think JoLayne would shoot the kid point-blank; the two shitkickers, maybe, but not Shiner.

Unless he tried something stupid.

> An unidentified convenience store clerk was shot to death Monday in a bizarre attack on a remote island off the Florida Keys.
>
> Police said the victim apparently was ambushed by a disgruntled customer who believed she had been cheated out of a $14 million lottery ticket. Arrested for first-degree murder was JoLayne Lucks, 35, who works at a veterinary clinic in Grange.
>
> Neighbors described her as a quiet, gentle person, and expressed shock and disbelief at the homicide charge.

Krome said to Shiner: "If you're the least bit fond of those testicles, I'd tell the lady what she wants to know."

"But I ain't even seen the damn thing, and that's the God's truth!" Shiner, hissing through his teeth.

JoLayne looked at Tom. "You believe him?"

"I hate to say so, but yeah."

"Well, I'm still not sure."

She took a step back. True to form, Shiner chose the moment to lunge for the Remington. He was surprised that JoLayne released it without a struggle. He was further surprised to find himself unable to hold on to it, as both his thumbs were abruptly dislocated and rendered useless.

While Shiner flopped on the ground like a mullet, JoLayne thanked Tom for teaching her the trick. He calmly grabbed Shiner around the neck and urged him in the strongest terms to suffer in silence, so as not to alert his travel companions.

"Now, where's the videotape?"

"It's hid in my car," Shiner whispered hoarsely, "back at Chub's trailer."

"Chub is the man with the ponytail?"

"And a tire patch on his eye, yessir. Plus a big ole crab on his hand."

Krome let go of Shiner's neck and yanked him upright. "What's his real name?"

"Chub? I never heard him tell." The kid was moist-eyed and panting. When he snuck a peek at his crooked thumbs, he almost passed out.

"What would your momma say about all this? Lord, I can just imagine." JoLayne's tone was scorching. She picked up the shotgun and sat on the sand beside Shiner. He recoiled as if she were a tarantula.

"Why'd you do this?" she asked. "Why'd you help those bastards?"

"I dunno." Shiner turned away and clammed up. It was the same strategy he tried whenever his mother hassled him about skipping his hymns or sneaking beer to his room.

Tom Krome said, "He's hopeless, Jo. Let's go."

"Not yet." Gently she put a fingernail under the young man's chin and turned his head, so their eyes met.

Shiner said, "It's just a club, OK? They asked did I wanna join up and I said sure. A brotherhood is what they tole me. That's all."

"Sure," said Tom. "Like Kiwanis, only for Nazis."

"It ain't what you think. Least it dint start out that way." Shiner, mumbling in a childish tone.

JoLayne's eyes glistened. "You know what your 'brothers' did to me? Want me to show you?"

Wordlessly the skinhead pitched forward and threw up. JoLayne Lucks took this as an unqualified no.

Unlike some women her age, Amber held a realistic view of life, love, men and her prospects. She knew where her good looks could carry her and how far to let things go. She would not fall for the blond modeling routine (drawing the line at calendar tryouts), and she would not dance tables (de-

spite the staggering sums involved). She would remain a waitress at Hooters and finish junior college and get a respectable job as a cosmetologist or
perhaps a paralegal. She would stay with jealous
Tony until someone better came along, or until she
could no longer tolerate his foolishness. She would
not become the mistress of any man old enough to
be her father, no matter how much money he had
or how great a bay-front apartment he offered to
rent for her. She would borrow from her parents
only in emergencies, and she would pay back every
dime as soon as she could. She would keep only
one credit card. She would not fake an orgasm two
nights in a row. She would stay off cigarets, which
had killed her uncle, and avoid Absolut vodka,
which caused her to misbehave in public. She
would not be automatically impressed by men
with black convertibles or foreign-language skills.

Yet even the most centered and well-grounded
young woman would have been rightfully terrified
to be kidnapped by an armed militia. However,
waitressing in ludicrously skimpy shorts had given
Amber an unshakable confidence in her ability to
handle jerks of all kinds. Of the three rednecks,
Shiner was the weak link and consequently the
chief target of her attentions. Amber of course
had never actually worked in a tattoo parlor and
knew nothing about the art, but she'd correctly
surmised that young Shiner was so hungry for her

touch that he would allow her to poke holes in his flesh with a rusty fishhook.

Early on, she'd sensed that Shiner's heart wasn't in hate crimes and that he'd joined up with Chub and Bodean Gazzer mainly out of small-town boredom and curiosity. After Shiner confided about the stolen Lotto ticket and the $14 million prize, Amber realized his two buddies intended to ditch him at their earliest convenience. Which meant she'd be left alone with the camouflaged colonel and the one-eyed panty-sniffing stoner, both of whom she perceived as more brutish and less malleable than the novice skinhead. Almost certainly they were not averse to the notion of forcible sexual intercourse.

Amber believed that keeping Shiner in the equation would improve her chances of avoiding a rape, and also of escape.

To that end, she'd devised for the young man a strategy of rudimentary blackmail. She was astounded he hadn't thought to demand a cut of the lottery prize—he was like a half-witted busboy, too thick or too shy to ask for his tip-out at the end of the night. The hammer (as Amber patiently explained to Shiner) was the security video from the Grab N' Go.

She had only one misgiving about helping the kid get a piece of the Lotto jackpot: It was somebody else's money. Some black chick, according to

Shiner. A girl from his hometown. Amber felt crummy about that, but decided it was premature to get the guilts.

For now the priority was emplacing the blackmail plan. It wasn't a bad one, either, concocted on short notice under adverse conditions, with an accomplice of limited cognitive range. The made-up business about the phone call to Shiner's mother, about her readiness to retrieve the videotape in the event of a double cross—those were nifty touches. The plan's chief flaw, as Amber now realized, was the time line. It gave Bode and Chub almost a whole day's grace, enough of a window to leave the island, destroy the incriminating tape and bolt to Tallahassee to claim the lottery.

Which is what they were preparing to do when she confronted them at the boat after her morning swim.

"Take those ridiculous pants off your face." One hand zipping up the top of the jumpsuit, the other clenching Chub's pistol, which earlier Amber had removed from the *Reel Luv* and concealed in some bushes near the campfire.

"Take 'em off. You look like a pervert." Then shooting once at Chub's feet, just to find out what it felt like; a huge heavy gun going off. And also to make the rednecks understand she was serious and would not negotiate with any grown man wearing shorts over his face.

"Now, what did you guys do with Shiner?"

Nothing, they replied.

"He went off to have a piss," Bodean Gazzer said.

"Well, he's gone."

"Bull," said Chub.

"Let's go find him. Get some clothes on," Amber said.

"Not jest yet." Chub, grinning lopsidedly. "Sure you don't see somethin' you like? Somethin' hot 'n' tasty?"

He waggled his sunburned peter, inspiring Amber to fire once again. This time the Colt nearly jumped out of her hand. The slug passed between Bode and Chub, snapping through the mangroves and splooshing in the water.

As leaves and twigs fluttered into the boat, the demon crab unaccountably dropped off Chub's ripening hand. The animal was long dead, it turned out. Chub jabbed the rancid blue husk with a bare toe and muttered, "Motherfucker."

Bode Gazzer raised his arms for Amber. "OK, sweet thing, quit with the damn gun. You made yer point."

"Tell your friend."

"Don't worry. He's on board."

Chub said, "Like hell. Not till we play some lollipop, her and me."

Bode scowled disgustedly. The man was unbelievable; no sense of priorities. No sense at all.

Amber said, "He's pushing it, Colonel."

"What can I say? Sometimes he's a complete fuckhead."

"Think I should shoot him?"

"I'd rather you didn't."

Chub was studying his infected hand like it was a busted carburetor. "I still got the damn claw, though."

"One thing at a time," Bode Gazzer told him. "Put on your clothes and let's go find the skinhead."

"Not until my darling Amber blows me."

"She's gonna blow you, awright. She's gonna blow your sorry ass to kingdom come."

Chub said, "No, I don't believe so. I believe I'm due for some good luck."

"Hell's *that* mean?"

"It means Amber ain't gone shoot nobody. That's azackly what it means."

He stepped toward her; an exaggerated Hitler-style goose step. Then another. By now she was gripping the pistol with both fists.

"He's asking for it," she warned Bode.

"So I see. My opinion, it's the damn glue."

Chub clucked. "It ain't the glue, Colonel. It's true fucking love."

With a giddy warble he attacked. Amber pulled the trigger but all she heard was a flat harmless click. The gun didn't fire—the cylinder turned, the hammer fell, but no slug came out.

Because there was no bullet in that particular

chamber; instead, a small piece of sand-gritted paper, bleached by sweat and saltwater, and folded tightly to fit the small round hole. If she'd been able to remove the paper and examine it, Amber would have seen that it bore six numerals and the likeness of a pink flamingo, official mascot of the Florida lottery.

"I tole you!" Chub crowed.

He was naked on the ground, and waving with his undamaged arm the recaptured Colt Python. Pinned in the sand and seaweed beneath him was Amber, struggling in silence.

"I tole you, yes I did." Chub, broke into coarse, vicious laughter. "I tole you fuckers I was due for some decent luck!"

Bodean Gazzer hadn't had sex in eleven months, his excuse for celibacy being that it was against the Bible to consort with nonwhite women, and all the white women he met demanded too much money. Still, his feverish pent-up desires regarding the fragrant and available Amber were clouded by misgivings.

Her unwillingness to service the White Clarion Aryans was evident from her vigorous resistance to Chub as he ungently disrobed her. And although Bode was intoxicated by the vision of Amber's breasts spilling out of the Mossy Oak camo, he nonetheless was disturbed to be par-

ticiping in the rape—and that's where this was
headed—of a white Christian woman of European descent. In fact, Bode would've been reluc-
tant even if she were a Negro or a Cuban, not so
much for the immorality of the crime but for the
legal risks. Unlike Chub, Bode Gazzer had spent
enough months behind bars to know it wasn't
worth knocking off a Burger King or boosting
a Cadillac, or even two minutes of humping
natural-blond pussy. Rape was felony time, and in
Florida the rape of a white woman—even by a
white man—could mean a long stretch in not-so-
scenic Starke.

Bode also knew that Chub, in his current frame
of mind, was immune to such logic. All Bode
could do was hold the Colt revolver and stand
there, hoping it wouldn't take long, hoping they
wouldn't make much noise. The shiver of arousal
sparked by Amber's nudity had already died of
distraction at the heaving, pink-butted spectacle
of Chub; grimy and grunting and drool-flecked.
The arresting sights and smells graphically reminded Bode Gazzer of his partner's many hy-
gienic lapses and killed any spark of temptation to
join in the fun.

"Hol' still! Hol' still!" Chub kept huffing.

But the agile Amber would not.

"Hurry up," Bode said, checking over his shoulder. The skinhead Shiner would go ballistic if he
saw what was happening.

"I can't get it in! Goddamn, make her hol' still!" Chub used his weight to constrain her. Ribbons of brown turtle grass clung to his thighs.

"Use the damn gun!" he hollered at his partner.

"Shit." Bode knelt and placed the barrel to Amber's head. She stopped squirming. Behind a tangle of yellow-blond hair, her eyes narrowed with acceptance; not coldness and wild anger, like that crazy Negro woman up in Grange.

This is the way it's supposed to be, Bode mused. You see the gun, you quit trying to fight. "Be still now," he said. "It'll be over soon."

"Listen to the man." Chub seized Amber's wrists, pulling them away from her chest. "And do your lips . . . all pushed out and pouty . . . you know, like how Kim Basinger does."

Amber said, "OK, on one condition. Tell me your name."

"What for!"

"I can't make love to a man," she said, "unless I know his name. I just can't do it, I'd rather die."

Bode Gazzer told Chub: "Don't be a idiot."

Chub, pinning Amber's arms over her head, catching his breath. "Gillespie," he said. "Onus Gillespie."

Bode was relieved—it was such a strange name, he thought his partner had made it up.

Coolly Amber said, "Pleased to meet you, Otis."

"Naw, it's *Onus*. O-n-u-s."

"Oh. Mine's Amber." She blinked innocently. "Amber Bernstein. That's B-e-r-n-s-t-e-i-n."

It was as if Bodean Gazzer had been mule-kicked in the gut.

"Get off!" he shrieked at Chub.

"No sir!"

"But didn't you hear? She's . . . she's a Jew!"

"I don't care if she's Vietcong, I'm gone stick my weenie in."

"No! NO! Get off, and that's an order!"

Chub closed his eyes and tried to block out Bode's carping. *Hilton Head,* he told himself. *You and Blondie are at Hilton Head, doin' it on the beach. Naw, even better—you're doin' it on the balcony of your brand-new condo!*

But Amber's obstinate wriggling was giving him fits; it was like trying to screw an eel. Plus, in his glue-dazed condition, Chub found himself wielding something less than a world-class, diamond-cutter erection.

"No white Christian man"—Bode, somber as a coroner, leaned over them—"no white Christian man shall give his seed to an infidel child of Satan!"

Amber interrupted her evasions to mention that her father was a rabbi. Bode Gazzer emitted a mournful groan. Chub glared up at him. "You worry about your own damn seed. Now back off so's I kin plant mine."

"Negative! As commanding officer of the White Clarion—"

Chub rose to his knees and, with his clawless hand, snatched the pistol from the colonel. He jammed it to Amber's throat and told her to spread her legs.

Bode remembered the Colombian's Beretta in his belt. He considered drawing the gun, not so much for Amber's sake but to reinforce his superior rank. Without a steep improvement in discipline, Bode felt, the fledgling militia would soon go to pieces.

His consternation was heightened by the unexpected arrival of Shiner, the young blackmailer himself, stumbling through the trees. His cheeks were puffy and his pants were soiled and his twisted-looking fists were extended oddly at his sides, like a scarecrow's. Upon seeing Major Chub naked atop Amber, Shiner roared into a headlong assault.

Bodean Gazzer was poised to tackle the hapless skinhead when something exploded from the shoreline behind him. Chub was lifted off Amber as if there were springs in his ass. Then Bode heard a frightfully heavy thump, which he later learned was the butt of a Remington shotgun impacting his own skull.

When he regained consciousness, Bode was aware of being constricted. A white man he didn't know was tying him with a length of anchor rope to a buttonwood stump. Still flat on the ground was Chub, gurgling curses and drenched in his own blood. Shiner sat downcast in the bow of the stolen boat; his melancholy gaze was fixed on the bruised scabby mess of a tattoo. Amber stood back, wrapped in the oilskin tarpaulin. Irritably she plucked leaves and turtle grass from her hair.

All the militia's weapons had been piled on the ground. The captured arsenal was being inspected by a muscular young Negro woman with neon-green nails and a Remington shotgun. Bode Gazzer recognized her immediately.

"Not you!" was all he could say.

"That's right, bubba. Say hi to the Black Tide."

The sky and earth and universe began to spin madly for Bode Gazzer, as his fate appeared to him with sickening lucidity. The white man finished with the knots and stepped away from the tree. The Negro woman came forward, carrying the gun so casually as to cause a spasm in Bode's fragile sphincter.

"What do you want?" he asked.

JoLayne Lucks slipped the shotgun between his lips.

"Let's start with your wallet," she said.

25 The case of *LaGort* v. *Save King Enterprises, Allied-Cagle Casualty, et al.* was settled in a courthouse hallway after a pretrial conference lasting less than two hours. The attorneys for the supermarket's insurance carrier, having detected in Judge Arthur Battenkill Jr. a frosty and inexplicable bias, chose to pay Emil LaGort the annoying but not unpalatable sum of $500,000. The purpose was to avoid a trial in which the defense clearly would get no help from the judge, who'd already vowed to prohibit any testimony attacking the past honesty of the plaintiff, including but not limited to his very long list of other negligence suits. Emil LaGort attended the conference in a noisy motorized wheelchair with maroon mica-fleck armrests, and wore around his neck a two-tone foam cervical brace. The brace was one of nine models available in Emil LaGort's walk-in closet, where he saved all medical aids acquired during the phony recoveries from his many staged accidents.

After the settlement papers were signed and the sourpuss insurance lawyers filed into the elevator and Emil LaGort rolled himself across James Street to a topless luncheonette, his lawyer discreetly obtained from Judge Arthur Battenkill Jr. the number of a newly opened Nassau bank account, into which $250,000 would be wired secretly within four weeks.

Not exactly a king's ransom, Arthur Battenkill knew, but enough for a fast start on a new life.

The judge's wife, however, wasn't packing for the tropics. While Arthur Battenkill was tidying up the details of the Save King payoff, Katie was on her knees in church. She was praying for divine guidance, or at least improved clarity of thought. That morning she'd read in *The Register* that Tom Krome's estranged wife had come to town to receive a journalism award on her "late" husband's behalf. Regardless of Tommy's ill feelings toward the elusive Mary Andrea Finley, it seemed possible to Katie Battenkill that the woman might be mourning an imagined loss; that she still might love Tom Krome in some significant way.

Shouldn't somebody tell her he's not really dead? If it were me, Katie thought, I'd sure want to know.

But Katie had assured Tommy she wouldn't say a word. Breaking her promise would be a lie, and lying was a sin, and Katie was trying to give up sinning. On the other hand, she couldn't bear the thought of Mrs. Krome (whatever her faults) needlessly suffering even a sliver of widow's pain.

Knowing Tom was alive became a leaden weight upon Katie's overtaxed conscience. There was a second secret, too; equally troubling. She was reminded of it by another item in *The Register,* which reported that the human remains believed to be those of Tom Krome were being shipped to an FBI laboratory "for more sophisticated analysis." This meant DNA tests, which meant it wouldn't be long before the dead man was correctly identified as Champ Powell, law clerk to Circuit Judge Arthur Battenkill Jr.

The devious shitheel with whom Katie was about to flee the country forever.

"What do I do?" she whispered urgently. Head bowed, she knelt alone in the first pew. She prayed and waited, then prayed some more.

God's answer, when it eventually came, was typically strong on instruction but weak on details. Katie Battenkill didn't push it; she was grateful for anything.

As she walked out of church, she removed her diamond solitaire and deposited it in the slot of the oak collection box, where it landed with no more fanfare than a nickel. Lightning didn't flash, thunder didn't clap. No angels sang from the rafters.

Maybe that'll come later, Katie thought.

After the last of the pilgrims were gone, Shiner's mother approached the besheeted Sinclair, who was sloshing playfully with the cooters in the moat. She said, "Help me, turtle boy. I need a spiritual rudder."

Sinclair's unshaven chin tilted toward the heavens: *"Kiiikkkeeeaay ka-kooo kattttkin."*

His visitor failed to decipher the outcry (KICK-ING BACK WITH ULTRA-COOL KATHLEEN—from a feature profile of the actress Kathleen Turner).

"How 'bout giving that a shot in English?" Shiner's mother grumped.

Sinclair beckoned her into the moat. She kicked off her scuffed bridal heels and stepped in. Sinclair motioned her to sit. With cupped hands he gathered several baby turtles and placed them on the billowing white folds of her gown.

Shiner's mother picked one up to examine it. "You paint these suckers yourself?"

Sinclair laughed patiently. "They're not painted. That's the Lord's imprint."

"No joke? Is this little guy 'posed to be Luke or Matthew or who?"

"Lay back with me."

"They paved my Jesus this morning, did you hear? The road department did."

"Lay back," Sinclair told her.

He sloshed closer, taking her shoulders and lowering her baptismally. Shiner's mother closed her eyes and felt the coolness of the funky water on her neck, the tickle of tiny cooter claws across her skin.

"They won't bite?"

"Nope," said Sinclair, supporting her.

Soon Shiner's mother was enfolded by a preternatural sense of inner peace and trust, and possibly something more. The last man who'd touched her so sensitively was her periodontist, for whom she'd fallen head over heels.

"Oh, turtle boy, I lost my son and my shrine. I don't know what to do."

"Kiiikkkeeeaay ka-kooo," Sinclair murmured.

"OK," said Shiner's mother. *"Kiki-kakeee-kooo.* Is that the Bible in, like, Japanese?"

Unseen by the meditators in the moat was Demencio, who stood with knuckles on hips at a window. To Trish he said: "You believe this shit—she's in with the turtles!"

"Honey, she's had a rough day. The D.O.T. paved her road stain."

"I want her off my property."

"Oh, what's the harm? It's almost dark."

Trish was in the kitchen, roasting a chicken for supper. Demencio had been mixing a batch of perfumed water, refilling the tear well in the weeping Madonna.

"If that crazy broad's not gone after dinner," he said, "you go chase her off. And be sure and count them cooters, make sure she don't swipe any."

Trish said, "Have a heart."

"I don't trust that woman."

"You don't trust anybody."

"I can't help it. It's the nature of the business," said Demencio. "We got any red food coloring?"

"For what?"

"I was thinking . . . what if she started crying blood? The Virgin Mary."

"Perfumed blood?" said his wife.

"Don't gimme that face. It's just an idea is all," Demencio said, "just an idea I'm playing with. For when we don't have the turtles no more."

"Let me check." Trish, bustling toward the spice cabinet.

Under less stressful circumstances Bernard Squires might have enjoyed the farmhouse quaintness of Mrs. Hendricks' bed-and-breakfast, but even the caress of a handmade quilt could not dissolve his anxiety. So he took an evening walk—alone, in his sleek pin-striped suit—through the little town of Grange.

Bernard Squires had spent a tense chunk of the afternoon on the telephone with associates of Richard "The Icepick" Tarbone and, briefly, with Mr. Tarbone himself. Squires considered himself a clear-spoken person, but he'd had great difficulty making The Icepick understand why Simmons Wood couldn't be purchased until the competing offer was submitted and rejected.

"And it *will* be rejected," Bernard Squires had said, "because we're going to outbid the bastards."

But Mr. Tarbone had become angrier than Squires had ever heard him, and made it plain that closing the deal was requisite not only for Squires' future employment but for his continued good health. Squires had assured the old man that the delay was temporary and that by week's end Simmons Wood would be secured for the Central Midwest Brotherhood of Grouters, Spacklers and Drywallers International. Squires was instructed not to return to Chicago without a signed contract.

As he strolled in the cool breezy dusk, Bernard Squires tried to guess why the Tarbones were so hot to get the land. The likeliest explanation was a dire shortfall of untraceable cash, necessitating another elaborately disguised raid on the union pension fund. Perhaps the family intended to use the Simmons Wood property as collateral on a construction loan and wanted to lock in before interest rates shot up.

Or perhaps they really *did* mean to build a Mediterranean-style shopping mall in Grange, Florida. As laughable as that was, Bernard Squires couldn't eliminate the possibility. Maybe The Icepick had tired of the mob life. Maybe he was trying to go legit.

In any case, it truly didn't matter why Richard Tarbone was in such a hurry. What mattered was that Bernard Squires acquire the forty-four acres as soon as possible. In tight negotiations Squires was unaccustomed to losing and had at his disposal numerous extralegal methods of persuasion. If there were (as Clara Markham asserted) rival buyers for Simmons Wood, Squires felt certain he could outspend them, outflank them, or simply intimidate them into withdrawing.

Squires was so confident that he probably would've drifted contentedly into a long afternoon nap, had old man Tarbone not uttered what sounded over the phone like a serious threat:

"You get this done, goddammit! You don't wanna end up like Millstep, you'll fucking get this done."

At the mention of Jimmy Millstep, Bernard Squires had felt his silk undershirt dampen. Millstep had been a lawyer for the Tarbone family until the Friday he showed up twenty minutes late at a bond hearing for Richard Tarbone's homophobic nephew Gene, who consequently had to spend an entire weekend in a ten-by-ten cell with a well-behaved but flamboyant he-she. Attorney Millstep blamed a needful mistress and an inept cabbie for his tardiness to court, but he got no sympathy from Richard Tarbone, who not only fired him but ordered him murdered. A week later, Jimmy Millstep's bullet-riddled body was dumped at the office of the Illinois Bar Association. A note pinned to his lapel said: "Is this one of yours?"

So it was no wonder Bernard Squires was jumpy, a condition exacerbated by the abrupt appearance of a rumpled stranger with bloody punctures in the palms of his hands.

"Halt, sinner!" said the man, advancing with a limp. Bernard Squires warily sidestepped him.

"Halt, pilgrim," the man implored, waving a sheaf of rose-colored advertising flyers.

Squires snatched one and backed out of reach. The stranger muttered a blessing as he shuffled off into the twilight. Squires stopped beneath a street-lamp to look at the paper:

ASTOUNDING STIGMATA OF CHRIST!!!!
Come see amazing Dominick Amador,
the humbel carpenter who woke up one day
with the exactly identical crucifiction wounds of
Jesus Christ himself, Son of God!
Bleeding 9 a.m. to 4 p.m. daily.
Saturdays Noon to 3 p.m. (Palms only).
Visitations open to the publix. Offerings welcomed!
4834 Haydon Burns Lane
(Look for The Cross in the front yard!)

And in small print at the bottom of the paper:

As feachered on Rev. Pat Robertson's
"Heavenly Signs" TV show!!!

Bernard Squires crumpled the flyer and tossed it. Sickos, he thought, no matter where you go on this planet. Sickos who never learned to spell. Squires stopped at the Grab N'Go, where his request for a *New York Times* drew the blankest of stares. He settled for a *USA Today* and a cup of decaf, and headed back toward the b-and-b. Somewhere he made a wrong turn and found himself on a street he didn't recognize—the chanting tipped him off.

Squires heard it from a block away: a man and a woman, vocalizing disharmoniously in some exotic tongue. The tremulous sounds drew Squires to a floodlit house. It was a plain, one-story concrete-and-stucco, typical of Florida tract developments in the 1960s and '70s. Squires stood out of sight, behind an old oak, watching.

Three figures were visible—four, counting a statue of the Virgin Mary, which a dark-haired man in coveralls was positioning and repositioning on a small illuminated platform. Two other persons—the chanters, it turned out—sat with legs outstretched in a curved trench that had been dug in the lawn and filled with water. The man in the trench was cloaked in dingy bed linens, while the woman wore a formal white gown with lacy pointed shoulders. The pair was of indeterminate age, though both had pale skin and wet hair. Bernard Squires noticed v-shaped wakes pushing here and there in the water; animals of some kind, swimming . . .

Turtles?

Squires edged closer. Soon he realized he was witness to an eccentric religious rite. The couple in the trench continued to join arms and spout gibberish while scores of grape-sized reptile heads bobbed around them. (Squires recalled a cable-television documentary about a snake-handling cult in Kentucky—perhaps this was a breakaway sect of turtle worshipers!) Interestingly, the dark-haired man in coveralls took no part in the moat-wallowing ceremony. Rather, he intermittently turned from the Madonna statue to gaze upon the two chanters with what appeared to Bernard Squires as unmasked disapproval.

"Kiiikkkeeeaay ka-kooo kattttkin!" the couple bayed, sending such an icy jet down Squires' spine that he crossed the street and hurried away. He was not a devout man and certainly didn't believe in omens, but he was profoundly unsettled by the turtle handlers and the stranger with blood on his palms. Grange, which initially had impressed Squires as a prototypical tourist-grubbing southern truck stop, now seemed murky and mysterious. Weird vapors tainted the parochial climate of sturdy marriages, conservatively traditional faiths and blind veneration of progress—*any* progress—that allowed slick characters such as Bernard Squires to swoop in and have their way. He returned straightaway to the bed-and-breakfast, bid an early good night to Mrs. Hendricks (taking a pass on her pork roast, squash, snap beans and pecan pie), bolted the door to his room (quietly, so as not to offend his hostess), and slipped beneath the quilt to nurse a hollow, helpless, irrational feeling that Simmons Wood was lost.

. . .

The *Reel Luv* smelled of urine, salt and crab parts. How could it not?

Shiner slouched over the wheel. They were cruising at half-speed to conserve gas. Bode Gazzer's marine chart was unrolled across Amber's lap. The route to Jewfish Creek had been marked for them in ballpoint pen by the helpful Black Tide lady.

Florida Bay had a brisk chop; no rollers to make the travelers queasy. Still, Shiner's cheeks took on a greenish tinge, and there were dark circles under his eyes.

"You all right?" Amber asked.

He nodded unconvincingly. The pudge on his arms and belly jiggled with each bump. He steered gingerly; the Black Tide lady had popped his dislocated thumbs back into the sockets, but they remained painfully swollen.

"Stop the boat," Amber told him.

"I'm OK."

"Stop it. Right now." She reached across the console and levered back the throttle. Shiner didn't argue because she had the gun; Chub's Colt Python. The tip of the barrel peeked from beneath the chart.

As soon as the boat stopped moving, Shiner leaned over the side and puked up six of the eight Vienna sausages he'd wolfed down for breakfast on Pearl Key.

"I'm sorry." He wiped his mouth. "Usually I don't get seasick. Honest."

Amber said, "Maybe you're not seasick. Maybe you're just scared."

"I ain't scared!"

"Then you're a damn fool."

"Scared a what?"

"Of getting busted in a stolen boat," she said. "Or getting the shit beat out of you by my crazy jealous boyfriend back in Miami. Or maybe you're just scared of the cops."

Shiner said, "What cops?"

"The cops I ought to call the second we see a phone. To say I was kidnapped by you and nearly raped by your redneck pals."

"Oh God." Noisily Shiner launched the remainder of breakfast.

Afterwards he restarted the engines and off they went, the hull of the *Reel Luv* pounding like a tom-tom. Amber was still trying to sort out what had happened on the island. Shiner hadn't been much help; the more earnestly he'd tried to explain it, the nuttier it sounded.

This much she knew: The woman with the shotgun was the one the rednecks had robbed of the lottery ticket.

"How'd she find you guys all the way out here?" Amber had wondered, to which Shiner had proposed a fantastically muddled scenario involving liberals, Cubans, Democrats, commies, armed black militants, helicopters with infrared night scopes, and battalions of foreign-speaking soldiers hiding in the Bahamas. Wisely Shiner had refrained from tossing in the Jews, although he couldn't stop himself from asking Amber (in a whisper) if her last name was actually Bernstein, as Chub had raged.

"Or d'you make that up?"

"What's the difference," she'd said.

"I don't know. None, I guess."

"You'd still marry me, wouldn't you? In about ten seconds flat." Amber winking at her joke, which had caused Shiner to redden and turn away.

That was after Chub had been shot and the colonel had been knocked out and Amber had fixed herself up and put on some clean clothes. Then the black woman and the white guy had collected the militia's guns—the AR-15, the TEC-9, the Cobray, the Beretta, even Shiner's puny Marlin .22—and heaved them one after another into the bay. The only thing that didn't get tossed was a can of pepper spray, which the black woman placed in her handbag.

Afterwards she'd told Shiner and Amber to take the stolen boat back to the mainland. The black woman (JoLayne was her name) had marked the way on the chart and had even given them bottled water and cold drinks for the journey. Then the white guy had pulled Shiner aside, into the woods, and when they'd returned Shiner was ashen. The white guy had handed Chub's Colt Python to Amber with instructions to "shoot the little creep if he tries anything funny."

Amber didn't have much faith in the big revolver since it had misfired once already, but she didn't mention that to Shiner. Besides, he looked too sick and dejected for mischief.

Which he was. The white guy, JoLayne's friend, hadn't laid a hand on him in the mangroves. Instead he'd looked the kid square in the eyes and said, "Son, if Amber doesn't get home safe and sound, I'm going straight to your momma in Grange and tell her everything you've done. And then I'm going to put your name and ugly skin-headed picture on the front page of the newspaper, and you're going to be famous in the worst possible way."

And then he'd calmly escorted Shiner back to the shore and helped him into the boat. JoLayne Lucks had been waiting with the shotgun, watching over Bodean Gazzer and Chub. The white guy had waded in, shoving the stern into deeper water so Shiner and Amber could lower the outboards without snagging bottom.

"Have a safe trip," the black woman had sung out. "Watch out for manatees!"

An hour later Shiner finally heard what he'd been dreading—a helicopter. But it was blaze orange, not black. And it wasn't NATO but the U.S.

Coast Guard, thwock-thwocking back and forth in search of a woman overdue in a small rental boat; a woman who'd said she was going no farther than Cotton Key.

Shiner had no way of knowing this. He was convinced the chopper had been sent to strafe him. He dove to the deck, yanking Amber with him.

"Look out! Look out!" he hollered.

"Would you please get a grip."

"But it's them!"

The helicopter dipped low over the boat. The crew spotted the couple entwined on the deck and, accustomed to such amorous sightings, flew on. Clearly it wasn't the vessel they'd been sent to find.

Once the chopper disappeared, Shiner sheepishly collected himself. Amber shoved the chart under his chin and told him to quit behaving like a wimp. An hour later, the Jewfish Creek drawbridge came into view. They nosed the *Reel Luv* into the slip farthest from the dockmaster (its owner would be puzzled but pleased to find it there, and the theft would be ascribed to joyriding teenagers). Mindful of his throbbing thumbs, Shiner struggled to tie off the bow rope. Amber scouted for the marine patrol, just in case. She was relieved to spot her car, undisturbed in the parking lot.

Shiner gave a glum wave and said, "See ya."

"Where you going?"

"To the highway. Try and hitch a ride."

Amber said, "I'll drop you in Homestead."

"Naw, that's OK." He was worried about her boyfriend, jealous Tony. Maybe she was setting him up for an ass-whupping.

"Suit yourself," she said.

Shiner thought: God, she's so pretty. To hell with it. He said, "Maybe I will bum along."

"That's a good way to describe it. You drive."

They were halfway up Highway One to Florida City when Amber took Chub's pistol out again, leading Shiner to believe he'd misjudged her intentions.

"You're gone kill me, ain't you?"

"Oh right," Amber said. "I'm going to shoot you in broad daylight in all this traffic, when I had all morning to blow your head off in the middle of nowhere and dump your body in the drink. That's what a dumb bimbo I am. Just drive, OK?"

The way Shiner was feeling, a hot slug in the belly couldn't have hurt much worse than her sarcasm. He clamped his eyes on the road and tried to cook up a story for his Ma when he got back to Grange. The next time he glanced over at Amber, she'd gotten the Colt open. She was spinning the cylinder and peering, with one eye, into the chambers.

"Hey," she said.

"What's that?"

"Stop the car."

"OK, sure," said Shiner. Carefully he guided the gargantuan Ford to the grassy shoulder, scattering a flock of egrets.

The gun lay open on Amber's lap. She was unfolding a small piece of paper that had fallen from one of the bullet chambers.

Shiner said, "Lemme see."

"Just listen: Twenty-four . . . nineteen . . . twenty-seven . . . twenty-two . . . thirty . . . seventeen."

Shiner said, "God, don't tell me it's the damn Lotto!"

"Yup. Your dumb shitkicker buddies hid it inside the gun."

"Oh man. Oh man. But—d-damn, what do we do now?"

Amber snapped the revolver shut and slipped the lottery coupon in a zippered pocket of her jumpsuit.

"You want me to keep drivin'?" Shiner asked.

"I think so, yes."

They didn't speak again until Florida City, where they stopped at a McDonald's drive-thru. They were fifth in the line of cars.

Amber said, "We've got a decision to make, don't we?"

"I always get the Quarter Pounder."

"I'm talking about the Lotto ticket."

"Oh," said Shiner.

"Fourteen million dollars."

otᵗ m

"God, I know."

"Sometimes there's a difference," Amber said, "between what's right and what's common sense."

"Good."

"All I'm saying is, we need to think this out from all angles. It's a big decision. Order me a salad, would you? And a Diet Coke."

Shiner said, "You wanna split some fries?"

"Sure."

Later, sitting at the traffic light near the turnpike ramp, Shiner heard Amber say: "What do you think they did to your buddies? Back on the island, I mean. What do you think happened after we left?"

Shiner said, "I don't know, but I can guess." Sadly he examined the mutilated militia tattoo on his arms.

"Light's green," Amber said. "We can go."

26 Bodean Gazzer watched the Negro woman pick through his wallet until she found the condom packet. How could she have possibly known?

Another mystery, Bode thought despondently. Another mystery that won't matter in the end.

As nonchalant as a nurse, the woman unrolled the rubber and plucked out the lottery ticket, which she placed in a pocket of her jeans.

"That ain't yours," Bode Gazzer blurted.

"Pardon?" The Negro woman wore a half smile. "What'd you say, bubba?"

"That one ain't yours."

"Really? Whose might it be?"

"Never mind." Bode didn't like the way her eyes kept cutting to the shotgun, which she'd handed to the white guy while she searched the wallet.

"Funny," she said. "I checked the numbers on that ticket. And they were *my* numbers."

"I said never mind."

Chub began to moan and writhe. The white guy said, "He's losing lots of blood."

"Yes, he is," said the Negro woman.

Bode asked, "Is he gone die?"

"He most certainly could."

The white guy said to the woman: "It's your call."

"I suppose so."

She walked briefly out of Bode's view. She reappeared carrying a flat white box with a small red cross painted on the lid. She knelt beside Chub and opened it.

Bode heard her saying: "I wish I could stand here and let you die, but I can't. My whole life, I've never been able to watch a living thing die. Not even a cockroach. Not even a despicable damn sonofabitch like you. . . ."

The words lifted Bode's hopes for reprieve.

Covertly he began rubbing his wrists back and forth, to loosen the rope that held him to the tree.

The shotgun blast had excavated from Chub's left shoulder a baseball-sized chunk of flesh, muscle and bone. He was not fortunate enough to pass out immediately from pain. The woman's touch ignited splutter and profanity.

Firmly she told him to be still.

"Get away from me, nigger! Get the hell away!" Chub, wild-eyed and hoarse.

"You heard the man." It was the white guy, holding the Remington. "He wants to bleed out. You heard him, JoLayne."

Another agitated voice. Sounded like Bode Gazzer. "For God's sake, Chub, shut up! She's only trying to save your life, you stupid fuck!"

Yep. Definitely the colonel.

Chub shook himself like a dog, spitting blood and sandy grit. The bicycle patch had peeled, so now he had two open eyes with which to keep a bead on the nigger girl; more like one and a half, since the unhealed lid drooped like a ripped curtain.

"What're you gone do to me, if I might ast?"

"Try to clean this messy gunshot and stop your bleeding."

"How come?"

454

"Good question," the woman said.

Craning his head, Chub saw it was attached to a striped, sand-caked body that could not possibly be his. The cock, for example, was puckered to the size of a raspberry; definitely not a millionaire's cock.

Had to be a nightmare is all, a freak-out from the boat glue. That must be how come the nigger girl looks 'zackly like the one they'd robbed upstate, the one clawed the shit outta us with those hellacious electric-looking fingernails.

"You ain't no doctor," Chub said to her.

"No, but I work in a doctor's office. An animal doctor—"

"Jesus Willy Christ!"

"—and you're about the dumbest, smelliest critter I ever saw," the woman said matter-of-factly.

Chub was too weak to hit her. He wasn't even a hundred percent sure he'd heard it right. Delirium slurred his senses.

"Whatcha gone do with all that lottery money, nigger?"

"Well, I thought I'd buy me a Cadillac or two," JoLayne said, "and a giant-screen color TV."

"Don't you talk down to me."

"And maybe a watermelon patch!"

"You gone kill me, girl?" Chub asked.

"Well, it's tempting."

"Why can't you jes answer me straight."

The white guy's face appeared over the woman's shoulder. He whistled and said, "Hey, sport, what happened to your eye?"

Chub exerted himself to make a sneer. "You muss be some kind a nigger-lover."

"Just a beginner," the white man said.

The last thing Chub heard before blacking out was Bodean Gazzer bellowing: "Hey, I changed my mind! You kin let him die! Go 'head and let the asshole die!"

JoLayne Lucks couldn't do it.

Couldn't, although the stench of the robber had brought everything rushing back, the bile to her throat and the stinging to her eyes. All that had happened that night inside her own house—the horrible words they'd used, the casual way they'd punched her, the places on her body where they'd put their hands.

She still could taste the barrel of the man's revolver, oily and cool on her tongue, yet she couldn't let him die.

Even though he deserved it.

JoLayne willed herself to think of Chub as an animal—a sick confused animal, not unlike the raccoon she'd patched up the night before. It was the only way she could suppress her rage and concentrate on the seeping crater in the man's shoulder; cleaning the wound as best she could, squeezing out the whole tube of antibiotic and dressing the pulp with wads of thin gauze.

The bastard finally passed out, which made it easier. Not having to listen to him call her nigger: that sure helped.

At one point, maneuvering to get the tape on, JoLayne wound up with his head in her lap. Instead of feeling repulsed, she was overwhelmed by an anthropological curiosity. Studying Chub's slack unconscious face, she searched for clues to the toxic wellspring. Was the hatred discernible in his deep-set eyes? The angry-looking creases in his sunburned brow? The dull unhappy set of his stubbled jaw? If there was a telltale mark, a unique congenital feature identifying the man as a cruel sociopath, JoLayne Lucks couldn't find it. His face was no different from that of a thousand other white guys she'd seen, playing out hard fumbling lives. Not all of them were impossible racists.

"Are you all right?" Tom Krome, stooping beside her.

"Fine. Brings back memories of my trauma-unit days."

"How's Gomer?"

"Bleeding's stopped for now. That's about all I can do."

"You want to talk with the other one?"

"Most definitely," JoLayne said.

As Krome approached the buttonwood stump,

he sensed something was different. He should've stopped right away to figure it out, but he didn't. Instead he picked up the pace, hurrying toward Bodean Gazzer.

By the time Krome saw the limp rope and noticed the prisoner's legs were tucked under his butt—boot heels braced against the tree trunk—it was too late. With a martial cry the stubby thief vaulted from the ground, spearing Krome in the chest. He toppled backward, sucking air yet clinging madly with both fists to the shotgun. From a bed of damp sand he raised his head to see Bode Gazzer running away, into the mangroves.

Running toward the other end of Pearl Key, where Tom and JoLayne had hidden the other boat.

Which was, now, the only transportation off the island.

Krome hadn't slugged anybody for years. The last time it happened was in the Meadowlands stadium, where he and Mary Andrea were watching the Giants play the Cowboys. The temperature was thirty-eight degrees and the New Jersey sky looked like churned mud. Sitting directly behind Tom Krome and his wife were two enormous noisy men from somewhere in Queens. Longshoremen, Mary Andrea speculated with a scowl, although they would later be revealed as com-

modities brokers. The men were alternating vodka
screwdrivers and beer, and had celebrated a Giants
field goal by shedding their coats and jerseys and
pinching each other's bare nipples until their eyes
watered. By the second quarter Krome was scouting the stands for other seats, while Mary Andrea
was packing to go home. One of the New Yorkers
produced a pneumatic boat horn, which he de-
ployed in sustained bursts six to ten inches from
the base of Krome's skull. Irately Mary Andrea
wheeled and snapped at the two men, impelling
one of them—he sported a beer-flecked walrus
mustache, Krome recalled—to comment loudly
upon the modest dimensions of Mary Andrea's
breasts, a subject about which she was known to
be sensitive.

The colloquy quickly degenerated (despite the
distraction of a blocked Dallas punt) until one of
the men aimed the boat horn at Mary Andrea's
flawless nose and let 'er rip. Krome saw no other
option but to punch the fat fuck until he fell down.
His bosom buddy of course took a wide sloppy
swing at Krome's noggin, but Tom had plenty of
time to duck (Mary Andrea was way ahead of
him) and unleash a solid uppercut to the scrotal
region. The decking of the rude men drew flurries
of cheers, the other football fans mistaking
Krome's outburst for an act of husbandly chivalry.
In truth it was pure selfish anger, as Krome
demonstrated by grabbing the boat horn, placing

it flush against the right ear of fallen Walrus Face, and blasting away until the canister emptied, its plangent blare ebbing with a sequence of comical burps.

Cops arrived, jotted names, arrested no one. Krome himself fractured two knuckles in the fight but had no regrets. Mary Andrea scolded him for flying off the handle, but phoned every one of her friends to brag on him. A month later the Kromes heard from an attorney representing one of the commodities brokers, who claimed to be suffering from chronic headaches, deafness and myriad psychological problems resulting from the beating. A companion lawsuit was being hatched by the other fan, who was said to be in need of delicate surgery for cosmetic repair of a displaced left testicle. Tom Krome's own lawyer strongly advised him to avoid a trial, which he did by agreeing to purchase Giants season tickets for each of the aggrieved brokers and also providing (thanks to the connections of a sportswriter pal) official-looking NFL footballs personally autographed by Lawrence Taylor.

Krome anticipated no such nuisance suits from Bodean Gazzer and would take all steps necessary to prevent the robber from escaping Pearl Key and stranding Tom and JoLayne without a boat. To prevent shooting off his own toes, Krome prudently set down the shotgun before he started running. The redneck had a fifty-yard head start but he wasn't hard to track, crashing through

branches like a crazed rhinoceros. Any conceal-
ment provided by Gazzer's camouflage outfit was
offset by his unstealthiness. The longer-legged
Krome was able to gain ground and at no time
mistook the fleeing felon for a mangrove tree.

He overtook Gazzer in a clearing and tackled
him. The redneck extracted one chunky leg and
slammed his boot smartly into Tom Krome's
cheekbone. Quickly Gazzer was up and running
again. He got to the Boston Whaler, which he was
laboring to drag into the water when Krome again
overtook him. They went down in a splash, the
camouflaged man windmilling his arms.

Krome felt a lifetime of emotional detachment
dissolve in a stream of bubbles and galvanizing,
uncontrollable fury. It was the first purely murderous impulse of his life, and for a split second it
gave a perverse clarity to all the murderous acts
he'd written about for newspapers. Krome understood that he ought to be terrified, but he felt only
a primitive rage. He wrapped Bodean Gazzer in a
brutal headlock and held him underwater with the
gravest intention. When a wildly flung elbow
struck Krome in the throat, he realized that he was
(at age thirty-five) engaged in his first life-or-death
struggle.

He would have preferred it more neatly choreo-
graphed, like the altercation at Giants Stadium,
but that was unusual. In his work Krome had attended enough crime scenes to know that violence

was seldom cinematic. Usually it was clumsy, careless, chaotic: a damn mess.

Exactly like this, he thought. If I can't get my head up even for half a second, I'm probably going to drown.

In four lousy feet of water, I'm going to drown.

They'd stirred up so much marl that Krome couldn't see anything but a greenish haze in suspension. He released his hold on Gazzer's neck but they remained tangled—he and the crook, no longer fighting each other but flailing for air.

As the mortal darkening began, words came unspooled in Tom Krome's brain.

REPORTER FOUND DEAD . . .

REPORTER BELIEVED DEAD FOUND DEAD . . .

REPORTER BELIEVED DEAD FOUND DEAD ON MYSTERY ISLAND . . .

Krome thinking: Headlines!

He pictured them vividly as they would appear in the paper, below the fold of the front page. He beheld a vision of scissors flashing, the article about his drowning meticulously being clipped by a faceless someone—his father, Katie, JoLayne or even Mary Andrea (strictly for insurance purposes).

Tom Krome envisioned the span of his life condensed to one shitty, potentially ungrammatical newspaper caption. The prospect was more depressing than death itself.

With a last measure of strength, he pulled away

from Bodean Gazzer and thrashed to the surface. Wheezing and half choked, Krome now saw that the darkness was spreading not in his mind but in the water; a deep-reddish cloud, lustrous and undulant around his legs.

Blood.

Krome thinking: God, don't let it be mine.

One moment Bode Gazzer had the boat, the next he was being heaved in the drink. He'd been outrun, naturally; the curse of short legs and tar-gummed lungs. Thank you, Mom and Dad. Thank you, Philip Morris.

Who else could he blame?

Chub, for being stoned, blind-horny and incompetent.

The government, for allowing Negro terrorists to purchase Lotto tickets.

And his own bad fortune, for unknowingly robbing and assaulting a card-carrying member of the feared Black Tide, whatever the hell that was; a woman who obviously used her NATO cohorts to track the White Clarion Aryans to the remotest of islands so she could pick off his troops one by one, like baby harp seals.

Not me, Bode vowed, submerging in the grasp of the Negro woman's white accomplice. Nosir, you ain't leavin' me out here to starve with that sorry-ass Chub.

Major, my ass. Major fuckup is more like it.

Bode battled with no style but loads of determination. The heavy shitkicker boots were an encumbrance, filling rapidly with saltwater—he might as well have strapped cinder blocks to his feet. Nor was the sodden camo suit an ideal choice for swimwear, but Bode coped as well as he could. Having been choked two or three times before, in prison fights, he recognized the onset of oxygen deprivation.

The white guy was stronger than Bode Gazzer expected, so Bode undertook a strategy of mad pawing and thrashing. The effect was to muddy the bay bottom so thoroughly that Bode initially failed to see the stingray lying there, as flat as a cocktail tray.

Like most criminals who relocate to South Florida, Bodean Gazzer had spent little time familiarizing himself with the native fauna. He was keenly aware that lobsters had a weakness for lobster traps, but otherwise his knowledge of marine wildlife was sketchy. A minimal amount of scholarship—say, a visit to the Seaquarium— would have provided two lifesaving facts about the common southern stingray.

One: It doesn't actually sting. The detachable barb on the end of its tail, although coated with an infectious mucus, is used defensively as a lance.

Two: Should one encounter a ray dozing in the shallows, the worst possible thing to do is kick it.

Which is what Bodean Gazzer (mistaking it for an extremely large flounder) did. The agony he experienced was the result of the stingray barb penetrating deep flesh. The blood he saw in the water jetted from his own femoral artery.

Once Bode poked up for air, he saw the white guy wading doggedly in pursuit of the boat, which was drifting away. Bode aimed himself toward dry land but discovered he couldn't stand upright, much less walk. A chill shook him to the marrow, and suddenly he felt woozy.

What now? he thought. Then he keeled sideways.

"Wake up," JoLayne said to the moaning redneck.

"It might be too late," Tom Krome told her.

"No, it's not."

Bodean Gazzer cracked his eyelids. "Get the fuck away."

"Told you," JoLayne said.

"Get away!"

"No, I've got a question. And I'd like an honest answer, Mr. Gazzer, before you die: Why'd you pick me? Of all people, why me? Because I'm black, or because I'm a woman—"

Tom said, "He's out of it."

"Hell I am," the redneck murmured.

"Then please answer me," JoLayne said.

"It wasn't none a them reasons. We picked you on account a you won the damn Lotto. It just worked out you was a Negro—hell, we didn't know." Bode Gazzer chuckled weakly. "It just worked out that way."

"But it made it easier, didn't it? That I was black."

"We believe in the s-s-supremacy of the white race. If that's what you mean. We believe the Bible preaches genetic p-p-purity."

They'd hauled him up on shore and peeled off his hunting camos. Once they saw the gushing leg wound, they knew it was over.

The redneck said, "You tell me I'm dyin'—I look dumb enough to fall for that?" His eyelids closed. JoLayne cupped his cheeks and urged him to stay awake.

"Please," she said, "I'm trying to understand the nature of your hatefulness. Let's sort this out."

"Oh, I got it. You ain't gonna shoot me, you're gonna talk me to death."

"What did I ever do to you?" she demanded. "What did any black person ever do to you?"

Bodean Gazzer grunted. "Prison once, there was a Negro stole the magazines out from under my whatchacallit. My bunk. Plus some NRA decals."

Tom said, "He's going into shock."

JoLayne nodded disappointedly. "I wish I

understood—there was no cause for all this. Man doesn't even know me, comes to my house and does what he did—"

" 'Nother time they got my car stereo." Bode's voice trailed. "Happened in Tampa, either them or Cubans for sure. . . ."

Tom said, "It won't be long, Jo. Let's go."

She stood up. "Lord have mercy," she said to the dying man. "There's nothing I can do for you."

"No shit." The redneck tittered. "Nothin' anybody can do. I'm on God's shit list, that's the story my whole damn life. Numero uno on God's shit list."

"Goodbye, Mr. Gazzer."

"You ain't gonna shoot me? After all this?"

"Nope," said JoLayne.

"Then I sure don't understand."

Tom Krome said, "Maybe it's just your lucky day."

The helicopter pilot decided to make one more pass and call it quits. The ride-along said he understood; the Coasties were on a bare-bones budget like everybody else.

Search conditions were ideal: a cloudless sky, miles of visibility and a light clean chop on the water. If the lost boat was anywhere on Florida Bay, they probably would've found her by now.

The pilot was certain of one thing: There was no sixteen-foot Boston Whaler near Cotton Key. Either the woman who'd rented it had gotten lost in the foul weekend weather or she'd lied to the man at the motel marina.

Flying at five hundred feet, the pilot took the chopper on a sinuous course from the Cowpens along Cross Bank toward Captain Key, Calusa, the Buttonwoods and Roscoe. Then he arced back across Whipray Basin toward Corinne Key, Spy and Panhandle. He was coming up fast on the Gophers when he heard his spotter say: "Hey, we've got something."

It was an open skiff, zipping through a stake channel on Twin Key Bank. The Coast Guard pilot throttled down and put the bird in a hover.

"Whaler sixteen?"

"Roger," said the spotter. "Two aboard."

"Two? Are you sure?"

"That's a roger."

The ride-along said nothing.

"They OK?" the pilot asked the spotter.

"Seem to be. Heading for Islamorada, it looks like."

The pilot leaned toward the jump seat. "What do you think, sir?"

The ride-along had brought his own binoculars, weatherproof Tascos. "A little closer if you can," he said, peering.

468

Perched in the chopper door, the spotter reported it was a man and a woman. "She's waving. He's giving us a thumbs-up."

The Coast Guard pilot said, "Well, Mr. Moffitt?"

"That's her. Definitely."

"Good deal. You want us to hang by?"

"Not necessary," the agent said. "She's as good as home."

27 Shiner never contemplated stealing the Lotto ticket from Amber and cashing it for himself. He was too infatuated; they'd spent so much time together, he felt they were practically a couple. Moreover, he was by nature an accomplice; a follower. Without someone to boss him around, Shiner was adrift. As his mother often said, this was a young man who needed firm direction. Certainly he hadn't the nerve to travel alone to Tallahassee and attempt to claim the lottery jackpot. The idea was petrifying. Shiner knew he made a poor first impression, knew he was an unskilled and transparent liar. The vile tattoo could be concealed, but how would he explain his corkscrew thumbs and the skinhead haircut? Or the crankcase scar? Shiner couldn't conceive a circumstance in which the State of Florida willingly would hand him $14 million.

Amber, on the other hand, could pull off anything. She was smooth and self-confident, and her
dynamite looks sure couldn't hurt. Who could say
no to a face and a body like that! Shiner figured the
best thing to do was concentrate on the driving
(which he was good at) and let Amber handle the
details of collecting the Lotto winnings. Certainly
she'd cut him in for *something*—probably not fifty
percent (on account of the kidnapping and then
what happened on the island with Chub), but
maybe four or five million. Amber did need him,
after all. It would be foolish to turn in the lottery
ticket without first destroying the videotape from
the Grab N'Go, and only Shiner could take her
where it was hidden. He resolved to be the best
damn chauffeur she ever saw.

"Where's this trailer?" she asked.

"We're almost there."

"What's all that, corn or something?"

"The colonel said corn, tomatoes and I think
green beans. You grow up on a farm?"

"Not even close," Amber said.

Shiner thought she seemed a little cranky. To
loosen her up, he sang a few lines from "Nut-
Cutting Bitch," tapping a beat on the dashboard
and hoping she'd join in. He gave up when he ran
out of lyrics.

Amber blinked impassively at the passing crop
fields. "Tell me about the black girl," she said.
"JoLayne."

"What's to tell."

"What does she do?"

Shiner shrugged one shoulder. "Works at the vet. You know, with the animals."

"She got any kids?"

"I don't think so."

"Boyfriend? Husband?" Amber, biting her lower lip.

"Not that I heard of. She's just another girl around town, I don't know much about it."

"Do people like her?"

"My Ma says so."

"Shiner, are there many black people where you live?"

"In Grange? Some. What's 'many'? I mean, we got a few." Then it occurred to him that she might be considering a move, so he added: "But not many. And they stick pretty much to theyselves."

Showing good sense, Amber thought.

"You all right?"

"How much farther?"

"Just up the road," Shiner said. "We're almost there."

He was relieved to see his Impala next to the trailer, where he'd parked it, although he'd apparently left the trunk ajar. Dumb-ass!

Amber said, "Nice paint job."

"I done the sanding myself. When I'm through, it'll be candy-apple red."

"Look out, world."

She stood and stretched her legs. She noticed an opossum curled on the trailer slab; the mangiest thing she'd ever seen. It blinked shoe-button eyes and poked a whiskered pink snout in the air. When Shiner clapped his hands, it ambled into the scrub. Amber wished it had run.

She said, "I can't believe anybody lives like this."

"Chub's tough. He's about the toughest I ever met."

"Yeah. Look where it got him—a dump." Amber meant to shatter any notions Shiner might have about inviting her inside. "So where's the tape?" she asked impatiently.

He stepped to the Impala and opened the passenger-side door. The glove compartment was open, and empty.

"Oh shit."

"Now what?" Amber leaned in to see.

"I can't fucking believe this." Shiner wrapped his arms around his head. Someone had been inside his car!

The videotape was gone. So was the bogus handicapped parking emblem, which Shiner had hung from the rearview. Also missing was the Impala's steering wheel, without which the car was scrap.

"It's them again. The goddamn Black Tide!" Shiner gasped out the words.

Amber looked inappropriately amused. He asked her what was so damn funny.

"Nothing's funny. But it *is* sort of perfect."

"Glad you think so. Jesus, what about the Lotto!" he said. "And what about my car? I hope you got Plan B."

Amber said, "Let's get going." When he balked, she lowered her voice: "Hurry. Before 'they' come back."

She made Shiner drive, an enforced distraction. Soon he blabbered himself into a calm. In Homestead she instructed him to pull over by a drainage canal. She waited for a dump truck to pass, then tossed Chub's Colt Python into the water. Afterward, Shiner stayed quiet for many miles. Amber knew he was thinking about all that money. She was, too.

"It wasn't meant to be. It wasn't right," she said, "not from any angle."

"Yeah, but for fourteen million bucks—"

"Know why I'm not upset? Because we're off the hook. Now we don't have to make a decision about what to do. Somebody made it for us."

"But you still got the ticket."

Amber shook her head. "Not for long. Whoever came for that video knows who really won the lottery. They *know,* OK?"

"Yeah." Shiner went into a sulk.

She said, "I've never been arrested before. How about you?"

He said nothing.

"You mentioned your mom? Well, I was thinking about my dad," Amber said. "About what my dad would do if he turned on the TV one night and there's his little blond princess in handcuffs, busted for trying to cash a stolen Lotto ticket. It'd probably kill him, my dad."

"The rabbi?"

She laughed softly. "Right."

Shiner wasn't sure how to get back to Coconut Grove, so Amber (who needed to pack an overnight bag, check in with Tony and arrange for her friend Gloria to cover her shift at Hooters) told him to stick with U.S. 1, even though there were a jillion stoplights. Shiner didn't complain. They were stopped in traffic at the Bird Road intersection when the car was approached by an elderly Cuban man selling long-stemmed roses. Impulsively Shiner dug a five-dollar bill from his camos. The old man grinned warmly. Shiner bought three roses and handed them to Amber, who responded with a cool dart of a kiss. It was the first time he ever got flowers for a woman, and also his first experience with a genuine Miami Cuban.

What a day, he thought. And it still ain't over.

The videotape gave Moffitt a headache. Typical convenience-store setup: cheapo black-and-white with stuttered speed, so the fuzzy images jerked along like Claymation. A digitalized day/date/time flickered in the bottom margin. Impatiently Moffitt fast-forwarded through a blurry conga line of truckers, traveling salesmen, stiff-legged tourists and bingeing teenagers whose unwholesome diets and nicotine addictions made the Grab N'Go a gold mine for the Dutch holding company that owned it.

Finally Moffitt came to JoLayne Lucks, walking through the swinging glass doors. She wore jeans, a baggy sweatshirt and big round sunglasses, probably the peach-tinted ones. The camera's clock flashed 5:15 p.m. One minute later she was standing at the counter. Moffitt chuckled when he saw the roll of Certs; spearmint, undoubtedly. JoLayne dug into her purse and gave some money to the pudgy teenage clerk. He handed her the change in coins, plus one ticket from the Lotto machine. She said something to the clerk, smiled, and went out the door into the afternoon glare.

Moffitt backed up the tape, to review the smile. It was good enough to make him ache.

He'd left Puerto Rico a day early, after the de la Hoya cousins wisely discarded their original explanation of the three hundred Chinese machine guns found in their beach house at Rincón (to wit: they'd unknowingly rented the place to a band of leftist guerrillas posing as American surfers). Attorneys for the de la Hoyas realized they were in trouble when they noticed jurors smirking (and, in one case, suppressing a giggle) as the surfer alibi was presented during opening statements. After a hasty conference, the de la Hoyas decided to jump on the government's offer of a plea bargain, thus sparing Moffitt and a half dozen other ATF agents the drudgery of testifying. Once the case was settled, Moffitt's pals headed straight to San Juan in search of tropical pussy, while Moffitt flew home to help JoLayne.

Who was, naturally, nowhere to be found.

Moffitt had known she wouldn't take his advice, wouldn't back off and wait. There was nothing to be done; she was as stubborn as a mule. Always had been.

Finding her, if she was still alive, meant finding the Lotto robbers whom she undoubtedly was tracking. For clues Moffitt returned to the apartment of Bodean James Gazzer, which appeared to have been abandoned in a panic. The food in the kitchen was beginning to rot, and the ketchup message on the walls had dried to a gummy brown crust. Moffitt made another hard pass through the rooms and came up with a crumpled eviction notice for a rented trailer lot in the boonies of Homestead. Scratched in pencil on the back of the paper were six numbers that matched the ones on JoLayne's stolen lottery ticket.

Moffitt was on his way out the apartment door when the phone rang. He couldn't resist. The caller was a deputy for the Monroe County sheriff's office, inquiring about a 1996 Dodge Ram pickup truck that had been found stripped near the Indian Key fill, on the Overseas Highway. The deputy said the truck was registered to one Bodean J. Gazzer.

"That you?" the deputy asked on the phone.

"My roommate," Moffitt said.

"Well, when you see him," said the deputy, "could you ask him to give us a holler?"

"Sure thing." Moffitt thinking: So the assholes ran to the Keys.

Immediately he began calling marinas, working south from Key Largo and asking (in his most persuasive agent-speak) about unusual rentals or thefts. That's how he learned about the Whaler overdue in Islamorada, rented to a "nigrah girl with a sassy tongue," according to the old cracker at the motel dock. The Coast Guard already had a bird up, so Moffitt made another call and got cleared to tag along. He was waiting at Opa-Locka when the chopper came in for refueling.

Ninety minutes later they'd spotted her—JoLayne with her new friend, Krome. Tooling along in the missing skiff.

Watching through the binoculars, Moffitt had felt sheepish for worrying so much about her. But who in his right mind wouldn't?

After the helicopter dropped him off, Moffitt drove to Homestead to locate the house trailer from which a man known to his landlord as

"Chub Smith" was being evicted. It was a dented single-wide on a dirt road way out in farm country. Inside, Moffitt came across piles of old gun magazines, empty ammo boxes, a WHITE POWER T-shirt, a FRY O.J. sweatshirt, a GOD BLESS MARGE SCHOTT pennant, and (in the bedroom) a makeshift forgery operation for handicapped-parking permits—the quality of which, Moffitt noted, was pretty darn good.

The mail was sparse and unrevealing, bills and gun-shop flyers addressed to "C. Smith" or "C. Jones" or simply "Mr. Chub." Not a scrap of paper offered a hint to the tenant's true identity, but Moffitt felt certain it was the ponytailed partner of Bodean James Gazzer. A clot of grimy long strands in the shower drain seemed to confirm the theory.

Parked outside the trailer was an old Chevrolet Impala. Moffitt made a note of the license tag before popping the trunk (where he found a canvas rifle case and a five-pound carton of beef jerky), checking under the seats (two roach clips and a mangled *Oui* magazine) and unlatching the glove box (the video cassette now playing in his VCR).

Moffitt turned off the tape player and opened a beer. He wondered what had happened while he was out of the States, wondered where the white-trash robbers were. Wondered what JoLayne Lucks and her new friend Tom had been up to.

He dialed her number in Grange and left a message on the machine: "I'm back. Call me as soon as you can."

Then he went to sleep wondering how much he ought to ask, and how much he really needed to know.

Mary Andrea Finley Krome sparkled like a movie star.

That's what everyone at *The Register* was saying. Even the managing editor admitted she was a knockout.

She'd gotten her short hair highlighted and her nails done, put on tiny gold hoop earrings, pale-rose lipstick, sheer stockings and a stunningly short black skirt. The coup de grâce was the rosary beads, dangling sensually from Mary Andrea's fingertips.

When she entered the newsroom, the police reporter turned to the managing editor: "Tom must've been nuts to walk out on *that.*"

Maybe, thought the managing editor. Maybe not.

The elegant widow walked up to him and said, "So, where are they?"

"In the lobby."

"I just came through the lobby. I didn't see any cameras."

"We've got ten minutes," the managing editor said. "They'll be here, don't worry."

Mary Andrea asked, "Is there a place where I can be alone?"

The managing editor glanced helplessly around the newsroom, which offered all the privacy of a bus depot.

"My office," he suggested, unenthusiastically, and headed downstairs for a Danish. When he returned, he was intercepted by an assistant city editor.

"Guess what Mrs. Krome is doing in there."

"Weeping uncontrollably?"

"No, she's—"

"Doubled over with grief?"

"Get serious."

"Rifling through the desk. That's my bet."

"No, she's rehearsing," the assistant city editor reported. "Rehearsing her lines."

"Perfect," said the managing editor.

When they got to the lobby, crews from three local television stations were waiting, including the promised Fox affiliate. A still photographer from *The Register* arrived (properly sullen about the assignment), boosting the media contingent to four.

"Not exactly a throng," Mary Andrea griped.

The managing editor smiled coldly. "It is, by our modest standards."

Soon the room filled with other editors, reporters and clerks, most of whom didn't know Tom Krome very well but had been forced to attend by their supervisors. There were even clusters from Circulation and Advertising—easy to spot, because they dressed so much more neatly than the newsroom gang. Also among the audience were curious civilians who had come to *The Register* to take out classified ads, drop off pithy letters to the editor or cancel their subscriptions because of the paper's shameless left- or right-wing bias.

One person missing from the award ceremony was the publisher himself, who hadn't been especially shattered by the news of Tom Krome's probable incineration. Krome once had written a snarky article about a restricted country club to which the publisher and his four golfing sons belonged. After the story appeared, the membership of the country club had voted to spare the sons but expel the publisher for not firing Tom Krome and publicly apologizing for exposing all of them to scorn and ridicule (Krome had described the club as "blindingly white and Protestant, except for the caddies").

The managing editor would have loved to use that line (and a dozen other zingers) in his tribute to Krome, but he knew better. He had a pension and stock options to consider. So instead, when the TV lights came on, he limited himself to a few innocuous remarks, gamely attempting to invest the first-place Amelia with significance and possibly even prestige. The managing editor of course invoked the namesake memory of the late Ms. Lloyd, noting with inflated irony that she, too, had been cut down midcareer in the line of journalistic duty. Here several reporters exchanged doubtful glances, for the prevailing gossip held that Tom Krome's death was in no way connected to his job and was in fact the result of imprudent dating habits. Fueling the skepticism was the conspicuous absence of Krome's own editor, Sinclair, who normally wouldn't pass up an opportunity to snake credit for a writer's good work. Obviously something was screwy, or Sinclair would have been in the lobby, buoyantly awaiting his turn at the lectern.

The managing editor was aware of the rumors about Tom's death, yet he'd made up his mind to venture out on this limb. One reason was his strong belief that local authorities were too incompetent to sort out the true facts (whatever they were) about the fatal blaze at Krome's house. And in the absence of competing explanations, the managing editor was willing to promote his newspaper's first Amelia as a posthumous homage to a fallen star. If, come spring, Krome's tenuous martyrdom still hadn't been shot down in a hail of embarrassing personal revelations, the managing editor might just try to float it past a Pulitzer committee. And why the hell not?

"My regret—*our* regret," he said in conclusion, "is that Tom couldn't be here to celebrate this moment. But all of us here at *The Register* will remember him today and always with pride and admiration. His dedication, his spirit, his commitment to journalism, lives on in this newsroom. . . ."

Inwardly the managing editor cringed as he spoke, for the words came out corny and canned. It was a tough audience, and he expected to hear a muffled wisecrack or a groan. Quickly he pushed on to the main event.

"Now I'd like to introduce someone very special—Tom's wife, Mary Andrea, who came a very long way to be with us and share some memories."

The applause was respectful and possibly heartfelt, the most vigorous burst erupting (out of gung-ho reflex) from the crisp-shirted advertising reps. Slightly more reserved was the newsroom crew, although the managing editor snapped his head around upon hearing a crude wolf whistle; one of the sportswriters, it turned out. (Later, when confronted, the kid would claim to have been unaware of the occasion's solemnity. Bearing late-breaking news of a major hockey trade, he'd been hurrying through *The Register*'s lobby toward the elevator when he had spotted Mary Andrea Finley Krome at the podium and was overcome by her rocking good looks.)

As she stepped to the microphone, the managing editor presented her with the standard slab of lacquered pine, adorned by a cheap gold-plated plaque. An appalling etching of the late Amelia J. Lloyd, full-cheeked and chipper, was featured on the award, which Mary Andrea enfolded as if it were a Renoir.

"My husband . . . ," she said, followed by a perfect pause.

"My husband would be so proud."

A second burst of applause swept the lobby. Mary Andrea acknowledged it by hugging the Amelia to her breasts.

"My Tom," she began, "was not an easy man to know. During the last few years, he threw himself into his work so single-mindedly that, I'm sad to say, it pushed us apart. . . ."

By the time Mary Andrea got to their imaginary backstage reunion in Grand Rapids (which, she'd decided at the last moment, sounded more romantic than Lansing), the place was in sniffles. The TV cameras kept rolling; two of the crews even reloaded with fresh batteries. Mary Andrea felt triumphant.

Twenty seconds, my ass, she thought, dabbing her cheeks with a handkerchief provided by the managing editor.

Most surprising: Mary Andrea's tears, which had begun as well-practiced stage weeping, had bloomed into the real deal. Talking about Tom in front of so many people made her truly grief-stricken for the first time since she'd learned about

the fire. Even though she was largely fictionaliz-
ing their relationship—inventing anecdotes, intimacies and confidences never shared—the act
nonetheless thawed Mary Andrea's heart. Tom
was, after all, a pretty good guy. Confused (like all
men) but decent at the core. It was a pity he hadn't
been more adaptable. A damn pity, she thought,
blinking away the teardrops.

One person who remained unmoved during the
ceremony was the managing editor of *The Register.* The other was Tom Krome's lawyer, Dick
Turnquist, who politely waited until Mary Andrea
was finished speaking before he edged through
the well-wishers and served her with the court
summons.

"We finally meet," he said.

And Mary Andrea, being somewhat caught up
in her own performance, assumed he was a fan
from the theater who wanted an autograph.

"You're so kind," she said, "but I don't have a
pen."

"You don't need a pen. You need a lawyer."

"What?" Mary Andrea, staring in bafflement
and dismay at the documents in her hand. "Is this
some kind of sick joke? My husband's dead!"

"No, he's not. Not in the slightest. But I'll pass
along all the nice things you said about him today.
He'll appreciate it." Turnquist spun and walked
away.

The managing editor stood frozen by what he'd

overheard. Among the onlookers there was a stir, then a bang caused by lacquered pine hitting terrazzo. The managing editor whirled to see his prized Amelia on the lobby floor, where the non-widow Krome had hurled it. Only inches away: a discarded rosary, coiled like a baby rattler.

The last conscious act of Bodean Gazzer's life was brushing his teeth with WD-40.

In a survivalist tract he'd once read about the unsung versatility of the popular spray lubricant, and now (while exsanguinating) he felt an irrational urge to brighten his smile. Chub pawed through the gear and found the familiar blue-and-yellow can, which he brought to Bode's side, along with a small brush designed for cleaning pistols. Chub knelt in the blood-crusted sand and tucked a camouflage bedroll under his partner's neck.

"Do my molars, wouldya?" Groggily Bode Gazzer opened his mouth and pointed.

"Jesus Willy," Chub said, but he aimed the nozzle at Bode's brown-stained chompers and sprayed. What the hell, he thought. The fucker's dying.

Bode brushed in a listless mechanical way. He spoke from the uncluttered side of his mouth: "You believe this shit? We just lost twenty-eight million bucks to a Negro terrorist and a damn waitress! They got us, brother. NATO and the Tri-

Lateral Negroes and the damn com'nists . . . You believe it?"

Chub was in a blinding misery, his bandaged shoulder afire. "You know . . . you know what I *don't* believe?" he said. "I don't believe you still won't say 'nigger' after all she done to us. God-damn, Bode, I wonder 'bout you!"

"Aw, well." Bodean Gazzer's eyelids drooped to half-staff. One hand flopped apologetically, splatting in a puddle of blood. His face was as pallid as a slab of fish.

"She shot you. She *shot* you, man." Chub hunched over him. "I wanna hear you say it. 'Nigger.' Before you go and croak, I want you to act like a upright God-fearin' member of the white master race and say that lil word just once. Kin you do that for me? For the late, great White Clarion Aryans?" Chub laughed berserkly against the pain.

"Come on, you stubborn little prick. Say it: N-i-g-e-r."

But Bodean James Gazzer was done talking. He died with the gun brush in his cheeks. His final breath was a soft necrotic whistle of WD-40 fumes.

Chub caught a slight buzz from it, or so he imagined. He snatched up the aerosol can, struggled to his feet and staggered into the mangroves to mourn.

28

The pilgrims were restless. They wanted Turtle Boy.

Sinclair wouldn't come out until he had a deal. Shiner's mother sat beside him on the sofa; the two of them holding hands tautly, as if they were on an airplane in turbulence.

The mayor, Jerry Wicks, had rushed to Demencio's house after hearing about the trouble. Trish prepared coffee and fresh-squeezed orange juice. Shiner's mother declined the pancakes in favor of an omelette.

Demencio was in no mood to negotiate, but the crazy fools had him pinned. Something had gone awry with the food-dye formula and his fiberglass Madonna had begun to weep oily brown tears. Hastily he'd hauled the statue indoors and shut down the visitation. Now there were forty-odd Christian tourists milling in the yard, halfheartedly snapping photos of baby turtles in the moat. Sales of the "holy water" had gone flatline.

"Lemme get this straight." Demencio paced the living room. "You want thirty percent of the daily collection *and* thirty percent of the concessions? That ain't gonna happen. Forget about it."

Sinclair, still numb and loopy from his revelations, had been taking his cues from Shiner's mother. She pressed a smudged cheek against his shoulder.

"We told you," she said to Demencio, "we'd set-tle for twenty percent of the concessions."

"What's this 'we' shit?"

"But only if you find a place for Marva," Sin-clair interjected. Marva was the name of Shiner's mother. "A new shrine," Sinclair went on, brush-ing a clod of lettuce from his forelock, "to replace the one that was paved."

He hardly recognized his own voice, a trillion light-years beyond his prior life. The newsroom and all its petty travails might as well have been on Pluto.

Demencio sagged into his favorite TV chair. "You people got some goddamn nerve. This is *my* business here. We built it up by ourselves, all these years, me and Trish. And now you just waltz in and try to take over. . . ."

Shiner's mother pointed out that Demencio's pilgrim traffic had tripled, thanks to Sinclair's mystical turtle handling. "Plus I got my own loyal clientele," she said. "They'll be here sure as the sun shines, buying up your T-shirts and sodey pops and angel food snacks. You two'll make out like bandits if only you got the brains to go along."

Trish started to say something, but Demencio cut her off. "I don't need you people, that's the point. You need *me.*"

"Really?" Shiner's mother, with a smirk. "You

got a Virgin Mary leakin' Quaker State out her eyeballs. Who needs who? is my question."

Demencio said, "Go to hell." But the loony witch had a point.

Even in his blissfully detached state, Sinclair wouldn't budge off the numbers. He knew a little something about business—his father ran a gourmet cheese shop in Boston, and there were plenty of times he'd had to play hardball with those blockhead wholesalers back in Wisconsin.

"May I suggest something?" Mayor Jerry Wicks, playing mediator. The manager of the Holiday Inn, fearing a dip in the bus-tour trade, had implored him to intervene. "I've got an idea," said the mayor. "What if . . . Marva, let me ask: What would you need in the way of facilities?"

"For what?"

"Another manifestation."

Shiner's mother crinkled her brow. "Geez, I don't know. You mean another Jesus?"

"I think that's the ticket," the mayor said. "Demencio's already got dibs on the Mother Mary. The turtle boy—may I call you Turtle Boy?—he's got the apostles. That leaves a slot wide open for the Christ child."

Shiner's mother wagged a bony finger. "No, not the baby Jesus. The growed-up one is what I favor."

"Fine," said the mayor. "My point is, this place

would make a helluva shrine, would it not? Talk about having all your bases covered!" He cocked his chin toward Demencio. "Come on. You gotta admit."

Demencio felt Trish's hand on his shoulder. He knew what she was thinking: *This could be big.* If they did it right, they'd be the number one stop on the whole Grange bus tour.

Nonetheless, Demencio felt impelled to say: "I don't want no stains on my driveway. Or the sidewalks, neither."

"Fair enough."

"And I won't give up no more than fifteen percent on the collections."

Sinclair looked at Shiner's mother, who smiled in approval. "That we can live with," she said.

They gathered at the dining table to brainstorm a new Christ shrine. "Wherever He appears, that's where it is," Shiner's mother explained, raising her palms. "And maybe He won't appear at all, not after what happened out on the highway—them heathens from the road department."

Ever the optimist, Mayor Jerry Wicks said: "I bet if you went outside and started praying real hard . . . Well, I just have a feeling."

Shiner's mother squeezed Sinclair's arm. "Maybe that's what I'll do. Get down on my knees and pray."

"Not in my driveway," Demencio said curtly.

"I heard you the first time, OK? Geez."

Trish said: "Who needs more coffee?"

From where he sat, Demencio had a clear view of the scene out front. The crowd was thinning, the pilgrims bored to tears. This was bad. The mayor noticed, too. He and Demencio exchanged apprehensive glances. Unspoken was the fact that Grange's meager economy had come to rely on the seasonal Christian tourist trade. The town couldn't afford a downturn, couldn't afford to lose any of its prime attractions. Around Florida there was growing competition for the pilgrim dollar, some of it Disney-slick and high-tech. Not a week went by when the TV didn't report a new religious sighting or miracle healing. Most recently, a purported three-story likeness of the Virgin Mary had appeared on the wall of a mortgage company in Clearwater—nothing but sprinkler rust, yet three hundred thousand people came to see. They sang and wept and left cash offerings, wrapped in handkerchiefs and diapers.

Offerings, at a mortgage company!

Demencio didn't need Jerry Wicks to tell him it was no time to slack off. Demencio knew what was out there, knew it was vital to keep pace with the market.

"Wait'll you see," he told the mayor, "when I got my Mary cryin' blood. You just wait."

The telephone rang. Demencio went to take it in

the bedroom, where it was quiet. When he came out, his expression was dour. Shiner's mother asked what was wrong.

"You said you were gonna pray? Well, go to it." Demencio waved an arm. "Pray like crazy, Marva, because we'll need a new miracle, ASAP. Any new Jesus'll do just fine."

Jerry Wicks sat forward, planting his elbows on the table. "What happened?"

"That was JoLayne on the phone. She's coming home," Demencio reported cheerlessly. "She's on her way home to pick up her cooters."

Sinclair went pale. Shiner's mother stroked his forehead and told him not to worry, everything was going to be all right.

They bought some new clothes and went to the best restaurant in Tallahassee. Tom Krome ordered steaks and a bottle of champagne and a plate of Apalachicola oysters. He told JoLayne Lucks she looked fantastic, which she did. She'd picked out a long dress, slinky and forest green, with spaghetti straps. He went for simple slate-gray slacks, a plain blue blazer and a white oxford shirt, no necktie.

The lottery check was in JoLayne's handbag: five hundred and sixty thousand dollars, after Uncle Sam's cut. It was the first of twenty annual payments on JoLayne's share of the big jackpot.

Tom leaned across the table and kissed her. Out of the corner of an eye he saw a starchy old white couple staring from another table, so he kissed Jo-Layne again; longer this time. Then he lifted his glass: "To Simmons Wood."

"To Simmons Wood," said JoLayne, too quietly.

"What's wrong?"

"Tom, it's not enough. I did the math."

"How do you figure?"

"The other offer is three million even, with twenty percent down. I promised Clara Markham I could do better, but I don't think I can. Twenty percent of three million is six hundred grand—I'm still short, Tom."

He told her not to sweat it. "Worse comes to worse, get a loan for the difference. There isn't a bank in Florida that wouldn't be thrilled to get your business."

"Easy for you to say."

"JoLayne, you just won fourteen million bucks."

"I'm still black, Mr. Krome. That *do* make a difference."

But after thinking about it, she realized he was probably right about the loan. Black, white or polka-dotted, she was still a tycoon, and bankers adored tycoons. A financing package with a fat down payment could be put together, a very tasty counteroffer. The Simmons family would be drooling all over their foie gras, and the union boys from Chicago would have to look elsewhere for a spot to erect their ticky-tacky shopping mall.

JoLayne attacked her Caesar salad and said to Tom Krome: "You're right. I've decided to be positive."

"Good, because we're on a roll."

"I can't argue with that."

They'd returned the overdue Boston Whaler with a minimum of uproar, blunting the old dock rat's ire by pleasantly agreeing to forfeit the deposit. After grabbing a cab down to the boat ramp, they'd retrieved Tom's Honda and sped directly to Miami International Airport, where they lucked into a nonstop to Tallahassee. By the time they arrived, the state lottery office had closed for the day. They'd gotten a room at the Sheraton, hopped in the shower and collapsed in exhaustion across the king-sized bed. Dinner was cocktail crackers and Hershey's kisses from the minibar. They'd both been too tired to make love and had fallen asleep laughing about it, and trying not to think of Pearl Key.

When the Lotto bureau opened the next morning, JoLayne and Tom were waiting at the door with the ticket. A clerk thought she was joking when she matter-of-factly remarked it had been hidden inside a nonlubricated condom. The paperwork took about an hour, then a photographer from the publicity office made some pictures of JoLayne holding a blown-up facsimile of the flamingo-adorned check. Tom was pleased they'd avoided TV and newspaper coverage by showing up unannounced. By the time a press release was issued, they'd be back in Grange.

"This is all going to work out," he assured Jo-Layne, pouring more champagne. "I promise."

"What about you and me?"

"Absolutely."

JoLayne studied him. "Absolutely, Tom?"

"Oh brother. Here it comes." Krome set down his glass.

She said, "I think you deserve some of the money."

"Why?"

"For everything. Quitting your job to stay with me. Risking your neck. Stopping me from doing something crazy out there."

"Anything else?"

"I'd feel so much better," she said, "giving you something."

Tom tapped a fork on the tablecloth. "Boy, that guilt—it's a killer. I sympathize."

"You're wrong."

"No, I'm right. If I won't take the money, it'll make it harder for you to dump me later. You'll feel so awful you'll keep putting it off, stringing me along, probably for months and months—"

"Eat your salad," JoLayne said.

"But if I *do* take a cut, then you won't feel so lousy saying goodbye. You can tell yourself you didn't use me, didn't take advantage of a hopelessly smitten sap and then cut him loose. You can tell yourself you were fair about it, even decent."

"Are you finished?" JoLayne inwardly ached at the truth of what he said. She definitely was looking for an escape clause, in case the romance didn't work. She was looking for a way to live with herself if someday she had to break up with him, after all he'd done for her.

Tom said, "I don't want the damn money. You understand? *Nada.* Not a penny."

"I believe you."

"Finally."

"But just for the record, I've got no plans to 'dump' you." JoLayne kicked off a shoe and slipped her bare foot in Tom's lap, under the table.

Tom's eyes widened. "Oh, *that's* fighting fair."

"I've had a bad run with men. I guess I'm conditioned to expect the worst."

"Understood," he said. "And just for the record, you should feel free to string me along. Drag it out as long as you can stand to, because I'll take every minute with you that I can get."

"You're pretty polished at this guilt business."

"Oh, I'm a pro," Tom said, "one of the best. So here's the deal: Give us six months together. If you're not happy, I'll go quietly. No wailing, no racking sobs. The only thing it'll cost you is a plane ticket to Alaska."

JoLayne steepled her hands. "Hmmm. I suppose you'll insist on first class."

"You bet your ass. Up front with the hot towelettes and sorbets, that's me. Deal?"

"OK. Deal."

They shook. The waiter came with the steaks, big T-bones done rare. Tom waited for JoLayne to take the first bite.

"Delicious," she reported.

"Whew."

"Hey, I just thought of something. What if you dump *me*?"

Tom Krome grinned. "You just thought of that?"

"Smart-ass!" she said, and poked him with her big toe in quite a sensitive area. They wolfed their steaks, skipped dessert and hurried back to the room to make love.

Judge Arthur Battenkill Jr. came home to an empty house. Katie was probably at the supermarket or the hairdresser. The judge put on the television and sat down to savor a martini, in celebration of his retirement. The early news came on but he didn't pay much attention. Instead he absorbed himself with the challenge of selecting a Caribbean wardrobe. Nassau would be the logical place to shop; Bay Street, where he'd once bought

Willow a hand-dyed linen blouse and a neon thong bikini, which he'd brutishly gnawed off in the cabana.

Arthur Battenkill tried to imagine himself in vivid teal walking shorts and woven beach sandals; him with his hairy feet and chalky, birdlike legs. He resolved to do whatever was needed to be a respectable exile, to blend in. He looked forward to learning the island life.

The name Tom Krome jarred him from the reverie. It came from the television.

The judge grabbed for the remote and turned up the volume. As he watched the footage, he stirred the gin with a manicured pinkie. Some sort of press conference at *The Register.* A good-looking woman in a short black dress; Krome's wife, according to the TV anchor. Picking up a journalism plaque on behalf of her dead husband. Then: chaos.

Arthur Battenkill rocked forward, clutching his martini with both hands. God, it was official— Krome was indeed alive!

There was the man's lawyer on television, saying so. He'd just served the astonished and now flustered Mrs. Krome with divorce papers.

Ordinarily the judge would've smiled in admiration at the attorney's cold-blooded ambush, but Arthur Battenkill wasn't enjoying the moment even slightly. He was climbing the stairs, taking three at time, anticipating what he'd find when he reached the bedroom; preparing himself for the catastrophic fact that Katie wasn't at the grocery or the salon. She was gone.

Her drawers in the bureau were empty; her side of the bathroom vanity was cleaned out. A suitcase was also missing, the big brown one with foldaway casters. A lavender note in Katie's frilly handwriting was Scotch-taped to the headboard of their bed, and for several moments it paralyzed the judge:

Honesty, Arthur. Remember?

Which meant, of course, that his wife, Katherine Battenkill, had been to the police.

The judge began packing like the frantic fugitive he was about to become. Tomorrow's front-page newspaper headline would exhume Tom Krome but, more important, rekindle the mystery of the corpse found in the burned house. Detectives who might otherwise have dismissed Katie's yarn as spousal bile (and done so without a nudge, being longtime courthouse acquaintances of Arthur Battenkill) would be impelled in the scorching glare of the media to take her seriously.

Which meant a full-blown search would begin for Champ Powell, the absent law clerk.

I could be fucked, thought Arthur Battenkill. Seriously fucked.

He filled their second-string suitcase, a gun-metal Samsonite, with underwear, toiletries, every short-sleeved shirt he owned, jeans and khakis, a windbreaker, PABA-free sunscreen, swim trunks, a stack of traveler's checks (which he'd purchased that morning at the bank) and a few items of sentimental value (engraved cuff links, an ivory gavel and two boxes of personalized Titleists). He concealed five thousand in cash (withdrawn during the same sortie to the bank) inside random pairs of nylon socks. He packed a single blue suit (though not the vest) and one of his judge's robes, in case he needed to make an impression on some recalcitrant Bahamian immigration man.

One thing Arthur Battenkill found missing from the marital bureau was his passport, which Katie undoubtedly had swiped to thwart his escape.

Clever girl, the judge said to himself.

What his wife did not know (and Arthur Battenkill did, from his illicit travels with Willow and Dana) was that U.S. citizens didn't need a passport for entry into the Commonwealth of the Bahamas. A birth certificate sufficed, and the judge had one in his billfold.

He latched the suitcase and dragged it to the living room, where he got on the phone to a small air-charter service in Satellite Beach. The owners owed him a favor, as he'd once saved them a bundle by overruling a catastrophic jury verdict. The case involved a 323-pound passenger who'd been injured by a sliding crate of roosters on a flight to

Andros. Jurors blamed the air-charter service for the mishap and awarded the passenger $100,000 for each of her fractured toes, which numbered exactly four. However, it was Arthur Battenkill's view, based on the expert testimony, that the woman herself shared much of the blame since it was her jumbo presence in the rear of the aircraft that had caused the cargo to shift so precipitously upon takeoff. The judge sliced the jury award by seventy-five percent, a decision upheld on appeal and received buoyantly by the air-charter firm.

Whose owners now assured Arthur Battenkill Jr. that it would be no trouble flying him to Marsh Harbour, none whatsoever.

As the judge showered and shaved for the last time as an American resident, he imagined how it would be, his new life in the islands. It would have been better with Katie, for a single middle-aged man surely would attract more notice and even suspicion. Still, he could easily picture himself as the newly arrived gentleman divorcé—no, a widower. Polite, educated, respectful of native ways. He'd have a small place on the water and live modestly off investments. Discreetly he would let it drop that he'd held a position of prominence in the States. Perhaps eventually he would take on some piecework, advising local attorneys who had business with the Florida courts. He also would learn how to snorkel, and would order some books to help him identify the reef fish. He would go barefoot and get a nut-brown tan. There would be time for painting, too (which he hadn't done since his undergraduate days)—watercolors of passing sailboats and swaying palms, bright tropical scenes that would sell big with the tourists in Nassau or Freeport.

Leaning his forehead against the tiles in the steamy shower, the Honorable Arthur Battenkill Jr. could see it all. What he couldn't see was the plain blue sedan pulling into his driveway. Inside were three men: an FBI agent and two county detectives. They'd come to ask the judge about his law clerk, whose name had been helpfully provided by the judge's wife and secretaries, and whose toasted remains had been (less than one hour ago) positively identified by a series of DNA tests. If, as Mrs. Battenkill stated, the judge had assigned the late Champ Powell to the arson in which he'd perished, then the judge himself would stand trial for felony murder.

It was a topic that would arise soon enough, after Arthur Battenkill toweled off, got dressed, picked up his suitcase and—gaily humming the tune of "Yellow Bird"—walked out his front door, where the men stood in wait.

"What'll happen to your husband?"

Katie Battenkill said, "Prison, I guess."

"God." Mary Andrea Finley Krome, thinking: This one's tougher than she looks.

"There's a Denny's off the next exit. Are you hungry?"

Mary Andrea said, "Tell me again where we're going. The name of the place."

"Grange."

"And you're sure Tom's there?"

"I think so. I'm pretty sure," Katie replied.

"And how exactly do you know him? Or did you already say?"

Mary Andrea wasn't in the habit of road-tripping with total strangers, but the woman had seemed trustworthy and Mary Andrea had been frantic—spooked by Tom's divorce lawyer and rudely shouted at by the reporters. She would never forget the heat of the TV lights on her neck as she fled, nor the dread as she fought for a path through the crowd in the newspaper lobby. She'd even considered feigning another medical collapse but decided against it; the choreography would've been dicey amid the tumult.

All of a sudden a hand had gripped her elbow, and she'd spun to see this woman—a pretty strawberry blonde, who'd led her out the door and said: "Let's get you away from all this nonsense."

And Mary Andrea, stunned with defeat and weakened from humiliation, had accompanied the consoling stranger because it was the next best

thing to running, which was what Mary Andrea
felt most like doing. The woman introduced herself as Katie something-or-other and briskly took
Mary Andrea to a car.

"I tried to get there sooner," she'd said. "I
wanted to tell you your husband was still alive—
you deserved to know. But then I got tied up at the
sheriff's office."

Initially Mary Andrea had let pass the last part
of the woman's remark, but she brought it up later,
as an icebreaker, when they were on the highway.
Katie candidly stated that her husband was a local
judge who'd committed a terrible crime, and that
her conscience and religious beliefs required her to
rat him out to the police. The story piqued Mary
Andrea's curiosity but she was eager to steer the
conversation back to the topic of her scheming
bastard husband. How else to describe a man so
merciless that he'd burn down his own house to set
up his own wife—even an estranged one—for publicly televised ridicule!

"You're mistaken. It wasn't like that," said Katie
Battenkill.

"You don't know Tom."

"Actually, I do. See, I was his lover." Katie was
adhering to her newfound doctrine of total honesty. "For about two weeks. Look in my purse,
there's a list of all the times we made love. It's on
lavender notepaper, folded in half."

Mary Andrea said, "You're serious, aren't you?"

"Go ahead and look."

"No, thanks."

"Truth matters more than anything in the world. I'll tell you whatever you want to know."

"And then some," Mary Andrea said, under her breath. She considered putting on a show of being jealous, to discourage the woman from further elaboration.

But Katie caught her off guard by asking: "Aren't you glad he's alive? You don't look all that thrilled."

"I'm . . . I guess I'm still in shock."

Katie seemed doubtful.

Mary Andrea said, "If I weren't so damn mad at him, yes, I'd be glad." Which possibly was true. Mary Andrea knew her peevishness didn't fit the circumstances, but young Katie couldn't know what the Krome marriage was, or had become. And as good a performer as Mary Andrea was, she wasn't sure how an ex-widow ought to act. She'd never met one.

Katie said, "Don't be mad. Tom didn't set you up. What happened was my husband's fault—and mine, too, for sleeping with Tom. See, that's why Arthur had the house torched—"

"Whoa. Who's Arthur?"

"My husband. I told you about him. It's a mess, I know," said Katie, "but you've got to understand that Tommy didn't arrange this. He had no clue. When it happened he was out of town, working on an article for the paper. That's when Art sent a man to the house—"

"OK, time out!" Mary Andrea, making a T with her hands. "Is this why your husband's going to jail?"

"That's right."

"My God."

"I'm so glad you believe me."

"Oh, I'm not sure I do," said Mary Andrea. "But it's quite a story, Katie. And if you *did* cook it up all by yourself, then you should think about a career in show business. Seriously."

They were thirty minutes outside Grange before Katherine Battenkill spoke again.

"I've come to believe that everything happens for a reason, Mrs. Krome. There's no coincidence or chance or luck. Everything that happens is meant to guide us. For example: Tom. If I hadn't made love thirteen times with Tom, I would never have seen Arthur for what he truly is. And likewise he'd never have burned down that house, and you wouldn't be here with me right now, riding to Grange to see your husband."

For once Mary Andrea was unable to modulate her reaction. "Thirteen times in two weeks?"

Thinking: That breaks *our* old record.

"But that's counting oral relations, too." Katie, attempting to soften the impact. She rolled down the window. Cool air streamed through the car. "I don't know about you, but I'm dying for a cheeseburger."

"Well, I'm dying to speak to Mr. Tom Krome."

"It won't be long now," Katie said lightly. "But we do need to make a couple of stops. One for gas."

"And what else?"

"Something special. You'll see."

 On the morning of December 6, Clara Markham drove to her real estate office to nail down a buyer for the property known as Simmons Wood. Waiting in the parking lot was Bernard Squires, investment manager for the Central Midwest Brotherhood of Grouters, Spacklers and Drywallers International. As Clara Markham unlocked the front door, JoLayne Lucks strolled up—jeans, sweatshirt, peach-tinted sunglasses and a baseball cap. She'd done her nails in glossy tangerine.

The dapper Squires looked uneasy; he shifted his eelskin briefcase from one fist to the other. Clara Markham made the introductions and started a pot of coffee.

She said, "So how was your trip, Jo? Where'd you go?"

"Camping."

"In all that weather!"

"Listen, hon, it kept the bugs away." JoLayne moved quickly to change the subject. "How's my pal Kenny? How's the diet coming?"

"We've lost two pounds! I switched him to dry food, like you suggested." Clara Markham reported this proudly. She handed a cup of coffee to Bernard Squires, who thanked her in a reserved tone.

The real estate broker explained: "Kenny's my Persian blue. Jo works at the vet."

"Oh. My sister has a Siamese," said Squires, exclusively out of politeness.

JoLayne Lucks whipped off her sunglasses and zapped him with a smile. He could scarcely mask his annoyance. *This* was his competition for a $3 million piece of commercial property—a black woman with orange fingernails who works at an animal hospital!

Clara Markham settled behind her desk, uncluttered and immaculate. JoLayne Lucks and Bernard Squires positioned themselves in straight-backed chairs, almost side by side. They set their coffee cups on cork-lined coasters.

"Shall we begin?" said Clara.

Without preamble Squires opened the briefcase across his lap, and handed to the real estate broker a sheaf of legal-sized papers. Clara skimmed the cover sheet.

For JoLayne's benefit she said, "The union's offer is three million even with twenty-five percent down. Mr. Squires already delivered a good-faith cash deposit, which we put in escrow."

They jacked up the stakes, JoLayne brooded. Bastards.

"Jo?"

"I'll offer three point one," she said, "and thirty percent up front." She'd been to the bank early. Tom Krome was right—a young vice president in designer suspenders had airily offered an open line of credit to cover any shortfall on the Simmons Wood down payment.

Squires said, "Ms. Markham, I'm not accustomed to this . . . informality. Purchase proposals on a tract this size are usually put into writing."

"We're a small town, Bernard. And you're the one who's in the big hurry." Clara, with a saccharine smile.

"It's my clients, you see."

"Certainly."

JoLayne Lucks was determined not to be intimidated. "Clara knows my word is good, Mr. Squires. Don't you think things will move quicker this way, all three of us together?"

Disdain flicked across the investment manager's face. "All right, quicker it is. We'll jump to 3.25 million."

Clara Markham shifted slightly. "Don't you need to call your people in Chicago?"

"That's not necessary," Squires replied with an icy pleasantness.

"Three three," JoLayne said.

Squires closed the briefcase soundlessly. "This can go on for as long as you wish, Miss Lucks. The pension fund has given me tremendous latitude."

"Three point four." JoLayne slipped from worried to scared. The man was a shark; this was his job.

"Three five," Bernard Squires shot back. Now it was his turn to smile. The girl was caving fast. *What was I so worried about?* he wondered. *It's this creepy little hole of a town—I let it get to me.*

He said, "You see, the union has come to rely upon my judgment in these matters. Real estate development, and so forth. They leave the negotiations to me. And the value of a parcel like this is defined by the market on any given day. Today the market happens to be, quite frankly, pretty good."

JoLayne glanced at her friend Clara, who appeared commendably unexcited by the bidding or the rising trajectory of her commission. What *was* evident in Clara's soft hazel eyes was sympathy.

Gloomily JoLayne thought: *If only the lottery paid the jackpots in one lump sum, I could afford to buy Simmons Wood outright. I could match Squires dollar for dollar until the sweat trickled down his pink midwestern cheeks.*

"Excuse me, Clara, may I—"

"Three point seven!" Bernard Squires piped, from reflex.

"—borrow your phone?"

Clara Markham pretended not to have heard Squires. As she slid the telephone toward JoLayne, it rang. Clara simultaneously lifted the receiver and twirled her chair, so she could not be seen. Her voice dropped to a murmur.

JoLayne snuck a glance at Bernard Squires, who was flicking invisible dust off his briefcase. They both looked up inquisitively when they heard Clara Markham say: "No problem. Send him in."

She hung up and swiveled to face them. "I'm afraid this is rather important," she said.

Bernard Squires frowned. "Not another bidder?"

"Oh my, no." The real estate agent chuckled.

When the door opened, she waved the visitor inside—a strong-looking black man wearing round glasses and a business suit tailored even more exquisitely than Squires' own.

"Oh Lord," said JoLayne Lucks. "I should've known."

Moffitt pecked her on the crown of her cap. "Nice to see you, Jo." Then, affably, to Squires: "Don't get up."

"Who're you?"

Moffitt flipped out his badge. Bernard's reaction, Clara Markham would tell her colleagues later, was so priceless that it was almost worth losing the extra commission.

When he hadn't heard from JoLayne, Moffitt had driven to Grange, jimmied the back door of her house and (during a neat but thorough search) listened to the voice messages on her answering machine. That's how he'd come across Clara Markham, a woman who (unlike some Florida real estate salespersons) wholeheartedly believed in cooperating with law enforcement authorities. Clara had informed Moffitt of JoLayne's interest in Simmons Wood and brought him up to speed on the negotiations. Something ticked in the agent's memory when he learned the competing buyer was the Central Midwest Brotherhood of Grouters, Spacklers and Drywallers International. Moffitt had spent the early part of the morning talking to the people in his business who talked to the computers. They were exceptionally helpful.

Clara Markham invited him to sit. Moffitt declined. His hovering made Bernard Squires anxious, which was for Moffitt's purpose a desirable thing.

Squires examined the agent's identification. He said: "Alcohol, Tobacco and Firearms? I don't understand." Then, for added smoothness: "I hope you didn't come all this way on government business, Mr. Moffitt, because I don't drink, smoke or carry a gun."

The agent laughed. "In Florida," he said, "that puts you in a definite minority."

Bernard Squires was compelled to laugh, too— brittle and unpersuasive. Already he could feel his undershirt clinging to the small of his back.

Moffitt said, "Do you know a man named Richard Tarbone?"

"I know who he is," Squires said—the same answer he'd given to three separate grand juries.

"Do you know him as Richard or 'Icepick'?"

"I know *of* him," Squires replied carefully, "as Richard Tarbone. He is a legitimate businessman in the Chicago area."

"Sure he is," Moffitt said, "and I'm Little Richard's love child."

JoLayne Lucks covered her mouth to keep from exploding. Clara Markham pretended to be reading the fine print of the union's purchase offer. When Moffitt asked to speak to Mr. Squires privately, the two women did not object. JoLayne vowed to hunt down some doughnuts.

Once he and Squires were alone in the office, Moffitt said: "You don't really want to buy this property. Trust me."

"The pension fund is very interested."

"The pension fund, as we both know, is a front for the Tarbone family. So cut the crap, Bernie."

Squires moved his jaws as if he was working on a wad of taffy. He heard the door being locked. The agent was standing behind him now.

"That's slander, Mr. Moffitt, unless you can prove it—which you cannot."

He waited for a response: Nothing.

"What's your interest in this?" Squires pressed. He couldn't understand why the ATF was snooping around a commercial land deal that had no connection to illegal guns or booze. Gangsters bought and sold real estate in Florida every day. On the infrequent occasions when the government took notice, it was the FBI and Internal Revenue who came calling.

"My interest," Moffitt said, "is purely personal."

The agent sat down and scooted even closer to Bernard Squires. "However," he said, "you should be aware that on May 10, 1993, one Stephen Eugene Tarbone, alias Stevie 'Boy' Wonder, was arrested near Gainesville for interstate transportation of illegal silencers, machine-gun parts and unlicensed firearms. These were found in the trunk of a rented Lincoln Mark IV during a routine traffic stop. Stephen Tarbone was the driver. He was accompanied by a convicted prostitute and another outstanding public citizen named Charles 'The Gerbil' Hindeman. The fact Stephen's conviction was overturned on appeal in no way diminishes my interest in the current firearms trafficking activities of the young man, or of his father, Richard. So officially *that* is my jurisdiction, in case I need one. You with me?"

A metallic taste bubbled to Squires' throat from places visceral and ripe. Somehow he mustered a stony-eyed demeanor for the ATF man.

"Nothing you've said interests me in the least or has any relevant bearing on this transaction."

Moffitt jovially cupped his hands and clapped them once, loudly. Sinclair jumped.

"Transaction? Man, here's the transaction," the agent said with a grin. "If you don't pack up your lizard valise and your cash deposit and go home to Chicago, your friend Richard the Icepick is going to be a front-page headline in the newspaper: 'ALLEGED MOB FIGURE TIED TO LOCAL MALL DEAL.' I'm not a writer, Mr. Squires, but you get the gist. The article will be real thorough regarding Mr. Tarbone and his family enterprises, and also his connection to your union. In fact, I'll bet Mr. Tarbone will be amazed at the accuracy of the information in the story. That's because I intend to leak it myself."

Bernard Squires struggled to remain cool and disdainful. "Bluffing is a waste of time," he said.

"I couldn't agree more." From a breast pocket Moffitt took a business card, which he gave to Squires. "That's the reporter who'll be doing the story. He'll probably be calling you in a few days."

Squires' hand was trembling, so he slapped the card flat on the table. It read:

Thomas P. Krome
Staff Writer
The Register

"A real prick," Moffitt added. "You'll like him."

Bernard Squires picked up the reporter's card and tore it in half. The gesture was meant to be contemptuous, but the ATF agent seemed vastly entertained.

"So Mr. Tarbone doesn't mind reading about himself in the press? That's good. Guy like him needs a thick hide." Moffitt rose. "But you might want to warn him, Bernie, about Grange."

"What about it?"

"Very conservative little place. Folks here seem pretty serious about their religion. Everywhere you go there's a shrine to one holy thing or another—haven't you noticed?"

Dismally Squires thought of the gimp with the bloody holes in his hands and the weird couple chanting among the turtles.

"People around here," Moffitt went on, "they do not like sin. Not one damn bit. Which means they won't be too wild about gangsters, Bernie. Gangsters from Chicago or anyplace else. When this story breaks in the paper, don't expect a big ticker-tape parade for your man Richard the Icepick. Just like you shouldn't expect the Grange town fathers to do backflips for your building permits and sewer rights and so forth. You follow what I'm saying?"

Bernard Squires held himself erect by pinching the chairback with both elbows. He sensed the agent shifting here and there behind him, then he heard the doorknob turn.

"Any questions?" came Moffitt's voice.

"No questions."

"Excellent. I'll go find the ladies. It's been nice chatting with you, Bernie."

"Drop dead," said Squires.

He heard the door open, and Moffitt's laughter trailing down the hall.

Without rising, Demencio said: "You're early. Where's the lucky lady?"

"She's got an appointment," said Tom Krome.

"You bring the money?"

"Sure did."

Trish invited him inside. It was a peculiar scene at the kitchen counter: she and her husband in yellow latex gloves, scrubbing the shells of JoLayne's baby turtles.

Krome picked up one the cooters, upon which a bearded face had been painted.

"Don't ask," Demencio said.

"Who's it supposed to be?"

"One of the apostles, maybe a saint. Don't really matter." Demencio was despondently buffing a tiny carapace to perfection.

Trish added: "The paint comes right off with Windex and water. It won't hurt 'em."

Tom Krome carefully placed the cooter in the tank with the others. "Need some help?"

Trish said no, thanks, they were almost done. She remarked upon how attached they'd become to the little buggers. "They'll eat right out of your fingers."

"Is that right."

"Lettuce and even raw hamburger."

"What my wife's trying to say," Demencio cut in, "is we'd like to make JoLayne an offer. We'd appreciate the opportunity."

"To do what?"

"Buy 'em. All forty-five," he said. "How's two grand for the bunch?"

The man wasn't joking. He wanted to own the turtles.

Trish chirped: "They'll have a good home here, Mr. Krome."

"I'm sure they would. But I can't sell them, I'm sorry. JoLayne has her heart set."

The couple plainly were disappointed. Krome took out his billfold. "It wouldn't be hard to catch your own. The lakes are full of 'em."

Demencio said, "Yeah, yeah." He finished cleaning the last turtle and stepped to the sink to wash up. "I told you," he muttered to his wife.

Tom Krome paid the baby-sitting fee with hundred-dollar bills. Demencio took the money without counting it; Trish's job.

"How about some coffee cake?" she offered.

Krome said sure. He figured JoLayne would be tied up at the real estate office for a while. Also, he felt the need to act friendly after squelching the couple's cooter enterprise.

To give Demencio a boost, he said: "I like what you did with the Madonna. Those red tears."

"Yeah? You think it looks real?"

"One-hundred-proof jugular."

"Food coloring," Trish confided. She set two slices of walnut cinnamon coffee cake in front of Krome. "It took a day or so for us to get the mixture just right," she added, "but we did it. Nobody else in Florida's got one that cries blood. *Perfumed* blood! You want butter or margarine?"

"Butter's fine."

Demencio said the morning's first busload of Christian pilgrims was due soon. "From South Carolina—we're talkin' hellfire and brimstone, a damn tough crowd," he mused. "If *they* go for it, we'll know it's good."

"Oh, it's good," Trish said, loyally.

As Krome buttered the coffee cake, Demencio asked: "You see the papers? They said you was dead. Burned up in a house."

"So I heard. It was news to me."

"What was that all about? How does somethin'

screwy like that happen?" He sounded suspicious.

Tom Krome said, "It was another man who died. A case of mistaken identity."

Trish was intrigued. "Just like in the movies!"

"Yep." Krome ate quickly.

Demencio made a skeptical remark about the bruise on Krome's cheek—Bodean Gazzer's last earthly footprint. Trish said it must hurt like the dickens.

"Fell off a boat. No big deal," Krome said, rising. "Thanks for the breakfast. I'd better run— JoLayne's waiting on her cooters."

"Don't you wanna count 'em?"

Of course, Krome already had. "Naw, I trust you," he said to Demencio.

He grabbed the corners of the big aquarium and hoisted it. Trish held the front door open. Krome didn't make it to the first step before he heard the cry, quavering and subhuman; the sound of distilled suffering, something from a torture pit.

Krome froze in the doorway.

Trish, staring past him: "Uh-oh. I thought he was asleep."

A slender figure in white moved across the living room toward them. Demencio swiftly intervened, prodding it backward with a long-handled tuna gaff.

"*Nyyahh froohhmmmm! Hoodey nyyahh!*" the frail figure yodeled.

Demencio said, sternly: "That'll be enough from you."

Incredulous, Tom Krome edged back into the house. "Sinclair?"

The prospect of losing the cooters had put him into a tailspin. Trish had prepared hot tea and led him to the spare bedroom, so he wouldn't see them swabbing the holy faces off the turtle shells. That (she'd warned Demencio) might send the poor guy off the deep end.

To make sure Sinclair slept, she'd spiked his chamomile with a buffalo-sized dose of NyQuil. It wasn't enough. He shuffled groggily into the living room at the worst possible moment, just as the baby cooters were being carried away. Sinclair's initial advance was repelled by Demencio and the rounded side of the gaff. A second lunge aborted when the crusty bedsheet in which Sinclair had cloaked himself became snagged on Demencio's golf bag. The turtle fondler was slammed hard to the floor, where he thrashed about until the others subdued him. They lifted him to Demencio's La-Z-Boy and adjusted it to the fully reclined position.

When Sinclair's eyes fluttered open, he blurted at the face he saw: "But you're dead!"

"Not really," Tom Krome said.

"It's a blessed miracle!"

"Actually, the newspaper just screwed up."

"Praise God!"

"They should've waited on the DNA," said Krome, unaware of his editor's recent spiritual conversion.

"Thank you, Jesus! Thank you, Lord!" Sinclair, crooning and swaying.

Krome said: "Excuse me, but have you gone insane?"

Demencio and his wife pulled him aside and explained what had happened; how Sinclair had come to Grange searching for Tom and had become enraptured by the apostolic cooters.

"He's a whole different person," Trish whispered.

"Good," Krome said. "He needed to be."

"You should see: He lies in the water with them. He speaks in tongues. He . . . what's that word, honey?"

Demencio said, " 'Exudes.' "

His wife nodded excitedly. "Yes! He exudes serenity."

"Plus he brings in a shitload of money," Demencio added. "The pilgrims, they love it—Turtle Boy is what they call him. We even had some T-shirts in the works."

"T-shirts?" said Krome, as if this were an everyday conversation.

"You bet. Guy who does silk screen over on Cocoa Beach—surfer stuff mostly, so he was hot for a crack at something new." Demencio sighed. "It's all down the crapper now, since your girlfriend won't sell us them turtles. What the hell use are T-shirts?"

Trish, in the true Christian spirit: "Honey, it's not JoLayne's fault."

"Yeah, yeah," said her husband.

Krome eyed the linen-draped lump in the recliner. Sinclair had covered his head and retracted into a fetal curl.

Turtle Boy? It was poignant, in a way. Sinclair peeked out and, with a pallid finger, motioned him closer. When Krome approached he said, "Tom, I'm begging you."

"But they don't belong to me."

"You don't understand—they're miraculous, those little fellas. You were dead and now you're alive. All because I prayed."

Krome said, "I wasn't dead, I—"

"All because of those turtles. Tom, please. You owe me. You owe *them*." Sinclair's hand darted out and snatched Krome by the wrist. "The inner calm I feel, floating in that moat, surrounded by those delicate perfect creatures, God's creatures . . . My whole life, Tom, I've never felt such a peace. It's like . . . an epiphany!"

Demencio gave Trish a sly wink that said: Write that one down. Epiphany.

Krome said to Sinclair: "So you're here to stay?"

"Oh my, yes. Roddy and Joan rented me a room."

"And you're never coming back to the news-paper?"

"No way." Sinclair gave a bemused snort.

"You promise?"

"On a stack of Bibles, my brother."

"OK, then. Here's what I'll do." Krome pulled free and went to the aquarium. He returned with a single baby turtle, a yellow-bellied slider, which he placed in his editor's upturned palm.

"This one's yours," Krome told him. "You want more, catch your own."

"God bless you, Tom!" Sinclair, cupping the gaily striped cooter as if it were a gem. "Look, it's Bartholomew!"

Of course there was no face to be seen on the turtle's shell; no painted face, at least. Demencio had sponged it clean.

Tom Krome slipped away from Sinclair and lifted the aquarium tank off the floor. As he left the house, Trish said, "Mr. Krome, that was a really kind thing to do. Wasn't it, honey?"

"Yeah, it was," Demencio said. One cooter was better than none. "JoLayne won't be pissed?"

"No, I think she'll understand perfectly."

Tom Krome told them goodbye and carried the heavy tank down the front steps.

. . .

The two women arrived in Grange on Tuesday night, too late for Katie Battenkill's sightseeing. They rented a room at a darling bed-and-breakfast, where they were served a hearty pot-roast supper with a peppy Caesar salad. Over dessert (pecan pie with a scoop of vanilla) they tried to make conversation with the only other guest, a well-dressed businessman from Chicago. He was taciturn and so preoccupied that he didn't make a pass at either of them; the women were surprised but not disappointed.

In the morning Katie asked Mrs. Hendricks for directions to the shrine. Mary Andrea Finley Krome pretended to be annoyed at the detour, but truthfully she was grateful. She needed more time to rehearse what to say to her estranged husband, if they found him. Katie was confident they would.

"In the meantime, you won't be sorry."

"Should we bring something?" Mary Andrea asked.

"Just an open mind."

The visitation was only a few blocks away. Katie parked behind a long silver bus that was disgorging the eager faithful. They carried prayer books and crucifixes and umbrellas (for the sun) and, of course, cameras of all types. Some of the men wore loose-fitting walking shorts and some of the women had wide-brimmed hats. Their faces were open and friendly and uncluttered by worry. Mary

Andrea thought they were the happiest group she'd ever seen; happier even than *Cats* audiences.

Katie said, "Let's get in line."

The Virgin Mary shrine was in the lawn of an average-looking suburban house. The four-foot icon stood on a homemade platform beyond a water-filled trench. A cordial woman in a flower-print pants suit moved among the waiting pilgrims and offered soft drinks, snacks and sunscreen. Mary Andrea purchased a Snapple and a tube of Hawaiian Tropic #30. Katie went for a Diet Coke.

Word came down the line that the weeping Madonna was between jags. The tourist ahead of Katie leaned back and said, "Cripes, I hope it's not another dry day."

"What do you mean?"

"That's what happened last time I was here, in the spring—she never cried once, not one darn teardrop. Then the morning after we leave, look out. Some friends mailed us pictures—it looked like Old Faithful!"

Mary Andrea was diverted by a weather-beaten woman in a bridal gown. Perched on a stool beneath a tree, the woman was expounding in low tones and gesticulating theatrically. A half dozen of the bus tourists stood around her, though not too close. As an actress Mary Andrea had always been drawn to such colorful real-life characters. She asked Katie Battenkill to hold her place in line.

Shiner's mother was alerted by the click of high heels, for the typical pilgrim didn't dress so glamorously. The brevity of the newcomer's skirt also raised doubts about her piety, yet Shiner's mother wasn't ready to pass judgment. Couldn't red-headed rich girls be born again? And couldn't they, even as sinners, be generous with offerings?

"Hello. My name's Mary Andrea."

"Welcome to Grange. I'm Marva," said Shiner's mother, from the stool.

"I love your gown. Did you make it yourself?"

"I'm married to the Word of the Lord."

"What've you got there," Mary Andrea inquired, "in the dish?"

Other tourists began moving in the direction of the Madonna statue, where there seemed to be a flurry of activity. With both arms Shiner's mother raised the object of her own reverence. It was a Tupperware pie holder; sea green and opaque.

"Behold the Son of God!" she proclaimed.

"No kidding? May I peek?"

"The face of Jesus Christ!"

"Yes, yes," Mary Andrea said. She opened her handbag and removed three dollar bills, which she folded into the slot of the woman's collection box.

"We thank you, child." Shiner's mother centered the Tupperware on her lap and, with a grunt, prized off the lid.

"Behold!"

"Isn't that an omelette?" Mary Andrea cocked her head.

"Do you not see Him?"

"No, Marva, I do not."

"Here . . . now look." Shiner's mother rotated the Tupperware half a turn. Instructively she began pointing out the features: "That's His hair . . . and them's His eyebrows . . ."

"The bell peppers?"

"No, no, the ham . . . Look here, that's His crown of thorns."

"The diced tomatoes."

"Exactly! Praise God!"

"Marva," said Mary Andrea, "I've never witnessed anything like it. Never!" Not since the last time I ate at Denny's, she thought.

The omelette looked like absolutely nothing but an omelette. The woman was either a loon or a thief, but who cared?

"Bless you, child." Shiner's mother, slapping the lid on the Tupperware and burping it tight. In this manner she announced that the high-heeled pilgrim had gotten her three bucks' worth of revelation.

Mary Andrea said, "I'd love for my friend to see. Would you mind?" Waving gaily at Katie, she thought: At least it beats sitting alone at the HoJo's.

"Katie, come over here!"

But Katie Battenkill was otherwise engrossed.

The queue at the weeping Madonna had dissolved into a loose and excited swarm, buzzing toward the moat.

Shiner's mother shrugged. "Crying time. You better get a move on."

Mary Andrea found herself feeling sorry for the wacko in the wedding dress. It couldn't be easy, competing with a weeping Virgin. Not when all you had was a plate of cold eggs in Tabasco. Mary Andrea slipped the woman another five bucks.

"You wanna see Him again?" Shiner's mother was aglow.

"Maybe some other time."

Mary Andrea began working her way to the house. She walked on tiptoes, trying to spot Katie among the surging pilgrims. Even in their fervor they remained orderly and courteous; Mary Andrea was impressed. In New York it would've been a rabid stampede for the shrine; like a Springsteen concert.

Suddenly Mary Andrea found the sidewalk blocked—a tall man lugging, of all things, an aquarium filled with turtles.

Boy, she thought, is this town a magnet for crackpots!

Mary Andrea stepped aside to let the stranger pass. He was lifting the tank high, at eye level, to protect it from the jostle of the tourists; apologizing to them as he went along.

Through the algae-smudged plate of aquarium glass Mary Andrea recognized the man's face.

"Thomas!"

Curiously he peered over the lip of the tank. Her husband.

"I'll be damned," he said.

Cried Mary Andrea Finley Krome: "Yes, you will! I believe you will be damned!"

Angrily she snapped open her pocketbook and groped inside. For an instant, Thomas Paine Krome wondered if irony could be so sublime, wondered if he was about to be murdered for real, with an unexplained armful of baby cooters.

30 Leander Simmons and Janine Simmons Robinson were miffed to learn Bernard Squires had withdrawn his offer for their late father's property. In a conference call with Clara Markham, the siblings said they didn't appreciate getting jerked around by some fast-talking Charlie from up North. They'd gotten their hopes sky-high for a bidding war, and now they were stuck with one buyer and one offer.

"Which," Clara reminded them, "is more than you had two weeks ago."

She didn't let on that JoLayne Lucks was sitting in the office, listening over the speakerphone.

Leander Simmons argued for rejecting the $3 million offer, as the old man's land obviously would fetch more. All they needed was patience. His sister argued strenuously against waiting, since she'd already pledged her share of the proceeds for a clay tennis court and new guest cottages at her winter place in Bermuda.

They went back and forth for thirty minutes, the bickering interrupted only by an occasional terse query to Clara Markham on the other end. Meanwhile JoLayne was having a ball eavesdropping. Poor Lighthorse, she thought. With kids like that, it was no wonder he spent so much time skulking in the woods.

Eventually Janine and Leander compromised on a holdout figure of $3.175 million, to which Jo-Layne silently assented (flashing an "OK" sign to Clara). The real estate agent told the siblings she'd bounce the new number off the buyer and get back to them. By lunchtime the deal was iced at an even three one. The new owner of Simmons Wood got on the line and introduced herself to Leander and Janine, who suddenly became the two sweetest people on earth.

"What've you got in mind for the place?" the sister inquired cordially. "Condos? An office park?"

"Oh, I'll leave the land the way it is," JoLayne Lucks said.

"Smart cookie. Raw timber is one helluva long-term investment." The brother, endeavoring to sound shrewd.

"Actually," JoLayne said, "I'm going to leave it exactly the way it is . . . *forever.*"

Baffled silence from the siblings.

Clara Markham, brightly into the speaker-phone: "It's been a joy doing business with all of you. We'll be talking soon."

Moffitt was waiting outside. He offered JoLayne a lift, and on the way apologized for searching her house.

"I was worried, that's all. I tried not to leave a mess."

"You're forgiven, you sneaky little shit. Now tell me," she said, "what happened between you and Bernie boy—how'd you scare him off?"

Moffitt told her. With a grin, JoLayne said, "You're so bad. Wait'll I tell Tom."

"Yeah. The power of the press." Moffitt wheeled the big Chevy into her driveway.

"How about some lunch?" she asked.

"Thanks, but I gotta run."

She gave him a kiss and told him he was still her hero; it was a running gag between them.

Moffitt said, "Yeah, but I'd rather be Tom."

Which gave JoLayne a melancholy pause. Sometimes she wished she'd fallen for Moffitt the way he'd fallen for her. He was one of the best men she'd ever known.

"Hang in," she said. "Someday you'll meet the right one."

He threw his head back, laughing. "Do you hear yourself? God, you sound like my aunt."

"Geez, you're right. I don't know what got into me." She slid from the car. "Moffitt, you were sensational, as usual. Thanks for everything."

He gave a mock salute. "Call anytime. Especially if Mister Thomas Krome turns out to be another sonofabitch."

"I don't think he will."

"Be careful, Jo. You're a rich girl now."

Her brow furrowed. "Damn. I guess I am."

She waved until Moffitt's car disappeared around the corner. Then she jogged up the sidewalk to the porch, where the mail lay stacked by the front door. JoLayne scooped it up and unlocked the house.

The refrigerator was a disaster—ten days' worth of congealment and spoilage. One croissant, in particular, had bloomed like a Chia plant. The only item that appeared safe for consumption was a can of ginger ale, which JoLayne cracked open while thumbing through letters and bills. One envelope stood out from the others because it was dusty blue and bore no address, only her name.

Ms. Jo Lane Lucks was how it had been spelled, in ballpoint.

Inside the blue envelope was a card that featured a florid Georgia O'Keeffe watercolor, and tucked inside the card was a piece of paper that caused JoLayne to exclaim, "Oh Lord!"

And truly, devoutly, mean it.

Amber kept the engine running.

"You feel OK about it? Tell the truth."

Shiner said, "Yeah, I feel pretty good."

"Didn't I tell ya?"

"You wanna come in? It don't look like she's home." All the lights were off, including upstairs.

Amber said, "I can't, hon. Gotta get back to Miami and see if I've still got a job. Plus I've already missed way too much school."

Shiner didn't want to say goodbye; he believed he'd found his true love. They'd spent two more nights together—one at a turnpike rest stop near Fort Drum, and the other parked deep in the woods outside of Grange. Nothing sexual had occurred (Amber sleeping in the back seat of the Crown Victoria, Shiner in the front) but he didn't mind. It was rapture, being so near to such a woman for so long. He'd become intimate with the scent of her hair and the rhythm of her breathing and a thousand other things, all exotically feminine.

She said, "We did the right thing."

"Yep."

"But I still wonder who that was in the other car."

I don't know, Shiner thought, but I guess I owe him. He bought me a few more hours with my darling.

The first time they'd cruised past JoLayne Lucks' place, the other car was idling at the curb: a squat gray Chevrolet sedan. The buggy-whip antenna said cop. Shiner had cussed and stomped the accelerator.

They'd tried again later, with Amber at the wheel. This time the watcher had been parked around the corner, by a newspaper rack. Shiner had gotten a pretty good look at him—a clean-cut black guy with glasses.

"Don't stop! Keep driving!" Shiner had urged Amber.

He'd been too freaked to go directly home. He feared that the Black Tide (and who else could it be, lurking around JoLayne's?) would ransack his house and kidnap his mother to the Bahamas. Amber had been anxious, too. To her, the guy in the gray sedan looked like heavy-duty law enforcement—and he could be looking for only one thing.

So she'd kept driving, all the way past the Grange city limits to a stretch of light woods off the main highway. She'd spotted a break in the barbed-wire fence, and that's where she'd turned. They'd spent a clear chilly night among the pines and palmettos; no big deal, after Pearl Key. Through the wispy fog at dawn they'd seen a herd of white-tailed deer and a red fox.

It was still early when they'd arrived back at Jo-Layne's place. The gray cop car was gone; they'd circled the block three times to make certain. Amber had backed the Ford up to the house, get-away style, and said: "Want me to do it?"

Shiner had said no, he wanted to be the one.

The way she'd looked at him, damn, he felt like an honest-to-God champ. When all he really was trying to do was make something right again.

She'd passed him the blue envelope and he'd trotted to JoLayne's porch—Amber watching in the rearview, to make sure he didn't get any cute ideas. Afterwards they'd gone to breakfast, and now home. Shiner wished it wouldn't end.

She motioned him closer in the front seat. "Roll up your sleeve. Lemme see."

His muscle was a marquee of contusions, the tattoo lettering crusty and unreadable.

"Not my best work," Amber remarked, with a slight frown.

"It's OK. Least I got my eagle."

"For sure. It's a beauty, too." With a fingertip she lightly traced the wings of the bird. Shiner felt strangled with desire. He squeezed his eyes closed and heard the pulse pounding in his ears.

"Whoa," Amber said.

A stranger was peering through the windshield—an odd fellow with fuzzy socks on his hands.

"Hey, it's Dominick," said Shiner, pulling himself together. He rolled down the window. "How's it goin', Dom?"

"You're back!"

"Yeah, I am."

"Who's your friend? Geez, what happened to your thumbs?"

"That's Amber. Amber, this here's Dominick Amador."

The stigmata man reached into the car for a handshake. Amber obliged politely, although her face registered stark alarm at the creamy glop that oozed from the stranger's sock-mitten.

Shiner told her not to worry. "It's only Crisco."

"That would've been my second guess," she said, wiping it brusquely on his sleeve.

Dominick Amador was unoffended. "You lookin' for your ma, Shiner?" he asked. "She's over at Demencio's. They hooked up on some kinda co-op deal."

"What for?"

"The state come in and paved her stain. Didn't you hear?"

"Naw!"

"Yeah, so she's over with the Turtle Boy."

"Who?"

"Y'know, it was me that first give Demencio the idea for the cooters—a Noah-type deal. Now you should see what they done with JoLayne's bunch! It's a damn jackpot."

Amber had heard enough. She whispered emphatically to Shiner that she had to leave. He acknowledged with a lugubrious nod.

"That's where I'll end up, too," Dominick rambled, "workin' for Demencio, I 'xpect. He's got a good setup, plus on-street parking for them pilgrim buses. Him and me got a 'pointment tomorrow. We're pretty close on the numbers."

Amber was about to interrupt even more forcefully when the man flung himself on the grass and thrust both legs in the air. Proudly he displayed his bare soles. "Look, I finally got 'em done!"

"Nice work." Shiner forced a smile.

Amber averted her eyes from the stranger's punctured feet. Surely this could be explained—a radiation leak in the maternity ward; a toxin in the town's water supply.

Dominick hopped up and gave each of them a pink flyer advertising his visitations. Then he limped away.

Shiner felt himself being nudged out of the car. Slump-shouldered, he circled to the driver's side and rested his forearms on the door.

He said to Amber, "I guess this is it."

"I hope things are OK between you and your mom."

"Me, too." He brightened at the sight of the

three roses in the back seat. They were gray and dead, but Amber hadn't discarded them. To this slender fact Shiner attached unwarranted significance.

Amber said, "If it doesn't work out, remember what I told you."

"But I never bused tables before."

"Oh, I think you can handle it," she said.

Certainly it was something to consider. Miami scared the living piss out of Shiner, but a gig at Hooters could be the answer to most, if not all, of his problems.

"Are they like you?" he asked. "The other waitresses, I mean. It'd be cool if they all was as nice as you."

Amber reached up and lightly touched his cheek. "They're all just like me. Every one of them," she said.

Then, leaving him wobbly, she drove off.

Later Shiner's mother would remark that her son seemed to have matured during his mysterious absence from Grange, that he now carried himself with purposefulness and responsibility and a firm sense of direction. She would tell him how pleased she was that he'd turned his heathen life around, and she'd encourage him to chase his dreams wherever they might lead, even to Dade County.

And not wishing to cloud his mother's new-found esteem for him, Shiner would elect not to tell her the story of the $14 million Lotto ticket and how he came to give it back.

Because she would've kicked his ass.

It wasn't a loaded firearm in Mary Andrea's purse. It was a court summons.

"Your attorney," she said, waving it accusingly, "is a vicious, vicious man."

Tom Krome said, "You look good." Which was very true.

"Don't change the subject."

"OK. Where did Slick Dick finally catch up with you?"

"At your damn newspaper," Mary Andrea said. "Right in the lobby, Tom."

"What an odd place for you to be."

She told him why she'd gone there. "Since everybody thought you were dead—including yours truly!—they asked me to fly down and pick up your stupid award. And this is what I get: ambushed by a divorce lawyer!"

"What award?" Tom asked.

"Don't you dare pretend not to know."

"I'm not pretending, Mary Andrea. What award?"

"The Emilio," she said sourly. "Something like that."

"Amelia?"

"Yeah, that's it."

He shot a wrathful glare toward the house, where Sinclair was holed up. That asshole! Krome thought. The Amelias were the lamest of journalism prizes. He was appalled that Sinclair had entered him in the contest and infuriated that he hadn't been forewarned. Krome fought the impulse to dash back and snatch the yellow-bellied slider from the editor's grasp, just to see him whimper and twitch.

"Come on." Tom led his wife away from the bustle of the shrine, around to the backyard. He set the bulky aquarium in the sun, to warm the baby cooters.

Mary Andrea said, "I suppose you saw it on television, Turnquist's big coup. You probably got a good laugh."

"It made the TV?"

"Tom, did you set me up? Tell the truth."

He said, "I wish I were that clever. Honestly."

Mary Andrea puffed her cheeks, which Tom recognized as a sign of exasperation. "I don't think I'm going to ask about those turtles," she said.

"It's a very long story. I like your hair, by the way. Looks good short."

"Stop with that. You hear me?" She very nearly admitted she'd started coloring it because it had become shot full of gray, no thanks to him.

Tom pointed at the summons, with which Mary Andrea briskly fanned herself. He had to grin.

Fifty-nine degrees and she's acting like it's the Sahara.

"So when's our big day in court?"

"Two weeks," she said curtly. "Congratulations."

"Oh yeah. I've already ordered the party hats."

"What happened to your face?"

"A man stomped it. He's dead now."

"Go on!" But she saw he wasn't kidding. "My God, Tom, did you kill him?"

"Let's just say I was a contributing factor." That would be as much as he'd tell; let her make up her own yarn. "Well," he said, "what's it going to be? Are you going to keep fighting me on this?"

"Oh, relax."

"Gonna take off again? Change your name and all that nonsense?"

"If you want the truth," Mary Andrea said, "I'm tired of running. But I'm even more tired of road tours and working for scale. I need to get back East and jump-start this acting career of mine."

"Maybe look for something off Broadway."

"Exactly. I mean, God, I ended up in the middle of *Montana*."

"Yeah?" Krome thinking: Not a megamall for a thousand miles.

"Me in cowboy country! Can you imagine?"

"All because you didn't want a divorce."

"I'll be the first Finley woman in five centuries to go through with it."

"And the sanest," Tom said.

Mary Andrea gave a phony scowl. "I saved your goodbye note. The lyric you ripped off from Zevon."

"Hey, if I could write worth a lick," he said, "I wouldn't be working for schmucks like Sinclair."

"What about your novel?" she asked.

Stopping him cold.

"Your girlfriend told me about it. *The Estrangement.* Catchy title."

Mary Andrea's tone was deadly coy. Tom angled his face to the sky, shielding his eyes; pretending to watch a flight of ducks. Buying time. Wondering when, why and under what unthinkable circumstances JoLayne Lucks and Mary Andrea Finley Krome had met.

"So how far along are you?"

"Uh?" Tom, with a vague, sidelong look.

"On your book," prodded Mary Andrea.

"Oh. Bits and pieces are all I've got."

"Ah."

A knowing smile was one of her specialties, and now she wore a killer. Just as Tom was about to surrender and ask about JoLayne, Katie Battenkill came around the corner, humming contentedly. Then he understood.

"*Ex*-girlfriend," he whispered to Mary Andrea.

"Whatever."

Katie rushed up and unabashedly hurled her arms around his neck. "We rode over together," she said. "Your wife and I."

"So I gather."

The information had a paralytic, though not entirely disagreeable, effect. Tom had never before been bracketed by two women with whom he'd slept. Though awkward, the moment enabled him to understand perfectly why he'd been attracted to each of them and why he couldn't live with either one.

"Tell her she looks great," Mary Andrea said archly to her husband. "We *all* look great."

"Well, you do."

Katie said, "I think you guys need to be alone."

Tom snagged her around the waist before she could slip away. "It's all right. Mary Andrea and I have finished our serious chat."

His wife asked: "What's that on your hand, Katie? Did you cut yourself?"

"Oh no. That's an actual teardrop from the world-famous weeping Madonna." Katie gaily displayed a red-flecked ring finger. "My guess is tap water, food coloring and perfume. Charlie, it smells like."

After a discreet sniff, Mary Andrea concurred.

Krome said to Katie: "I hope you're not too disappointed."

"That it's not real? Geez, Tommy, you must

think I'm a total sucker. It's a beautiful shrine, that's what matters. The tears are just for hype."

Mary Andrea was on the verge of enjoying herself. "His book," she reported confidentially to Katie, "is still in the very early stages."

"Eeeeek." Katie covered her face in embarrassment. She knew she shouldn't have mentioned to Tom's wife his idea for a divorce novel.

"What else did you tell her," he said, "or am I foolish to ask?"

Katie's green eyes widened. Mary Andrea responded with a quick shake of the head.

Krome caught it and muttered: "Oh, terrific." Katie and her carnal scorecard. "You should get a job on the sports desk," he told her.

She smiled wanly. "I might need it."

Mary Andrea gave her new friend's arm a maternal pat and suggested it was time to leave. "We've got a long drive, and you need to get home."

"It's Art," Katie volunteered to Tom. "He's been arrested—it was all over the radio."

Krome couldn't fake so much as a murmur of sympathy. His house burned down because of Arthur Battenkill; burned down with a man inside. The judge deserved twenty to life.

"The police want to talk to me some more," Katie explained.

"It's good you're cooperating."

"Of course, Tommy. It's the only honest thing.

Oh, look at all the little cooters—they're adorable!"

Lugging the turtle tank, Tom Krome escorted the two women through the ebullient pilgrims, past the blood-weeping Virgin and the runny Jesus Omelette, and out to the street.

Katie Battenkill was delighted to learn what was planned for the baby reptiles. "That's so lovely!" she said, kissing Tom on the nose. She primly scissored her long legs into the car and told him she'd see him at Arthur's trial. Tom waved goodbye.

Mary Andrea stood there looking tickled; savoring the sight of her long-lost spouse trying to balance his swirling emotions and an exotic cargo. The only possible explanation for the turtle project was a new woman, but Mary Andrea didn't pry. She didn't want to know anything that might weaken the story in the retelling.

"Well," Tom said, "I guess we'll be seeing each other at a different trial, won't we?"

"Not me. I don't have time."

She sounded sincere but Krome remained wary; Mary Andrea could be so smooth. "You mean it?" he said. "We can finally settle this thing?"

"Yes, *Tommy.* But only if I get a first edition of *The Estrangement.* Autographed personally by the author."

"Christ, Mary Andrea, there's no book. I was just ranting."

"Good," she said to her future ex-husband.

"Then we've got a deal. Now put down that damn aquarium so I can give you a proper hug."

Bernard Squires was a light drinker, but after supper he accepted one glass of sherry from Mrs. Hendricks at the bed-and-breakfast; then another, and one more after that. He wouldn't have drunk so much liquor in front of other guests, particularly the two attractive women who'd arrived the previous night. But they'd already checked out, so Squires felt that seemly comportment was no longer a priority.

The poor fellow was suffering, Mrs. Hendricks could see that. He told her the deal had fallen through, the whole reason he'd come all the way to Grange from Chicago, Illinois.

Kaput! Finished!

Mrs. Hendricks sympathized—"Oh dear, these things happen"—and tried to nudge the conversation toward cheerier topics such as the Dow Jones, but Mr. Squires clammed up. Slouched on the antique deacon's bench, he stared dolefully at his shoe tops. After a while Mrs. Hendricks went upstairs, leaving him with the sherry bottle.

When it was empty, he snatched up his briefcase and went wandering. Crumpled in a pocket of his coat were three telephone messages in Mrs. Hendricks' flawless penmanship. The messages had come from Mr. Richard Tarbone and were progressively more insistent. Bernard Squires could not summon the courage to call the hot-tempered gangster and tell him what had happened.

Squires himself wasn't sure. He didn't know who the black girl was, or where she'd gotten so much dough. He didn't know how the hard-ass ATF agent got involved, or why. All Bernard Squires knew for certain was that neither the pension fund nor the Tarbone crime family could afford another front-page headline, and that meant the Simmons Wood deal was queered.

And it wasn't his fault. None of it.

But that wouldn't matter, because Richard the Icepick didn't believe in explanations. He believed in slaying the messenger.

Each passing minute reduced the odds of Bernard Squires' surviving the week. He knew this; drunk or sober, he knew.

In his career as a mob money launderer, Squires had faced few predicaments that a quarter million dollars cash could not resolve. That was the amount he'd brought to Grange, to secure the Simmons Wood parcel. Afterwards, when the deal officially turned to dogshit, Clara Markham had made a special trip to the bank to retrieve the money and had even helped Squires count the bundles as he repacked the briefcase.

Which he now carried nonchalantly through the sleeping streets of Grange. It was a lovely, still autumn evening; so different from how he'd always pictured Florida. The air was cool, and it smelled earthy and sweet. He stepped around an orange tomcat, snoozing beneath a streetlamp, which barely favored him with a glance. Occasionally a dog barked in a backyard. Through the windows of the homes he could see the calming violet flicker of televisions.

Squires hoped the stroll might clear his muddled brain. Eventually he would figure out what to do—he always did. So he kept walking. Before long he found himself on the same street where he'd been two nights before, under the same oak in front of the same bland one-story house. From behind the drawn curtains he heard lively conversation. Several cars were parked in the driveway.

But Bernard Squires was alone at the glazed shrine of the Virgin Mary. No one attended the spotlit statue, its fiberglass hands frozen in benediction. From his distance it was impossible for Squires to see if there were teardrops in the statue's eyes.

Edging forward, he spotted a lone figure in the moat; the linen-clad man, his knees pulled up to his chest.

Hearing no chanting, Squires ventured closer.

"Hello, pilgrim," the man said, as if he'd been watching the entire time. His face remained obscured by a shadow.

Squires said, "Oh. Am I interrupting?"

"No, you're fine."

"Are you all right in there?"

"Couldn't be better." The man lowered his knees and reclined slowly into the water. As he spread his arms, the white bedsheet billowed around him, an angelic effect.

"Isn't it cold?" Squires said.

"Sah-kamam-slamasoon-noo-slah!" came the reply, though it was more a melody than a chant.

SOCCER MOMS SLAM SUNUNU FOR SLUR— another of Sinclair's legendary headlines. He couldn't help it; they kept repeating themselves, like baked beans.

Bernard Squires asked, "What language is that?"

"Into the water, brother."

Sinclair welcomed any company. A noisy meeting was being held in the house—Demencio and his wife, Joan and Roddy, dear lusty Marva, the mayor and the plucky stigmata man. They were talking money; commissions and finder's fees and profit points, secular matters for which Sinclair no longer cared.

"Come on in," he coaxed the visitor, and the man obediently waded into the shallow moat. He did not remove his expensive suit jacket or roll up his pants or set aside his briefcase.

"Yes! Fantastic!" Sinclair exhorted.

As Bernard Squires drew closer, he noticed in the wash of the floodlights a small object poised on the floating man's forehead. At first Squires believed it to be a stone or a seashell, but then he saw it scoot an inch or so.

The object was alive.

"What is it?" he asked, voice hushed.

"A sacred cooter, brother."

From the shell a thimble-sized head emerged, as smooth as satin and striped exquisitely. Bernard Squires was awestruck.

"Can I touch it?"

"Careful. He's all that's left."

"Can I?"

The next day, during the long flight to Rio de Janeiro, Bernard Squires would fervidly describe the turtle handling to a willowy Reebok account executive sitting beside him in business class. He would recount how he'd experienced a soul soothing, a revelatory unburdening, an expurgation; how he'd known instantly what he was supposed to do with the rest of his life.

Like a cosmic window shade snapping up, letting the sunlight streak in—"blazing lucidity" is how Bernard Squires would (while sampling the in-flight sherry) describe it. He would tell the pretty saleswoman about the surrealistic little town—the weeping Madonna, the dreamy Turtle Boy, the entrepreneurial carpenter with the raw holes in his hands, the eccentric black millionaire who worked at the animal clinic.

And afterwards he would tell the woman a few personal things: where he was born, where he was educated, his hobbies, his tastes in music and even (sketchily) his line of work. He would under no circumstances, however, tell her the contents of the eelskin briefcase in the overhead compartment.

EPIPHANY

Tom Krome carried the turtle tank up the porch and backed it slowly through the front door. The house was warm and fragrant with cooking; spaghetti and meatballs.

JoLayne was sampling the sauce when he came in. She was barefoot and blue-jeaned, in a baggy checked shirt with the tails knotted at her midriff.

"Where've you been?" she sang out. "I'm in my Martha Stewart mode! Hurry or you'll miss it." She breezed over to check on the cooters.

"We're one shy," Tom said. He told her about Demencio's "apostles" and the weirdness with Sinclair. "I felt so sorry for the guy," he said, "I gave him a slider. He thinks it's Bartholomew."

JoLayne, with consternation: "What exactly does he do with them? Please tell me he doesn't . . ."

"He just sort of touches them. And chants like a banshee, of course."

She said, "You've gotta love this town."

The remaining forty-four seemed perky and fit,

although the aquarium needed a hosing. To the turtles JoLayne crooned, "Don't worry, troops. It won't be long now."

She felt Tom's arms around her waist. He said, "Let's hear the big news—are you a baroness, or still a wench?"

JoLayne knighted him grandly with the sauce spoon. He snatched her up and twirled with her around the floor. "Watch the babies! Watch out!" she said, giggling.

"It's fantastic, Jo! You beat the bastards. You got Simmons Wood."

They sat down, breathless. She pressed closer. "Mostly it was Moffitt," she said.

Tom raised an eyebrow.

"He told the guy you were writing a big exposé on the shopping-mall deal," JoLayne said. "Told him it was bound to make the front pages—Mafia invades Grange!"

"Priceless."

"Well, it worked. Squires bolted. But, Tom, what if they believe it? What if they come after you? Moffitt said they won't dare, but—"

"He's right. The mob doesn't kill reporters anymore. Waste of ammo, and very bad for business." Krome had to admire the agent's guile. "It was a great bluff. Too bad . . ."

"What?"

"Too bad I didn't think of it myself."

JoLayne gave him a marinara kiss and headed for the kitchen. "Come along, Woodward, help me get the food on the table."

Over dinner she went through the terms of the land sale. Tom worked the math and said: "You realize that even after taxes and interest payments, you'll still have quite a comfortable income. Not that you care."

"How comfortable?"

"About three hundred grand a year."

"Well. That'll be something new."

OK, JoLayne thought, here's the test. Here's when we find out if Mr. Krome is truly different from Rick the mechanic or Lawrence the lawyer, or any of the other winners I've picked in this life.

Tom said, "You could actually afford a car."

"Yeah? What else?" JoLayne, spearing a meatball.

"You could get that old piano fixed. And tuned."

"Good. Go on."

"Decent speakers for your stereo," he said. "That should be a priority. And maybe a CD player, too, if you're really feeling wild and reckless."

"OK."

"And don't forget a new shotgun, to replace the one we tossed overboard."

"OK, what else?"

"That's about it. I'm out of ideas," Tom said.

"You sure?"

JoLayne, hoping with all her heart he wouldn't get a cagey glint in his eye and say something one of the others might've said. Colavito the stockbroker, for instance, would've offered to invest her windfall in red-hot biotechs, then watched the market dive. Likewise, Officer Robert would've advised her to deposit it all in the police credit union, so he could withdraw large sums secretly to spend on his girlfriends.

But Tom Krome had no schemes to troll, no gold mines to tout, no partnerships to propose. "Really, I'm the wrong person to give advice," he said. "People who work for newspaper wages don't get much experience at saving money."

That was it. He didn't ask for a penny.

And JoLayne knew better than to offer, because then he'd suspect she was setting him up to be dumped. Which was, now, the farthest thing from her mind.

Bottom line: From day one, the man had been true to his word. The first I've ever picked who was, she thought. Maybe my luck *has* changed.

Tom said, "Come on—you must have your own wish list."

"Doc Crawford needs a new X-ray machine for the animals."

"Aw, go nuts, Jo. Get him an MRI." He tugged on the knot of her shirttail. "You're only going to win the lottery once."

She hoped her smile didn't give away the secret. "Tom, who knows you're staying here with me?"

"Am I?"

"Don't be a smart-ass. Who else knows?"

"Nobody. Why?"

"Look on top of the piano," she said. "There's a white envelope. It was in the mail when I got home."

He examined it closely. His name was hand-printed in nondescript block letters. Had to be one of the locals—Demencio, maybe. Or the daffy Sinclair's sister, pleading for an intervention.

"Aren't you going to open it?" JoLayne tried not to appear overeager.

"Sure." Tom brought the envelope to the table and meticulously cut the flap with the tines of a salad fork. The Lotto ticket fell out, landing in a mound of parmesan.

"What the hell?" He picked it up by a corner, as if it were forensic evidence.

JoLayne, watching innocently.

"Your numbers. What were they?" Tom was embarrassed because his hand was shaking. "I can't remember, Jo—the six numbers you won with."

"I do," she said, and began reciting. "Seventeen . . ."

Krome, thinking: This isn't possible.

"Nineteen, twenty-two . . ."

It's a gag, he told himself. Must be.

"Twenty-four, twenty-seven . . ."

Moffitt, the sonofabitch! He's one who could pull it off. Print up a fake ticket, as a joke.

"Thirty," JoLayne said. "Those were my numbers."

It looked too real to be a phony; water-stained and frayed, folded then unfolded. It looked as if someone had carried it a long way for a long time.

Then Krome remembered: There had been two winners that night.

"Tom?"

"I can't . . . This is crazy." He showed it to her. "Jo, I think it's the real thing."

"Tom!"

"And this was in your mail?"

She said, "Unbelievable. *Unbelievable.*"

"That would be the word for it."

"You and me, two of the most cynical people on God's green earth . . . It's almost like a revelation, isn't it?"

"I don't know what the hell it is."

He tried to throttle down and think like a reporter, beginning with a list of questions: Who in their right mind would give up a $14 million Lotto ticket? Why would they send it to him, of all people? And how'd they know where he was?

"It makes no damn sense."

"None," JoLayne agreed. That's what was so wondrous. She'd been over it again and again— there were no sensible answers, because it was impossible. What had happened was absolutely impossible. She didn't believe in miracles, but she was reconsidering the concept of divine mystery.

"The lottery agency said the other ticket was bought in Florida City. That's three hundred miles away."

"I know, Tom."

"How in the world . . ."

"Honey, put it away now. Someplace safe."

"What should we do?" he asked.

" 'We'? It's your name on that envelope, buster. Come on, let's get moving. Before it's too dark."

It was a few hours later, after they'd returned from their mission and JoLayne had drifted to sleep, when Tom Krome found the answer to one of the many, many questions.

The only answer he'd ever get.

He slipped out of bed to catch the late TV news, in case the men on Pearl Key had been found. He knew he shouldn't have been concerned—dead or alive, the two robbers wouldn't say much. They couldn't, if they wished to stay out of prison.

Nonetheless, Krome was glued to the tube. As though he needed independent proof, a confirmation that the events of the past ten days were real and not a dream.

But the news had nothing. So he decided to surprise JoLayne (and demonstrate his domestic suitability) by washing the dinner dishes. He was scraping a tangle of noodles into the garbage when he spotted it in the bottom of the can:

A blue envelope made out to "Ms. Jo Lane Lucks."

He retrieved it and placed it on the counter.

The envelope had been opened cleanly, possibly with a very long fingernail. Inside the envelope was a card, a bright Georgia O'Keeffe print.

And inside the card . . . nothing. Not a word.

And Tom Krome knew: That's how the second lottery ticket had been delivered. It was sent to Jo-Layne, not him.

He could've cried, he was so happy. Or laughed, he was so mad.

Again she'd been one step ahead of him. It would always be that way. He'd have to get used to it.

She was too much.

Vultures starred in his nightmares, and Chub blamed the nigger woman.

Before boarding the skiff, she'd warned him in harrowing detail about black vultures. The sky over Pearl Key was full of them. "They're gonna come for your friend," she'd said, kneeling beside him on the shore, "and there's nothing you can do."

People think all buzzards hunt by smell, she'd said, but that's not so. Turkey vultures use their noses; black vultures hunt purely by sight. Their eyeballs are twenty or thirty times more powerful

than a human's, she'd said. When they're circling
like that—the nigger woman pointing upward
and, sure enough, there they were—it means
they're searching for carrion.

"What's that?" Chub, fumbling to open his
ragged eyelid, so he might see the birds better.
Every part of him burned with fever; he felt infected from head to toe.

"Carrion," the woman had replied, "is another
word for dead meat."

"Jesus Willy."

"The trick is to keep moving, OK? Whatever
you do, don't lie down and doze off," she'd said,
"because they might think you're dead. That's
when they'll come for you. And once they get
started, Lord . . . Just remember to do like I said.
Don't stop moving. Arms, legs, whatever. As long
as they see movement, buzzards'll usually keep
away."

"But I gotta sleep."

"Only when it's dark. They feed mainly in the
daytime. At night you should be safe."

That's when she'd pressed the can of pepper
spray into his crab-swollen fist and said, "Just in
case."

"Will it stop 'em?" Chub peered dubiously at
the container. Bode Gazzer had purchased it at the
Lauderdale gun show.

"It's made to knock grizzly bears on their
asses," the woman had told him. "Ten percent con-

centration of oleoresin capsicum. That's two million Scoville Heat Units."

"What the fuck's that mean?"

"It means big medicine, Gomer. Good luck."

Moments later: the sound of an outboard engine revving. Sure as shit, they'd left him out here. She and the white guy—deserted him on this goddamn island with his dead friend, and the sky darkening with vultures.

They'd come down for Bode in the midafternoon, just as the woman predicted. At the time, Chub was squatting in the mangroves, huffing the last of the WD-40. It didn't give a fraction of the jolt that boat glue did, but it was better than nothing.

Teetering from the woods, he'd spotted the buzzards picking eagerly at his partner's corpse—six, seven, maybe more. Some had held strings of flesh in their beaks, others nibbled shreds of camouflage fabric. On the ground the birds had seemed so large, especially with their bare, scalded-looking heads and vast white-tipped wings—Chub had been surprised. When he ran at them they'd hissed and spooked, although not far; into the treetops.

On the bright sand around him he'd noticed the ominous shrinking shadows of others dropping closer, flying tighter circles. That's when Chub decided to run far away from Bode's dead body, to a safer part of the island. He grabbed the pepper

562

spray and half lurched, half galloped through the mangroves. Finally he came to a secluded clearing and keeled in exhaustion, landing on his wounded shoulder.

Almost immediately the first nightmare began: invisible beaks, pecking and gouging at his face. He bolted upright, sopped in sweat. In his next dream, which followed quickly, the rancid scavengers encircled him and, by aligning wing to wing, formed a picket from which he couldn't escape. Again he awakened with a shiver.

It was all her fault, the nigger girl from the Black Tide—she'd put the crazy buzzard talk in his head. They were only birds, for chrissake. Stupid, smelly birds.

Still, Chub kept his good eye trained on their glide pattern, the high thermals.

At dusk he made his way back to the abandoned campsite, in hopes of finding a dry tarp and some beer. When he spotted the paper grocery bag in the bushes, he got an idea about how to pass the long nerve-racking night. He dumped out the crinkled tube of marine adhesive and gave one last squeeze, to make sure he hadn't missed any. Then he shook the can of pepper spray and shot a stream inside the empty bag.

Thinking: Stuff's gotta be heavy-duty to take out a fuckin' grizzly.

Chub had never heard of "Scoville heat" but he assumed from its potent-sounding name that a whiff of two million units would produce a deliriously illicit high—exactly what he needed to take his mind off the buzzards and Bodean Gazzer. Chub further assumed (also mistakenly) that the pepper spray was designed to impair only an attacker's vision and that the fumes could be ingested as easily as those of common spray paint, and that he'd be safe from the caustic effects if he merely covered his eyes while inhaling.

Which is what he did, sucking the bag to his face.

The screams lasted twenty-five minutes; the vomiting, twice as long.

Chub had never known such volcanic misery— skin, throat, eyes, lungs, scalp, lips; all aflame. He slapped himself senseless trying to wipe off the poison, but it seemed to have entered chemically through his pores. Daft from pain, he clawed at himself until his fingertips bled.

When his strength was gone, Chub lay motionless, mulling options. An obvious one was suicide, a sure release from agony, but he wasn't ready to go that far. Possibly, if he'd had his .357 . . . but he surely couldn't work up the nerve to hang himself from a tree or slice his own wrists.

A sounder choice, Chub felt, was to club himself unconscious and remain that way until the acid symptoms wore off. But he couldn't stop thinking about the vultures and what the nigger woman had told him: Keep moving! Once the sun came up, blacking out would be dangerous. The deader you looked, the faster the hungry bastards would come for you.

So Chub made himself stay awake. In the end, what he most wanted was to be saved, plucked off the island. And he wasn't picky about whether the rescue helicopter was black or red or canary yellow; or whether it was being flown by niggers or Jews or even card-carrying communist infiltrators. Nor did he give two shits whether they carried him back to Miami or straight to Raiford prison, or even to a secret NATO fortress in the Bahamas.

The main thing was to get away from this horrible place, as soon as possible. *Away.*

And if, at dawn the next morning, there actually had been a rescue chopper searching Florida Bay, and if it had flown low over Pearl Key, the crew would have noticed something that would have brought them banking around sharply for a second pass:

A lone naked man waving for help.

The spotter in the helicopter would've seen through his high-powered binoculars that the stranded man had a lank gray ponytail; that his body was dappled with dried blood; that one shoulder was heavily bandaged and one hand was swollen to the size of a catcher's mitt; that his sunburned face was raw and striated, and that one eye appeared scabbed and black.

And the crew would have been impressed that, despite the stranded man's severe injuries and evident pain, he'd managed to construct a device for signaling aircraft. The crew would've admired how he had lashed together mangrove branches to make a long pole, and on the end of it he had fastened a swatch of shiny fabric.

But in the end, there was nobody to see the stranded man. No helicopters were in the sky over Pearl Key at dawn the next day, or the day after, or for many days that followed.

No one was searching for Onus Gillespie, the person known as Chub, because no one knew he was missing.

Every morning he stood in the sunniest spot on the island and feverishly waved his makeshift flag at glistening specks in the blue—727s from Miami International, F-16s from Boca Chica, Lears from North Palm Beach, all of which were flying far too high over Florida Bay to see him.

Finally the beer was gone, then the beef jerky and then the last of the fresh water. Not long afterwards, Chub lay down in the coarse bleached sand and did not move. Then the vultures came, just like the bitch had said they would.

Nine months later a poacher would find a skull, two femurs, a rusty can of pepper spray and an oilskin tarpaulin. He would be appropriately intrigued by the doomed man's handmade pole and the unusual streamer tied to it:

A pair of skimpy orange shorts, just like babes at Hooters wore.

On the drive to Simmons Wood, they went back and forth with the radio. Tom got a Clapton, while JoLayne took a Bonnie Raitt and a Natalie Cole (on the argument that "Layla" was long enough to count as two songs). They wound up in a discussion of guitarists, a topic as yet unexplored in the relationship. JoLayne was delighted to hear Tom include Robert Cray in his personal pantheon, and as a reward yielded the next two selections. "Fortunate Son" was playing, full blast, when they arrived.

JoLayne bolted from the car and ran to the FOR SALE sign, which she yanked triumphantly from the ground. Tom took the baby cooters out of the tank one at a time and placed them in a linen pillowcase, which he knotted loosely at the neck.

"Careful," JoLayne told him.

A chapel-like stillness embraced them as soon as they entered the woods, and they didn't speak again until they got to the creek. JoLayne sat on the bluff. She patted the ground and said, "Places, Mr. Krome."

The sun was almost down, and the pale dome of sky above them was tinged softly with magenta. The air was crisp and northern. JoLayne pointed out a pair of wild mergansers in the water and, on the bank, a raccoon prowling.

Tom leaned forward to see more. His face was bright. He looked like a kid at a great museum.

"What are you thinking?" she asked.

"I'm thinking anything is possible. Anything. That's how I feel when I'm out here."

"That's the way it's supposed to feel."

"Anyway, what's a miracle? It's all relative," he said. "It's all in somebody's head."

"Or in their heart. Hey, how're my babies?"

Tom peeked in the pillowcase. "Excited," he reported. "They must know what's up."

"Well, let's wait till Mister Raccoon is gone."

JoLayne smiled to herself and wrapped her arms around her knees. A flight of swallows came top-gunning out of the tree line, gulping gnats. Later Tom was certain he heard the whinny of a horse, but she said no, it was just an owl.

"I'll learn," he promised.

"There's another piece of land, not far from here. Once I found a bear track there."

In the twilight Tom could barely make out her expression.

"A black bear," she said, "not a grizzly. You'll still need to go to Alaska for one of those."

"Any old bear would be fine."

She said, "It's also for sale, that land where I saw the track. I'm not sure how many acres."

"Clara would know."

"Yes. She would. Come on, it's time."

She led him down to the creek. They walked along the bank, stopping here and there to place baby turtles in the water.

JoLayne was saying, "Did you know they can live twenty, twenty-five years? I read a paper in *BioScience* . . ."

Whispering all this—Tom wasn't sure why, but it seemed natural and right.

"Just think," she said. "Twenty years from now we can sit up there and watch these guys sunning on the logs. By then they'll be as big as army helmets, Tom, and covered with green moss. I can't wait."

He reached into the sack and took out the last one.

"That's a red-belly," she said. "You do the honors, Mr. Krome."

He placed the tiny cooter on a flat rock. Momentarily its head emerged from the shell. Then out came the stubby curved legs.

"Watch him go," JoLayne said. The turtle scrambled comically, like a wind-up toy, landing with a quiet plop in the stream.

"So long, sport. Have a great life." With both hands she reached for Tom. "I need to ask you something."

"Fire away."

"Are you going to write a story about all this?"

"Never," he said.

"But I was right, wasn't I? Didn't I tell you it would be a good one?"

"You did. It was. But you'll never read about it in the paper."

"Thank you."

"In a novel, maybe," he said, playfully pulling free. "But not in a newspaper."

"Tom, I'll kill you." She was laughing as she chased him up the hill, into the tall pines.

Look for these and other Random House Large Print books at your local bookstore

Berendt, John, *Midnight in the Garden of Good and Evil*
Brinkley, David, *David Brinkley*
Brinkley, David, *Everyone Is Entitled to My Opinion*
Carter, Jimmy, *Living Faith*
Chopra, Deepak, *The Path to Love*
Crichton, Michael, *Airframe*
Cronkite, Walter, *A Reporter's Life*
Daly, Rosie, *In the Kitchen with Rosie*
Dexter, Colin, *Death Is Now My Neighbor*
Flagg, Fannie, *Daisy Fay and the Miracle Man*
Flagg, Fannie, *Fried Green Tomatoes at the
        Whistle Stop Cafe*
Gilman, Dorothy, *Mrs. Pollifax, Innocent Tourist*
Guest, Judith, *Errands*
Hailey, Arthur, *Detective*
Hepburn, Katharine, *Me*
Koontz, Dean, *Sole Survivor*
Koontz, Dean, *Ticktock*
Landers, Ann, *Wake Up and Smell the Coffee!*
le Carré, John, *The Tailor of Panama*
Lindbergh, Anne Morrow, *Gift from the Sea*
Mayle, Peter, *Chasing Cezanne*
Michael, Judith, *Acts of Love*
Patterson, Richard North, *Silent Witness*
Peck, M. Scott, M.D., *Denial of the Soul*
Phillips, Louis, editor, *The Random House Large Print
        Treasury of Best-Loved Poems*
Powell, Colin with Joseph E. Persico, *My American
        Journey*
Rampersad, Arnold, *Jackie Robinson*
Shaara, Jeff, *Gods and Generals*
Snead, Sam with Fran Pirozzolo, *The Game I Love*
Truman, Margaret, *Murder in the House*
Tyler, Anne, *Ladder of Years*
Updike, John, *Golf Dreams*
Whitney, Phyllis A., *Amethyst Dreams*